# ONE BULLET AWAY

DALE M. NELSON

SEVERN RIVER

PUBLISHING

Severn River Publishing
www.SevernRiverBooks.com

This is a work of fiction. Names, characters, businesses, places, events and incidents are either the products of the author's imagination or used in a fictitious manner. Any resemblance to actual persons, living or dead, or actual events is purely coincidental.

ISBN: 978-1-64875-620-7 (Paperback)

# ALSO BY DALE M. NELSON

**The Gage Files**

No Prayers for the Dying

One Bullet Away

Lightning Strikes Twice

**With Andrew Watts**

Agent of Influence

A Future Spy

Tournament of Shadows

All Secrets Die

Never miss a new release!

Sign up to receive exclusive updates from author Dale M. Nelson.

**severnriverbooks.com**

# 1

Los Angeles had just endured one of its worst winters on record, and the whole city seemed wired for trouble. It'd been raining steadily for days, and the sea was angry. Not even the locals would go out in that surf, so we all huddled over coffees at Cosmic Ray's and waited for it to pass. Ray's was the Santa Monica tiki bar on the beach that I'd adopted as my office. Work had been slow. If people were having the kinds of problems they typically hired a private eye to fix for them, they'd been keeping it to themselves.

I liked Cosmic Ray's, and it was better than cooling my heels in an office alone.

The staff mostly tolerated my presence, and the locals put up with me, as long as I didn't try to offend the ocean by surfing.

Besides, with as slow as work had been lately, I had a hard enough time making rent without having to worry about footing an office on top of it.

Carrie, who was the server on shift that morning, refilled my coffee and harassed me about not having a real job—this coming from someone who waited tables at a dive bar so she could surf before and after her shifts. Carrie wore cutoff shorts regardless of the temperature and had the legs to back the decision. She flirted with me, even though it was vaguely patronizing. And she called me "gramps," because to a twentysomething, a dude in his mid-forties probably had witnessed the building of the pyramids.

"I'm expecting a prospective client today," I said. "Can you let him know where I'm at?"

Carrie looked around the bar in an exaggerated mimicry of conducting a sweep. Apart from the aging surfers in wetsuits lined up along the bar shooting the shit with the owner, the place was empty.

"Yeah, I'll let him know," she said dryly and walked off.

My private investigator license was new enough I was worried the ink would rub off. I'd finally taken the exam last fall, on the advice of some friends in law enforcement. The same people who told me my office shouldn't be a table at a tiki bar. Just goes to show they don't know everything. The license wasn't just to keep me in the good graces of the FBI, I needed the work. Most of the time, I freelanced for an international group of investigative journalists called the Orpheus Foundation. Their work often required skills that few other than ex-spies possessed. However, my contact with that outfit, an old friend named Jennie Burkhardt, was out of the country working on a story she'd been after for a long time. Until she got back, I needed to find my own way.

Which was why I was taking this meeting.

My prospective client arrived just after noon. Jimmy Lawson looked like his job. He was six feet tall, black, with a tight fade haircut. He wore a gray sharkskin suit that cost more than my entire wardrobe, a silver shirt, and cobalt blue tie. A razor thin Van Dyke framed his mouth, which was already breaking into a smile honed for the cameras. The guy looked like what people who don't live here think Hollywood looks like.

"Mr. Gage?" he said, in a low, sonorous tone that sounded like distant thunder in summer.

I stood and offered a hand. He took it and had a hell of a grip.

"Jimmy Lawson," he said, looking around. He did a good job hiding his skepticism at the surroundings. Jimmy and I hadn't spoken before. He was a referral from a previous client, and she'd told him how to find me.

"Don't suppose you've got an office we could go to," Jimmy said.

"This is my office."

"This is a bar."

He didn't miss much.

I waved a hand at the chair opposite me. "Have a seat. If you decide to hire me, you won't want me hanging out in a fancy office anyway. You'll want me on the streets, doing my job. How can I help you?"

"I'm a friend of Elizabeth Zhou. She suggested I look you up."

Elizabeth had been a client. She'd also been...more. We shared something, though it ended fast and left me with more questions than answers. After the case was done, she took a leave from her Hollywood law firm to "figure things out." I'd hoped at the end of that, it would mean maybe we'd get a legitimate shot. I knew her well enough to know that setting me up with a job probably was her way of telling me she was moving on.

"How do you know Elizabeth?" I asked.

"Law school."

"Are you with WCMA as well?" I said, meaning her firm. Elizabeth was, or had been, an entertainment lawyer.

"No. I'm an agent, and I'm not based here. I'm out of Miami, was in town to meet with some clients. I asked Elizabeth if her firm had anybody they used, like a troubleshooter. She told me about you."

"Elizabeth's case was...complicated," I said. In the way landmines are "complicated," right before they blow up. "You're based out of Miami, you said?"

"That's right?"

"Presumably, that's where the job is. Before we get started, can I ask why you're looking for a private eye in Los Angeles?"

"How about I explain what's going on first? But, yeah, I've got a good reason for coming out here. Miami is like a small town in that everyone kind of knows everyone else in certain circles. I'm looking here because I've got to know it's someone I can trust."

"I understand," I said, even though I really didn't. "Tell me what's going on."

"I have a situation with one of my clients. Maybe it's nothing. I don't know." Carrie came over and asked if we wanted anything. I took a refill on my coffee. Lawson said he was good. "What do you know about NIL?"

I did know that NIL, or "Name, Image, and Likeness" rights, was the biggest change to collegiate sports probably in my lifetime.

"I think I understand the basics, but you should probably give me a crash course if this conversation is going to make any sense."

Lawson laughed at that. "So, there are a few different permutations, but the majority of them basically work like this. There are these organizations called 'collectives,' which exist so there is a legal way to pay student athletes. People can donate money to their school's collective, and then the collective will make a deal with a particular athlete. The rules prohibit people paying an athlete directly, so these collectives exist to create a medium for that. Some of them also broker endorsement deals. Players get money from the collective, primarily donations from boosters, fans, and alums. Then, if they get endorsement deals out of it, they get that money too. As you'd expect, the football and basketball players get the most money. Though you're starting to see gymnastics and swimming and some others get big contracts as well. The idea is to bring all this activity into the daylight and give athletes their fair share of the profits schools make because of them."

"I'm guessing that latter part is the reason we're having this conversation," I said.

"Yeah, pretty much. One of the other big changes is that now student athletes can sign with an agent. I represent a kid named Brashard Brown. He's a quarterback at Miami. Redshirted his freshman year, and there was some legal trouble with the school's primary collective that year, so Brashard didn't see any money. He ended up signing with this new outfit called Sunshine Sports Collective. Fast forward to last fall. Midway through the season, the starter gets blown up in a game against Florida State. Brashard comes in and finishes the season, sets an in-game passing record. We expect he probably starts in the fall. He's a good kid. Now, he signed with SSC before I took him on as a client. They sold Brashard on a bunch of high-end endorsements, none of which have materialized yet."

"Other than the endorsements, what's the problem?"

Lawson opened his hands as if to show the nothingness in them. "They locked up his NIL rights in perpetuity. Fine-print stuff. Any lawyer would've caught it, but the Browns didn't."

"I take it this young man comes from a modest background—family probably makes enough to make ends meet, but sure as hell not enough for an attorney. Even if they'd have thought to hire one."

"They've never owned a home," Lawson said. "Three kids, Brashard is the oldest. Parents have never done better than hourly wages."

"And they'd like out of the contract?"

"Once I took a look at it, I told them it was a bad deal. SSC gets fifteen percent of Brashard Brown for the rest of his life."

"That's bullshit," I said. Lawson nodded. "You're the lawyer, though. If you could beat it in court, you wouldn't be talking to me."

"Elizabeth said you didn't miss much. The contract is legit, even though it's predatory as shit. I don't think it holds up in the long run, though Brashard will lose a lot of money between now and then."

"What is it exactly you think I can do for you?"

"I'd like you to look into SSC for me. I want to see if you can find something I can use to get Brashard out of this contract."

"You mean like if SSC is breaking the law?"

"Right."

"Have you spoken with the police or the NCAA?"

"Miami PD, Miami-Dade Police, and Florida Department of Law Enforcement have all said that without clear evidence of malfeasance or corruption, there's nothing for them to do. NCAA says they can't enforce anything, that it's up to the university. The school says they are prohibited by the NCAA's current rules to advise student athletes and that they have their 'official' collective."

"So, your guess is with everyone saying it's someone else's responsibility, SSC is able to get away with something."

"Yes."

"What makes you think they're doing something illegal? Jimmy, if you're a friend of Elizabeth's, I'd like to help you out. To me, though, it doesn't sound like you need a private detective, you need a contracts lawyer."

Lawson gave me a look that could've boiled lead. It dissolved quickly into something like weary frustration, and he said, "I had our contracts people look at it. It's manipulative and intentionally underhanded, but it's perfectly legal. Rather than paying Brashard all the money they promised, they sold him on some 'investment opportunities.' They gave him some of it and then redirected the rest to real estate and some high-risk investment funds. Said it was to diversify his income. 'Future proof' it, they said. They gave him some of the cash, which his family used as a down payment on a home. Then they pushed the rest of it into these investments."

"And the family is about to miss some house payments?"

Lawson nodded.

I could imagine how this the scheme might come together. Sunshine Sports Collective grabs naïve kids without representation and dangles a big payday in front of them. They'll recoup most of that money by getting them to invest in sketchy businesses. It couldn't be that easy, though, or the police would've swooped in and shut it down. With just these data points, a local reporter would be all over this kind of thing.

"Have you spoken with the *Herald*?" I asked.

Lawson shook his head. "I did. And the *Orlando Sentinel*. I mostly got a lukewarm response from everyone I spoke with. The *Herald* at least admitted to me that they don't have much budget for in-depth investigations anymore."

That didn't surprise me. Newspaper budgets had all but dried up over the last twenty years as those institutions had to deal with the public's changing news consumption, readership habits, twenty-four-hour cable news, and social media. Even major papers had to cut whole departments and outsource some sections to news services.

"I hate to say it, but I would also bet there isn't much sympathy for a kid that makes a million dollars playing college football when most people leave school with six-figure debt." Much of the argument against student athletes being paid came from those citing the value of a scholarship and room and board, particularly as tuition costs erupted over the last twenty years.

Jimmy didn't respond, he just pointed at me, adding a knowing nod.

"So, where do you factor into this?" I asked. "You've signed the kid, right? You represent him now? What's the difference between what you do and what the collective does?"

"That's a good question. My job is to represent players to the market. As a college athlete, mostly that means getting them endorsements, so there can be a little overlap with a collective. Once he gets closer to going pro, then I start working with teams that might be interested to make sure he lands in the right place. It's mostly development on future potential. I think he could be a breakout player, like a genuine superstar. Reminds me a lot of Mahomes. After I signed Brashard, I heard about this NIL deal he'd gotten himself into, and I wanted to try and help his family out. Whether it's legal or not, SSC is taking advantage of this kid, his talent, and his family's lack of financial savvy. The collective advised him not to sign with an agent. Told him, 'Why would you want someone to get three percent of you for the rest of your life?'"

"When they're getting fifteen?"

"Exactly."

I thought Lawson genuinely wanted to see if something illegal was going on here. If it was, he hoped that would get his client out of this contract. There was also the possibility that the act of hiring an investigator to kick over some stones might be enough to convince these guys to knock off whatever they were doing.

"It certainly seems there could be something questionable going on. A lifetime royalty lockup is predatory, reminds me of the stuff record companies used to pull. Unethical, but probably legal. I still think you can handle that in court. However, the push to investment vehicles is what has me concerned. That screams 'Ponzi scheme' to me. They attract some big-name athletes, which presumably brings in other donors."

"My thoughts exactly," Lawson said.

"That seems obvious to me, though. Hard to believe they'd be that careless."

"Why do you say that?"

"Because the way you describe, they're acting like they aren't afraid of getting caught—doing whatever they might be doing," I added. Things that appeared obvious so rarely were. There was something else to this, because it couldn't be as simple as it seemed.

"So, will you take the case?"

I looked at Jimmy Lawson for a string of breaths. "You didn't even ask what I charge."

"If it turns out SSC's people are just a bunch of assholes and there isn't anything illegal going on, I'll pay you whatever your rate is. Time and expenses is how it goes with you guys, right?"

"And if they're running a scam?"

"Then I'll pay you $250,000 cold if you can get evidence that helps me get Brashard out of his contract."

Lawson didn't need to explain his logic. This kid was a redshirt freshman at Miami. If his performance matched expectations, it's not impossible to see a seven-figure endorsement deal while he's still in college. A first-round pick could get a contract anywhere between twelve and forty million, depending on where they went in the draft. Lawson was gambling on this kid—and on his hunch something dirty was going on with Sunshine Sports Collective. If he was right, the money he paid me to prove it would be a rounding error. And he could probably write it off as a business expense.

Two hundred fifty thousand was a hell of a payout for a private detective.

I didn't even have health insurance.

I told him an investigation like this could take some time, and he didn't balk, just reminded me that the longer it lasted, the more entrenched these guys got. I didn't ask him if he was footing the bill for this or his firm was. Which only mattered as far as intent went, which was to say, it didn't much matter so long as the checks cleared.

---

I decided to drive.

When I'd left the Agency, I had quite a lot of money saved up since I'd worked so much and rarely took vacations. I burned most of that restomodding a '93 Land Rover Defender. The vehicle was updated with all the modern tech you'd find in any high-end vehicle, and a few things you wouldn't. My favorite was the concealed panel in the driver's side door that perfectly hid a Glock 34. There were additional hidden lockboxes in the back where I could stash my laptop, camera, and other gear. Taking my own vehicle during casework also meant I could bring the additional equipment I used to round out my investigative kit.

Considering the number of times I worried about making my rent as a detective, a six figure SUV might not have been the smartest investment, but holy hell was she fun to drive.

The downside was that even pushing it, it would still take me three days to get to Miami. With the price of gas, I was kind of banking on that $250k just to make this a profitable trip.

Since Jennie was out of the country, I texted her and asked if she had any contacts in sports journalism. We'd met in college in Florida, so I was hopeful she'd still have someone in-state I could speak with.

She replied a few hours later.

*OMG!! I have the perfect guy.*

Jennie introduced me to a J-school colleague, Mike Pusatera, who'd worked at ESPN for about fifteen years until their mass layoffs a few years ago. He was now an indie sportswriter and blogger based out of Tampa. If he agreed to meet, I could see him on my way. Jennie introduced us over email, and I waited for his reply.

As I drove, I tried to frame my investigation, to piece together what the missing information might be, so I'd know where to direct my efforts. The first part was to speak with Brown and, if possible, other student athletes. Then, I'd need to get inside Sunshine Sports. That was part of the reason Jimmy wanted someone from outside of Miami. I'd formulated a plausible way in. The part I hadn't figured out yet was, what was I looking for?

Mike wrote me back on the second day of the trip. We exchanged phone numbers and made plans to meet once I got in-state.

I spent most of the trip listening to podcasts reporting on NIL and the evolving business of sports management. This was a horrendously confusing landscape, and more than once, I wondered what I'd gotten myself into. The only part of this I did understand was that there was a lot of money flying around and very few rules governing how.

I stayed in the panhandle on my second night and was on the road shortly after sunrise. Even though I'd crossed into Florida, I still had thirteen hours in front of me. People forget how long this state is.

I grew up south of Tampa and, even though I don't get back much, I'll always think of it as home. Mike lived in Tarpon Springs now, a community on the western side of Tampa, next to the Gulf. We met at a neighborhood bar that had weathered picnic tables over white sand.

"We met once, actually," Mike said. "In college."

"Really?"

"Yeah, you and Jennie were in the 'on again' phase. I had a house on the north side of University Avenue. It was, like, two blocks behind the Purple Porpoise."

"No shit," I said. I had no memory of this.

"Anyway, the usual college house party."

"Red solo cups and a keg of Southpaw?"

"Yeah." Our server brought the beers and asked if there was anything else we needed. I told her we were good. Over the first beer, Mike talked about how he'd gotten a job at the sports desk of the *Miami Herald* out of college. He spent seven years with the paper, until he was hired by ESPN to join their rapidly growing website division in the mid-2000s. He stayed with them until the series of layoffs in recent years that jettisoned scores of veteran sports journalists. The buyout money got him enough for a down-payment on a house in Tampa, where he now lived with his wife and their two kids. Today, Mike was a freelance sportswriter and blogger, contributing to a host of syndicated publications and the *Tampa Bay Times*. Not only did Mike primarily cover college sports, but he was an emerging expert on the tornadic chaos that was the Name, Image, and Likeness situation.

"So, Jennie said you're working as a private detective now?"

"That's right." Now I was curious to know how much she'd told him outside of the email where she introduced us. "I'm not the kind of person who deals in NDAs. I also know how valuable a scoop is. I'd love to be able to ask you some direct questions and have it all remain confidential."

"Of course. I'm not going to leak anything. Jennie trusts you." Mike lifted his beer and gave a dry smile. "She also said not to fuck with you."

This was somebody I could work with.

"I'll make you a deal," he said. "I'll tell you everything I know. If it turns out there's a story here, I want first crack."

"That's fair. Mike, are you familiar with Sunshine Sports Collective?"

He chuckled. "Everyone who's spent a minute in the Miami sports scene knows Raymond Ruiz."

"Really?"

"Oh yeah. So, I get to Miami in '99 to start my gig with the *Herald*. Ruiz went to Miami and then Florida International for law school, graduates in

'98. He lands a gig in the Sports Management Group mail room. Raymond is a hustler. What I mean is, he puts in the work, but he also works the angles. Even in the mail room, he figures out who is meeting with whom, what agents are on the rise, so he knows whose phones he wants to answer. He's smart too. He starts building relationships with the reporters—TV, newspaper, radio, which is how I met him. He also talked his way into the circles of all the front offices with the Dolphins, the Marlins, and the Heat. By 2001, he's out of the mail room and is an assistant to one of the agency's heaviest hitters. Two years later, he's a full agent with his own roster.

"He's living high. Expensive clothes, dinners, parties, everything. In 2008, I'm now working out of ESPN's Miami office, writing web stories and starting as a producer. A year later, Ruiz was involved in a recruiting scandal with the Canes. The NCAA already cited him for improperly contacting an amateur athlete on two occasions, so once this third scandal emerged, SMG cut him loose. None of the other agencies would touch him. I sort of lost track of him after that. I was moving back and forth between Bristol and Miami as ESPN dictated. I heard he tried to start a sports management company, had some other ventures that didn't quite land. Fast forward to 2022. The ink is just drying on the NCAA's NIL policy, and Ray hangs out the Sunshine Sports Collective shingle. I reconnected with him and interviewed him about it when he first opened." He paused. "That expression on your face, what is it?"

"Sorry, back in LA, I hang out at this place called Cosmic Ray's, and whenever you say that name, I have a hard time picturing anything but an ex-pro surfer turned bartender who grows weed in the room I'm supposed to use as an office."

Mike gave me a very blank stare.

"Anyway, what did you find out," I asked.

"That's the thing." Mike paused for a sip from his beer. "NIL exists to allow players to make money off athletic participation, right? Fans, alums, boosters can donate money to these collectives, and the collectives pay the players. But they're all associated with a school. Sunshine Sports is institution agnostic."

"Meaning they aren't tied to any one school."

"Exactly, and I can't figure out how that makes sense. Or why even do it.

Like, if we wanted our school to do better in a sport, we'd donate a bunch of money to our collective. Ray gave me this story about investing in players and using it as a tool to recruit."

"I thought that was illegal, using money to entice players to a school."

"Matt, these rules change so fast, and there's really no oversight until someone files a lawsuit. That's the only way anything gets attention."

"Meaning, Ruiz could be taking advantage of a new, unregulated market."

"Look, I don't want to accuse him of anything. Or imply that he's doing something wrong. It's hard to break the law when there isn't a law, right? I've been acquainted with the guy for twenty years, but it's not like we're friends. I was a reporter. He told me what he wanted me to know. He just always struck me as the kind of person who would get away with just enough."

"Do you know how SSC makes money?" I asked. "My understanding is that some of these collectives are nonprofits, others operate kind of like businesses."

"That's a great question. I asked him that too. He gave me a song-and-dance about keeping a low overhead and maximizing profit for the athletes. I also know he's got a nice house on Miami Beach and hasn't lost his taste for the good life. He said any time I wanted to come down and do a story on him, he'd take me to a Heat game—in his box."

"I bet if you asked him about the money he spends, he'd tell you a rising tide lifts all boats, right?"

"His exact words to me were, 'Celebrities don't give money to paupers unless it's for charity.'"

"Is Ruiz doing anything novel here? Is this any different from what any other collective is doing?"

"As far as I can tell, all NIL did was take the most insidious part of college sports and put it out in the open. Only they failed to put the guardrails up when they did it. I couldn't tell you if what Ruiz is doing is wrong, because the NCAA, or the government, or whomever, never told us what 'right' is. I tend to be a pessimist about this sort of thing, so take this for what it's worth, but I can't see any good coming from this."

"From SSC?"

"From any of it."

Mike gave me more insight into the rapidly evolving business of college athletics, particularly the multiple lawsuits underway that he thought would shape the landscape. We finished a second round, and I agreed to keep him posted on my progress. From what I'd learned so far, it sounded like he'd get a story out of this.

---

Jimmy Lawson set me up with a hotel in downtown Miami. I checked in around seven that evening and did a few laps in the pool to work out the tension from being in a seat for three days straight. Then I got a beer and a burger from the bar. It was March, and they had the basketball tournament on.

Jimmy called to make sure I'd made it okay and said we'd be meeting the Browns the following evening. "I should mention, when Brashard hired me, he didn't talk to his parents about it first."

"Kid's an adult," I said.

"Yeah, I guess Ruiz later got in their ear about their son not needing representation in college, splitting the pot and all that. Anyway, the dad isn't particularly keen on me and less keen on you."

"Then why are we even meeting with them?"

"I'm not working behind people's backs, Matt. I've also been working on Mr. Brown. I think I've convinced him that Ruiz pushing back on an extra set of eyes is suspicious, and forcing them into investments rather than paying them isn't normal either."

Looked like I was starting right from the jump. *Buckle up, folks. We're expecting turbulence.*

## 2

The Browns now lived in an upper-middle-class neighborhood as close to Coral Gables as you could get without leaving Miami proper. It was only a few miles from the University of Miami campus. The home was a two-story, 1980s construction and recently renovated.

I assumed the Range Rover out front belonged to Lawson, though these days you could never be sure.

It was about seventy degrees and tropical. Los Angeles is an informal town, and people spend way too much money to make it look like they're too lazy to dress up. In Miami, it was usually too hot for anything more than a tank top, though that's not what I wanted to greet clients in. Instead, I'd opted for dressing in clothes I assumed people thought private detectives wore—a brownish herringbone blazer, white oxford shirt, and jeans. I carried a lightweight ballistic nylon briefcase.

Mr. Brown greeted me at the door, his face a mixture of skepticism and wariness. He was an inch or two taller than me, mostly bald with the thick, ropy build that was used to hard work. He wore a Hurricanes polo and gray pants.

"Matt Gage," I said and offered a hand.

The man sized me up and gave no indication one way or the other about his conclusion. Instead, he took my handshake and nearly ground my bones into powder. I guess that was a welcome and a warning.

"Cyrus Brown. Come on in."

It wasn't exactly unwelcoming, it was just...distant.

We made no small talk as he escorted me into the dining room.

The house was nice, but something about it seemed off to me. By the time we'd reached the dining room, I'd guessed what it was. The furniture and the decor, right down to the bowl of fake fruit on the table, all looked generic. It wouldn't surprise me if this was the exact setup the realtor had used to stage the house, and the Browns had bought it lock, stock, and barrel.

Mrs. Brown ordered the two younger children upstairs, who reluctantly left on the third reminder. No doubt, they wanted to see why there was a white guy with a jacket in their dining room.

A young man I assumed was Brashard and Jimmy Lawson sat at the table talking quietly. The air was heavy with the lingering aromas of their dinner. Whatever it was, it smelled delicious. Mrs. Brown stood in the kitchen—the design was sort of an open-air concept—wiping her hands anxiously on a towel. Brashard sat next to Lawson at the table, and they were conversing when I entered with Cyrus. All conversation stopped as I walked in, as though they were expecting me to drop some unwelcome news on the table. The air was tight.

"Good evening," I said. "Mrs. Brown, you have a lovely home."

A look of restrained anguish passed over her face. She covered it quickly by offering me a cup of coffee, which I accepted despite the hour, because things were awkward enough. She moved over to the table with a tray of brownies and cookies and set that down before pouring me a mug of coffee.

"You must be Brashard," I said and moved over to greet the Browns' son. He stood and took my offered hand. He had a look of ambivalent disinterest I'd expect out of a nineteen-year-old who knows something important is going to be discussed but who also wanted very little to do with it. I already knew Brashard's stats from my initial research, six-three and 230. A true dual threat quarterback, Brashard had some serious wheels and could scramble as well as throw darts. He was built like the running backs of my generation.

"Thank you for coming to see us, Mr. Gage," Mrs. Brown said, joining us at the table.

"I guess I'll get us started," Jimmy began. "Mr. Gage here is a private investigator. Like we discussed last week, I share your concerns that there are some irregularities with how Sunshine Sports Collective is handling Brashard's affairs. The concerns were substantial enough that I made a call to Mr. Gage. He'd done some work for a law-school classmate of mine and comes highly recommended."

"What was the work?" Mr. Brown asked.

"I'm sorry?"

"That you did for his friend. What was the work?"

"I exposed a foreign spy ring in Silicon Valley," I said. There was a lot of detail we'd be leaving out of *that* story.

"I see," said Mr. Brown.

"Mr. and Mrs. Brown, Brashard, I'd like to start by asking some questions. Some of these may be difficult to answer. My intent is not to press too deeply into personal matters, and I don't mean to offend you. It's important that I have as complete a picture as possible." I took a notepad and pen out of my bag. "I'd like to understand your relationship with SSC first. Brashard, can you tell me when you first communicated with them?"

Brashard looked to his father, who nodded. "About a year ago. It was a few months into spring practice my freshman year."

"Why didn't you sign with the NIL collective associated with the school?"

"They didn't do anything for me," he said, as if rising to some unspoken challenge.

"The Canes had three quarterbacks on the roster and Brashard was QB3," Cyrus said. "The other collectives weren't interested in offering him anything. SSC made theirs after his freshman year. The other collectives were being conservative, I guess you'd say."

"This is because one of them had gotten into trouble?"

"Not the collective, but the guy who managed it, yes," Jimmy said.

"Cane Collective offered fifteen thousand. Then the gentleman from SSC called us and offered substantially more."

"How much more?"

"One million dollars," Mr. Brown said. "They also promised endorsements."

"With whom?"

"They said they had connections with Nike, Gatorade, and some apparel companies."

"I assume you never heard from any of those people," I said.

Mr. Brown just shook his head in response. Brashard had been mostly quiet so far. His expression was hard to read, other than I still had the opinion he wanted to be anywhere else but here.

"Brashard, have you gotten any endorsements to date?" I asked.

"Just some local stuff. A restaurant, a gym equipment chain. Car dealership," Brashard said. The kid's tone and posture said more than his sparse response did.

"There was that prep academy," Mrs. Brown said.

"It wasn't a prep academy, Mom. It was a gym where kids can work out to get better at football."

"SSC is not associated with the school, right?"

"That's correct," Lawson said. "They are allowed to say they represent student athletes at the school and to display the school's logo on their website, as long as that's true. They just can't say they're the school's official collective."

My understanding was that most schools had their own "official" sports collective. Some schools had a few, focusing on groups of sports, though each were licensed by their respective universities. SSC wasn't linked to any one school. As far I could tell, this was the only instance of a collective sponsoring athletes at multiple institutions. It seemed to break the model of attracting big-name boosters to dump huge sums of cash in support of their chosen program.

"Has SSC introduced you to any of their donors?"

"A few. They're mostly local businessmen. One of 'em was like a senator or something."

"A state senator representing Miami," Lawson amended.

"Why did you sign with SSC?" I asked.

"Anyone ever hand you a check for a million dollars?" Mr. Brown asked.

"Just a Russian oligarch," I said. "But that was supposed to be a bribe."

The looks around the table ranged from blank to stupefied.

"He was trying to buy me off. I didn't take it," I added. Okay, national security jokes weren't going to play at this table. "So, you get a contract for an NIL deal. They agree to pay you a million dollars. Is that lump sum?"

While I had a lot of questions about the contract itself, asking them now wasn't going to help. This wasn't a family with the resources to hire a contract lawyer, and they may not have even thought to do it. Bringing it up again would just come across as rubbing their nose in it, and that wouldn't help them, or me. However, detail on how this had paid out would be important.

"The money was spread out," Mr. Brown said. "They gave us a check when he signed with them."

"How much?"

When Brown didn't answer, Lawson said, "It's okay, Cyrus. You can trust Mr. Gage."

"It was $250,000," Mrs. Brown said. I noted a steel rod of pride running through those words.

"Do you know why they offered your son so much?" This is where it was going to get contentious.

"You seen him play?" Mr. Brown said.

I had. I'd watched every YouTube highlight I could. To my amateur eyes, the kid definitely had talent.

"What I mean, Mr. Brown, is that the average NIL contract—now this is across all sports—is between one and ten thousand dollars. The top D1 starting quarterbacks, almost all of them were Heisman candidates, all made about one point five million."

"They know how good my boy is," Mr. Brown said, again with hard conviction.

This was interesting, if paradoxical. They'd questioned SSC's legitimacy, up until the collective talked about how valuable their son was. The conversation broke down into the Brown family pummeling me with game statistics for a few minutes to make sure there was no question in my mind of their son's value.

"Mr. Ruiz, the guy who runs the collective, said the reason they gave me so much was they wanted to attract bigger investors," Brashard finally said. "He said their model or whatever is based on the athlete and not the school. If they make *me* a name, then businesses that aren't associated with the school will want to be associated with me. That's why they did it. Betting on my potential. He said if there's a car dealership that's the official car dealership of the university—you know how they say that in commercials during the game?—well, that eliminates every other dealership from the mix."

"How many payments have you received so far?"

I heard the air conditioning kick on and nothing else.

Mr. Brown said there was one, but his wife contradicted that statement. The two of them bickered a bit over what constituted a payment, and then Brashard weighed in. I got the impression his father didn't appreciate that much. There was more playing out here than just answering the question I'd asked. I looked to Lawson for help, but he was stone-faced. His eyebrow lifted a notch, and that was all the explanation I got.

"I'm sorry," I said. "I hope I didn't confuse things. Have they just paid you the one, or is there something about the way they're paying that's a problem?"

"They took the second payment of $250,000 and invested it. That Ruiz said investing the money was the best way to protect it. Make the money grow in case Brashard ever got hurt. He said we should plan like this is the only money we'd see. It made sense at the time, the way he explained it."

I could tell that Cyrus Brown knew he'd been swindled and was deeply embarrassed. That check was likely the most money he'd ever seen at one time in his life. Talking about this with a stranger—and their son's full-of-swagger agent—in front of his family drained him of his self-worth.

"What about the remaining five hundred?" I asked.

"Paid out in year three and year four," Jimmy said. "Which is not normal."

"Could you get me the information on the investments they made on your behalf? I should look into those."

Cyrus nodded. I pulled a card out of my bag and set it on the table.

I had what I needed to get started.

I thanked them for their time and said I'd be in touch if there were other questions.

Jimmy hung back a minute for a few words with the family before meeting me in the half-moon-shaped carport.

I looked back at the house for a few moments. "They bought this with the first check, didn't they?"

Lawson nodded slowly.

"One point two?"

"One point one," he said. "Two hundred down to secure the loan. First home they'd ever owned."

"Both parents work?"

"Cyrus is in construction. Janelle works at a school cafeteria. Brashard has two younger sisters. You have an idea how you're going to approach this?"

"Some. The thing I need you to understand, Jimmy, is that financial investigations take time. Usually with a full staff with forensic accountants and systems to trace the money. I've done this kind of thing before, but I had both time and resources."

"Who were you going after?"

I don't know how much Elizabeth Zhou told Jimmy about my life before being a private investigator. I'd admitted to her that I'd spent close to twenty years in the CIA. That was not something I shared with a lot of people. "Terrorists, transnational criminal organizations, arms dealers, and the people who enable them by moving their money around. We also had support from the FBI and Treasury Department. I've got none of that. The only way I see to do it is to get inside SSC and get them to show me something illegal."

With what I'd learned so far, it seemed the one plausible option. What I hadn't told him was that on Elizabeth's case, after we continued to get stonewalled by the police and given part of the story, I'd broken into her father's house.

I had a bad habit of rewriting the rule book when it suited me.

Well, *I* didn't consider it a bad habit, but cops seemed to. I identified as "investigatorially progressive."

Jimmy asked, "How are you going to get them to show you something illegal?"

"That, my friend, is what I do best." Lawson's expression said he was looking for something more than a quip, so I said, "The easiest way in is to make myself look like a big donor. Or, better yet, a representative of a collection of them. I'm not above sticking my neck out to poke around, especially if I know you're going to back me up with representation should things go south."

"Hey, we didn't talk about..."

"I'm talking about bending the law, not breaking it. We need to be clear on what the outcome is here. Do we just want Brashard to get out of his contract, or do we want to make it so these guys can't do this to anyone else?"

"We can't do both?"

"Not without cops," I said. "Unless I'm working with them in an official capacity, nothing I uncover is admissible as evidence. Now, you came to me because the police wouldn't take you seriously. So, I dig around and see what I can find. If Sunshine Sports is running a scam, having a private investigator looking around might be enough to get them to fold it up. Different organizations use people like me—lawyers, reporters, financial firms. Most of my work comes from an investigative journalism outfit. If SSC is small time, this is probably enough to make them disappear. We might not get all Brashard's money, but he'll be free to sign deals with whomever he wants."

"And if they're not small time?"

"Then I take everything I've got to the police. I have a friend in the FBI who used to work financial crimes. She might be able to make some introductions on my behalf."

Lawson nodded.

The door opened, and Mr. Brown appeared there. He stepped into the warm night, a folded piece of paper in his hands. He walked up to me, tentatively, and held the paper out.

"This is the list of the businesses that endorsed my son," he said.

I took the list. "Thank you. This is useful."

"Can you help us, Mr. Gage?"

Brown and Lawson traded a look.

"I'm certainly going to try, sir. Your son seems like a good kid and a talented athlete. He deserves his shot. I get angry when people like you get taken advantage of."

"What do you mean 'people like us'?"

"Regular people who maybe don't have access to lawyers and things like that."

"How long have you been a private detective?"

"About a year," I said.

Brown pivoted to face Lawson, looking like a statue coming alive. "You said—"

"Mr. Brown, I was a case officer in the CIA for almost twenty years. This is sort of a second career. Is it more important to you that I have the job title or that I know how to find the kinds of things people like Raymond Ruiz tend to bury?"

Cyrus locked eyes with me and gripped them with some invisible tether. "Don't take advantage of my boy. I had enough of that," he said. I didn't know if it was a threat or a plea, or maybe a little of both.

"You have my word that I'll do everything I can for you."

Cyrus nodded, mollified, and returned to the house. I told Jimmy I'd speak to him in a day or two, once I had my arms around my approach.

The next day, I worked mostly out of my hotel room. I put in calls to the *Miami Herald* sports desk and the local television stations. I'd made a little traction by lunchtime. The *Herald*'s college football beat writer called me back and said he didn't know much about SSC. I also put emails in to the Hurricane's writer at the *Athletic* and a few websites specializing in college football and NIL coverage. These were longshots and mostly intended to validate my suspicions on the collective. Likely, I wouldn't learn more than I already had from Mike, but it was worth it to check.

I decided not to call the other Miami-based collectives. At least not yet. I didn't know the relationship between them and SSC, and I didn't want to risk tipping Ruiz that someone was looking at him.

Later that afternoon, I called an old friend.

Mikhail Iliescu had been a consultant to the intelligence community for many years, which is how I knew him. He was an information security expert and had built several novel technologies, which he'd sold off to larger firms. Much of his work now was as a white-hat hacker, breaking into organizations' networks to show them where the holes were. We used him for something else.

If you needed a digital persona that could stand up to brutal scrutiny, Mikhail Iliescu was the gold standard. We used Mickey for any number of dirty tricks and electronic shell games. As with most of the players in this space, it was best not to ask how they got their skills, though we knew from our own backgrounding that he'd once worked for an organized crime outfit in his native Romania.

"Mickey," I said into the phone. We communicated over Signal, an encrypted chat tool that had voice capability.

"Matthew, it's good to hear your voice. What laws are you breaking today?"

"That's funny coming from you. I was hoping to get your help on a project. Shouldn't be too big a lift. Are you free right now?"

"I can be. Usual rates and all that."

"I need some artifacts to backstop a cover. How fast can you create a digital presence for a company and a personal profile for me?"

"What kind of scrutiny does it need to hold up to?"

"Probably just web traffic and some reference calls," I said.

Mickey got quiet, and I heard clacking keys on the other end. He banged on a key twice with some vigor and said, "I can probably get you something by the morning. Are you looking for social media too?"

Working undercover in the online age added tremendous complexity. There were innumerable places where people's lives and histories were displayed for all to see. You could play the "privacy enthusiast" card just so many times. Even when posing as a State Department foreign service officer, people expected you to have the usual social media profiles online. The federal intelligence service in Argentina once spent a lot of time digging into the background we'd created on LinkedIn. Of course, we'd had the company's permission to use it. Mickey wouldn't in this case.

"No, I think I've got a way around it. The guy I'm thinking about will be too rich to care about networking."

"Sounds good," he said.

I had Mickey build a website for a Dallas-based private equity firm called "Apogee Partners." The firm's landing page would have the kind of digital velvet rope that people with money expected to see, hints at the types of investment they did without overtly disclosing it. The subtle "if you know, you know" cues. This allowed us to fabricate something that looked legitimate and slightly secretive, which was the point. Mickey would create profiles of the C-suite, using digitally altered headshots. I would be listed as "Chief Strategy Officer." The 800 number would get routed to a voice-cloned, generative AI bot that could field simple questions and take a number to call a person back. Mickey had also built an app that I could load onto my phone, allowing me to send emails from a specific domain—in my case, it would be "Apogee Partners." The app would also have a VOIP calling feature that rendered my alias and Apogee's name on caller ID.

"Give me about eighteen hours, and everything will be up and running."

The app for my phone was something he could give me now. He'd built this a while ago, and I'd used it on cases before. All it took was about an hour of configuration to match what we were building for Apogee. He directed me to an IP address to download it and install on my phone.

Once it was loaded and configured, I dialed another number.

"Sunshine Sports Collective, this is Marcia," the voice said.

"Hi, my name is Jameson Carter. I represent a PE firm called Apogee Partners, and we're interested in learning a little more about your athletes."

I didn't have the time or the team to do a full forensic accounting investigation, so I opted for what I could do.

Force SSC into tripping up.

The first call to SSC didn't get me much.

Marcia directed me to their website which offered investment levels to match any budget. I asked to speak with their leadership team about something a little more substantial. She took my number down and said someone would get back to me.

Apparently, I wasn't the only one employing bots to field phone calls.

# 3

I picked up Raymond Ruiz's tail as he was leaving the office. SUV that went for about $250k. Stevie Wonder could find that thing.

The office for Sunshine Sports Collective was in a new building in Coconut Grove. The open-air shopping plaza and parking garage gave me ample places to stage stakeouts from different locations so as not to establish patterns that might get me seen.

Ruiz moved a lot. I followed him to meetings across Dadeland, most of which seemed to be with businesses and people with expensive tastes. Ruiz took few meals by himself. Most found him at Miami's high-end restaurants, and those were often difficult for me to get into without a reservation.

During one surveillance, I convinced a maître d' that I was a writer for *Food and Wine*, doing a profile on the chef. That got me through the doors and gave me cover to take photos inside. I captured Ray and his guest so I could run it through my image recognition software later. Another time, I found him dining outside, and I posted nearby where I vamped taking pictures of the skyline. The practice had become ubiquitous, so no one notices people taking pictures anymore—it's just part of the background— and Ray certainly didn't. A good camera is an invaluable espionage tool, and not just for the pictures it takes. With some rightly placed words, it can grant you the ability to conduct surveillance in the open.

After dinner the second night, Ray went to a Miami Heat game, and I lost him completely. There were ways I could've gotten in, but without knowing where he'd be, it'd be nearly impossible to find him in the stadium. Instead, I staked out the valet and waited for him to come out.

Night three found him going to one of the strangest places I'd ever seen. Sky Club was a members-only club built as a skybridge between two towers. It was a wedge of steel and glass, fifty-five feet above Miami's Brickell neighborhood, and it was clear that I wasn't getting past the lobby without help. I spoke to a concierge to inquire about membership. By then, I'd started dressing up for the stakeouts because I often found myself inside. Miami's only true dress code was "expensive," so I'd done some shopping in the afternoon and hoped Jimmy would be tolerant of the expense report.

Before they'd even entertain the idea of giving me a tour, the "membership consultant" wanted a detailed background on who I was, so I wouldn't waste "our" time. I'd had business cards printed up and overnighted to my hotel with the Apogee Partners logo and contact information. We trudged through an interminable thirty minutes of this guy getting into atomic detail about how exclusive membership was and, if I were lucky enough to be chosen, everything it'd do for me. I began to think this was part of a prospective member hazing ritual—you had to spend it locked in a room with this guy, "Rafe."

"Listen, I haven't decided if I want to join. What I have decided is that I'm done listening to the pitch. I'd like to see something a little more impressive than your iPad if I'm going to consider applying."

Rafe sat there for a moment in confused silence as he tried to process what he'd just heard. Was that right? Did someone have the temerity to question him? Holy shit, they did. His haughty veneer crumbled quickly as he realized his approach was about to cost him a commission. "I'm so sorry, Jameson. You're absolutely right."

"Ah, ah," I said, wagging a finger at him. "It's 'Mr. Carter' until I sign."

"Yes, sir. Of course."

Rafe stood in a hurry and made best speed to an elevator, where he took me up in awkward silence. When we were three quarters of the way up,

Rafe attempted his recovery. "The club is ten thousand square feet, suspended between two buildings."

"I'm from Texas, son. If this were in Dallas, it'd be twenty thousand square feet, and we'd have a building on top of it."

"Right." We'd covered the amenities in his office, but Rafe told me again about the spa, the rooftop pool, and thirteen guest suites members could avail themselves of to entertain guests.

"I'd like to see those," I said.

"Of course, Mr. Carter." We exited the elevator, and Rafe led me onto the sky bridge. The building faced south with a breathtaking view of Biscayne Bay. And that was at night. I could only imagine what this looked like in full daylight. Rafe guided me through the club's main floor, subtly noting the extraordinary things I'd only find here. He asked me what clubs I belonged to in Dallas.

"The Ranch," I said.

"I'm not familiar with that," Rafe said.

"Exactly."

We walked to a line of doors along one of the exterior walls. He chose one that was unoccupied, and we stepped inside. It was all recessed bookshelves, ultramodern décor, and chairs suitable for the most diabolical of Bond villains. And, naturally, privacy curtains. If Ruiz was a member here, I suspected he'd be in one of those. I hadn't seen him in the bar as we passed by it.

"Shall we see the pool?" Rafe asked.

"Let's," I said.

We stepped out, and he led me to a wide, curving helix-shaped staircase, which we took up two floors for the purpose of seeing the view from the inside. Then Rafe walked us out to the rooftop patio. This was incredible—and I'd seen a few things in my day. Though, to be fair, 90 percent of my job was souks, back alleys, probable minefields, and the occasional embassy party. Contrary to Hollywood portrayal, spies didn't usually work in places like this.

The pool was in the center of the patio, which occupied the entire roof. Two towers, which held the upper residences, loomed over the pool deck, glowing brightly, like a pair of avenging angels. The deck's exterior wall was made up of twenty-foot sheets of glass facing the bay. There were large planters with palms growing from them, spaced at precise intervals, which created natural barriers almost like open air rooms. I spotted Ray immediately.

Ray and two guests stood along the glass wall, drinks in hand and laughing. One of the men was Caucasian, sixties, white hair and a beard, bright blue jacket with a pocket square with colors that didn't exist in nature. He wore a charcoal-colored shirt and white pants. The second guest was a black man who had the look of a retired athlete. His face was familiar, though I couldn't place it. He wore the kind of thing that only a celebrity with his kind of build could get away with—a mauve suit with a white tee shirt.

"He used to play for the Dolphins," Rafe said.

Then I had it. Hall of Fame linebacker and six-time Pro Bowl selection, he'd retired a decade ago and still held the franchise sack record.

Staring at the guy would've undermined the notion of hushed secrecy this place conveyed, so I took a mental picture and let Rafe continue with the tour. We made an orbit around the pool—with me noting the class of people I would not become in two lifetimes—and then returned to the bar.

"How about I have a martini and think over my membership?"

"I'm sorry, Mr. Carter, the bar is reserved exclusively for our members and their authorized guests."

I wanted to ask him if there was such a thing as an "unauthorized guest" but decided the juice wasn't worth the squeeze. Leaving me unaccompanied was a long shot anyway. Rafe took me to the elevator, and we rode it back down. I remained silent while he burned oxygen building up the hard sell. Once he hit the lobby, I took two long strides, turned halfway around, like I had *just* enough time for that and nothing more. Half over my shoulder, I said, "Thanks for the tour, Rafe. My assistant will be in touch."

I left him wondering if a comped martini would have made a difference between closing me or not.

Three days down.

So far, what I'd concluded was that Raymond Ruiz was a well-connected hustler. Which is to say, he was exactly what I'd expected someone in his position to be. If I'd expected Ruiz to meet with some shady-looking, obviously underworld character who helpfully handed him a burlap sack with a dollar sign on it...I'd be disappointed.

At the end of my stakeout, I had a solid pattern of life for Raymond Ruiz, but nothing that I could really use.

Meanwhile, I was digging into his background.

Open Source Intelligence was an emerging field of analysis that some speculated might surpass clandestine collection. OSI was based on all data in the public domain—traditional and social media; non-proprietary commercial data like satellite imagery; government documents such as police, tax, and court records; transcripts of official testimony; grey literature; and literally everything on the internet. If something was publicly available and legally accessible, it was considered "open source." Increasingly, data found on the dark web was being included in OSI collection.

There were several open-source aggregators available to law enforcement, corporate security outfits, and investigative agencies with tools not available to the public. Now that I was a licensed private detective, I could purchase one. I used a program called EchoTrace. I'd actually run the search queries on Ray one night on the drive here, though I'd only had time to skim it. Now that I felt I had a solid pattern of life, I figured it was time to dig a little deeper.

Never married and no children. A waterfront home in North Miami Beach with a boat. Member of the most exclusive private clubs in Miami. He entertained and courted—what I assumed to be—investors almost every night of the week, often multiple times throughout the day. EchoTrace confirmed that in addition to the box seats Mike told me about, Ray also had them at the Hard Rock Stadium. EchoTrace had an image recognition function, and I used that to analyze the surveillance photos I'd taken of Ruiz. I wanted to know who he was meeting with. Most of the returns were from social media and local news sites, showing prominent Miami business leaders and major donors to University of Miami Athletics. High rollers and local influencers.

The one conclusion I could conclusively make—Ray Ruiz lived large.

There wasn't much in the public domain about Sunshine Sports Collective. The collective didn't share what businesses they were associated with, nor did they share the athletes they sponsored. Some collectives registered with the IRS as tax-exempt organizations, and a few of them were even registered to lobby. I couldn't find anything on SSC, however. So far as I could tell, there wasn't anything illegal about a collective being a for-profit entity, even though they existed solely to funnel money to players. I did know that it took time for the paperwork to go through. I wondered which of those paths would get less scrutiny from the government.

Speaking of government, I kept bouncing off the city's tax office. I was frustrated and tired of the stalled progress, so I called and pretended to be a state regulator from Tallahassee. I told them I was doing records checks and needed to verify ownership of a few local entities. There's nothing classified or secretive about corporate ownership, it's just that at the municipal level it's typically buried beneath a few layers of paperwork and civic malaise. With most public corporations, that information is available online.

It took some time, but they eventually got me the ownership verification for each of the businesses that sponsored Brashard Brown. The football prep program was registered to the owner and in his name. The restaurant and sports equipment chain, however, were both registered to LLCs. I wrote those down, thanked the lady for her time, and disconnected.

I burned the fourth day of the stakeout following Ruiz to West Palm Beach.

When tailing someone, patterns are what get you spotted. Usually, you run surveillance with a team of people, coordinated over the radio. You leapfrog coverage, handing it over to a new car periodically. You also don't do it in a thirty-year-old SUV whose silhouette would be described as "distinctive and iconic."

Thankfully, I wasn't driving the Defender that day.

I arranged with the hotel to have daily driver rentals dropped off at 8:30 a.m. I didn't want Ruiz to spot the $200,000 restomod and catch on, so I drove rentals. That day, I happened to be in a BMW 3 series. Ruiz didn't leave his condo at the regular time, and for a while, I'd thought I missed him. My vantage point was the parking lot to catch him leaving the condo. There wasn't a great way to see if he was leaving on foot, and I had no other forms of surveillance. I did have some AirTags with magnetic holders that I have used to slide onto vehicles before, but I'd decided not to do that here.

If my case was ultimately meant to push the police or a state investigator off their assess, everything I did had to be completely legal. And even though Florida recognizes my California PI license, I wasn't familiar with the state's laws regarding surveillance and didn't want to risk it. Better to assume the same standard as California, which was "nothing without a warrant."

I caught Ruiz leaving the Miami Beach peninsula around ten that morning. He headed north and picked up I-95. Tailing him through the morning traffic crawl was easy enough, and I settled in for what turned out to be an hour's drive north to West Palm. On the plus side, it was easy to follow an Aston Martin. And as an ex-spy, I'm required to be able to spot one immediately in the wild. Union rules. On the downside, it's a hell of a lot faster than a 335i, and I lost him more than once as he opened it up. Eventually, the physics of traffic played in my favor, and I was able to catch up.

Ruiz left the interstate and crossed over Lake Worth Channel to Palm Beach proper. His Aston fit in a lot better there. My BMW, not so much. He pulled into a mansion on the Lake Worth side of Palm Beach and spent two hours inside. While he was in the home, I tried looking up the owner, but no dice. Not surprising really. People with this kind of money also had the resources to keep their identities hidden. Odds were that Ruiz was courting a wealthy donor. Still, it was worth checking out.

I burned the time watching the house, listening to a podcast through my AirPods.

He left shortly after one and drove back to Miami.

My phone rang when I was on I-95, five cars back from Ruiz's Aston. I was about to let it go to voicemail, when I realized the ringtone was different. It was the app Mickey had given me. I answered the call, toggling the noise cancellation on the AirPods to muffle the car's ambient noise.

"This is Jameson," I said.

"Mr. Carter, my name is Raymond Ruiz."

A cold shock ran through me. I'd been tailing Ruiz for several days and was, even now, within sight of him. "Raymond, it's great to hear from you."

"Ray, please. Sorry it took me so long to get back to you, Mr. Carter. You know how it is. I'm in the car now and had a few minutes to spare. What can I do for you?"

"Ray, I represent a group of investors called Apogee Partners. We're a PE firm, primarily focusing on the energy and tech sectors."

"How did you hear about us?"

I gave him a perfunctory laugh. "Brashard Brown. One of my partners and I are both Aggies, and we were real excited when we thought we were going to land Brashard Brown. You can imagine we were crushed when the young man switched to the U."

There was a chuckle on the other end, and Ruiz said, "I think I know where this is going."

"I understand your collective has a relationship with the kid. Personally, I'm more of a realist, but I think Dean has some hopes that we might be able to lure him away from Miami."

"I doubt that very much. He's going to start in the fall. Always happy to have a conversation, though."

"More broadly, we're about to go through a coaching change, and I'm not sure our booster group is planning effectively for..."

"That's exactly the problem I'm trying to solve. The beauty of our collective, Jameson, is that we aren't tied to any one school."

"You aren't?"

"No, we're tied to the athlete. So, this would be the perfect vehicle for you. Now, I don't have any relationships with your alma mater as yet—I'm a small operation, concentrating on south and central Florida. That's not to say we stay that way. I'd love to get you in and talk more about it in person. We're leaning into the current fluidity in college athletics. As a booster, you can certainly contribute to your school's athletic program through a traditional NIL vehicle. What *we* offer is an opportunity to invest in the player."

"I don't follow," I said.

"Just in the last few months, the courts have stated that collectives can be used to recruit players to schools. So, if you wanted to offer Brashard Brown, or any other player, money to play at A&M, there's nothing stopping you from doing it. SSC exists to facilitate those types of transactions. As a booster, you can have direct influence over a player. With every other collective in the country, you're paying into the fund and trusting them to make decisions."

"What happens if I make a bid for Brashard to come to A&M and another booster pays double to keep him here?"

"We act as an intermediary, but the player makes the final decision on which offer he takes. If he doesn't take the deal, you get your money back."

"It's like fantasy football, just for real."

"It's exactly like that."

Ruiz said he'd have his assistant call me in a few hours to set up a time to come in.

I casually followed him back to Miami and broke off the tail shortly before getting downtown, taking a different route to my hotel. I turned the car in and went back to my room.

Lawson had texted while I was on the road, asking if I was free for dinner. I called him back, and he said, "Carne, on South Beach."

"Jimmy, it might be a good idea for us not to be seen in public together."

"Why?" He sounded genuinely confused.

"I spoke with Ruiz today. I'm setting a meet with him in a few days, under an alias."

"Oh man, that's awesome. Real cloak-and-dagger shit. I love it. Listen, don't sweat it. We have more high-end restaurants per square foot than New York City. Even if Ruiz is out, the odds of him seeing us together are so low, Draft Kings wouldn't even touch it."

I assumed that was an inside baseball way of saying we were clear, but I didn't know anything about sports betting.

Against my better judgment, I put my jacket on and went to meet Jimmy.

# 4

Carne was not subtle.

From the bright-red leather chairs and leopard-print booths to the pineapples on the drapes, all collapsing around a bar that could have been yanked off Flagler's Folly, the whole place looked like Tony Montana decorated a WeWork. I'd looked up the chef before coming and saw that he was one of the most renowned in Argentina, which was saying something.

I gave my name to the hostess, and she brought me to Jimmy's table. "Your guest is here, Mr. Lawson," she said.

He winked at her. "Thank you, Monique."

I sat.

Jimmy already had a cocktail, and a waiter materialized to take my order. At the risk of being typecast, I ordered a martini.

We weren't getting out of here for less than five hundred apiece. I'd already racked up nearly a thousand-dollar hotel stay, and that didn't include my fee. So far, I hadn't gotten much for Jimmy's money. There were a lot of reasons for being reluctant to take an out-of-state job like this. I had no connections in local government or law enforcement. Or the darker ones that you often needed in this line of work. Nor was I conversant with the state's laws to the level that I knew how far I could push them.

I knew how to recruit assets and to entice people to reveal their deepest darkest. I knew how to move without being seen in a crowd. I'd made a career of breaking other countries' laws. I was less sure that I could find and prove others were breaking laws here.

Jimmy offered me damned good money, enough that it'd buy me another year at this PI thing if I was successful. After a week without much more to go on, I worried I might not be.

My drink arrived, and Jimmy said, "So, you spoke with Ruiz?"

"We spoke on the phone, and I'll be going into the office under the guise of being a potential investor. I've also been tailing him for the last three days and looking into the businesses that sponsor him. He's got an extravagant lifestyle, to say the least. Waterfront house on Miami Beach, drives an Aston Martin. He's entertaining prospective clients sometimes twice a day, and none of them touch the check. I saw him with a retired Hall of Famer the other day."

"That sure sounds like a Ponzi scheme to me," Jimmy said.

"Yeah. A Ponzi is a lot like playing craps, right? Where most people screw up is they let it ride too long and they get found out. It doesn't seem like that's what he's doing to me. Again, all this is from a distance. The only way I really figure out that he's breaking the law is by looking at his books."

"How do you plan to do that?"

"I don't know yet. I just don't see what the angle is."

"What do you mean?"

"Where is Ruiz breaking the law? I think him talking kids like Brashard into lifetime contracts is unethical as all hell, but it's not illegal. To all outward appearances, he's living beyond his means. Is he, though? We don't know where the money is coming from. What if he's got a couple megadonors who kicked a lot of cash in to create the collective. He said they were investing directly in the players. I told him it sounded like fantasy football for real, and he said it was exactly like that. From what I can tell, there's so little regulation around this, Ruiz might just have found a loophole and is milking it as hard as he can for as long as he can."

"Unethical but not illegal, like you said. You'll figure something out."

I decided to play for honesty. "I hope so. I don't take work lightly, and I don't want to waste your money. Or the Browns' hope. I mean that."

Oddly, Jimmy smiled at that.

"I know you do. Look, Matt, I spoke to Elizabeth at length about this and about you. She said there were a lot of things about her case she couldn't talk about and a few more that she wouldn't. However, Elizabeth did share a few important details. One, that you risked your life during that case, a few times. And you saved hers. All that stuff sounds cool and would probably make a damn cool movie." Jimmy set his drink down and looked me in the eye. "The thing I care most about, though, is when she said you wouldn't give up, even when the FBI threw you in jail because they were trying to scare you off." A low, rumbling chuckle rolled out of his mouth. "She said that just pissed you off and got you to dig your teeth in. So, don't sweat it. Ray Ruiz is up to something. You'll figure out what it is. And when you do, we'll get my client the fair shake he deserves." Jimmy picked up his cocktail. "I didn't call you here for a debrief. I mean, I wanted to know how the case is going. But I also wanted to break bread, you know?"

Jimmy telling me about his conversation with Elizabeth meant something to me. I appreciated hearing it.

There was something else, though. His demeanor was entirely different than when I'd first met him and when I'd seen him with the Browns. He wasn't the slick, dapper agent. Tonight, though still dapper (I didn't dress in this guy's league...or even his sport), he was laidback, funny, and engaging. He was the exact opposite of what I'd seen during all our prior interactions.

"How'd you end up in LA for law school?" I asked.

"Baseball mostly. I grew up in Minneapolis, and if you know anything about Minnesota in the winter..." He chuckled behind the words. "I bet the tire marks are still on the road from when I left. Anyway, I played ball most of my life. Wasn't good enough for a scholarship, but I really wanted to go to UCLA. Or, rather, I really wanted to go to Los Angeles. I had this kind of mythological view of the place that was probably from the movies."

"I know the feeling," I said.

"So, anyway, I'm at UCLA, and I'm pestering the baseball coach like crazy. Hanging around all the time. Played on some club teams my freshman year. Eventually, I bothered the coaches enough that they let me on the team as a walk-on. I was friends with some of the players and got them to vouch for me. I played three years, last two were on scholarship.

Senior year, coach called me into his office and told me, 'Jimmy, all the coaches here think the world of you, and we all agree you hustle like nobody else. You're just not going to play in the majors.' He talked to me like a man, said I was a good ball player, I just wasn't a great one. He said I could probably have a decent career in the minors if I really just wanted to play ball. Though he thought—and I'll never forget this—he said I'd be wasting a lot of other potential if I settled for being a minimum-wage ballplayer. He said, 'You worked your way into a scholarship in a D1 program and played in the College World Series twice. You have nothing to prove to anyone, you can hang your head high anywhere you go.'"

"You regret not trying to go pro?"

Jimmy shook his head. "I don't. By the time I hit my senior year, I was played out. Coach was right—I had nothing left to prove. I knew I didn't have the dedication or the ability required to play at a higher level." He laughed again. "Or enough of a love for the game that I'd do it for peanuts. So, I went to law school instead. Being an agent lets me stay connected to sports, and at this age, I'm better at negotiating deals than fielding balls. Having played, though, I get the mindset these athletes have, and I can represent them better. They know I did it and respect me for it."

"How long did you stay in LA after school?"

"Almost ten years. That's still the mecca for representation, and I'm back a couple of times a year. The firm wanted to expand its presence here, and I was a little tired of the LA scene, so I moved to Miami. And the Pacific is too damn cold, even in the summer."

I laughed at that.

"Which do you like better, LA or Miami?" I asked.

"I'm happy here. Pace is different. People still front, but it's nowhere near LA levels. Easier to meet people. I met someone, and we got serious for a while. Ended up not working out, part of me kind of hopes it still might. What about you?"

I gave him an abbreviated version. A senior person at the Agency ordered me to something questionable and, when it blew up in his face, blamed me for it. I took the fall for an international incident and quit. Or was fired, depended on who you asked. I didn't tell Jimmy about the death

I'll carry with me for the rest of my life. "I got into this line of work because there was a time when I needed someone with my background in their corner, and I was alone."

The waiter appeared and asked if we were ready for our main course. Jimmy ordered for the both of us, some sampler of their best cuts and a few token vegetables so we didn't go fully primal afterward. He asked me if I wanted to select the wine, and I deferred.

"I'm looking forward to this meal. I've been to Argentina. There are few things they take more seriously than steak," I said.

"What's it like?"

"Beautiful. Imagine the best parts of Europe with a Latin American flair." And a relentless federal security service that assumes every American on an official passport is worthy of suspicion.

A sommelier appeared and poured our wine with an unnecessary flourish

"So, you're going to go meet with Ray undercover. What are you looking for?"

"My suspicion is that Ruiz doesn't have the money to pay these athletes, so he pretends to vector their money into investment vehicles. That's the classic Ponzi move, right? Don't know if there's anything there, but I've got the ownership records for the businesses that sponsored Brashard. I'm assuming these are people that Ruiz suckered into backing his collective. Worth running down."

"I almost hope it's *not* that," Jimmy said, his voice suddenly tired.

"Why do you say that?"

"That's like another twelve months of investigation by the Treasury Department or the FBI or whomever."

"That's true. However, I mentioned before that I've got a friend in the FBI who used to work financial crimes. I'm calling her tomorrow. We can also use that to our advantage to get the Browns out of their contract." Which is, after all, what Jimmy was paying me for, not necessarily to break up a Ponzi scheme. "So far, I've found what we'd call 'indicators.' Clues, basically, to suggest SSC isn't being honest with their athletes. The pressure test will come when I roll in there as a high-value investor. Then we'll see how all this holds up. They aren't a nonprofit yet, are they?" My research showed that some percentage of NIL collectives registered as nonprofits for tax exempt status.

"Not as far as I can tell," Jimmy said. "Why?"

"Less scrutiny."

The meat arrived and took a team of waiters to set it up, still sizzling on its cast iron bed. Irrespective of contextual clues, one of them admonished us not to touch it because it was hot.

Jimmy and I dug in.

"There's something else you might want to look into," he said. "I just found this out."

His words carried a weight.

"Friend of mine, Elena Mendoza—she's another agent at my firm—was talking with a gymnast at UF. Elena got a phone call from someone who said this girl already had representation. The way Elena described it, it was one of those 'polite but not polite' conversations. Her words exactly. Elena double checks with the young lady, who confirms she's not represented. She did say that SSC reached out to her with a deal: five hundred thousand, mostly to do athleisure apparel modeling. She keeps the conversation with the gymnast going. She's having lunch with a client downtown, this guy walks up to her and says if she tries poaching one of his clients again, he'll see her in court."

"That sort of thing happens all the time in your business, right?"

"It's not exactly like *Entourage*, but yeah. And the bottom feeders will make approaches. It's also not a big community, especially here. We all know each other, and we talk. Figured out, this guy calls himself an NIL agent, and it looks like he works exclusively with SSC. That doesn't necessarily make him guilty, but...I'm just saying."

"You mentioned the agent before," I said.

"It gets better. Or, rather, worse. Elena is driving home a couple of days ago. The guy in front stops short at a yellow light, and she rear-ends him. In this town, 100 percent of people would have made that light. Now, she's already got her guard up, because the latest carjacking tactic is to cause a minor collision, and when you get out to inspect the damage, they steal your car. So, Elena walks up to inspect the damage, and she's making a show of having her phone out. She says she's going to call a traffic cop to take a look. The driver isn't this would-be agent but a thug-looking guy. Cuban, built like a fire hydrant. He looks her dead in the eye and says, 'You want to be more careful, miss.'"

"That's not normal," I said.

"No way. I've seen agents do some underhanded shit to land a client, or to take one away. No one ever goes to violence."

"She call the police?"

"She did. They told her until someone made an actual threat against her, they couldn't do anything."

I noticed a recurring theme on this case, which was that people in authority seemed to confuse "couldn't" and "wouldn't."

I said, "If this is a criminal conspiracy of some kind, it's smart. There's nothing to connect the agent's actions with SSC. Everyone has deniability. I'll dig more into this NIL agent, though I also wouldn't be surprised to learn that's a red herring."

"What do you mean? He threatened my colleague."

"Without question. You just can't prove it was connected to Sunshine Sports."

We ate in silence for a few moments.

"Can I ask you a personal question?" I asked.

"Of course."

"Why the bother with Brashard? And don't tell me you're a crusader. We can spot our own. Also, Brashard Brown doesn't strike me as a windmill to tilt."

Jimmy speared a perfectly medium-rare cut with his fork and popped it in his mouth. He savored that as he thought on my question. Then, he took a sip of wine.

"I think he could be big, and that's the truth. The kid is built like Mahomes, and he's pinpoint accurate with the ball. I've spoken with the coach—and this is off the record, so if this gets out I'll fire you in a flat second—but camp is going to be competitive. QB1 is up for grabs officially. Unofficially, they are leaning hard toward Brashard. They don't think their original starter is going to be back and healthy. Coach won't admit that publicly. He told me because he wants to make sure Brashard isn't going to rabbit if he doesn't get the starting position. Canes have been either a bubble team or an unmitigated disaster for fifteen, twenty years now. Even if they don't blow up, Brashard has first or high second-round potential. I'm investing in him." Jimmy stabbed another piece of meat. "But don't discount my desire to do the right thing. Someone looked out for me once. I think he's a good kid, and I don't want to see him get screwed over." Jimmy lifted his wineglass and stared at the contents a moment. "This business is only sharks, and there's always blood in the water."

---

Jimmy wouldn't let me see the check, which was probably just as well.

I told him I'd update him as soon as I got inside SSC then went to grab my Uber. The driver took me back across the neon-lit bridge to Miami's electric, glowing skyline.

The next day, I hit the bricks.

First, I went to the car dealership that had endorsed Brashard Brown. Turned out, the dealership was a local chain selling pre-owned imports. I asked for the manager, hoping I could learn about their relationship with SSC. An older, smarmy salesman intercepted me before I could make the bank of glass-walled offices in the back of the showroom.

Deflecting him, I found a receptionist, who told me the store manager wasn't in. So, I redirected and asked for the manager. The salesman hovered just off my shoulder, a creepy specter. The receptionist immediately assumed I was a dissatisfied customer going full Karen. While that kind of existential fear can be useful on occasion, it just caused the woman to turtle on me. I reassured her there was no problem and that I just wanted to speak to him about business. She took my information down and said Mr. Selby would get back to me as soon as he could, but that she didn't expect him to return until later that day.

*Odd reaction*, I thought.

My next stop was the Miami Fitness Source, "Dadeland's most complete retailer of high-quality fitness equipment to meet all of your wellness goals." The first thing I wanted to tell them was if something was already "complete," they couldn't then be the "most complete."

Charlie Garcia had an office in the flagship store in North Miami. He was not what I expected. Mid-fifties, glasses, gray business-athletic pants and a branded Miami Fitness Source polo that didn't hide the weight around his middle. He did not have the look of an ex-athlete put out to pasture. The office was cluttered with promotional material—his and others—and stacks of paper bulging out of folders that seemed unnecessary in the current age.

"What can I do for you, Mr. Gage?" He motioned to the chair opposite his desk. I sat.

As a PI, I'd be using my real name and credentials. If it ever got back to Ruiz that someone was looking around, Jameson Carter would just claim he always used an investigator for due diligence before making an investment.

"You recently signed an endorsement deal for Brashard Brown, quarterback with the Hurricanes, didn't you?"

"Yes, we did. We cut a commercial and everything," he said with some exuberance.

"Did you know Brashard?"

"Not before the TV spot. I do try to keep up with the local talent, though. I've been trying to land a contract with the school district for years. The university too."

"How did you come to know Sunshine Sports Collective?"

You'd have thought an arctic blast had blown through, based on how his expression frosted.

"I'm sorry, what's this about?"

I am a disciplined man, but sometimes, my lesser angels win out. A tired and irritated sigh escaped my lips. I managed not to eye-roll him, and for that, I think I deserve a little credit. "I was asking how you came to know Sunshine Sports Collective."

"Oh, someone came to see me about investing in local players." Garcia's eyes went to his computer screen, and his mouth screwed into a tight expression.

"Was it Raymond Ruiz?"

"I think so. Maybe. Probably."

"You signed a contract with his collective, but you don't remember the name of the person you spoke to?"

"I didn't really deal with him," he said, and the words came out just a mile or two over the speed limit. "I dealt with the ad agency."

"But the contract was with the collective, right? I'm sure the ad agency just organized the commercial."

"Can I ask what this is about?"

"I represent a group of investors. They're considering an arrangement with the collective and hired me to conduct some due diligence. Nothing is wrong, I assure you. They just wanted to understand the business from every angle."

"I don't know anything about their business. I just sell fitness equipment. Now, if you'll excuse me, I've got a sales meeting." I'd be willing to bet that Charlie Garcia could recite the stats and MSRP on every piece of equipment in his showroom, including whether it was the same model that Arnold Schwarzenegger had in his home gym. What he couldn't do was think fast on his feet about anything else. As soon as I asked him something he didn't want to answer, the guy short-circuited.

"Just one more question, if I could."

"Sorry, I just don't have the time. If you'll excuse me."

I made no move to leave. "If you don't mind me saying, Mr. Garcia, you seem nervous all of a sudden. As soon as I mentioned SSC, you became agitated. Is there a reason for that?"

"No, I just don't appreciate your asking questions about my business associates when it's none of *your* business. Now, please leave."

---

I dropped by the restaurant that Brashard had done a spot for. Family restaurant in Hialeah. The manager's English wasn't great, or at least he wanted me to think it wasn't. I asked to speak with the owner, and he smiled and nodded and said "yes" a lot.

People have many reasons for not wanting to speak with an authority figure, even a presumed one. In their defense, I looked like the establishment. Thanks to the CIA, I speak four languages pretty well. Unfortunately, not one of them is Spanish. You want someone to navigate French Africa or buy Russian guns in their native tongue, I'm your guy.

Miami's traffic was a force multiplier in all the worst ways. The places I'd gone were spread out across the greater Dadeland area, which made for a long day. After my fourth stop, I was beginning to feel like this was a dead end, a lot of footwork for little gain. I went back to my hotel for a beer and some dinner. I found a spot at the end of the bar, ordered a pint and a Cuban sandwich. March Madness was in full swing, and the bartender had the game on. Florida Gulf Coast versus Tennessee. When I was in school, the Vols were one of our big rivals, so it was easy to root for FGCU. I found myself staying at the bar for my entire meal and a few more beers than I planned.

The bartender, whom I'd gotten to know over my week and change at the hotel, leaned across the bar and hit my arm to get my attention. "Check this out," he said, pointing to the TV screen I was already watching. "The center, Cody Portman, is a local kid. My cousin played against him in high school. He's unreal. Led Pembroke Pines to a conference championship. Probably could've gotten state if they'd had more of a team around him."

"Yeah? Surprised a bigger school didn't scoop him up," I said.

There's ten seconds left, and the Vols are up by a point.

"Well, he didn't really blow up until his senior year. I mean, literally, kid grew three inches. Guess there wasn't enough of a resume for a Florida or a Miami."

FGCU grabs a rebound and rockets down the court. Clock time dissolves to a couple of seconds. They got a guy outside the field goal line, looking like he's going to go for a three, but instead, he passes it to the center, the local kid. Two seconds left. Center makes the shot. Sinks it as time expires. FGCU wins. Cinderella gets her crown.

*Everyone* is shocked as shit. It takes a full second for the Gulf Coast bench to realize what happened and flood the court.

Cody Portman, the center, hasn't moved. He's dumbfounded.

"He did that against my cousin too," the bartender marvels.

"Can't believe that thing even hit the backboard," I say.

"Yeah, it's an ugly shot, but it went in."

The commentators are all losing their minds. Both benches erupt—one is "shock," and the other is "awe." After a few, furious seconds, the commentators get ahold of themselves and reiterate that Cinderella just found her glass slipper.

The cameras naturally zoom in on Cody for a reaction shot. Commentators talking about how stunned he looks.

I know that look.

He's not stunned—he's scared.

## 5

I had an appointment to meet Raymond Ruiz the following afternoon.

I didn't look the part of a venture capitalist who'd be willing to drop thousands of dollars on a college football player *just because*. Thankfully, I'd spent some time in Silicon Valley and saw how people with startup exit money dressed themselves.

After a few hours in some downtown Miami boutiques, I rolled out with a bright blue linen jacket, white polo, white pants, and loafers allegedly handmade in Italy. Assuming I'd be meeting Ruiz more than once, I had a few outfits put together. Jimmy was either going to shit an egg roll when he saw my expense report or go "game recognizes game."

The Sunshine Sports Collective was in a just-opened office complex on Grand Avenue in Coral Gables, a block from the water. It was a two-story facility with a high, arched roof and glass panels that reminded me of the Hall of Justice from the *SuperFriends*. There was an electronic kiosk and a fountain surrounded by palms in the entry foyer. I found SSC on the second floor and walked up the curving staircase. The receptionist greeted me by name, which I hoped was just a good guess based on the day's schedule. She guided me back to a conference room with a large monitor that showed a slideshow of college athletes in various stages of effort and triumph.

She offered me a seat, water, and a coffee. I asked for an espresso to be difficult. The girl obliged.

I'd mentioned earlier that Jimmy Lawson looked like his job. Well, so did Raymond Ruiz.

I put him at five foot ten, fit, and upper forties, though he looked a good ten years younger. Black hair with a slight shine and the kind of eyes that could drill holes in a wall. Intense and focused. Ruiz had sharp, angled features that age had rounded out just slightly. He flashed a bright, broad smile as he entered the room with a hand extended.

"Ray Ruiz. Welcome to Sunshine Sports Collective," he said with a gaze like it came from klieg lights.

"Jameson Carter," I said. "James to my friends. Great to meet you, Ray. Thanks for having me."

He poured a couple of mineral waters and asked if I wanted a coffee. I told him the girl up front had already taken care of it. Then he shocked me. What I'd expected was a monologue worthy of at least a daytime Emmy, bolstered by stories of how they were literally lifting kids out of poverty. All delivered by the kind of guy who spends a quarter of a million on a car.

Instead, he went full fan boy.

He talked, in detail, about Texas A&M's football program going all the way back to the four years in the 1950s when Bear Bryant coached there. He talked in detail about how they resurrected their program when they joined the SEC in 2012 and the impact Johnny Manziel had as a player and a personality. The challenges they had under Jimbo Fisher, always bouncing against that glass ceiling—they could beat Alabama, but not take home the national title. He talked about Jameson Carter's alma mater the way I knew my real one. Sure, I'd bet Ruiz had studied up for the meeting. Though I gathered it was more a refresher of facts he already knew. All this was delivered with a wide-eyed and honest enthusiasm of a true fan and student of the game.

To be honest, one of the hardest things I'd ever done was to keep up in that conversation and show that I knew what in the hell I was talking about. That I was the kind of person who not only had the money to just give away to players, but that I understood what it would get me.

"Listen, I'm not an armchair coach," I said after Ray asked me directly what I wanted to do with my prospective investment. "I'm not talking about trying to convince players to go to A&M, players the staff doesn't even want. I'm looking for ways to help them out, using whatever tools are available to me today."

Ray smiled at that. "That's exactly what we're here for at SSC," he said.

"All right, so why you? What does Sunshine Sports get me that my school's collective does not?" I asked, attempting to steer the conversation away from sports statistics that I clearly didn't know.

"Do you have a relationship with the coaching staff?"

I flashed a dry smile. "We give enough that people will take our calls, yeah."

"Honestly, James, that is where we come in. We're the tool you use to build the roster your coach wants. The other thing we can do is use the transfer portal to make it attractive for certain players to look elsewhere."

"Pay them to leave? Why not just cut them?" I said.

"Oh, coaches can certainly do that. Though it gets ugly. Offering a little incentive to players who don't match the system makes roster-building much simpler."

Ray spent a few minutes talking about the membership tiers and the perks—how if we spent a certain amount, we'd get photos with the athletes we sponsored and other things like sideline access. As before, Ray spoke with genuine enthusiasm. If he was putting on an act, he was as good at this as I was.

"What can you tell me about your donors, so far? What kind of company am I going to be in?"

"Well, you know many donors want to remain anonymous," he said.

"Except from the IRS," I added.

"Well, right. I won't disclose our boosters. People tend to be sensitive about that sort of thing, as I'm sure you can appreciate. I'm especially mindful of protecting identities in the current environment." Ruiz left that floating in the air between us, as though I was to know what he meant. "All that said, I know names are a draw, and I'm courting some big ones that I think would help."

"You're talking professional athletes?"

"Exactly. People with the kinds of careers that our athletes and prospectives want to emulate. It's a big draw, for sure. I was just talking with an NFL Hall of Famer this week, and we're close. Of course, I have connections with the U and our alumni network. I've got calls in to a slew of retired football and basketball players. Frankly, this is where a relationship with you and your partner would be interesting to us. This expands us across the Gulf, gets us into another top-tier school."

"What's the draw for them? For Cane Collective, I get why someone like, say, Warren Sapp or the Rock would invest in that. Why SSC?"

"That's a great question, James. For the pros, it's often about being able to sponsor an athlete they think has potential, someone who reminds them of themselves a bit. Remember, these guys never had those options. Again, when you contribute to a school's collective, you have less of a say in what happens with the individual athletes. We're trying to change that paradigm. SSC is also working with the lower-profile athletes who tend not to get as much attention. We've talked a lot about Brashard Brown, but what about his offensive line? Who's looking out for the players casual fans can't name?"

"That's great," I said. "I love it. I can't quote them, but I think the statistics on second-round draft picks going on to have Hall of Fame careers are interesting."

"Yes," Ray agreed, exuberantly.

I'd made that up entirely, though it was a decent guess.

"So, how do you make money?" I asked. "Presumably, it costs a couple of bucks to court these major donors, right?"

Ray forced a tired smile, as if the high-roller life exhausted him. "It does. Couple of ways. First, I run a lean business, and there are only five permanent employees here. Myself, Olivia McEvoy, who runs investor relations and is my de facto COO, an office manager, a talent scout, and an investment manager. We use some virtual assistants for the admin work and the bookkeeping. As to your first question, we take a percentage from the endorsement deals we help secure, assuming they clear a certain threshold. And there's a small administrative fee baked into our contracts to cover office expenses. I do take a nice salary—though as you say, our entertainment budget is quite high, and that comes out of my pocket."

The business model he'd just detailed didn't quite jive with what Jimmy described. He'd said they took money from the athlete's contracts. Ruiz made it sound like the sponsors covered it.

There was a rap on the door, and a man poked his head into the conference room.

"Not interrupting, am I?" he asked in the practiced way of someone who didn't care if he was or not. Five foot ten, slicked-back hair, and ten pounds too many packed inside a tailored, tropical-weight, gray suit.

"No, of course not, Frank." Ray stood. "James, I'd like you to meet Frank Rizzo. He's a state senator representing Miami and one of our biggest advocates in the capitol."

I stood and shook his offered hand. "Jameson Carter," I said.

"I was just in to drop some things off with Olivia and wanted to pop in, say hi."

Ray gave Rizzo a perfunctory rundown of who he thought I was and what we were doing here. Then, he moved on to the advocacy work Rizzo did in Tallahassee on behalf of collegiate athletics and what Ray termed an "athlete's right to fair compensation."

"What do you do, Jameson?" Rizzo asked.

"I run strategy for a private equity firm in Dallas. I am in town for a few days, heard about the interesting things Ray is doing here, and popped in to see if Sunshine Sports could help my Aggies out."

"Love it," Rizzo said, the way politicians do. "I won't keep you. If you need a reference or want to talk about how we're influencing things at the state level, drop by my office."

"I'll do that," I said.

Rizzo and Ruiz exchanged some words about an engagement they had, and Rizzo oozed back into the hallway.

Ray said, "I'm going to connect you with Olivia McEvoy before you leave."

"Sounds great," I said.

"I hope I've answered all your questions. Maybe we can grab a drink before you leave town."

"Let's do that," I said.

Olivia materialized in the doorway as if summoned. She cut a striking figure. Her outfit clung as close to her body as it could and still be considered business attire, while showing off the muscled curvature beneath. She was blond with dark roots and brown eyes.

Ray introduced us and said, "I'll let you two connect. Olivia, please take good care of Jameson here. I've got that call with Mr. Edwards. Jameson, it was a pleasure. I hope we'll be in touch." Ray turned the klieg-light stare to me, full wattage, before strutting out of the room.

I didn't think it was coincidental that Senator Frank Rizzo just happened to be in the building or that Olivia McEvoy would appear out of thin air. This was rehearsed, and I wouldn't be surprised to learn Ray had a way of communicating with them other than his phone.

"So, you're here to talk me into spending some money?" I asked Olivia.

"Oh, I think you already know what you want," she said.

Putting myself in Ruiz's position, if I were trying to recruit an asset, this would be how I'd do it.

"In all seriousness, Jameson, I think we offer good opportunities to invest in future superstars and contribute to an undervalued community." Olivia had dropped the flirty, pseudo-sexual tone and gone zero-to-business so fast she may have left tire marks. "We're in an uncharted regulatory space, and anything could change. That being said, we believe strongly it will be some years before meaningful regulation happens. We've also raised a nonprofit arm of the business to lobby state and federal officials on behalf of our and the student athlete's interests."

"I think I just met part of that activity?"

"Ahh, Frank stopped by," she said. Olivia McEvoy then handed me her card. "I'd love to get a drink sometime, and we can discuss what an investment might look like for Apogee."

"I'd like that," I said.

As a case officer, I'd have months to develop an asset before I asked them to spy for us. As a private detective, I had days, sometimes only hours, to convince someone to help. Ray believed Jameson Carter was a player with money to throw around. Now I'd shift my focus to Olivia. In that one meeting, I'd need to determine if she'd be an asset. If so, a conscious one or an unwitting one?

There was nothing in the meetings today that suggested anything here was below board. Though, admittedly, I hadn't seen their finances. If it weren't for that strange interaction with Charlie Garcia and his whiplash shift in demeanor that felt like panic, I might have thought Jimmy was just being paranoid.

I took her card and said tomorrow night looked good.

Satisfied with my progress, I left.

Once I was back in my hotel, I made a phone call.

"Are you in jail?" FBI Special Agent Katrina Danzig asked. I didn't even get a "hello" first.

"Why is that always your first question?"

"I mean..."

"I'll remind you that the last time I was *in* jail, you put me there. *And* it was your fault. For which you apologized. Profusely."

Amazing how you can sometimes almost hear an eye-roll on the phone.

"How can I help you, Matt?"

"You got a minute?"

"I do. What's up?"

"You used to be based in Miami, right? Investigating financial crimes or something."

"Correct. You're not thinking of committing any, are you?"

I realized my demeanor tended to draw that kind of response from people. This wasn't the time, though. "Katrina, this is serious." I'd met Agent Danzig during Elizabeth's case. I had some baggage with the FBI, courtesy of my inglorious exit from the Agency, and she, perhaps, took that a little too much to heart. Like thinking I may have been a Chinese asset. We got over that, and I helped her round up the *actual* Chinese agents trying to plumb our nation of its precious technology secrets...and murder people who spoke out against Beijing. Now, we were friends.

"I'm working on a case, and I think I may have stumbled onto a Ponzi scheme. Could I run this by you and see what you think?"

"Go for it."

"All right. My client is a sports agent representing a University of Miami football player. Are you familiar with name, image, and likeness rights?"

"A little. The Bureau has investigated college sports in the past. You might remember a big case about twenty years ago. There were some boosters with links to organized crime funneling money to the Ohio State program."

"I do remember that. So, this kid gets a million-dollar NIL deal from a collective here in Miami. Now, there's only about twenty or so college athletes across the country making that kind of money. Also, this collective is not tied to the school."

"I thought that was the whole point of a collective."

"These guys claim they are school agnostic. Their investment scheme is that you get to support individual players."

"I don't totally see why anyone would do that," Danzig said.

"I said it sounded like fantasy football with real people."

"Huh. That makes sense, I guess. Still, I also don't see how it's a Ponzi. Have they paid any of their players?"

"I only know one of them, my client's client. He's received two hundred fifty thousand of the million they signed him for. The rest of it, the collective vectored into investments on his behalf. According to them, it's so the student athletes don't blow all their money."

"That might be something," Danzig said. "Still...what was it they hired you to do?"

"The kid, Brashard Brown, signed a lifetime royalty contract with this collective before he had an agent. Apparently, it stays in place even after he goes pro. Once the family realized what had happened, they got an agent and tried to get out of the deal. So far, no dice. They hired me to see if I could find any evidence of illegal activity at the collective to get Brashard out of his contract. They think there might be something sketchy going on with these investments."

"It certainly sounds unethical, but I'm not sure it meets the bar for illegal. What I mean is, if you were presenting this to me, I'm not sure there would be enough evidence to open a case."

I was afraid of that.

Then Danzig said, "That's not what this is, right? You're not trying to backdoor me into taking up a new case? Because this isn't my jurisdiction."

"Christ no. I've got too much money riding on this to turn it over," I said, mostly joking. "So, you don't think there's enough to go on?"

Danzig continued. "Well, you might be onto something. This NIL stuff is all uncharted territory. With all the money flying around, it wouldn't shock anyone to find out that someone had figured out how to run a scam. I know the Bureau is keeping an eye on it, though that's not my department. Let me do this. When I was in Miami, I was on a financial crimes task force. We had state and local law enforcement as well as prosecutors. I know a lieutenant with Miami-Dade from my time there. Michelle Silvestri. She's a good cop. We worked a case together, and I think she went on to lead an organized crime unit. I can put you in touch with her. One of her informants used to be the money guy for the Russian mob in Miami. She may be willing to connect you with him to ask some questions. My gut is, if this collective has invented a new way of scamming people, this guy probably knows about it. Wouldn't surprise me if it was his idea." The way she said it, I got the sense that last bit was saying the quiet part loud.

"I'd appreciate the connection. Having a friendly with local law enforcement would be helpful."

"Tread carefully with this guy. Thanks to him, the Bureau tagged one of Fidel Castro's favorite hit men, and we closed about a dozen political assassinations going back to the 1970s. He tipped us to this Russian mob outfit that, to be fair, the Bureau didn't know about. He will bring this up when you mention me."

"So, why do I tread lightly?"

"Well, for one thing, he's a con artist and should've been arrested for fraud. I also got the sense there was something between Silvestri and him."

"Awesome," I said. "I was actually hoping this case could get murkier."

"One other thing, Matt."

"What's that?"

"Be careful. Maybe smoke here means fire, but maybe it doesn't. If this is just a case of people playing fast and loose with the rules, you could be screwing up this kid's chances and costing his family a lot of money. You can walk away if this blows up in your face, but they can't."

# 6

Danzig said she'd get back to me after she'd spoken with this Lieutenant Silvestri.

Informant baggage aside, having a connection with local law enforcement was invaluable. Miami wasn't my town. I had no network here. Besides, if this case did indeed break, I'd need the police's help anyway.

I called Jimmy and caught him between meetings. I updated him on my visit to SSC and the presumed follow-up with Olivia McEvoy. We agreed to meet up later and debrief.

Olivia was my best way in. There was a delicate balance here, because I didn't want to appear too eager. In addition to the time I'd already mentioned, asset cultivation also entailed significant behavioral profiling. And we had to tell them we were representatives of the United States government and wanted them to collect information on our behalf. I'd do none of that.

This would only be lies.

I had to convince Olivia McEvoy to admit to me her company was running a con.

I called her and asked if she was free to meet later. She suggested drinks at a place downtown. We agreed to meet for happy hour.

My phone rang at lunchtime, the call coming from a local number.

"Matt Gage?"

"This is. Who's calling?"

"This is Michelle Silvestri with Miami-Dade. I just spoke with Katrina Danzig, and she said we should chat."

"Thanks for calling, Lieutenant. Do you have a few minutes?"

"Let's do this in person. Where are you staying?"

"I'm at the JW Marriott downtown."

"I'm in the wrong line of work," she said.

"My client is springing for it. I typically stay in cinderblock shit houses."

That didn't even get a laugh. Silvestri said, "You free now?"

"I am."

She suggested Bayfront Park, a few blocks from my hotel. I walked out, eager to stretch my legs. Silvestri texted me fifteen minutes later to tell me she was parking. She asked me what I was wearing so she knew what to look for, and my first instinct was to make a crack about this feeling like an internet date, but I decided against it. I described my outfit, general build, and the bench upon which I'd parked myself.

There are people who are fit, and there are people who look like cross-fit evangelists.

Michelle Silvestri was the latter.

I wasn't sure if she had to run suspects down on foot anymore, but I felt a pang of regret for them if she did. She was five-nine, South Florida tanned, brown hair pulled back in a short tail, and incredibly fit. She wore aviator sunglasses. You do this long enough, you can feel someone sizing you up even if you can't see their eyes.

I stood. "Matt Gage," I said and extended a hand.

Silvestri wore a tan suit and navy blouse. She shook my hand. "Michelle Silvestri," she said. "So, how can I help you?"

I gave her the same rundown I did Danzig.

"Wouldn't shock me," she said when I'd finished. "What's your goal here?"

I kept it objective. "These guys are taking advantage of a kid and his family. My client, this kid's agent, wants me to prove that Sunshine Sports

Collective is running a scam with the athlete's money. If I can, my client can use that as leverage to void this contract. However, if I find evidence of illegal activity, I'm happy to turn anything and everything over to you, so you can go after them."

"That's not really what my group does," she said, shaking her head. "However, if you have evidence, definitely let me know, and I can get it to someone. I can't promise anything. We're seriously undermanned."

"Seems like a common problem," I said.

"Defund everything," she said grimly. "Danzig said you wanted to talk to one of my informants?"

"If it's possible. Two questions that are top of mind. First, based on what I've described, does this sound like a Ponzi scheme? And, two, has he heard of anything? Not sure if he still has active contacts,"

"I'm sure he does, even though I told him not to."

Well, I wouldn't be picking *that* thread up. Silvestri pulled her phone out. "Good morning, Francis," she said. It was one o'clock in the afternoon.

Listening to one side of this conversation was...interesting.

"Yes, it's a favor...shut up...goddamnit, Francis. Yes, ten minutes." She hung up, looked at me, and said, "Let's go."

Silvestri led me to her orange four-door Wrangler. "Katrina said you guys worked together on a case?"

"Sort of. Not sure how much background she gave you. I'm a Los Angeles-based private investigator. Last fall I had a case in the Bay Area. Started out with a grieving daughter wanting me to prove her father's suicide wasn't. Turned into something a lot worse. Katrina and her team eventually got involved."

"How much worse?"

"Chinese-espionage-and-murder-ring worse."

Silvestri turned her head to look at me, as if assessing me in new light. She said, "huh," and that was it.

We drove north about a mile to the Venetian Marina and Yacht Club. Silvestri gave her name to a security guard, and he allowed us to pass. She led us down the walkway to the curved docks built like outstretched arms of some sea god. I noted Silvestri had no problem finding it.

"He lives on a boat? They don't make waterbeds anymore?"

Silvestri just sighed, as though it were some significant weight she carried. We stopped at a berth with a craft called *The Green Flash*. It was a power yacht, about fifty feet long with a metallic-gray paint job and dark windows that ran the length of the hull. Its shape was that of an aggressive wave rolling into some tropical port.

"Francis," Silvestri barked.

The figure that emerged from the cabin looked like a gene-splicing experiment to combine Sonny Crockett with a carnival barker. He was about my height, though more wiry than muscular, dirty-blond hair that probably took ten minutes to look sloppy, and a dusting of facial hair. He wore a purple-and-blue floral print shirt, white shorts, and a pair of Maui Jims.

"You vouch for this guy?" I said, *sub rosa*.

"I do, and stop it." Silvestri raised her voice, clearly indicating I hadn't known her long enough to question her judgment. "Francis Madigan, meet Matt Gage."

"Everyone calls me Flash. Come on board," he said.

*Flash?*

I followed Silvestri onto the boat. "Matt, here, is a private investigator from California. We have a friend in common, Special Agent Katrina Danzig." I noted Silvestri had added the helpful reminder of Danzig's status as a federal agent, as though that were the kind of thing easily forgotten.

"This oughta be good," Flash said. I climbed the stairs and sat in the booth at the boat's stern. Silvestri didn't move from the diving platform.

"Gents, I'm going to leave you to your playdate. Matt, good luck with your case. If I can be of help, let me know. And if you find anything…" She extended her pinky and thumb miming a phone.

With Lieutenant Silvestri disappearing down the dock, Flash said, "Okay, so what the hell is this about?"

By now, I was pretty good at summarizing the case. I also told him how I'd posed as a potential investor. Maybe it was a good idea Silvestri wasn't here for this.

At the end of it, Flash said, "That doesn't sound like a Ponzi to me."

"Why not?" I asked, genuinely curious, not questioning him.

"Well, the point of those are to draw in as many clueless people as possible with the promise of too-good-to-be-true-but-still-believable returns. The way you described it, it didn't really sound like they were promising your client a massive payout on those investments. A Ponzi works like this: you've got a fake investment vehicle you get people to contribute to. Some of the savvier ones might even make a few people rich, people who aren't in on it, so you get some social proof. Ultimately, they're all hollow. Straight Peter to pay Paul. Usually, the person running it will give them fake statements to show the 'millions' their marks made. The goal is to keep it going long enough that you can disappear forever. Or, if you were Madoff, keep it going in perpetuity and live off the hog, knowing you'd either get away with it or die in prison. What you're describing doesn't sound like that. They don't have 'investors' in the traditional sense. They have donors. And donors don't expect a return on investment. The part that does sound fishy is pushing these kids to invest their money in these funds you mentioned. Even that, though...they're using money the athletes never had to begin with. The money is all coming from people who don't expect a financial benefit."

"So, you're saying this doesn't look like a scam?"

"No, I'm saying it doesn't look like a Ponzi scheme. This is a perfect setup for money laundering," Flash said. "Look at it this way. This is a completely unregulated business right now. Since they aren't a nonprofit, they don't have to disclose who the contributors are. I bet they've got a stream of dollars they want to legitimize, so they have people like you," he waved a hand at me, "pump money in. They pay some of the athletes just enough to make it look legitimate and defer the rest of it to these other investments. That buys them time to make the athletes whole later on. If it were me, I'd use the laundered money to invest in legitimate enterprises, real estate, stuff like that. Legitimate investments so they've got something to show for it."

"Well, they did convince this kid to park a portion of the money they were supposed to pay him in some investment fund."

"That's perfect," Flash said, a cynical laugh trickling out of his mouth. "Mix the dirty money with the clean, and no one is the wiser."

"Let's say you're right. How do you prove it? What do you look for?"

"That's the problem. It's going to be nearly impossible for someone like you. Unless there's an insider tipoff, the way these things are usually uncovered is through forensic accounting. Data." Flash, not having the benefit of my backstory, started to describe all the ways that money is moved around illegally. I let him talk. I wondered if we knew some of the same people. "You could look for shell companies. If you can figure out where they're parking their money or maybe the name of the group handling these investments, that might be something."

"I don't want to offend you, Flash, because you've been very helpful."

"But," he said in a loaded tone, pulling the word apart like a nine-year-old with bubblegum.

"Are you still connected to that world? My guess is this is why Silvestri didn't stick around."

Flash didn't answer right away. He studied the boat in the slip next to us, and I could see him chewing on his response, by the motion of his jaw.

"Not really. I had a chance to get out, and I took it. I used to work for this Russian gangster named Konstantin Kuznetsov. He was the big player here in Magic City for a few years. The FBI, represented by our mutual acquaintance, probably would've nailed him had he not been murdered by a Cuban gang leader named Enrique Aragon. Most people assumed I had dimed Kuznetsov out to him. I didn't. Aragon took him out for his own reasons. I bring this up to say that most people in the underworld won't talk to me anymore, which is how I want it. Most of those people would also kill me if they got the chance, which is why I tend to stick close to Lieutenant Silvestri."

I didn't think that was the *only* reason but wasn't going to press it.

I got the sense Francis "Flash" Madigan was saying this for the record. Almost as if he assumed someone was listening.

He held up a finger and disappeared inside the boat. I heard a little bit of shuffling inside and tried not to pay too much attention to it. He reemerged and sat, dropped his hand below the table, and set something on the bench. I looked down and saw it was a folded piece of paper. I slid it into my pocket.

Flash stood and smiled. "Sorry I couldn't be of more help."

Picking up on the act, I said, "No problem at all. It was a long shot."

I didn't shake his hand, just nodded and left.

When I was well outside the marina and back on a city street, I pulled out the piece of paper. A phone number had been scribbled on it. I dialed.

Flash answered.

"Good. Now we can have a proper conversation."

## 7

"I don't necessarily know if I can be helpful, but I can ask around. I still know a few people and more importantly, I know what to look for," he said.

"Hold on," I said. I'd even stopped walking, even though Flash couldn't see it. "Before we go any further, I have questions."

"I figured you might."

"First of all, why the secrecy? Is someone watching you, and do I now need to be concerned with someone watching *me*?"

"The price of liberty is eternal vigilance," he said, and I didn't respond. "I'm pretty sure someone is looking at me all the time. Listen, I did some bad shit for worse people and got away with it. I tried to make up for it with some undercover work that almost got me killed on multiple occasions. I'm not asking for societal forgiveness. I'm also not asking for judgment. If you're going to come off high and mighty, you can take whatever problems you've got with you."

"Sorry, I didn't mean to be an asshole. My client is a kid, football player, like I said. Good kid, just made some stupid decisions. I don't want there to be any blowback on him."

"That's fair," Flash said. "For whatever this is worth to you, I don't think anyone peeping me is going to be interested in you."

"Is it law enforcement types or the mob?"

"My guess is the latter."

"Then why am I talking to you on a burner?" I didn't know that I was—just a good guess.

"Call it an abundance of caution. I haven't done anything since Michelle got me out. That doesn't mean there isn't a state or federal agency that would take a swing at me to get me to kick on people I know."

"What's the organized crime scene like here now?" I'd known the Russians were here, even before Flash mentioned it. A lot of those guys were ex-KGB, so we tended to keep track. The history of Cuban organized crime in Miami can mostly draw its roots to the Bay of Pigs, which the Agency was all over. The largest and most powerful Cuban mob, at least through the 2000s, were all veterans of that disaster. On top of that, you've got the Columbian cartels moving in during the '70s and '80s. Doing business with and simultaneously fighting against Cuban, Haitian and other gangs for turf. Then the Columbian cartels fell, and the Mexican ones ascended. They're all here. CIA kept tabs on that as well, as did the FBI and DEA.

I'd tried to distance myself from the War on Terror when I was in the Agency. My mentor didn't think that was the fight the CIA should be in, and I'd taken to his logic. Not to say it wasn't a righteous struggle. It just wasn't necessarily *our* righteous struggle. I spent a lot of my career in Asia and South and Central America. As a result, I was more conversant with the issues that pervaded those regions—narcotics and weapons trafficking, money laundering, transnational crime, and smuggling, to name a few.

Miami had always had this reputation of being a modern-day Casablanca. It was spies—foreign and domestic—mixing with mobsters, drug cartels, arms dealers, smugglers, and counterfeiters, all existing just below the surface. It was as fascinating as it was terrifying. Somehow, at least since the early '90s, the pot rarely boiled over.

"Big players are still the Russians, though it's fragmented now," Flash said. "You have a ton of Cuban gangs. Many of them are working for the Russians in some capacity. The Cuban outfits tend to be smaller. I'd experience an abbreviated life expectancy if they ever heard me refer to them as such, but you could think of them as mini mafias. And no one seems to be paying attention to them. When I was an informant on Michelle's undercover task force, I got a crash course in what the local cops and the Feds care about."

"And it's not them?"

"It's not them. They tend to get away with murder," Flash said. There was nothing much I could say to that. "If you can get me the name of that investment corporation, I can run it down pretty fast and see if it's legitimate. I know what to look for. I will also ask around to see if my contacts know of any new schemes."

"Thanks, Flash. I appreciate that. What do you want in return?"

"You know why I still live on a boat? So I can leave at the drop of a hat. I would love nothing more than to not have to do that."

"How can I help?"

"Danzig seems to like you." How in the hell would he know that already? "If you can convince her to get some of her friends to look into things around here with information that didn't come from me, I might have a chance to put down something more than an anchor."

"I'll see what I can do."

I walked back to my hotel and realized I didn't have the Browns' phone number. I called Jimmy and updated him on what I'd learned. He gave me Cyrus's phone number. Cyrus was at work, and all the information he had on the investment vehicle was at home. He promised to call as soon as he got home and could take a look.

I cooled a few hours before I went to meet McEvoy.

---

Olivia suggested a bar in Little Havana called Café La Trova. The interior was tobacco and cream, red leather stools, and wrought iron. Olivia had a place at the bar staked out for us, which was helpful, given how packed it was.

Olivia was in a dress that didn't look like work attire.

She moved in for a hug and the cheek kiss. I could smell the daiquiri on her breath. I ordered a beer. After we'd drained half of our first round on small talk, she asked, "So, how are you feeling about it?"

"Unsure. It certainly sounds interesting. I think we'd like a little more confidence that, for the money, you could convince Brashard to enter the portal and that A&M would take him. Like, have you talked to him? Do you make the offer? How does it work?"

"We don't need to worry about specifics," Olivia purred. "We have a great relationship with all our athletes, and if the donation is right, I am confident he'd flip."

"Have you done this sort of thing before?"

"We have. I'm bound by confidentiality, of course. But we've facilitated such a transaction. Let's say you wanted to move forward. You put the donation into escrow. For sake of discussion, let's say it's one point two, based on what Brashard's valuation is. We approach him with the offer. If he's interested, then we reach out to the A&M coaching staff. Most of the time, we don't even broach the subject unless we know the player fits their scheme and they have roster space. Or are willing to make changes."

"What if they need convincing?" I asked.

She smiled with a feigned Victorian blush. "Sometimes an additional donation to the school's collective greases the wheels. I'll make sure you don't get taken for a ride." She flipped a glance over the rim of her glass, and I could see a wry smile behind it. "Unless, of course, that's what you want."

"Where did you guys get started? For a university-connected collective, I imagine they first round up some big-name alumni. How'd you do it?" If I hadn't met with Flash, who had turned my thinking around to this being a money-laundering operation, I'd have never thought to ask where the seed money came from.

"We had some angel investors."

"Who?"

"They'd like to remain anonymous benefactors."

"I'm sure you can tell me," I said. "Your industry might not be regulated, but ours is. The IRS has started scrutinizing private equity funds over the last few years. They're uptight because of how many PE funds are taking over businesses." I did my best to sound tired and annoyed by it. I had no idea at all if this was true. Seemed like something the IRS would plausibly be pissed at, though. "Now, they're digging into where we park our money. It's the current version of that S&L bullshit from the '80s."

"What is this, Jameson?"

"I just want to know where the money comes from. And where it's going."

"What do you mean?"

"Something Ray said to me. About how the collective is connecting players with investment opportunities to, as he put it, grow their money. Rainy-day fund if they don't make it as big as they hope. As part of our due diligence, we've spoken with some of the athletes. You guys don't advertise them, but some of the kids announced their deals on social media. It sounds like there are some who are being strongly encouraged to dump their money into a fund before they even see it."

Olivia held her glass up to her lips but didn't drink. Instead, she stared off at the action behind me, though from the look in her eyes, she didn't see any of it. "You're not with a PE fund, are you?"

"Why would you think that?" My voice was even, but my blood had iced.

She set her drink down on the bar. "We'd heard someone was looking at the collective, private investigator or something, calling around to some of our corporate sponsors. What's really going on, James?"

"Sure, I hired someone to look around. This can't be new to you," I said in a mildly scolding tone. "You're asking someone who doesn't know you by reputation to give you—what'd you suggest, one point two million? Into a unique sports investment activity, something that's currently unregulated? And you don't think I'd have a look around? Come on, Olivia, you're savvier than that."

"All you had to do was ask. We'd happily—"

"This is not uncommon in my line of work. Especially now that energy is getting a bad rap."

Olivia's expression softened, and she rested her free hand on mine. I took a drink and pretended not to notice. I also wanted the few seconds to plan out my next steps.

She said, "Maybe we can just have a conversation, and I can save you the trouble, and expense, of private security?"

"What do you have in mind?"

"Let's not talk here." She pulled her phone out of her bag, tapped a quick message, and replaced it. "I just need to cancel my plans."

"Lead the way," I said.

We left the bar, and I offered to drive. Olivia said she'd taken an Uber here. She guided me back downtown, about a block from my hotel.

There's a point when you're undercover, just before you're exposed, when you can bail. Maybe it's not enough to maintain the cover, but you can get out of the situation before the other person says, "I know who you really are."

Out of the corner of my eye, I could see Olivia tapping on her phone.

"Your plans from earlier?" I asked.

"Yeah," was all she said, clearly more focused on that than on me. A few minutes passed and she said, "Make a left here."

I turned off Second and onto Biscayne Bay Way, the JW rose to my left, and I was certain the game was up.

What better way to tell someone, "We caught you," than to guide them back to their hotel?

I'd been in this situation before and knew that I had seconds.

"It's the farthest one on the right," she said.

Wait, what?

*You have to be kidding me.*

Her condo was almost directly across the street from my hotel.

Chancing a look at her, Olivia was still staring at her phone, expression impassive. "Here," she said and handed me a badge from her purse. I tapped us into the garage and parked in a visitor spot. She guided me into the lobby with its west-facing glass wall. The sun was about to swan dive into the horizon.

Olivia had a two-story condo, facing the water on the building's second floor.

We rode the elevator up to Olivia's floor in a brief and nervous silence. I was still having a hard time processing the odds that her home was across the street from my hotel. What did that mean for my operations security going forward?

Olivia let us into her place. The interior was dark wood backlit with accent lighting, white marble surfaces, ultramodern décor, and a view of the ocean.

Olivia opened a bottle of wine and poured two glasses.

"Now, what do I need to do to reassure you?" she asked, handing me one of the wineglasses.

"You said your money came from some anonymous benefactors. I think Ray is connected to Dalton Bream. Was he one of them?"

I'd used my downtime over the last two days to follow up on some open items, like learning who lived in the Palm Beach house that Ruiz had visited when I was tailing him. I'd used EchoTrace to run a records search on the address, but the house was registered to a trust. Eventually, it took impersonating a state tax official to call the Palm Beach County records office, and they disclosed the owner was a Dalton Bream. Bream was a South Florida real estate baron and University of Miami megadonor. Certainly, a whale investor for SSC. EchoTrace confirmed Ruiz and Bream had attended college at the same time and had appeared together in some local news pieces over the years.

"He was an early donor, yes. Mr. Bream and Ray are good friends."

"I'm a little uncomfortable with the idea of treating this like fantasy football. Seems a little like treating people like commodities. Isn't it a little manipulative?"

"I guess it could seem that way. Honestly, you're an outlier. Most of the time, it's the coaching staff that reaches out to us looking for a legal way to incentivize a player. In the old days—and by that I mean, like, five years ago —major programs would have a donor they used to quietly facilitate payments to attract athletes. Now we're just able to do it in the open."

I lifted my wineglass. Then I set it down, as though I'd just had a thought that interrupted the action. "You ducked the question on where the investment came from," I said. "The other thing I'm a little uncomfortable with is this push to investments. I think this could get you guys in trouble. Think about it—the optics aren't great. You offer someone a million dollars, only give them a quarter of it, and put the rest in what, real estate? Mutual funds? Someone gets ahold of that information, it's going to look bad."

"Is that a threat?" she asked, and I genuinely couldn't tell if she was playing with me.

"No. If I'm a donor, I don't want to get caught up in anything that's going to reflect poorly on me, my business partner, or our school. Now, my investigator found a couple of anomalies."

Olivia didn't say anything and didn't touch her drink. She also didn't look me in the eyes. This was the critical moment, and I worried that I'd pushed her a little too far. And if she asked what the anomalies were, I didn't have a good answer, short of Charlie Garcia was acting dodgy.

"Ray won't tell me where the money came from. I've asked. He said they want to remain private, and that's the end of the discussion." She took a drink, and it was a deep one. "I don't know enough about how the money moves, and I don't like it."

"Have you spoken to anyone?"

"No. Listen, this is Ray's business. He's built this from nothing, and he's worked *hard*. I don't want to jeopardize that. I think it could be something special, something unique."

There was an unspoken "but" in her tone, and she was waiting for me to ask the follow-up question, give her permission to dish on her boss.

"Except there's something about this business that's making you uncomfortable," I said.

"Ray has his own private security. He's retained a detective named Felix Farrier. He's former military. An MP or intelligence or something. Ray uses him to vet donors to make sure they're on the level."

*Oh shit.*

"He's also worried about 'insider threat,' he calls it. I didn't want to say anything to anyone because I figured Farrier would find out. I'm telling you so you can be careful."

"Why should I have to worry about being careful?"

"Just that Ray can be a little paranoid."

I was having a hard time reconciling the earnestly stat-slinging sports geek I'd met yesterday with the person Olivia was describing now. Having a private detective on retainer for security wasn't novel. Maybe an odd move, given the size of SSC, though I could understand the logic if Ray was worried about getting swindled. In this environment, with as much money that was flying around, it wasn't hard to envision.

She said, "You're in private equity. You must have an MBA or a finance degree, right? Would you know what to look for if you saw it?"

"My firm thoroughly investigates the companies we invest in and the people we do business with. We usually use an outside firm for the deeper financial analysis, but I know how to spot some red flags." Like, say, a Russian "businessman" making political donations in mineral-rich Central African countries to get access to mining concerns. For instance.

"What if I left my laptop open and just happened to be logged into our banking software?"

"*If* such a thing happened, someone with my background could probably find an indicator of questionable activity."

"And if you don't find an indicator," she countered, "you can rest assured that your investment is safe, and we can get on with our evening."

She set her glass down, walked over to a bookshelf built into a wall, and picked up a laptop. She placed it on the dining room table, where there was a magnificent view of downtown from the north side of the Miami River inlet and the ocean. She opened her computer, tapped a few keys with her slender fingers, and then retrieved her wine. She left the room, looking over her shoulder once.

I wasn't sure how long I had with this. Instead of trying to read a ledger, I downloaded a copy of all financial transactions onto the desktop. I then opened a VPN and transferred them to a secure container on the internet. Now that I'd established a connection, had her computer's IP address, I could connect to it later and access all the information I needed. While the financial files were copying, I accessed some of the corporate records, specifically looking for lists of clients, prospects, corporate sponsors, and donors. I copied those too. I'd turn EchoTrace loose on these later, though I scanned them during the transfer. One name immediately stuck out to me —Cody Portman, the FGCU player who had knocked Tennessee out of the NCAA basketball tournament with a buzzer-beater two-pointer that no one expected him to make. Judging by the look on his face, Cody most of all. I copied any files relating to their investment vehicles.

Hearing footsteps in the hallway, I stepped away from the machine and left the screen facing away.

Olivia returned, glass in hand and wearing an expression I found difficult to read. She set the glass on the counter and took a few steps toward me.

"Do you mind if I ask you a few more questions?" I asked.

"I think I'm questioned out, James," she said, her voice just north of a purr.

"Did you ever ask where the money came from to initially attract the athletes, since it wasn't coming from a school's donor network?"

"He was up front about it. What I mean is, he told me right away that he had some wealthy donors who wanted to help him get started. He didn't elaborate, and I didn't ask."

"Why not?"

A coy smile. "This town, you don't always want to know."

I'd known a lot of otherwise good people who went along with very bad things because they were scared to stand up. Sometimes they didn't think it was their place. Others decided it was safer just to put their head in the sand and pretend everything was fine. It took courage to stand tall, especially if your safety might be at risk. Olivia may have had good cause to question the latter.

"What kind of reputation did Ray Ruiz have, back when he was an agent?"

She tittered and it sounded forced. "Like he just took the corners a little too fast. I think we've talked about this enough, don't you?" Olivia took a few steps toward me and placed her hand in the middle of my chest. She slid close to me, close enough that I could smell her perfume. She moved gracefully. Like you'd expect from a former swimmer who kept at it, or a jungle cat.

"Fair enough," I said. I'd learned long ago to be wary of everyone's intentions, and yes, it made maintaining relationships a challenge in my life. I also knew I was an average-looking guy, so when a woman that I knew to be clearly out of my league started coming on to me, my guard went up just a little. "I can count on you, can't I?"

"To do what?"

"We're talking about a lot of money here. I know the difference between finding an unexplored market and skirting the law. If I'm getting exposed here, you'll warn me," I said.

"What exactly are you asking?"

"I just want to know I've got a friend on the inside."

"I've done everything I'm willing to do. If you're asking me to spy on my boss for you, that's out of line, and I won't do it." Olivia's expression frosted, and she took a step back from me.

"My guy has been asking around. I think your boss, or this Felix Farrier, used some heavies to scare an agent named Elena Mendoza away from someone he wanted to sign. The way I understand it, it ended at a threat, though it seemed like it could've gone much worse. What happens if, next time, it does? You don't want that on your conscience, do you? Maybe it's private security that got a little overzealous protecting their boss's interests. Maybe it isn't."

"I don't know anything about that. And I doubt very much it's true."

No matter how well you profiled and prepared a potential asset, you still got turned down on occasion. Maybe you read their motivations wrong, or the assessment was incomplete and you missed something. Still, usually, if you were going to make the pitch and reveal yourself as an American intelligence officer, you had a strong sense they'd agree to it.

I had one night to convince Olivia McEvoy, and she'd rejected it.

Whatever reasons she'd had for sharing the financial information with me—and the data she didn't know she shared—was probably under the veneer of cooperation. She'd assumed this was low risk. Chess isn't a bad analogy. She'd taken out a pawn, but I'd moved a knight closer.

"I understand, and I appreciate your candor," I said. I left appreciation for anything else unsaid. "Suppose I should be going, then."

"Thank you for the drink," she said, giving me a friendly kiss on the cheek. All was forgiven and hinting at a future opportunity to pick up where we'd left off.

I saw myself out.

I spent twenty minutes getting back to my hotel across the street, driving a wending route of double-backs through downtown. Once I had the Defender safely in the garage, I stopped off at the bar. I'd become decent friends with Mario, the bartender, mostly talking about sports. It was a slow night, maybe ten people scattered about the place. Mario was watching the TV, his back to the bar. He turned his head as I entered, gave me a chin nod, and poured a beer. It was waiting for me by the time I got to the bar.

"You see the news?"

"No," I said. "What happened?"

"Remember Cody Portman, that kid who had the buzzer-beater three against Tennessee the other night?"

"Yeah?"

"His parents' house just burned down."

# 8

"Anything about how it happened?"

Mario shrugged. "Not really. They just had a short thing on it. Probably wouldn't have reported it at all if the kid wasn't a local celebrity because of the tournament. Anyway, we were talking about him the other night, so I thought I'd tell you. Shit luck, man. I hope he can still focus on the game."

"When do they play next?"

Mario pulled his phone out, and I could see him navigating to a sports app "Looks like a couple days. This weekend."

I'd told Mario to put the beer on my tab, left it on the bar, and dashed back to my room. I called Jimmy from the elevator.

"What's up, man?" Jimmy said.

"Do you know Cody Portman?" I asked.

"Yeah, he had that last-second score against the Vols the other night. That was wild. Why?"

"I was watching that game. The camera zoomed in for a closeup when Portman sank that shot. He looked shocked...and terrified."

"I imagine it was pretty emotional for him," Jimmy said. I could hear in his voice he wanted me to get to the point.

"No, he was scared. Like, *he* hadn't expected to make that shot. Hadn't wanted to."

"What are you talking about, Matt?"

"I saw SSC's client list today."

"How in the hell did you get that? They won't even share that with their athletes."

"In a minute. Portman signed with them."

"So?"

"So, his parents' house just burned down. It's all over the news."

Jimmy told me to hold on while he turned his TV on. "Man, that's awful. I don't see what this has to do with anything, though."

"Kid upsets a four seed in the tournament, a game which no one expected them to win. And that shot? He just winged the ball toward the basket. He wasn't trying—he was just making it look like he was. I know what deception looks like, especially when it's not done well."

"What are you saying exactly?"

"I think SSC might be involved in a little more than shitty contracts."

"You're talking point shaving?"

"Or fixing. Imagine if someone organized a betting pool against Gulf Coast."

"They'd have lost their shirts," Jimmy said. "I don't know, though. That feels like a stretch. Especially since they were underdogs anyway. It'd make more sense if they won. And anyway, why not just *not* take the shot at all if he's trying to lose?"

"Be a little too obvious, no? The best shooter on the team, and he's got a chance to win the game, but he doesn't take the shot? Think about it."

"Believe me, I am," Jimmy said in a heavy way. "Why would Ruiz even get into that? It doesn't make sense. If he's already skirting the rules with these sketchy contracts, why risk the exposure?"

I didn't have a great answer for that. It didn't make a lot of sense to me that Ruiz would jeopardize his business that way. I also know what I saw.

"I just met with Olivia McEvoy, the collective's chief operating officer."

"I know her."

"I tried to talk her into collecting for me, but she wouldn't go for it. She did open her laptop and then disappear into the other room."

"Why'd she do that?"

"Because she's trying to close the deal and thinks if she just lets me skim their bank data, I'll conclude everything is above board. She also thinks I'm a finance bro who wouldn't know what to look for. I got SSC's bank statements going back to their founding, all their clients, and information on where they're moving their money. I've got an AI tool that will trace their money. What I found already was the collective's initial investment came from two shell companies."

"Okay," Jimmy said, drawing out the word the way you do when you're skeptical but don't want to voice it.

"I've spoken with some law enforcement contacts. They put me in touch with an informant who walked me through a few scenarios. He said it's unlikely this is a Ponzi scheme. There didn't seem to be a clear way for anyone to make money, other than Ray skimming."

"What about the people who own these investments they're pushing Brashard to dump his money in?"

"So far, those all appear to be legitimate. They're all incorporated businesses."

"I don't know, man."

"For what it's worth, this consultant said it sounded much more like a front for a money-laundering operation and—"

"Hold on. Slow down, Matt. First you tell me they're point shaving, and now you're talking about money laundering. That's...that's a lot, man."

When you're in the thick of it and all this information resides in your head, it has a way of living with you. It's never far from thought, your mind works on the problem continually. You make connections. You develop an instinct for the patterns that form intelligence cases. As a case officer, if I'd have brought these indicators to my station chief, he would have said, "Keep going." Of course, that was a leader trained in intelligence work and used to dealing with ambiguity. Civilians liked to think they were, but they usually weren't—not to this level.

"I think there are clear indicators here that Sunshine Sports Collective is engaged in illegal activity."

"No shit, that's why I hired you."

"You had suspicions," I corrected. And honestly, they weren't grounded in much. I think Jimmy was looking for a way to get his client out of a bad contract more than he had grounded suspicions. Given that, I still harbored a lingering fear that I was trying to shoehorn the facts into a story that worked. And I had to reconcile my own impression of Ray with what I'd heard from Jimmy, the Browns, and my research. I wasn't convinced yet that this guy wasn't a sports nerd who was just looking for a way to work in a business he truly loved.

Then there was what I saw in Cody Porter.

"And you have what exactly?" Jimmy asked.

"I have some unaccountable money coming in and more money paid in the form of 'investments' to outside businesses. SSC also writes a lot of small checks to vendors. They seem to have a lot of cash on hand, yet they aren't paying that out to their athletes. Instead, they're redirecting it to investments. Now, with high-net-worth individuals, it's not uncommon to use trusts and corporations as vehicles for their money, so at this point, it's back-tracing all of those."

"Wait, you've got their donors?"

"Yes. Names of some, trust accounts and shell corporations for others. I'd like to get these records to your accountants and see what they can make of it."

"Whoa, whoa, whoa. I *cannot* commit agency resources to this. That's probably illegal, and even if it isn't, none of these guys are criminal investigators. They wouldn't know what to look for."

"This was given to me freely by an insider." Mostly.

"I'm not sure I'm entirely comfortable with this. You look through that stuff and tell me if there is anything we can use. That's what I'm paying you for. I just want to get Brashard out of this deal. That's it. Anything else? I do not want to get involved, understand?"

I told Jimmy I'd get back to him.

His reluctance surprised me.

Or maybe it didn't.

I stayed up late with the files, trying to make what sense of them I could. I put the light out around one o'clock. Sleep did not come easily, and I dreamed of burning buildings.

The next morning, I considered my next steps over coffee. The fastest way to do what Jimmy was paying me for was to find something that would get Sunshine Sports Collective in hot water so they would make a deal. Jimmy freed his client. I'd get a check for $250,000 and head home. Of course, if it turned out SSC really was up to something dirty, that didn't help the rest of the athletes in their stable or anyone they might snag in the future.

If I was wrong and I approached them, like Danzig had said, I could screw this kid's future.

My instinct said to follow the money. Even with AI assistance, a forensic accounting investigation would take weeks, possibly months, and would require specialized expertise I didn't have. I could get it, but Jimmy made it clear he wouldn't pay for it.

I couldn't shake the feeling about Cody Portman either. There were hundreds of nonverbal cues that revealed a person's true feelings and intentions. Shock came in many forms. There was a difference between being happily surprised, like "I didn't see that coming" and being terrified. Cody was definitely the latter. I was sure he hadn't expected to make that shot... hadn't wanted to. The only reason I could see was because his team wasn't supposed to win that game. There was no other explanation for that kid being terrified that he'd just made a hundred-to-one shot and pulled an upset that would make highlight reels for a decade. Portman tried to accomplish the task they'd forced on him—to lose the game without making it look like he was trying to lose the game—and it was a split-second decision. The ball went "win" because that kid probably spent three hours a day practicing making that exact shot, not to miss it. Not taking a shot in that moment would force so many more questions than trying and missing.

There would be consequences.

And there had been.

The common denominator was Sunshine Sports Collective.

I agreed with Jimmy's logic that it didn't seem right for Ray to also get into fixing games. That didn't make sense, sure, but we shouldn't shake the coincidence.

Once I got an idea in my head, it was hard for me to shake it loose without acting on it, or some mild explosives, so I got in the Defender and headed west.

Jimmy called while I was on the road.

"Hey, man," Jimmy said, his voice filling the cabin as though he were next to me. "Look, I was a little harsh last night and wanted to apologize. Digging is what I'm paying you to do, right? You just hit me with a lot at once. And this Cody Portman thing…I don't know, man."

"Thanks, Jimmy. I appreciate that. I'd received a lot of information in short order and was trying to process it all. Probably should've slept on it before sharing. The Portman thing shocked me. Maybe you're right, and there isn't a connection. Still, I need to run it down. If there is a genuine threat to someone's life, Brashard's or someone else's, I've got a duty to find out. If it's true, then you'll get what you want faster than if Ray Ruiz is laundering money for someone."

"Eh, I don't know. I mean, I hear what you're saying, but Portman isn't my client. And I'm not convinced that just because he looked weirded out after beating a higher seeded team on a one-in-a-million bucket means someone was trying to get him to tank the game. I watched the news. The police said it was a gas explosion at his house. It's a tragedy, for sure, and I hope the kid didn't do something dumb with his money, like buy a Porsche, so he can help his family out. That's not what I'm paying you for, so please drop it."

"I understand," I said.

"Where you at right now?"

"Out running some leads down." Actually, I was blasting down Alligator Alley, heading toward Ft. Myers and Florida Gulf Coast University to talk with Cody Portman. I guess I'd keep that to myself.

"Cool. Let's try to hook up later, and you can talk to me about this money thing in more detail. I'll fill you in on what I know about Ms. McEvoy too."

"Sounds good, Jimmy."

I disconnected the call. Guess I wouldn't be billing him for whatever I did today.

Alligator Alley, the section of I-75 that traversed the Everglades connecting South Florida's east and west coasts, was an eighty-mile stretch of straight, black asphalt with marsh on either side. Gave me a lot of time to think. Jimmy's comment about Olivia had me wondering what her endgame was. She admitted to being scared, but so much so she wouldn't tell me of what. The easiest answer was that the firm somehow knew a private investigator was looking into their business—actually, she'd admitted that much. As a small operation, if privileged information leaked, there could only be a couple of sources. Ruiz would rule himself out, leaving her and a select few others. If Olivia knew about them threatening Jimmy's colleague, Elena Mendoza, fear of reprisal for leaking was reasonable. She let me see their financial records, their client list, their internal documents. She wouldn't act as my agent. Why not? Why the half measure? Was it just as simple as deniability?

I'd left Miami early to beat the traffic and was in Ft. Myers by midmorning. I had no idea what kind of schedule a college basketball player would have. Presumably, academics was part of it, though I remembered an infamous player at my school having needed to be escorted to class by the athletic department to ensure he went.

FGCU's campus was on the southern end of the Ft. Myers area, nestled back in the lakes and wetlands. The buildings were gray with teal roofs, and several news sites had likened it to a resort. A quick internet search confirmed the team practiced at Alico Arena on campus, so I parked the Defender there and settled in to watch. While waiting, I spent some time looking at the expanding body of knowledge regarding college athletics.

Now that NIL deals were becoming common, programs were more open about how much work went into being a collegiate athlete. Based on what I'd learned, my best bet to find Portman would be between noon and one p.m., which was when I expected him to show up for afternoon practice. It seemed most programs had their students schedule classes in the morning so the rest of the day could be reserved for team activities—practice, strength and conditioning, rehab, whatever. I also didn't want to wait here until nine or whenever they finally knocked it off for the day.

I'd learned from a school sports fan site that the team had left Charlotte, where their group of teams played in the tournament's second round, to return to Ft. Myers the night of the victory. There were several posts about the fire at the Portman home, most of them amateur and rehashing what little news there was. The only thing notable was that Cody elected to remain with the team to prepare for their Sweet Sixteen appearance in five days, instead of going back home to be with his family.

At noon, I called the number SSC had as Portman's cellphone.

Not surprisingly, he didn't pick up. I imagined he was getting bombarded with phone calls right now. I hadn't bothered calling the police or the fire department, knowing they wouldn't disclose anything to me anyway. One of the challenges of taking a job where I had no connections.

While I was waiting for sight of Portman, I called my reporter friend, Mike.

"Hey, it's the private detective. How are things in Magic City?" he said.

"Hey, man. This case is...something. I'm going to have a story for you, for sure."

"Love to hear that."

"I know you're busy with the tournament going on, but I did have something I wanted to run by you," I said.

"No problem at all."

I had to be circumspect about this. First, I didn't want to bias him or lead him in one direction or another. I also didn't want to prejudice his coverage of this team if I was wrong. "Is there any record, that you know of, of point shaving or game fixing involving any Florida schools?"

"Are you talking about the basketball tournament?"

"Yes."

"Not that I know of. The big one was Boston College in the '70s. Most of the issues with Florida schools tend to involve booster money and player behavior. Out of an overdeveloped sense of school spirit, I'll leave it at that."

I laughed—which, I found, was needed. "Thank you. That's actually really helpful." I agreed to keep him updated and hung up.

Interesting.

Around twelve thirty, I saw players starting to roll into the practice facility. I tried Cody's number again, nothing. I got out of my car and positioned myself near the entrance I'd seen the players use. I knew what he looked like and that he was six foot five.

At ten to one, I saw him walking into the facility alone. I launched off the bench I was camping on and made fast steps to intercept him. Not an easy task given the six-inch height differential.

"Cody? Can I get a word?" I said when I was about fifteen feet from him.

His big head pivoted like a pissed-off colossus, sized me up, and rotated back to the front. He continued trudging forward.

"I want to talk to you about what happened to your parents' house. I'm a private investigator."

He stopped. "I don't have anything to say."

"Do you think someone intentionally set that fire?"

"I can't talk to you," he said, but the flare of shock in his eyes when I asked my question told me he absolutely thought that.

"Cody, I promise not to take up much of your time. I just want to ask you a couple questions. I'm not a reporter. Nothing you tell me goes anywhere but us. I'm looking into Sunshine Sports Collective."

"Man, I really can't talk to you. They told me not to say anything. They said their PR people would handle it."

"Handle what?"

"Anything with the newspapers or TV or whatever."

"This isn't that. Another SSC athlete hired me to look into them. They suspect SSC of engaging in illegal activity. I saw you make that shot against Tennessee. No one believed you would, least of all you. I know that look, Cody."

"I don't know what you're talking about."

"Did someone from SSC, or maybe someone else, try to get you to throw the game?"

The color drained out of his face, and he took a step back, subconsciously looking for a way out. He looked over his shoulder to see a couple of teammates walking into the facility. "Hey, guys, wait up," he said.

They stopped to wait for him.

Before he got too far away, I said, "If someone tried to force you to throw that game, I can get the police involved."

"Do *not* do that. I told you, I've got nothing to say. My mom and my little brother lost their fucking *house*, man! Now people are saying they torched it for the insurance money. I don't make shit from SSC, and they haven't paid me anything anyway. I gotta go."

I made sure to keep my voice down so his teammates wouldn't hear. "Cody, if someone forced you to throw the game, that's illegal. Your career will be over if that gets out. If you come forward, the police can help."

"Right," he said, bitterly. "Like they always do. Same police saying my mom lit her own house on fire. Fuck them and fuck *you*."

He didn't equivocate, I'll give him that.

Cody Portman joined his friends, and they disappeared into the practice facility.

He did not look back.

I walked to the Defender and got on the interstate for the return trip to Miami. I hadn't eaten since breakfast, but I had no appetite.

---

I'd called Silvestri on my way to Ft. Myers but had to leave a voicemail. She returned the call when I was finally on my way back to Miami.

"Thanks again for connecting me with Madigan," I said. I couldn't bring myself to call him *Flash*.

"Was he helpful?" Silvestri asked.

"Yeah. My hypothesis was all off. He pointed out right away how it didn't make sense as a Ponzi scheme. If anything, he said what I'd seen suggested money laundering."

All she said was, "Huh," in that way women have of not believing you, but being too polite to say it.

"I'm working on an internal source. If I can get them to disclose some information, would that be enough to get Miami-Dade to start an investigation?"

"Hold up there, Magnum. We're leading the country in violent crime. My organized crime task force was gutted and then shuttered so we could redirect those resources to home invasion, burglary, and theft. And this is at the same time as two different organized crime outfits got into a gunfight on the street." Her voice dropped, and all I heard was the sound of the truck's tires over pavement. "No one is going to lift a finger over some asshole ripping off college kids. I'm sorry. There's no way that becomes a priority here."

"What if they're also forcing them to throw games?"

"You're talking about point fixing?"

"Yes. I've got evidence someone tried to get a player to tank a game in the basketball tournament. Only he didn't, he made a last-second shot." Okay, *evidence* might be stretching it a little. Call it a good hunch. "Two days later, his parents' house burns to the ground. Yes, the kid had signed with this collective. All that has me thinking this group is a front for something else."

"I don't know, Gage. That all seems like a stretch. Still, for the sake of discussion, let's say you're right. *If* any of that were going on, it's probably a federal crime. The game wasn't played in Miami, so we don't even know if the threat was made in Miami."

"Yeah, we just know that's where their house was burned down."

Silvestri didn't have a response to that.

"Look, Gage, I'm sorry that I can't help you. You seem like a good guy, and you're trying to do the right thing by this kid. I have to wonder, though, if you aren't a cat barking up trees."

That one lost me. "Cats don't bark."

"Exactly," Silvestri said. She wished me a good rest of my day and hung up.

I drove back to Miami in silence. I didn't even put the radio on.

The thought that kept clawing at the back of my mind, like a burglar without tools, was that maybe the point to this was the design. Maybe Ray Ruiz found a scheme that fit right between the seams of the multitude of federal, state, and local law enforcement or regulatory agencies that might otherwise give a shit about what he was doing. Assuming he was actually violating some law and not just being an asshole who writes usurious contracts.

I had to concentrate on finding something to give me enough leverage that I could convince Ruiz to let Brashard loose. There was another angle, too, which was to amp up the pressure on Ray himself. Make him think there was a large-scale investigation on him and his collective. Create a false-flag operation, get him scared and see what he does. My hypothesis was that if Ray was breaking the law, he would make some hasty moves to protect himself. That could be another way to create the leverage I needed —once he was in a full panic, offer a way out.

## 9

I was back at my hotel in the late afternoon and had a plan formulated.

First, I looked up the management company who ran the building where SSC had their office. The building was recently constructed and owned by a local real estate developer. With a few minutes of link analysis on EchoTrace, I had the developer's backers. Interestingly, Ray's buddy, Dalton Bream, was a major investor.

"Good afternoon," I said when someone picked up. I'd used a tool Mickey developed to give me a randomly assigned 800 number on the caller ID. "My name is Phillip Nokes, and I'm with Eclipse Security. We're an investigative firm retained by Glades Development."

"Okay," the woman on the other end said, wariness evident in her tone.

"We're conducting some due diligence on Glades' investment in the Grand Avenue property. This is just a routine physical security audit. You're the building manager, is that correct?"

"I am, yes," she said.

"Excellent. As I said, this is just a routine audit. I'd like to ask you some basic questions about your physical security procedures." After she agreed, I spent a few minutes asking legitimate-seeming questions about their security. The purpose was to get her used to answering mundane questions.

"Great. You've been a big help. One last thing. Your visitor logs are electronic, correct?"

"That's right," she said.

"I'd like to see the logs for the building going back, oh...six months should do it."

"For everyone?"

"I only need a random sampling," I said.

"I think it's easier if I just give you everyone, if that's okay. I'm sorry if that makes it more difficult. It's a new system, and I don't really know how it works yet."

"No problem at all. We'll sort it out," I said. "That's what we're here for." I gave her an email address I'd just created for my fake security company and stayed on the phone as she exported the entry logs into a spreadsheet and emailed it to me. "You've been a big help," I said and hung up.

I accessed the spreadsheet and filtered out the other occupants. Now, I had everyone that had visited Sunshine Sports in the last six months. There were a few names I recognized right off the bat, and for the ones I didn't, I entered them into EchoTrace for a search. We had some former athletes, an infamous Miami rapper, and a professional wrestler. The EchoTrace returns all came back quickly and showed the expected results of Miami-based business figures and representatives from the athletic staffs of the University of Miami, Florida Gulf Coast, Florida International University, Florida Atlantic, and several junior colleges.

I noted Charlie Garcia, the owner of Miami Fitness Source.

"Oh, what's this?" I said aloud. There was a local courier company that made a delivery or a pickup at least once a week. A quick googling showed them to be just that, a delivery service. Interestingly, it was the same courier every time—Jamal Washington. A records check revealed Jamal had worked there for two years. He played two years of JuCo football, though nothing beyond that. Could that be anything? He also had three hits for possession with intent to distribute.

I filed Jamal Washington away for later.

I'd done some early passes with the local university athletic departments. It was time to do that again, adding local business associations and state offices to that list. It was getting to be late in the day, and I expected the latter two to be closed for the evening. I placed a few phone calls and sent emails out under my "Gage Investigative Agency" address. I'd toyed with calling my business the "California Investigations Agency," but that seemed a little too on the nose, even for me.

After getting back from the evening with Olivia, I remotely accessed her hard drive and imaged it, so I had a copy of everything she'd done up to that point. Then I entered the financial files into EchoTrace, which showed each of their corporate sponsors—businesses that wanted to endorse an athlete in exchange for some kind of advertising. It also showed the collective's donors. Interestingly, when I ran a cross-reference of the visitor logs with the financials, I found very little overlap and none of the celebrities. Of course, they'd likely donated through a trust, a corporation, or some other business. Still, Ray's closure rate for big names didn't seem very high. For the AI, that was just an additional step, because I'd already calibrated the tool to secure the incorporation documents for any trusts, LLCs, whatever.

He had several million dollars under management, which begged the question as to why he couldn't or didn't pay all the athletes what they'd agreed to.

Now that I was finally looking at data, my mind's natural aptitude for pattern matching started to fire. One thought came to me about Cody Portman. Ray might have gotten mixed up with some dangerous people, extended himself too far, and given up names to buy himself some time. Those bad actors may have tried to use that to set up a point-fixing scheme in the tournament.

Now that things were moving, I felt better.

Well, "better" wasn't the word, because I seemed to be wading into some ugly, polluted waters. I was making progress, though, and that was good.

My phone rang, and I looked up, eyes burning a little from staring at the screen so long. I realized I'd been at this a few hours. I saw Jimmy's face on the screen.

I picked up.

"Yo, Matty," he said.

*Yo, Matty?*

"Hey, man," I replied. I was tired and decided to let him know just how much.

"Are you free for a drink later?"

"I don't know, Jimmy. Long day, couple of hours in the car. I'm more in the mood for some laps in the pool and an early night."

"I get that. Our conversation from earlier has been bothering me. You're doing exactly what I asked you to do, and I jumped down your throat about it. I'm sorry for that. It was out of line."

"Thanks."

"I've been thinking, too, about what you said about fixing games. I'll be honest with you, that seems far-fetched...but if it *is* happening, I want to know about it."

"I really appreciate that, Jimmy." I pressed my eyes together against the strain from bearing down on my computer for the last few hours. Actually, a little friendly contact would be a welcome change. "You know, I think I'll take you up on the drink. I'd like to bounce some theories off you. You know this business way better than I do. I could use your help in separating the coincidence from the clues."

"I get you."

We made plans to meet at my hotel around eight.

Feeling like I was on a roll, I decided to skip dinner and keep at it. I wanted to do a deeper dive on the financial files. I'd had EchoTrace run a host of analyses, I just hadn't had time to dig into any of them yet.

Most of the money coming into Sunshine Sports Collective was from private donors, with just about seventy percent of those listed as LLCs, trusts, or some other type of corporate entity. That alone wasn't surprising. High-net-worth individuals rarely kept money in their own name. What was interesting was where the funds were going. SSC did pay their athletes. Courtesy of my document dump, I had their royalty contracts and payment schedules. The four- and low-five-figure contracts were typically paid out. The few larger ones were where they tended to redirect the payment to these investment opportunities. SSC also made regular payments on a free-lance job site called OneGig. I looked that site up, and it appeared to be like any of the other gig economy job sites. People would post a job, potential vendors would bid on them. Once selected, the buyer would transfer funds to the job site's account, which would hold them in escrow until completed. SSC appeared to be spending large sums of money, typically in one- to five-thousand-dollar increments, for consulting, marketing, and media services.

They had five million dollars under management, according to the bank documents I saw. They were paying their athletes about two million in total, spread across all athletes. Brashard's contract counted for a fifth of the collective's total funds. That explained why they wanted it diverted into a deferred payment scheme—they couldn't afford to shell out right now. Ray looked like he was bleeding cash. The lease on that office was stratospheric. I also discovered that the collective was registered as a subsidiary of a different corporation, called RCR Ventures. The principles of detection told me that stood for "Raymond C. Ruiz." RCR Ventures owned that Aston Martin and listed his North Miami Beach house as its headquarters, which it also owned.

Sunshine Sports paid between ten and fifty thousand a month for various services, primarily through this OneGig app. I researched how these gig economy job sites worked. For most of them, a person or business posted a need, and a freelancer would bid on it. The buyer would pay the gig site, who took a small admin fee, one to two percent in most cases, and the money was held in escrow until the job was complete.

Entirely electronic and below the level required to report to the IRS.

This looked like the infrastructure of a well-designed money-laundering scheme. The only part that didn't necessarily track was the relatively low amount of money moving through the system. If they were laundering, that didn't seem like a major payout, though even ten grand a month felt high for "consulting."

As I was reviewing this, my thoughts naturally went to how I'd gotten the information. I wouldn't have any of this without Olivia's help. Her motives weren't clear to me, and the justification that she felt something was off didn't wash. Why help? What does she gain from this?

That said, if it was a setup, I didn't think she would have shared all their banking information with me.

My phone rang again. This was not a number I had.

"Hello?"

"Mr. Gage?"

"Yes," I said. I recognized the voice but couldn't place it. He didn't say anything for a few seconds. I added, "This is the part where you introduce yourself, and tell me why you called."

"Right, sorry. This is Charlie Garcia. We spoke the other day at my office. You left me your card."

"That's right, Mr. Garcia. How are you?"

"I'm...o-kay." He tripped over the words like they were zipping by on a conveyor belt.

"How can I help you?" I said after another quiet bit.

"I was wondering if we could speak."

*Oh, for the love of Christ.* I wondered if I was going to have to dig the words out of his mouth with a shovel.

"We're doing that right now, Mr. Garcia. What can I do for you?"

"I don't want to, ah, talk on the phone."

"Can you at least tell me what this is about?"

"When you were at my office, you said you wanted to ask some questions about Sunshine Sports and my sponsorship arrangement. I'd like to talk to you about that. You said you were investigating them. I have...information. Maybe it's nothing, I don't know."

"Why can't we just do that now?" My patience was evaporating. I didn't have a lot of tolerance for people who couldn't get to the point.

As if sensing this, Garcia said, "Please, Mr. Gage. I'm not comfortable talking to you about this over the phone. I'd like to speak in person. I think there are some...irregularities. Are you free now?"

It was nearing six, and I wouldn't be meeting Jimmy for another two hours.

"I can be. If it's worth my time."

"Thank you. I think it will be."

"I can be at your office in about thirty minutes, depending on traffic."

"Oh, I'm at my warehouse in Opa-locka at 121st and 24th."

Oh, hell. During evening rush hour, that could easily be an hour. Turned out, Miami has the ninth worst traffic in the world. Which is saying something, and I've been to Delhi. I'd just be getting back in time to meet Jimmy.

"I'll be there within the hour," I said. God willing. I collected my things and wended my way through the labyrinthine hotel to the garage.

Jimmy texted as I slid behind the wheel of my Defender and said he'd be closer to nine. He'd just got a call from a prospect that he'd been trying to sign, and they wanted to meet with him in person. Well, at least I wouldn't be pushing it timewise now.

Thankfully, the route was almost entirely a straight shot north on 441, the same road Tom Petty immortalized in *American Girl*. I drove like an asshole and cut nine whole minutes off my trip. Advantage: Gage.

Opa-locka was an inland community northwest of Miami proper. The city was famous for its Moorish-revival architecture, its original design in the 1920s having been heavily influenced by *One Thousand and One Nights*. There was even a street named after Ali Baba. More recently, though, the city was infamous for having the highest rate of violent crime in the country and a notoriously corrupt police department.

Nearing seven, I pulled up to the industrial park, which was a collection of one- and two-story warehouses with a few token palm trees along the streets to break up the concrete-jungle aesthetic. I saw the Miami Fitness Source logo on the door and walked up.

The lights were off, and nobody was home.

The posted hours said the place closed at five.

I walked back to the Defender and looked around. There was no sign of Garcia.

"What the hell," I mumbled, pulling out my phone. I dialed. He didn't pick up. Called three more times in rapid succession, just to make the point.

I walked the perimeter, which burned about ten minutes, and there was no sign of Charlie Garcia.

"Asshole," I said and climbed back into the Defender. Though I supposed if you didn't have at least one bum steer, were you even a private eye? I checked traffic on my phone and saw that 441 Southbound was a complete shitshow, so I opted for taking the famed Ali Baba Avenue across to 27th and hit that south for a while until I could cut back over.

An Escalade pulled up behind me as I made the left on 27th, and it followed me through the turn. I wasn't particularly religious, but I hoped there was a special place in hell for the assholes that rode bumpers during rush hour. As if my wishing would give me some cosmic power I had over the line of cars in front of me. *Okay, I wasn't going to bend reality and move these cars, but since* you're *in a hurry, I'll do it.*

Unsurprisingly, the asshole smashed into my rear end when I stopped for a red.

Now, my vehicle is nigh-on indestructible. Like the original Jeep, this was what the British Army used in the field for decades and was made to endure punishment. Frankly, I was in a hurry and wasn't worried about whatever this guy did. His front end was likely in worse shape than my reinforced bumper. However, since he got out, I figured it was the least I could do. What I didn't want was to spend two hours here dicking around with each other's insurance carriers.

The person who emerged from the Escalade was a barrel with legs and construction equipment for arms stuffed into a white tank top and jeans. That wasn't what spooked me. Training taught me to check the passenger-side mirror, and I saw a friend emerge from the Cadillac's other side. Doesn't take three people to inspect a dinged bumper.

My left hand went to the concealed door panel where I kept the Glock 34. I pressed the panel, it popped open, and I pulled the gun out, shifting it to my right hand. I opened the door and stepped out, sliding the Glock into my waistband at the small of my back.

"Why'd you stop short, man?" he said, already aggressive.

"How about you have your friend get back in your car, and we can inspect the damages?"

I remembered what Jimmy told me about the latest carjacking tactic of slamming into someone, holding them up, and taking the car.

"How about you inspect this?" The guy, who was bald and a light-skinned Latino, pulled his shirt front up, revealing a pistol grip.

"If you knew the probability that you'd shoot your balls off, I'd bet you'd get a holster," I said.

His hand went to his crotch, presumably for the gun, but mine was out and aimed before what passed for his better judgment kicked in. "I wouldn't," I said, and really hoped he'd play this smart.

He did not.

His hand twitched, and my trigger finger responded.

I don't kill people as a matter of practice. I've only come close once, and he deserved it. You can't question someone if they're dead.

There's also the minor problem of death being one of the few things in this life you can never take back.

I dropped the barrel and fired a round at the pavement. The thug dove for the street. Cars went from honking at the obstruction to screeching for safety.

I'd seen the other guy trying to round the front of my truck out of the corner of my eye, so I was ready when he tried to ambush me. The first guy didn't take me seriously. This one did.

He put his pistol at the back of my skull, and if I hadn't been anticipating him, I'd have been dead. I spun on my right foot, pivoting away from the barrel and rotating around him, at the same time I grabbed the pistol with my free left hand. I forced the weapon down and brought my weapon up to level at his chest.

"Drop it and get down!"

His eyes flicked to his partner.

I extended my right arm out to the side, sighted, and fired. I didn't look to see if I'd hit him, already into my next move. I snapped my left hand, cross-chopping for the second guy's throat. It connected, and he started choking. Still next to him, I stepped in and grabbed his opposite shoulder. Using my left leg as a fulcrum, I sent him to the ground. Then I turned back to the first guy. Looked like I'd hit him, though it was a glancing shot. He was crouched and bleeding from the arm.

I shifted my aim and put two rounds through the front of the Escalade, just below the driver's-side window, hoping to hit the steering column. Then I put three into the engine block and a final round into the front tire.

The Defender was still idling, and I jumped in, dropping my Glock on the seat next to me. I threw the Defender into gear and mashed the accelerator. The engine roared to life, and the SUV lunged forward like a pissed-off bear startled out of a power nap. Shots followed.

This stretch of road had two intersections in close proximity that looked like a pair of hashtags on my car's GPS screen. I made the first light by the skin of my teeth, and the second one, not so much. My new friends had piled into their Escalade and powered after me, blasting through a pair of red lights.

I don't know what died first, the front tire or the engine, but they never made it out of the second intersection. The massive truck stalled out, and they got T-boned by a minivan.

One thing was clear. That wasn't a random carjacking. That was a hit.

Looks like I had more to be worried about than Ruiz's jumped-up security guard.

---

Twenty-seventh was a long, straight stretch with few exits for several miles. I got off as soon as I could and drove a series of loop-backs and stair-steps to see if anyone was following me. When I was sure that I was clear, I pulled into a gas station to check my truck for damage. My bumper was a little scratched, though given the condition of my would-be attackers and their vehicle, I could call it even. Then I headed back to my hotel. Once I was in the garage, I opened a compartment in the back and retrieved one of my surveillance detection tools. Normally, I kept these on hand in case a client asked for a sweep. Still, having found myself on the opposite side of federal law enforcement, I'd used them on myself on occasion. The device was tuned to find GPS signals, and I ran it over my Defender to confirm I wasn't being tracked that way. Satisfied, I put it back and headed up to my room, planning out a very uncomfortable conversation with Charlie Garcia.

He'd set me up.

Or at least told someone where I was going to be, and they took it from there. Didn't much matter. This confirmed he was complicit, or at least compromised.

What didn't make sense to me was *why*.

All I'd done was ask some questions. And so far, none of them had real answers. Which was to say, no one had reason to be scared enough to want to kill me.

And yet, here we are. Charlie Garcia had phoned it in. I wondered if this meant I was looking in the wrong spot. A meek fitness equipment peddler didn't seem like the stuff of criminal conspiracies, but then this was Miami and anything was possible. If anyone knew the value of a good cover, it was me.

There wasn't enough to bring to Silvestri, and there wasn't much point in reporting the incident to the police.

While I didn't have anything tangible connecting the two thugs with my investigation, it was clear to me that they were. This was a vertical escalation, considering what little ground I'd made so far.

Think about the timing. I'd just gone to see Cody Portman. Had he called Ruiz to say someone was asking questions? If he had more cause to be afraid of Ruiz (or whomever) than trusting of me, that seemed plausible.

I fought the urge to drive up to Charlie's house to confront him. Force him to admit what he'd done. And for whom. I stalked the floor in my hotel room, planning out how I'd do it.

"Damn it, stay objective," I said.

I walked over to the mini bar and cracked a whiskey, which I at least poured into a tumbler because I'm not an animal. It didn't do much for my nerves, but it gave me something else to focus on for a minute.

Driving up to Charlie Garcia's house while I was freshly pissed was a bad idea. Bordering on criminally stupid. For one, it would tip off whoever ordered the hit that I knew. I'd need to speak to Garcia soon, though it would keep for tonight.

I really needed to speak with Jimmy. He might help me make sense of this.

Nine came and went, and I didn't hear from Jimmy.

He was meeting with a prospective client, and I didn't want to call him. I texted at nine fifteen from the hotel bar to see if we were still on.

After an hour, it was clear he wasn't going to show.

# 10

I woke up angry.

The night had come and gone, and I never heard from Jimmy.

I wanted answers.

Charlie Garcia and I were going to have a little chat. The night before, I'd held off because I didn't want to let on that I knew. Now, though, I wanted to see what kind of chain reaction confronting Charlie might kick off.

Turn on the lights and watch the roaches run.

I'm glad I waited. If I'd pressed Garcia last night, there was a strong chance I'd have responded with a violent lack of objectivity.

I was up early enough to see the pastel painting of a tropical sunrise. I took a banana and a coffee from the hotel lobby and was on the road by six thirty. A half an hour later, I was sitting down the street from Garcia's house. Tax records showed he'd bought the place three years ago from a builder who'd bought it, renovated it, and then flipped it. His stores were all on the east side of Miami-Dade, and of course, there was the warehouse up in Opa-Locka.

The Audi Q8 in the driveway probably took the edge off the commute.

Charlie had done well for himself.

The property was listed at three million. Single story, modern style with a lot of vertical lines and black-metal accents, recessed lighting. Four bedrooms, four baths with a saltwater pool, a Jacuzzi, and a Neptune boat launch. I knew from a Facebook profile that Charlie was married, had three children ages fifteen, thirteen, and ten. He loved the Marlins.

The sky was a glowing lavender and would be a blazing orange in another ten minutes.

I hated it when a stakeout ruined a perfectly nice morning.

Miami Fitness Source was a nine-to-five operation, and Charlie would probably be leaving around eight to open up. EchoTrace found a profile in a local magazine which said that he had an office in each of the stores and rotated, though he tended to use the flagship location of North Miami most, as that was closest to his house.

Charlie walked out to the driveway from the double front door of frosted glass and art-deco accents to his Audi at eight twenty to find my Defender blocking his exit. I leaned against my truck, arms folded with a self-satisfied smirk.

To his credit, Charlie looked genuinely surprised to see me.

"W-what are you doing here?"

"Surprised to see me, Chuck? Or just surprised to see me alive?"

I closed the distance between us, but not all the way, and when I spoke, I made sure it was louder than necessary. "You've got a few questions to answer, pal."

"Will you keep it down?" he hissed.

"Imagine my surprise when you invited me up to your warehouse for a meeting that you didn't show up to."

"I had an emergency with one of my clients. They got the wrong equipment, and I was in South Beach all day sorting it out."

An undisciplined liar won't look you in the eyes when they do it. Charlie was studying the perfectly manicured strips of grass between the granite blocks on his driveway.

"Right. Too bad the meeting was scheduled fifty years before cell phones were invented and you had no way to contact me." Charlie's eyes traced an invisible line to some other point on the lawn. "No, Chuck, that's not what bugs me. What bugs me are the two guys who tried a bump-and-run just after I left your place. It was interesting timing. See, I'd just left your office, and they rammed me from behind at a red light. When I went out to inspect it, both of them pulled guns. Luckily for me, I've got extensive hand-to-hand combat training, specifically for situations where I'm outnumbered and outgunned. Less lucky for them. I imagine one of them is out of the hospital with a severe limp caused by a GSW and some uncomfortable conversations with the police."

Watching the precise moment that some deserving asshole realizes the exact degree they're out of their depth is one of my favorite hobbies. It's better than Must-See TV.

Charlie had no words.

Well, he did but was just too scared to say them out loud.

"Who told you to call me?" I asked.

"I don't know what you're talking about."

"You're not a good liar, Chuck, so you should stop doing it. You set me up. You wouldn't have been man enough to do it yourself."

"Go to hell," he said, finally looking up at me. *Ahh, hit him in the ol' machismo, and he bows right up.* Garcia had a mix of hate and fear in his eyes. Just didn't know if it was for me or somebody else. "I want you to get off of my property or I'm calling the police."

I laughed. "That's something you definitely don't want. Though probably not for the reasons you think. Your trespassing complaint probably loses out to attempted murder, but I like gambling, so let's give it a shot."

"Get. Off. My. Property. Leave me alone!"

"Who told you to set me up?"

"I told you, I don't know what in the hell you're talking about. Now, get off my property. I have to go to work."

"Or what? You're not calling the police. You're not going to try to kill me, or you wouldn't have outsourced it. Who set me up and why?"

The front door opened, and Mrs. Garcia's slim silhouette filled the door, tights and a fashion tank. At least someone in this house made use of the family business.

"What's going on, Charlie? I can hear you in the house. Who is this man?"

"He's just a client," Charlie said. "Go back inside, hon."

I lowered my voice so only he could hear. "Maybe she knows."

"You leave her out of this."

"What do you want with my husband? Do you know what time it is? What the hell is this?"

I stared Charlie Garcia down. He wasn't going to reveal anything, not here. But he knew something—that much was sure. Someone had made him make that call.

I turned to Mrs. Garcia and said, "I was asking Charlie, here, what he was doing with my wife."

---

Deciding I wasn't going to learn anything, I left the Garcias to explore the new complexities of their marriage and returned to my hotel.

Back at the hotel, there was enough anger pulsing in my veins that my hands were shaking.

In this particular case, I wasn't ready to rule out violence as the answer. Just not now.

While it was within the realm of cosmic possibility that it was exactly like it appeared—two gangbangers thought they could make an easy score and ended up picking the wrong fight. For his part, Garcia did seem confused.

What I needed was to clear my head and look at this objectively.

This wasn't the first time someone had taken a shot at me. One of the skills I'd honed over the years in the clandestine service was managing the fallout from violence.

I found that forcing myself into some kind of normalcy eased me back into a rhythm. Because so much of my adult life had been an act, sometimes blending in with the regular populace, doing normal things, had a way of easing me off the wave of tension. Jumping at shadows was a waste of time and energy. It also sapped your focus from solving the problem of who was trying to kill you. So, you compartmentalize and view it in the proper context.

Mario from the hotel bar recommended I check out this coffee shop on 15th Street, about six blocks away. The walk did me some good. I called Jimmy on the way, and I got voicemail. Maybe it was a little weird that I hadn't heard from him yet, though I also didn't know the guy all that well. That was another problem for later.

I arrived at the coffee shop. The exterior was bright red paint and a giant reproduction of a 1950s postcard from Havana. It had an off-white awning over the sidewalk covering the metal mesh tables and chairs, where I would spend the next hour.

The upside of this approach to life is that it enabled one to enjoy a nice breakfast the day after an attempted murder without your nerves ruining your appetite. But I still sat with my back to the restaurant's wall, my pistol clipped to a concealed holster under my shirt, and my eyes on the street.

The cafe served Cuban huevos rancheros consisting of a savory black-beans-and-rice dish alongside a poached egg over a tostada.

The most important thing I had to do today was ensure my cover as Jameson Carter was still in play. Acting as a private detective, I'd told Garcia and Cody Portman that I'd been hired to investigate Sunshine Sports Collective. As Jameson Carter, I'd told Olivia McEvoy that I used an investigative service to conduct due diligence. I'd also used that as a pretext for asking some questions around town, though I doubted the latter had gotten back to Ray Ruiz yet.

More to the point, if I didn't contact Ray today, he might connect Jameson Carter and Matt Gage.

There was something else to it, though. I wanted Ray's reaction. If he was behind the attempt, I might be able to pull that out of his response. Which was not to say this wasn't dangerous and risky as hell.

I ate my food and drank my coffee in silence, my eyes never straying far from the street.

Another skill I'd cultivated and honed to a keen edge over the years was knowing when I was being watched. Sometimes, some places, you don't need it. Moscow, Beijing, Hong Kong, Cairo, Damascus, Tehran. It's safe to assume you are, so you can save the sixth sense for later. Now, though, I couldn't shake the feeling.

I wondered if maybe Ray's security guy, Farrier, outsourced last night's entertainment. Could be it was a test, one they'd never intended to get lethal. Poke the fences, see where the holes are.

Maybe.

I called Ray's cell, and it went to voicemail.

"Ray—James Carter here. Had a great chat with Olivia the other night. My business partner and I are still interested. Hit me up, and let's talk next steps over drinks. Oh, and you're buying."

He returned the call by the time I'd made it back to the hotel.

"James, my man, how are you?" Ebullient for a weekday.

"Great, Ray. I have to say, I love this town. Super productive week with clients. Loving it here."

"I'm glad to hear that, man. There's no place in the world like Miami," Ray said. "So, you're interested in talking terms?"

"I am. Are you free later?"

"For you, anything. What say we have dinner at my club? You'll love it. It's in a sky bridge fifty stories off the ground. Unreal. Unlike anything you've ever seen."

I was hoping he'd say literally any place but there.

"Sounds great."

---

The middle part of my spy career was with a covert action team built to go after the worst of humanity. The kinds of diabolical Houdinis who always seemed to escape, the ones who armed both sides in a conflict or sold biological weapons to terrorists.

Aleksei Korolev was Putin's trouble broker. An arms dealer, dark-money financier, and global blackmailer, he was reported to have been the one who'd organized the sale of sarin gas to Bashar al Assad in Syria. But that wasn't why we wanted him. At least, not entirely. Korolev had also created a—if you'll excuse the pun—Russian nesting doll of shell companies that ultimately fronted a "global risk management firm." The simplest explanation was this allowed Korolev to purchase Western-made military technology and funnel it back to Russian military intelligence for them to reverse-engineer or use. We figured this was why the Russian forces had such a decisive technological advantage in their 2014 invasion and seizure of Crimea. In the summer of 2019, posing as a businessman looking to fund a small, clandestinely-supplied, private army to prop up an African dictator for the purposes of mining rights—something near and dear to a Russian oligarch's heart—I'd met Korolev in Monaco. The principality's government was notoriously poor at policing their residents.

Korolev employed a security staff consisting of ex-SVR, the KGB's successor service, and they were quite good. They'd figured out the CIA was onto them and that we may even have infiltrated their network. In a play eerily similar to what had happened last night, two hit men made a play for me. Or at least, for the cover I'd used to get into the country.

We didn't know for certain the next night whether my cover as British ex-pat businessman Douglas Wescott was burned or not. We also wouldn't get a second shot at Korolev without an MQ-9 and a Hellfire, so I had to chance it and go.

Now, as I rolled up to the looming tower of opulent glass and light, I couldn't help but remember that night stepping onto Korolev's yacht.

This, too, was a location with no easy way out if I was burned.

I'd used my Jameson Carter identity at the sky club, so I didn't have cause to be nervous about getting caught between lies. However, it would be at least awkward for a staff member to recognize me. Especially Rafe, who was no doubt waiting for my application.

Instead of driving my Defender with the California plates and risking it being identified as the ride belonging to a should-be-dead PI, I had the hotel concierge organize a not-quite limo for me to travel the roughly one mile. As with before, pulling into the tower's curved carport, I was struck by how much vertical glass could be stacked on top of itself. This place had strong *The Towering Inferno* vibes.

I entered and found the concierge, gave them my name, and said I was expected upstairs as Mr. Ruiz's guest.

"Right this way, sir."

Thanks to a few tours in the hotter parts of the world, I own a nice tropical-weight suit of the lightest gray imaginable. I'd paired that with a dark blue shirt and no tie. The concierge took me to the elevator, helpfully badged it open, and navigated the button sequence to get me to whatever fiftyish floor the club was on. Someone met me on the other side and guided me to Ray's table, where he had an unimaginable view of the setting sun. If you let your eyes lose focus on the minimal steel outline, you'd think you were Superman.

Probably not much of a stretch for the people who could afford to be members here.

Ray stood—light blue linen jacket, yellow shirt, and tan pants. A pocket square in a shade of purple I knew didn't exist in nature burst out of his pocket like an overripe fruit.

We shook hands and sat, and someone materialized instantly for a drink order.

Ray ordered a mojito, and I seconded.

If Ray expected me dead, he didn't show it.

Conversation started with sports. The tournament loomed large, though he also probed my knowledge of A&M's spring practices and depth-chart development, as any obsessive fan would. I tried to cover by saying I'd been traveling so much I couldn't follow as closely as I wanted. Ray's enthusiasm for the subject was infectious, and I had to force myself to remember that twenty-four hours ago, he may have tried to kill me.

"Man, Gulf Coast had a hell of an upset the other night," I said. "Of course, I'm always happy to see the Vols go down."

Ray sipped his drink, a mojito, and agreed. "Did you see the game?" he asked, and I said I had. "The kid who made that shot, Cody Portman...he's one of ours. No one else wanted to sign him."

"Bet you're going to have some competition now," I said.

Ray shrugged the statement off. "Maybe. I mean, I tend to sign long-term agreements with our athletes. Though if someone has a breakout season and their valuation increases, we're always willing to renegotiate terms. To my knowledge, there's nothing says anyone can't be in multiple collectives...especially if it's a setup like ours. Say Cody transferred from Gulf Coast to Florida, he could have an arrangement with us and with Florida Victorious. Far as I know. Now, in his case, and I haven't spoken to him yet...but I expect he's going to transfer. I also expect there's going to be an influx of interest and cash to make that happen."

Now that was interesting. If there was some kind of point-fixing scheme going on, I wondered how that would play out with the transfer portal dynamics. Did it end, or would they look at that as a chance to spread the cancer? Or was Ray just saying all this to throw off suspicion?

"You probably know from my conversation with Olivia," I said. "That Apogee Partners uses a retained investigative service to conduct due diligence on prospective investments."

"I heard something about that," Ray said, his voice crisp and brittle.

"You'd be surprised at some of the things we find when we're about to make an investment. Some of our work is corporate restructuring, though we try to avoid it. Most of what we do are promising ventures that maybe need a little help. Anyway, sometimes we find shady shit and have to pull the plug, and sometimes there are just more problems than we can solve."

"What'd your guy find?"

"Guys," I said. "And they're all with us in Dallas. Sometimes they travel, though not always. The point is, they did their work, asked hard questions in the right places. Spoke to the state regulators, things like that. Clean bill of health."

Surprise washed over Ray's face, though he recovered quickly.

"So, you never had anyone here locally?"

"Nope. Man, everything is online nowadays."

"Huh," was all he said, and then Ray drank.

"Honestly, they just had one real lingering question."

"What's that?"

"They wanted to know about these investments you set up for your athletes."

Ray's face brightened. "Oh, that. It's an experiment in altruism that I think is going to end up being more trouble than it's worth."

"How's that?"

"What would *you* have done if someone gave you a million dollars in college?"

I laughed a bit at that, remembering the chaotic force of nature that was twenty-year-old me. I would've done something so dumb with that amount of money they'd have needed to erect a permanent memorial to my stupidity to serve as a warning to others.

"Probably not spend it wisely," I said.

"Deion's kid bought a Lamborghini. That's my point. What's that kid going to do if his knee gets folded back on a bad play or if he just has a bad season? We don't do this with everyone. Just between us, I've only got five athletes that are making above twenty grand right now, though we are talking to several with that potential. Let's take Brashard Brown, since you're already familiar. Man, he's a good kid, good family. He had every opportunity to do the wrong things in life, and he never did. All my contacts in the athletic department say he's the first one there, last one to leave. Lives and breathes football. One of his coaches said if they took his scholarship and removed him from the depth chart tomorrow, they'd still expect to see him at practice the day after. I don't want to see someone like that end up broke because they got hurt and missed their shot to go pro."

That was a little different interpretation than I'd heard from Jimmy and from the Browns.

Ray took a sip from his drink—our second round—and said, "Something else I won't admit outside these walls, James. I don't know that Brashard is getting great advice at home. His dad, Cyrus, is a good man, and I think his heart is in the right place. It's just that he never made much of himself—didn't have a lot of opportunity to, really. But, man, I see the dollar signs in his eyes. We talk about endorsements and things, and Jesus, that guy is practically licking his lips."

"That bad?"

"Well, maybe that's not fair. I came from a very modest background too. I probably had some chances because of school that Cyrus Brown didn't. Still, every time I talk with him, it just seems like he's focused on the money as much as anything else, like his son's future. I know most of these kids. First thing they want to do is take care of their folks. Totally understand that. Support it. Shit, James, I've cosigned loans for kids. Just want to make sure the Brashards of the world have something to show for it and don't get taken. We talked about you in college with a million bucks, right? Would your parents have let you keep it, or would they tell you they sacrificed everything to put you there? Parents taking advantage of famous kids is not a new story."

"My dad ran fishing charters in the Gulf," which was true, just not the side of it that Ray was thinking. "We never had much money either. You've heard the fastest way to lose money is to buy a boat, right? Well, do that with three or four of them. I like to think my old man would've said, 'It's your money, son. Good job.' But who knows? He might just as easily tell me that if it wasn't for putting me through college, he'd have had however many more boats and crews to run them."

Ray telling me he was looking out for SSC's athletes certainly didn't jibe with what I'd learned about him so far—or with what Jimmy and the Browns had told me. Though Ray's assertion that Brashard wasn't getting good advice at home?

This, I could see. I felt a horrible sensation of guilt, thinking that about Cyrus. It also didn't feel that far off the mark.

"Something I wanted to talk to you about," Ray said, pregnant-pause style.

Now, it was my turn to have cold water crawl up my nerve endings.

"What's that?"

"This may be a little awkward, I'm not sure. We've talked a lot about you using SSC to vector players to A&M, which we can still totally do. I was thinking, though... would Apogee Partners be interested in investing in the business? There's a lot I could do with PE backing."

---

Dinner came and went, as did a bottle of wine, the price of which I could only guess. I told Ray to send a proposal to my Apogee email and I'd consider the offer. He suggested cigars on the patio, but I deferred, saying I had some early meetings.

In truth, I had *a lot* to process.

When I'd left Aleksei Korolev's yacht back in the day, there hadn't been any question about his guilt or what we'd do about it. We don't murder people, but as that TV painter might have said, "There are happy accidents."

With Ray Ruiz, I wasn't so sure. Flash had laid out a compelling argument that Ruiz could be laundering money. But for whom? And why? If Flash was wrong, and the extent of it was predatory royalty contracts, I wasn't sure there was anything I could do. After all, Jimmy's hypothesis was that SSC was engaged in illegal activity, and if I found out what it was, we could use that as leverage to get Brashard out of his contract.

After this evening, I was sure the Jameson Carter cover was still in place. And I'd come out of this with a better opportunity to look at SSC's operations than I'd ever had. My strategy of making Ray think he had threats from all sides appeared to be working, at least in that it gave me a way to mask my earlier probes into his activities. If he felt threatened, Ruiz might negotiate with us just to make this go away.

Still, *someone* had tried to murder me last night.

Right now, I just wasn't sure it was him. This didn't seem like an operation that you'd protect through murder. Though that didn't change the fact someone around here had a secret they were willing to kill to keep hidden.

I had a fistful of missed calls by the time I'd left dinner. Most would wait until morning. The one I decided to return, though, was Jimmy's colleague, Elena Mendoza. She was the fellow agent who'd said that an SSC-connected person had threatened her when she tried to sign a client he wanted.

It was about nine thirty, and I texted her, identifying myself and confirming it wasn't too late to call. She texted back that now was fine.

"Ms. Mendoza," I said. "Thank you for returning my call."

"Of course. I'm sorry it took so long. The last couple weeks before the NFL draft is always batshit crazy."

"I can only imagine."

"You're the investigator working with Jimmy, right?"

"That's right. I was wondering if I could ask you a couple of questions."

"I have a few minutes," she said. I heard a door close and the muffled click of the phone handing off to the car's audio. Late night for her too.

"Jimmy told me about a prospect you were looking to sign, and you ran into trouble with another agent?"

"Yeah, Blaise Palmas. He's set himself up as an NIL broker, sort of a cross between a traditional agent and a full-blown collective," she said.

"He works with Sunshine Sports Collective, is that right?"

"As I understand it. Some of their people who don't have full-time agents use him to negotiate their deals. Anyway, Palmas was talking with this girl on the UF gymnastics team, Vicky Lee. She's—"

"Ranked fifth in the country, right? Supposed to be short-listed for the next Olympic team?"

"That's right," Elena said. "The Gators had a little trouble with their first collective early on, so a lot of the athletes didn't have deals, and she was available. I knew of two women's sports apparel companies that wanted to talk to her, so I was trying to sign her. Palmas made some phone calls, showed up at a restaurant one time, and caused a scene. Said I was trying to steal his client and he'd refer me to the NCAA."

"But that wasn't everything, though?"

"No. It wasn't. This part isn't easy to talk about. A couple of days later, I got rear-ended. I got out to inspect it, and this big guy comes out. He says to me, and I'll never forget this, 'You want to be more careful.'"

"Do you remember what he looked like?"

"Cuban, bald, muscular."

"What, like an athlete? Powerlifter?"

"More like prison big."

"You remember what he was driving?"

"Cadillac Escalade."

A cold shock ran down my body.

It was the answer I'd expected to hear, but that didn't make it any more comforting to know.

God, I hate when I'm right.

"Mr. Gage?"

"Sorry. I'm still here. Was just thinking. Could we meet? Do you have time for a coffee or something?"

"I don't think that would be a good idea."

"Ms. Mendoza, I had a similar situation, same type of vehicle, person sounds the same. Together, we might be able to take this to the police."

"Mr. Gage, someone sent me a very clear message not to get involved. I talked to the police, and they said there was nothing they could do. I'm taking the hint. You want my advice? You should do the same."

"What if it doesn't stop with us?"

"That's not my problem. I'm getting another call. I have to go."

Elena Mendoza hung up, leaving me in the shadows of palm trees and mirrored-glass buildings.

---

Later, my phone rang again. A number I didn't recognize. It was about eleven, and I wasn't expecting any calls.

"This is Matt," I said.

"It's Brashard."

"Hey, hi. What can I do for you?"

"I, ah, just got a call. From Jimmy's agency." The kid's voice was thick with tension.

"What's going on, Brashard?"

"Jimmy's dead, man."

# 11

---

"He's what?"

I snapped up the remote and turned on the TV, scanning quickly for a local station.

"They just told me he was shot and killed tonight. It's all over the news. They said he went into Liberty City to buy drugs and things didn't go his way."

I had the local news on now, and they had Jimmy's headshot on screen next to footage of a chalk outline on the street and plastic bullet markers.

"Brashard, first of all, are you okay?"

"I don't even know."

"Let me call you back. I'll see if I can find out what's going on."

"Yeah," he said and hung up.

The noon anchor said Jimmy had gone into Liberty City, one of Miami's most dangerous neighborhoods, allegedly to buy drugs, when he got into an altercation with a dealer. Eyewitnesses said the dealer shot him with an automatic weapon and fled the scene.

I sat on the edge of my bed, too stunned to move or even think.

Jimmy Lawson, my client, was dead.

It took a lot of dark hours to process what had happened.

The next morning, I genuinely didn't know what to do. Without a client, I didn't have a case.

More importantly, a good man was dead. I hadn't known Jimmy long, though I'd quickly grown to like him. He was willing to take a few risks for Brashard, including trying to put himself between the kid and an over-bearing father, who likely meant well but didn't know a thing about the business side of sports. Worse, I think Cyrus Brown leaned on his son to accept the SSC offer. Yes, Jimmy thought the kid had breakout potential and could be a huge star if a lot of things broke his way. He was financially invested in the kid's future—that was true—but I'd also spent enough time with him to know his concern for Brashard was real. He believed in the kid and wanted him to get a shot. Jimmy told me that someone took a chance on him once and that meant something to him.

Brashard called again. He was shocked, maybe a little scared and looking for advice on what to do next. He said he had a little bit of time between lunch and practice, so I hauled ass over to campus.

The Canes' practice facility was a massive complex on the southern tip of campus that overlooked the Mahi Waterway in Coral Cables. I parked in front of one of the athletic buildings, and if collegiate parking lots hadn't changed since I was in school, I could expect a ticket in about five minutes for not having the right kind of tag.

Palms and other tropical trees covered the landscape. The campus looked to be emerging from a precisely manicured jungle like a Victorian explorer.

I messaged Brashard and saw him leave a cluster of palms by one of the buildings. He was already decked out in his practice gear. He threw out a couple of chin nods to people who passed him. That was impressive under the circumstances. Stress and pressure management was part of his job, sure, but I didn't think he'd seen anything like this before. He composed himself well.

Brashard shook his head as he walked up. "I don't know, man. Wouldn't have taken Jimmy for the type."

"I don't think he was."

"What do you mean?"

"Look, I didn't know him that well. I just didn't think he was into that sort of thing. This situation feels off to me. Call it an instinct."

"That all you got to go on?"

The words *someone tried to take a shot at me too* hovered in the front of my mouth, daring to be let out.

I held them back. I didn't know Brashard well enough to know what he'd do with that information.

"What are we gonna do now about my contract?"

That was a good and fair question, and I don't think Brashard asked it to be callous. There's only one way to take something like that, though. Still, we'd only met once, and it was business. This was the context in which he knew me. I wasn't the person he turned to for grieving about his dead agent. Jimmy had been my client, not the Brown family. I was helping them on Lawson's behalf. I'd had a lot of practice processing terrible news and learned to compartmentalize. There would be time for lamenting the loss of a friend and client. For now, my brain immediately went to answer the question of what I do next?

Which, to be honest, was "not much."

I had no client, so the investigation stopped.

"That's a complicated question, Brashard. Jimmy was my client, so without him, I can't do anything." That wasn't true in the strictest legal sense. There was nothing stopping me from investigating this as a concerned private citizen, though anything I uncovered might not have any weight. And there was the small matter of my not being paid.

"Lemme talk to my folks," Brashard said.

This was what I did not want.

"Brashard, your parents are behind on their house payments because SSC isn't paying you. How in the hell are you going to afford me?"

The kid flushed and looked away. He was angry and humiliated. The money Ray Ruiz had promised him was more than his parents would make in their entire life. It got them out of a cramped and moldy roach box and into the first home they'd ever owned. Brashard took that money, probably without thinking about the fine print, because it meant getting his family into a better situation now rather than in two or three years when he was drafted. The family who had scraped and saved and sacrificed so he could play ball, to get to *this* point. Then he made a mistake that may cost him millions in the future. Though not as Ray Ruiz would tell it.

That was a lot of weight for a nineteen-year-old to carry.

He asked, "What if you only got paid if you win? That's a thing, right?"

It wasn't appropriate for the moment, but I smiled anyway. I appreciated the kid's moxie. And it wasn't the worst idea.

"You mean, if I can get SSC to release you from your contract and get the money that you're owed, your family will pay me out of the money I recover?"

"Yeah."

"It's pretty fair, Brashard. I'll give you that. I also don't like the idea of quitting. We need to talk to your parents first. I would have to know they're on board before I'd agree to it. You also need to consider the fact that if you get out of your contract with SSC, they won't pay you the rest of that money. That has some implications for your family. You'd need a new deal with another collective...and fast."

"Why? I made that money," he said, in the defensive way only the youth can summon.

I held up my hands. "Because that's how contracts work. They may also try to take back what they gave you. I'm telling you all this so you and your family have the full picture. It's important to me they don't think I'm trying to take advantage of you."

"Yeah, okay. I get that."

"Are you able to meet them tonight?"

"I got practice at five, then dinner and study hall until, like, nine."

"They keep you guys pretty locked down, huh?"

"Can't get into trouble if they always know where you are."

"Actually, you don't necessarily need to be there when I talk to your folks. Call your dad. If he's willing to do it, I'll go see him tonight. I don't know if I'm going to do this yet, all right? I'm still processing all this too."

Who was I kidding?

There are people who have the cut-and-run gene. It's a life-saving skill as an intelligence officer.

I envy them.

I might have been able to quit before they tried to kill me. Now, I'm in this to the end. A mentor of mind would say that's the exact moment you know you need to walk away."

"Yeah, okay." Brashard turned and looked at the practice facility. He took a half-step then turned back to me. "Jimmy was my friend, man. He looked out for me. I just can't...I don't.... Shit, man. This ain't right. I can't believe it."

"Brashard, for whatever it's worth, most people are exactly who you think they are." Of course, I was referring to a Russian SVR officer who was a triple-crossing asshole, but why let that get in the way of the morality tale? "What I mean is, you believe Jimmy was a good guy and that he was looking out for you. I believe that too. I don't know if he was into drugs or not. It feels off to me. Even if he was, he cared about you and genuinely had your best interests at heart. I know that for fact."

I didn't know if that helped Brashard process what was happening. I hoped it did.

He still looked troubled, though.

"Was there something else you wanted to talk to me about?"

Brashard looked away. Whatever it was, it was difficult for him.

"Tell me on your time," I said.

"I'll call Dad," he said as he walked away.

I went back to my car just as the parking maven was rounding the row. I rolled out to Dixie Highway and back to the hotel.

---

The local news sites didn't have anything new on Jimmy's death, other than saying the Miami Police were looking into it. Which was helpful information to have. The City of Miami Police Department had responsibility for the city proper. The Miami-Dade Police Department had jurisdiction over the unincorporated areas of Dade County, or the communities too small to support their own police force.

Liberty City fell within the Miami Police Department's jurisdiction.

Lieutenant Silvestri worked for Miami-Dade, so she wouldn't be of help here.

I got the MPD's homicide squad number from their website and called.

It went straight to voicemail, so I left my name, number, and relation to Jimmy Lawson. I had little hope someone would call me back.

What I really wanted was to go exercise out some of the tension. And physical activity helped. When I was concentrating on a sport, my mind had a way of connecting dots in the background. I'd taken up open-water kayaking and mountain and road biking since moving to California. Made a few attempts at surfing, though the kind folks at Cosmic Ray's told me that I was as much a danger to myself as I was to others—and that my behavior on the waves was driving off their regulars.

I went for a run. The temperature was in the low seventies, humidity was manageable—for here. Compared to Los Angeles, it felt like I was at the bottom of a hot lake. I took off from the hotel and headed north toward Bayfront Park, being careful to take a route that wouldn't bring me in front of Olivia's building.

My phone rang three miles into the run. I stopped, chest heaving, to answer. I didn't recognize the number, though it had a Miami area code.

"This is Gage," I said.

"This is Detective Duane Parr, Miami Homicide. You called and left a message on the squad line about James Lawson?"

"I did, yeah."

"So, you've got some information for me or what?"

"I'm a private detective. Jimmy was my client. I don't think this was drug-related," I said.

"You have something to back that up?" Parr sounded tired and annoyed.

"Someone tried to kill me the same night. I have a hard time believing they aren't related."

"Where are you right now?"

"Jogging on Biscayne."

"I'll be there in ten minutes."

It was more like twenty. I met him at a public parking lot set in the median between Biscayne Boulevard's two halves. Parr was about my height, tan, late thirties, and blond. He did not have the archetypal detective mustache nor did he miss many sessions in the gym. He wore a blue suit off the rack. Parr had a folio opened on the trunk of his unmarked police ride. "Before we start, I have to take your picture, so I need your consent."

"Why?"

"Everyone gets their picture taken now. We have to put them with the FI cards."

FI, short for Field Interview, were the documents cops filled out when they collected information on a case. I'd never heard of cops taking photos to accompany the FIs before, but if officers had to have body cams now, there was a certain logic to taking a picture of an interview subject. I told him it was fine, and Parr took my picture on his phone. He took down my name and address.

"You're a long way from LA, aren't you? How'd you come to know Mr. Lawson?"

"A former client recommended me. They were law school classmates at UCLA."

Parr nodded and wrote that down as though it were insightful.

"What've you got for me, Mr. Gage?"

I'd backed myself into a corner without realizing it.

I hadn't reported the attempted murder, and I'd also fled the scene after discharging a deadly weapon. I know Florida had a Stand Your Ground law and was generously flexible when it came to self-defense with firearms, but I'd learned the hard way to be cautious with the information I shared with the police.

"Early in the case, I'd asked some questions to one of the people sponsoring Sunshine Sports Collective. He called me two nights ago saying he had additional information and wanted to speak at his warehouse in Opa-Locka."

"And this guy, he got a name?"

"Charlie Garcia," I said. I'd hoped to keep his name out of this, mostly because I didn't want to involve another jurisdiction and further muddy the case. "I showed up at the appointed time, he wasn't there. Called, no answer. I left. As I was leaving, a black Cadillac Escalade pulled up behind me. They hit my bumper at a light. I got out to check and two Cuban gangbangers—"

"Hold up. They tell you they were Cuban? You see a Cuban flag in the car?"

"No," I said.

"So you don't know."

"I don't."

"Right. I'm going to put this down as two Latin males. You say 'Cuban,' and you don't really know, we get the shit knocked out of us in the press for profiling." The cop shook his head. He seemed angry—at me, the system... probably both. "Then what happened?"

"One of them tried sneaking around my vehicle to get behind me. The other one showed me a gun he had stuck in his pants. I defended myself then got back into my car and left as soon as they were subdued."

"You fought off two men, one of whom was armed with a pistol?"

"I've been trained for this sort of thing," I said.

"What, like the Army?"

"Central Intelligence Agency," I told him.

Detective Parr closed his notebook. "Well, you should know that this is the new favorite thing in carjacking. Hitting a car and stealing it. You're lucky you got out alive. Next time, you need to call the police."

I'd had enough of this shit. Our entire conversation had focused on this attempt on me—which I'd clearly survived—and not on the *actual murder* this guy was allegedly investigating.

"What exactly would you have done, Detective? I call the cops, those two idiots are long gone. I didn't get a plate number."

"I don't think I like your attitude, *sir*. Mr. Lawson was killed in a known trafficking area. You were victim to one of the most common types of crime we have in this area. I think you're making a connection that isn't there."

"I don't think so," I said. "I think it's possible that someone was trying to silence him. And they succeeded." Parr's jaw tightened. He clearly didn't like being second-guessed by someone who couldn't hack it as a cop.

"Silence him about what?" Parr asked, not hiding his irritation.

"As I've been trying to explain to you, Jimmy hired me because he believed an outfit called Sunshine Sports Collective was tricking college athletes into a Ponzi scheme. Just as soon as I start asking questions, Jimmy gets a phone call and winds up dead. That same night, one of the people who gives money to SSC called me with 'information' he could only give me in person. I show up and he's not there, but two thugs are and they tried to kill me."

"Yeah, that still sounds like an attempted carjacking you were lucky to walk away from."

A hundred foul words bubbled up, and by the grace of God, training, and sheer obstinance, I wrestled them back down into my gut.

"Walk me through the evening," Parr said.

"Jimmy and I were supposed to meet that night. Couple of hours before that, he texted me and said a prospective client wanted to talk. Jimmy was going to see him first, and then we were going to meet up. I never heard from him again."

"Can I see the text?"

I opened my phone, pulled up Jimmy's texts, and scrolled to the last one. I held the phone out for him to read and made it clear I wasn't handing the phone to him. Annoyance flashed on his face.

"How'd you learn that he died?"

"Jimmy represents a Miami football player named Brashard Brown."

"Yeah, I know him. I mean, I know the name, sure."

"Brashard told me. Jimmy's agency called Brashard. They wanted him to find out before he heard it on the news."

"Gotcha," he said dispassionately.

Seriously? *Gotcha*?

"Can you give me this kid's number? I'll take the agency too, if you've got it."

"I'll have to look it up." I did and, again, held my phone out for him to look at. He took a picture of the contact card.

"We busted a manager last year for getting oxy for one of his clients. A running back for the Fish. My guess is, that's what this was with Lawson, unless he was trying to score for himself. Probably didn't want you to know."

"Detective, I don't think that's what this is."

"Gage, I humored you. Honestly, I was hoping you'd have something more for me."

"You're serious? That's it? I just gave you a solid lead that Sunshine Sports Collective is connected to one murder and another attempted one."

"What does this Sunshine Sports-whatever do again?"

"They facilitate endorsement deals for college athletes. So, they would likely know who the top prospects are in the area and would be able to name someone Jimmy Lawson would want to talk to. They might also know what kids did and didn't have agents. In the case of the latter, who they were talking to."

"Right. That's not really how I see this case, Gage. Just being honest with you. I get what you're saying, but it's a big leap to make, you know? Murder conspiracy to shut up the agent and the crusading private detective?"

That's literally exactly what this was.

Though, to be fair, when you put it like he did, the idea did sound a little stretched.

Knowing when to fold 'em should be in the private eye handbook. Good advice, Kenny. "I think there's more to this than you're making out."

"I think you need to leave this to the professionals," Parr said.

Parr stuffed his little cop's notebook back in his pocket. "Murder is big medicine, Gage. Don't go poking around and don't go looking for trouble. What I mean is, we've worked really goddamn hard to turn the murder rate in this city in a different direction. It's the lowest now since the '60s. Mr. Lawson was well known and wealthy. That gets attention. There's going to be a lot of pressure to close this. I don't need you poking around and making a bad situation more complicated. Understand?"

I understood. And I was glad I wasn't a Miami taxpayer.

--------

Cyrus Brown asked if I could come over at seven, after the family finished supper.

I arrived with my laptop and briefcase. Brashard greeted me at the door. So much for study hall. He led me to the dining room table. Mrs. Brown was guiding the younger children upstairs. Cyrus invited me to sit. I took up one spot in the middle, and he sat at the head. Brashard sat across from me.

Cyrus Brown looked weary, like he'd just climbed a mountain and realized he was only halfway up.

"Brashard told me about his idea," Cyrus said. "Would you be willing to do it?"

"I would," I said.

"So, we'd just take on the contract you negotiated with Jimmy?"

"Not quite." I opened the ballistic nylon briefcase and pulled out some papers. It contained a very simple contract I'd written up that day. "Jimmy's contention was that Sunshine Sports Collective was running a scam, and if I could prove it, we could use that as leverage to get Brashard out of his contract. If I was unsuccessful, he would pay my time and expenses. If I got Brashard free and clear, there was a substantially larger payment involved."

"How much?"

"It doesn't matter, because I'm not going to charge you that, under any circumstances."

The $250k would've been a great down payment on a house or enough to lease a proper office. Not that I have anything against tiki bars, mind you. An office is just optics for the haters.

Mrs. Brown returned to the dining room and sat next to her husband.

"What are your rates?"

"Six thousand a week plus expenses, and I only work for you," I said.

Odds were pretty good I was moving out of the JW Marriott now. Probably all for the best, given the proximity to Olivia's. With Jimmy dead, I'd be on the hook for what I'd spent so far and that was going to sting. I pushed the papers across the table. "This is a very simple contract, and there is no fine print. This says that you're engaging my services to get Brashard out of his contract with Sunshine Sports Collective and get any back pay you are owed. If that occurs, you pay me my weekly rate per the terms sheet on the back. I report to you weekly on progress, daily if you prefer. If, at any point, you wish to cancel, you may. If I am unsuccessful, you don't pay me anything."

"Do you think you can do that? Get him out?" Mrs. Brown said.

"If I didn't, I wouldn't have taken the case to begin with. Here's what I know. I have evidence that suggests the collective is laundering money. I don't know who yet, but I've gotten access to their financial data, and I know what that looks like. I've also brought in an independent expert, who has consulted with the police and FBI on money-laundering schemes. I have evidence that someone connected to SSC threatened another agent to scare them away from signing a client. And then someone tried to kill me."

"What?" Brashard and his father said at the same time, though Brashard added an expletive at the end of his.

"Watch your mouth, Brashard," his father admonished. "This isn't the practice field."

I explained the situation with Charlie Garcia. There was no way around it.

"I think someone set me up to be killed. The same night, Jimmy gets a call from a prospect and is gunned down. Both of these were made to look like something else. I don't think Jimmy went to buy drugs. Brashard, I didn't tell you when we spoke earlier because you were already processing Jimmy's death, I didn't want you worrying about what happened to me."

The two Brown men traded a look, and there was a lot passing between them, though I didn't have the backstory I needed to figure out just what.

"Is Brashard safe?" Mrs. Brown asked.

"I have no reason to believe he isn't."

"That's not a *no*," she said forcefully.

"It doesn't make sense for them to harm Brashard. Without him, they cannot get people to invest in the business."

"But what if it's all just a front for this money-laundering whatever?" Cyrus said.

"This is where I need to urge some patience, which I can appreciate is hard given what's just happened. I have indicators that SSC is laundering money, I haven't proven it yet. It could be that he's just skirting the rules, and Jimmy's death and the attempt on my life were horrible coincidences. Now, I don't believe that to be the case, but it's important that I'm truthful with you that it could come out that way." I paused and let them take all that in. The Browns asked no questions, though the looks traded between the three of them spoke volumes.

"So, let's say you're right," Cyrus said in his rockslide voice. "How do you get my boy out of his contract? Especially if...if what you say is true."

"I have two approaches. One, I take what I have to Ray Ruiz and make a deal. Let Brashard out, or I go to the cops. That's the first path. The second approach is that I continue my investigation and take what I have to the police. I have spoken with both Miami-Dade and MPD. I also have connections in the FBI. Those avenues will take longer. In that instance, I would work up to the point where I turned over my information to law enforcement, and you pay me if we are eventually successful."

Cyrus turned to his son. "Would you excuse us, Brashard?"

"This is about me, Dad. I should be here."

"I asked you to let us be, son."

I got the sense that not a lot of folks crossed Cyrus Brown.

Brashard shook his head, pushed back his chair, and stood. "I'll be at study hall."

"That's a better use of your time," Cyrus said.

Brashard scooped up his phone and lumbered toward the door. When it closed, Cyrus looked over to his wife and said, "Would you give us a minute?"

"If we're talking about Brashard, I want to be here."

"I need to have a word with Mr. Gage. Please."

Mrs. Brown gave her husband the kind of smoldering look that said this conversation was far from over, but she rose from her chair and left the room.

"He's a good boy, Mr. Gage. He doesn't deserve this."

"No, he doesn't. And neither do you," I said, even though as I spoke the words I couldn't help but weigh them against what I'd heard from Ray Ruiz. I left my conversation with Ray out of this. This situation didn't need more *gray*. I still couldn't reconcile the image I had of Ray, the eager sports geek, with a criminal mastermind who goes to murder as an opening move.

"Be honest with me—is what they say about Jimmy true? You have police connections. What are they saying?"

"Well, I need to be clear that my connections are with Miami-Dade. Miami PD is handling Jimmy's murder. I spoke with the MPD detective today, as I said. He may contact you. I didn't think he was very helpful, to be honest. Felt like he was phoning it in."

"Yeah," was all he said. A pause as he stared at the far wall. Then, "Is my son safe?"

"I stand by what I said earlier. It doesn't make any sense for them to harm Brashard."

"But what if you're successful? Will they come after him then? They can't have him so no one else can—that kind of thing?"

"I'm not going to let it come to that. The case has taken on a different dimension than when Jimmy hired me. The information that is going to get your son out of his contract is going to be the same information the police will need to put these people away."

"Sounds like a lot of *ifs* to me."

I wanted to tell him I'd made a career of daisy-chaining long shots, but that's not the reassurance I'd be looking for in his shoes.

"Yes, sir it is. I won't lie about that."

"You'll keep me posted on the situation with the police?"

"I will."

"And if you think Brashard is in danger?"

"I'll tell you right after I tell the cops."

"What if you're successful?" Cyrus asked.

"What do you mean?"

"Do we keep the money they've already given us?"

"That question is better for a lawyer, which I would strongly advise you to get. I told Brashard, and hopefully he relayed this to you, but I would imagine breaking the contract forfeits all future payment *and* you may be forced to pay back what they've already given you. I know that's a considerable amount."

Cyrus Brown's expression gave nothing away.

I wished him a good evening and left.

I found Brashard waiting for me outside.

"What's up?" I asked.

"Is this my fault? Did I get Jimmy killed?"

"No, of course not. Why would you think that?"

Brashard looked away again, as if he didn't want to meet my gaze. Right then, I knew this was why he'd called me earlier. What he'd wanted to say this afternoon and couldn't bring himself to.

Finally, he spoke. "Just after Jimmy hired you, Ruiz called me. He tried to get me to fire Jimmy, said I didn't need him because I already had the deal. It was just going to cost me money. I got mad. I flexed. I told him Jimmy hired you because he thought some shady shit was going on, and they'd be sorry if he was right."

"Brashard, Jimmy's murder is not on you. I mean that."

"How else could they have found out about him hiring you?"

"Ray Ruiz has a security guy, someone like me. He could've put it together. This is not on you, okay?"

He nodded, though it lacked conviction.

Well, that certainly clarified a few things.

# 12

Brashard had given me a lot to consider.

The kid carried the weight of Jimmy's death, and I tried to reassure him that it wasn't his fault. Maybe he even believed me a little.

First, damage control. What did this mean for the case?

As a detective, I'd made no secret that I was looking into Sunshine Sports Collective. I'd created a fabric of deception, in the form of a cover, that let me ask different kinds of questions. It created the kind of separation I needed to operate.

*Run down the facts.*

Ray knows that Jimmy Lawson hired a private detective named Matt Gage. *Someone* ordered me and Jimmy killed on the same night.

Ray knows that "Jameson Carter" has an investigative firm conducting due diligence on his operation, asking questions. He believes these people are in Texas and the investigation is entirely virtual.

Ray has a private security professional working for him.

Okay, now run down the unknowns:

Is my cover intact? Maybe. There isn't a definitive link between "Matt Gage" and "Jameson Carter."

Even if Ray had this Felix Farrier follow Jameson to vet him, I don't think there is anything they could use to connect my alias with my true name. The last time I saw Jimmy or the Browns was before I met with Ray as Jameson Carter.

Okay—assume the cover is still good.

For now, though, I needed to be diligent about running surveillance detection routes. Not only that, now that I knew someone who might have counterintelligence training could be watching me, I had to be mindful of the fact they'd know what an SDR was when they saw it. Something a private equity guy wouldn't know.

Olivia McEvoy was still my best way into SSC. She shared a lot of information with me, under the guise of being coy and trying to convince Jameson Carter to drop his due diligence. I hadn't yet decided whether she and Ray were working together on this or she'd gone behind his back. My gut read on her was that she would skirt the rules and would do whatever she could to make as much money as possible, but she couldn't pull a trigger.

Well, maybe I should amend that to *wouldn't*.

It's true that everyone has a price, and that integrity is sometimes a mathematical function. For the chronically honest, they just haven't met anyone with a pocketbook big enough to compromise them. I've seen enough of human behavior to know that everyone has a tipping point and that, if pushed hard enough, the question of "could kill" versus "would kill" is easier answered than you might think. It is usually a matter of leverage.

In most of the countries I worked in, prison is a fate worse than death. It could be equally true here.

All that is to say, I don't believe Ms. McEvoy knows someone ordered these killings and maybe I can use that to my advantage. I just had to be careful about how far I pushed it. If she feared capture more than she feared whoever was behind this, I had cards to play. If not, I could find myself in serious trouble.

My phone rang, and I was surprised to see it was Elena.

I hadn't gone back to my hotel right away after meeting with Brashard. Instead, I'd just driven around until I found a park near the water, where I now was.

"Mr. Gage?"

"Matt. What can I do for you?"

"You heard about Jimmy?"

"I did."

"I've known Jimmy for a long time," she said. "We came up at SRM together. He didn't do drugs."

Substance abuse is a problem in the clandestine service. Mostly alcohol, though not entirely. People have pain they don't know how to deal with, and sometimes they mask it with chemicals. They mask *that* with the kind of deception they employ every day. So, I know the lengths someone can go to hide an addiction. I couldn't say on a witness stand that Jimmy didn't use. It just didn't track.

"For the record, I agree with you. I didn't know him nearly as well, of course. It just didn't fit. I spoke with the homicide detective assigned to the case. When I told him I didn't think Jimmy used, he suggested Jimmy might have been trying to score for a client. Gave me some story about a manager who did that for a football player recently."

"That's bullshit. He'd never. I've seen him drive a client to rehab."

People can surprise you and usually not in a good way. Still.

"Well, I don't think Jimmy went to go score, for him or for someone else," I said. "I also don't think this cop is putting his whole ass into solving Jimmy's murder. I got the distinct impression they were looking for a drug dealer to pin it on as fast as they could."

The conversation stalled in a tense, charged silence. We were like two thunderheads about to crash into each other. Finally, Elena asked, "So, what are you going to do?"

"Jimmy hired me on behalf of Brashard Brown's family. They have agreed to pick up my expenses. So, I'm going to do what they hired me to do and try to prove something dirty is going on at Sunshine Sports. Hopefully, once I have enough proof, I can get the cops or the Feds involved. I've spoken with Miami-Dade and MPD. No one seems to be interested in SSC. That said, if I—" I stopped.

"If you what?"

"Forgive me for asking, but why'd you call?"

"I don't know. I guess I wanted to talk about my friend," she said. "And I wanted to see if you were doing anything about it. First, I got threatened, and now, this. I'm scared."

I was going to add that someone had taken a shot at me. I decided to hold that one until I could see the reaction in person.

"Why do you ask?"

The truth, which I wasn't going to share with her, was that the Browns were the only ones here I felt I could actually trust, and I'd learned that even with them, I needed to be judicious with the information I doled out.

"Can we meet in person?" I asked.

"Now?"

"Doesn't have to be."

"I think I could use a friend."

"I'm at the JW in Brickell. The regular one, not the Marquis."

"I'll be there in fifteen."

I cleaned up and went downstairs to speak with the hotel manager about the complications with my stay. I explained I was a private investigator here on a case and that my client put me up in the hotel. My client had been murdered. The manager expressed the appropriate amount of shock and horror, so at least I knew *he* wasn't in on it. Jimmy gave them a card for my stay, so everything up to his death would be charged to that. I estimated about two weeks of work, at least. I could not afford to burn $400 a night for a room, and it didn't feel right charging that back to the Browns. The manager offered to comp me for the night given the circumstances, though I'd need to find a new place in the morning. I thanked him for his generosity and went to meet Elena at the terrace bar.

She was there right on time in tight jeans, heels, and a black shirt, her hair pulled back into a tail.

We ordered drinks and sat at an outdoor table far away from anyone else. She had an Old-Fashioned, and I had a beer from a local brewery.

"What are you going to do?"

"The part I didn't tell you on the phone was that the night Jimmy was killed, someone tried to kill me."

Her eyes went wide in genuine shock.

"I'd been asking around at the businesses that sponsored SSC athletes. One of them called me up to Opa-Locka for a meeting, but he didn't show. A couple of thugs did in his place. I started to tell you about it."

"You did, and I didn't want to listen. I'm sorry for that."

I waved a hand to absolve her of the guilt.

"The two guys looked a lot like the ones you described. Same MO—bumped my car from behind, and when I got out, they tried to shoot me."

"How did you..."

"Let's just say I've been in worse situations with scarier people. One went to the hospital, and hopefully, the other is contemplating a career change. Like I said, that was the same night Jimmy was killed. I think whoever is behind this tried to take us both out in one go to make this thing go away."

"Oh, my God," she said, because that's about all you can say here.

"Yeah. So, tonight I learned that Ray Ruiz knows Jimmy hired me to investigate his collective. I put that up against what happened to you and me, and it's hard for me to conclude these things aren't related."

Elena set her glass down and just stared at it for a long time.

There was a lot for her to process, and I knew what that was like.

I remembered the first time I realized someone tried to kill me. I won't be macho and tell you it's something you get used to or get over.

Like they say, you never forget your first time.

"For what it's worth, Elena, I think you're clear. They tried to scare you off, and it worked. Given what we know, that seems like a wise move on your part."

"I can't understand why the police won't do anything," she said in a small voice.

"Well, there's a couple of new wrinkles I haven't shared with them yet." I could see the financial tentacles from EchoTrace in my mind's eye. Money coming in from shell corporations posing as athletic boosters and endorsement deals, then going out as some legitimate payments and these bogus investment deals. Elena had registered genuine shock when I told her someone had tried to take me out. That could come from any number of sources. Basically, I wasn't sure who to trust, and until I knew, I wasn't trusting anyone.

I hadn't told Elena anything Ruiz wouldn't already know.

We called this "blue dye" in the intel business. When you were looking for a mole, you fed different bits of information to different channels to see which one made it back to the source. Then you'd found your leak. Again, I didn't *think* Elena was in on it. I'd also learned the hard way to be cautious.

"Are you going to the police?" she asked.

"I thought I had enough already to make them sit up and take notice, but so far, no dice. Having a hard time wrapping my head around it. Think it's a matter of priorities. My Miami-Dade contact told me that even though the murder rate is down, violent crime is way above normal. Resources are stretched thin."

"And this doesn't make the cut."

"Sadly, no. I also have some connections with the FBI. They might be interested if I can prove there's a financial component." I didn't mention the finances because that would only come from one place, and I still needed McEvoy as a source.

"What about Jimmy?"

"It doesn't sit well with me," I said, "that he gets murdered and the cops try to bury it as a drug deal gone wrong. He deserves better than that."

Elena's dark eyes narrowed and took on the character of smoldering embers.

"Can I hire you to prove they killed him?" she asked.

Well, that changed things. I guess I knew what side she was on.

"This is a strange case," I said.

"How so?" she asked, apparently ignorant of the obvious.

"I can't see it. Normally, I can spot a conspiracy quickly. This one...I don't know what's up. On the surface, I think Ruiz has found a way around or, more accurately, in between the regulations, and he's exploiting it. I don't actually know if that part is illegal or not. My guess is *unethical* but not *unlawful*. Even the part where they're pushing kids to invest in things. I can't prove that's bent." My voice trailed off as I grabbed my drink. I was trying not to let too much defeat crawl into my voice. Given the last twenty-four hours, it was tough. "I've gotten access to some of their financial records, and I used some software to pattern match and run link analysis. That's—"

"I know what it is," Elena said.

"Right. So, I did that. I've got indications that SSC is moving money to and from a bunch of shell corporations. That could be indicators of money laundering or—"

"It could be rich people avoiding scrutiny," she interjected again.

"Exactly. I can't see what they're hiding. Even *if* it's money laundering, Jimmy and I weren't close enough to actual evidence that it makes sense for them to try and kill us. We didn't find anything yet worth the risk they took. Especially since I got away. Why not just ride it out, you know?"

"This business is as dirty and cutthroat as it gets, but no one would ever get violent," Elena said. "Even when Palmas tried to scare me off signing that gymnast, that was so far beyond the pale of anything I've seen in my career. Hearing your story and what happened to Jimmy, I agree with you. It seems like someone is trying to cover something up. Still, I just can't see Ray Ruiz murdering someone. Like, I *know* the guy."

We got another round of drinks, and I shifted the conversation to friendlier topics. Sometimes, this job required a level of compartmentalization that was either herculean or diabolical, depending on your perspective.

Even with all this happening in the foreground, Cody Portman's next game in the tournament was two days away, and I couldn't get anyone in authority to pay attention.

As maddening as it was, that wasn't the closest fire to throw water on.

I had to think through how I was going to manage this. The Browns wanted me to get Brashard out of his contract, and I'd said I'd only work for them. Elena wanted me to find out who'd killed her colleague. I wasn't looking for a way to double dip, but I wanted to solve both these problems. In my mind, it was a matter of uncovering enough evidence that the police could no longer ignore it.

Something dark and cancerous certainly seemed to be growing beneath the surface here.

I said, "The thing that shocks me about all this is that no one is really looking into it, you know?"

Elena cocked her head and seemed genuinely curious. "What do you mean?"

"All this money flying around under the radar."

That made her laugh. "Gage, this isn't even a drop in the bucket."

"A twenty-year-old getting a million dollars before he's even taken a snap of professional football?"

"You know what ESPN is paying to broadcast the college football playoff next year? One point six billion dollars." She picked up her drink and considered it for a moment. "You could buy a baseball team for that. I promise you, no one is paying much attention to NIL deals."

It had been a long day, and an emotional one, so I cut it off at two and walked Elena to the valet, where she picked up her car. She suggested that I visit the office tomorrow so we could finalize the agreement.

The Browns probably wouldn't care that I was working for her too, and I'd considered letting them out of the contract now that Elena was offering to pick up the tab.

Problems to be sorted out in daylight.

I returned to my hotel room, bone tired and just ground down into the dirt. I keyed myself into the room and flicked on the lights.

And I was not alone.

A man sat in a chair right in front of the window, one leg crossed over the other like he was waiting for a drink. Only there was a gun in his hand.

"Mr. Gage, I think it's about time we got acquainted."

## 13

I stepped into the room, and the door closed behind me.

You never get answers if you run, and I guessed the gun was for theatrics. If he was going to shoot me, it wouldn't be here on the twentieth floor. Or at least he'd have a suppressor. Still, I wished I'd kept the Glock instead of leaving it hidden in the truck.

"Hands up and turn around. Just going to make sure this stays friendly," he said.

"You kind of dicked that one up already," I said, but I did as he asked anyway. The man was six even, heavier than me and it looked like muscle. He looked to be of mixed race, dark hair cut close to the scalp, and a jawline that could cut glass, though what really threw me were the eyes. First off, they were hazel and that was immediately jarring with his darker complexion, but also the raw ferocity in them. Probably a bit cliché to say that he looked like a predator. Though he looked a hell of a lot like a predator.

"You're Felix Farrier, I take it?"

"Very good. You must be a detective," he said with a deep and sonorous voice that flowed like oil on glass. The pat-down complete, I turned back to face him.

Farrier wore brown gabardine pants of linen or silk and a short-sleeved blue camp shirt, which was tucked in. The shirt opened halfway up with a white tee underneath. A bit of a fashion plate for this kind of work.

"And you must have a casual relationship with the law if you're going to open with breaking-and-entering. Also, pleats went out in the '90s."

He just chortled, which I found terribly off-putting.

"Look, chief, it's been a long freaking day, and I have less patience for this kind of shit than I normally do. Which already isn't much. So, let's get to the point, huh?"

"The point, Gage, is that I wanted to make sure I had your attention."

"Oh, I think you guys have my attention. The two assholes in the Escalade made sure of that."

Now, Farrier is good, because he didn't react at all. "Coming here was stupid, Farrier, because now I know you guys are hiding something. Otherwise, you wouldn't have broken into my room trying to scare me off."

"This was to deliver a message."

"Phones also work," I said.

"I just wanted to tell you that you are not welcome here. Or needed. As to why I came to your room, I wanted your undivided attention. I wasn't about to roll up on you at some coffee shop...like that one on 15th."

*Oh.*

He continued. "No, I just wanted to have this here little chat. See, I think you and I understand each other. My client pays me to keep him out of trouble. Or to keep people from making trouble for him. He's got a new business going, and it's going to change the sports business landscape, and what this feels a lot like is someone trying to throw a wrench in that. Now, maybe young Brashard decided he doesn't like his contract, and this is an objective lesson in reading the fine goddamn print. Good life lesson there. What this is *not* is a chance for some muckraking, low-rent gutter dweller to run my client's name through the shit. You feel me?"

"Wait. You think I'm trying to cause problems for your client so he'll let Brashard out of his contract?"

"You here to tell me it's not that?"

Technically, it was exactly that, though I didn't want to give him any points for good guessing.

"Would you say that to Jimmy Lawson? I mean, if you could."

"That shit is a genuine tragedy. I hear Jimmy was a good dude. Too bad he let his judgment get on the wrong side of righteous."

"You seriously think that's what happened?"

"How can I put this, Matt? The police do not find your theory... credible."

Well, I could guess now why Detective Parr had been so half-assed earlier.

A few things snapped into brilliant clarity right now.

One—Felix Farrier was a damage controller. His job was to anticipate problems and eliminate them, and his boss probably didn't want too many details as to how.

Two—Ray did not know Felix was here.

Farrier was the breed of operative you didn't give orders to. You told them the outcome you wanted, and they gave you deniability and results in return.

Unclear to me was why Ray felt the need to have someone like Farrier on the payroll, so I thought I'd ask him.

"I think I get your message, Felix. Just one question before you go...and you *are* going."

"And what's that?" he said with a grin that was halfway between a sneer and a leer.

"If Ruiz isn't doing anything illegal, why does he need people like you running interference for him?"

"I already answered this one, but I can tell you're a slow learner. It's because of people like you, Gage. Ray is a good man, and I'm here to make sure it stays that way."

Felix Farrier holstered his pistol inside his waistband and shouldered his way past me and out the door.

---

The second I heard the door click, I dead-bolted it and called the front desk, asking for security. They connected me, and I told them about a man with a gun whom I'd caught in my room trying to rob me. They mobilized, though not fast enough to stop Farrier from leaving the building.

However, they did get a nice security camera shot of him entering, leaving, and using a device to access my room without my permission. The Miami Police Department was summoned, and I told them what had happened, more or less. I had to adjust the story so that I caught him leaving, which allowed me to obfuscate certain details like learning his identity, as that would only create questions I wasn't in the mood to answer.

The hotel manager was beside himself and upgraded me to the Presidential Suite, which required elevator access to get in.

Once I was installed in my new room, I fired up EchoTrace and went through the task of learning who Felix Farrier was, realizing this is something I should've done a long time ago.

What I learned was not encouraging.

Farrier didn't have public records that I could access, which told me something about him already. I did learn that he'd grown up in Brooklyn with a Jamaican mother and Puerto Rican father. He enlisted in the Army at seventeen and disappeared. EchoTrace didn't have access to classified systems, just publicly available information. This suggested he had an intelligence background and that most of his record was either redacted or just disappeared.

A flash of inspiration hit, and I turned EchoTrace onto SSC's internal files. I got some hits. Farrier was cagey, and he didn't share much with Ray over email. However, Ray, being who he was, basically disclosed everything Farrier offered privately as bona fides in emails Ray traded with Olivia and with Dalton Bream. Apparently, Bream worried about exposure. Ray told Olivia one of his investors wanted to keep his money parked somewhere his soon-to-be ex-wife couldn't get to it in the divorce. Of course, Ray lied about that being one of the offshores. I couldn't find anything in the public records about Bream getting a divorce, though he had the kind of money to keep that quiet.

After scanning Farrier's limited records and interpreting Ray's emails, I could read between the lines. Farrier started his career as an Army Human Intelligence specialist—a collector, like me—with a stint as an interrogator. Then he transferred to the Defense Intelligence Agency, and the records went dark there, though Farrier had suggested he'd done work in covert operations. After seven years at the DIA, he, oddly, transferred to the DEA and was posted to the Miami field office. He was there for...not long, quit, and became a private security specialist with a lot of high-profile clients on his website.

Looked like Felix had handled getting kicked out of government better than I had.

---

Back to business.

The next morning, I called Olivia McEvoy at open of business to see if she was free for lunch. I told her my business in Miami was concluding soon, but that we should finish our conversation.

She suggested a swanky sushi bar in South Beach.

I walked into the meeting, assuming my cover was still in play.

I couldn't know if she had any contact with Farrier. Or if Ray had told Farrier about Jameson Carter and Apogee Partners. It stood to reason that Farrier would do the kind of digging into my fake company that I'd told Ray my fake security firm had done on his. My alias would hold up against Ray Ruiz. It would not hold up against someone with training like mine.

One way to find out.

The restaurant was open to the outside, and I walked across the weathered hardwood floor to our table, beneath a lot of hanging greenery. It looked like a shipwreck on a tropical island. Olivia was already at the table with a glass of wine. She stood when I arrived, wearing tight black pants, a loose-fitting blouse, and a white jacket. She put an arm around my shoulder and told me she was glad I called.

My chair creaked as I sat down, and I had to wonder if it was because the ice was so thin beneath it.

I knew that I couldn't legally do much more with the collective unless I had someone on the inside. My one option left was to pitch Ms. McEvoy again. If she balked, all I had left was to give my evidence to the police and wish them good luck.

A plate of tuna tartare arrived, and Olivia swooped in with a pair of chopsticks.

I picked at it for show, though I didn't have much of an appetite.

We made small talk. Which is to say, she did. I layered in a few disposable comments to feign interest and mostly let her run. By the time the second round of sushi arrived, I could tell Olivia wanted to maneuver us toward business.

"Have you finished your due diligence yet?"

Time for a little colored truth of my own.

I'd tried recruiting Olivia during our first evening together, and that failed. As I played it back in my head, I realized my approach had been all wrong. The pitch centered on her betraying her boss for the sake of business. If she had any amount of humanity, that wouldn't work. However, appealing to her sense of right and wrong, the way I'd have done it with what we called "spies of conscience," might work.

The risk, of course, was this: if I calculated incorrectly, my cover was torched, and I would lose my only viable covert way into SSC's inner workings.

"Olivia, I need to tell you something important, and I want you to consider what I have to say carefully."

That coy smile drained into a confused look, for just a second, before she caught it and forced it back. "Something tells me this is a conversation I'm not going to like," she said, spearing another piece of fish.

"I'm not an investor, and my name isn't Jameson Carter. I'm a private detective. Jimmy Lawson hired me because he suspected something dirty was going on at the collective, and he didn't want his client caught up in it."

Olivia set her chopsticks down on her plate, harder than she may have intended—or maybe not—because the plate rattled against the table. "What a crock of shit. The kid signed a contract he didn't read, and now—"

"You people keep saying that. Here's what's happened since I started poking around. My client is dead, and I'll be goddamned if it was a drug buy. That same night, someone tried to kill *me*. Then last night, I find Ray's attack dog waiting for me in my hotel room. This feels a lot like someone is trying to scare me away, and we're long past the point where I'm willing to believe it's all coincidence. Now, my read on you is that you're a good person who maybe isn't aware of what she's caught up in. If that's right, you can help me."

"You snake son of a bitch. I'm not helping you with shit. I'd slap your face, but I haven't paid the check."

"You get one time to pop off at me, and that was it," I said. "It was one of SSC's sponsors who set me up. You want to be *real* careful with what you say next. Charlie Garcia called me up to his warehouse for a meeting. Two goons tried to jump me on the way home. Last night, Felix Farrier broke into my hotel room and threatened me."

Her eyes got wide, and I registered genuine shock. She grabbed her glass of wine and drained half of it.

I gave her a couple of seconds to compose herself before continuing. "You let me look at SSC's financials because you thought I was a private equity guy and would view it through that lens."

"What lens did you view it through?" she asked with hard, bitten words, refusing to look at me.

"Someone with long years going after bad people. I know what 'wrong' looks like on a financial ledger, put it that way. With what you showed me, I can make a compelling case that SSC is laundering money."

"What?" There was enough surprise in her voice that I took it to be genuine.

I continued. "So, when I couple that with what's happened over the last few days, it's impossible for me to conclude anything but someone is working hard to keep bad things secret. If it's not you, then it's Ray. Or people using him." I gave her a moment to take that in. In this situation, a cop would lay out the consequences and coerce the subject into helping out. My best guess, she could be looking at accessory to commit murder, a RICO charge, and money laundering. Depending on how they'd actually managed those contracts, fraud too.

Olivia McEvoy placed both of her hands on the table and considered a future that was suddenly less picturesque than it was when she walked in.

There were many times in my Agency career that I recruited people who genuinely wanted to do the right thing. They loved their countries despite the flaws and wanted to help us overthrow tyrannical governments, combat terrorists, whatever. On the other hand, some were opportunists looking for a way to take out a rival or to get a quick payout. It's a dirty, dark world, but I found a generally even split between good and bad.

In that moment, at that South Beach table, I could not tell which side of the line Olivia McEvoy fell on.

Sometimes, people surprised you.

"What would you need me to do?" she said, sooner than I'd expected her to.

"I don't believe Ray Ruiz would have me and Jimmy Lawson killed just because we tried to get Brashard Brown out of a bad contract. If he's involved, and I have to believe he is, he's protecting something bigger and darker than predatory contracts on college athletes."

Olivia didn't pick up the thread nor did she meet my gaze.

"That's not answering my question," she said.

"Who is he protecting?"

She shook her head.

"Who is he protecting, Olivia?"

"I don't know. That's the truth."

"Who donated the money to get him started?"

"Like I said before, Ray never told me. Just that it was a big booster that wanted to stay anonymous. I didn't ask again."

"How do you know him?"

"Ray? I worked in the finance department at Sports Management Group when they canned him. I thought it was bullshit. He wasn't doing anything any other agent wasn't already doing—Ray just got caught. Fast forward ten years, it's perfectly legal."

I wanted to ask her if the same was true about money laundering, but I didn't want her to lose her train of thought.

"Anyway, when Ray said he was starting up his own NIL collective, I wanted to be a part of it. So, Jameson, I'm not sure.... Wait, what is your real name anyway?" Olivia said and drained her glass of wine in one go. She caught the server's eye and got a reload. I stuck with my club soda.

"Matt Gage," I said.

"Well, Matt Gage, I'm not sure where the money came from. If I was, I doubt I would have shared our financials with you the other night."

"So, you know it's probably illegal?"

"I take it you earned the 'honest financing' merit badge in the Boy Scouts?" She'd need a moving crew to pack any more condescension into those words. She wasn't wrong, or more to the point, she wasn't *incorrect*. Because of its position as the unofficial capital of the Caribbean, gateway to Latin America, and central port of entry for the US drug trade, Miami had long been one of the world's money-laundering centers. A grim fact the Panama Papers confirmed when they broke in 2016. Olivia seemed to be using the "well, everybody's doing it" defense.

"That's cute. Here's what we've got. Sunshine Sports Collective gets an initial investment of five million dollars from two shell corporations chartered in the Caymans and Aruba. Please don't give me the tired line of rich people avoiding taxes. Ruiz then takes that money, and according to the records you showed me, he does pay some of the athletes on SSC's roster. Most of that money he cons them into investing in real estate schemes and other questionable investments. Now the money has changed hands a few times. Worse, he's got a handful of local businesses that are 'sponsoring' athletes, so there's more money coming in as payment for NIL endorsements. It'd be really interesting to trace the source of that seed money. Want to bet it's all the same source?"

The blood-drained expression suggested she did not.

I continued. "So, then, SSC pays out smaller transactions through a gig economy website that holds funds in escrow until the job is complete. The work is typically listed as consulting of one form or another. Except I looked into the people doing the jobs."

She cut in with, "We vetted them. *I* vetted them."

"No, you didn't. You looked at their hundred or so five-star reviews because, I'll bet, Ray said something like, 'I've found some consultants who look good. Let me know what you think.' If you dig into the reviews, you can see they're created by bot accounts. They're all dummies. Amazon has the resources to crack down on stuff like that, but a tiny website like OneGig does not. Since you worked in a finance department and have a top-twenty MBA, I won't go into a lengthy explanation of how money laundering works."

Olivia steadily drained her glass during my side of the discussion and was now calling for a third. We had rules against recruiting people under the influence in the Agency, sound mind and body and all that. So, when the server deposited her next round, I grabbed the stem before she did and moved it out of her reach.

"In a second," I said, and Olivia stared whole blades. "Your best bet is this stays with the police. If the Feds get involved, it goes RICO fast, and as an officer of the company, you can be charged with shit you didn't even know about. The best way to keep this local is to cooperate with me. I've already spoken with both the FBI and local authorities." Both technically true.

"You still haven't told me what you want me to do."

"You need to find out who Ray's backers are."

"I told you about that already! I asked, and he wouldn't tell me."

"Ask harder," I said, and then I took a healthy sip from her glass. "Or take your chances."

"How would I find anything out? If you're right, and he is doing something illegal, it's not like it's going to be written down."

"What happens to the collective if you leave?"

"He faceplants for a bit. He'll recover though."

"Tell him you want to know about the backers, that you're looking into the money and it looks suspicious to you. That shouldn't be a stretch, because it is suspicious. Tell him if he doesn't tell you, you walk. And tell him you connected the dots on Cody Portman."

"What about him?"

I told her.

Then she really needed that drink.

---

I picked up the check and guided her out of the restaurant to the art deco and sunlight. We found a coffee shop, picked up a pair to-go, and then found a bench. Olivia seemed like she could hold her booze, though I didn't want to send her back to SSC half-cocked. There wasn't a lot of time to prep. We rehearsed what she'd say to Ruiz, how to approach him. Given her background in finance, an audit of the company's funding streams in advance of a tax filing was the best line of attack. There were questions she'd have a legitimate right to ask, and when Ray expectedly pushed back on it, Olivia had sound justification to demand answers.

If things went sideways, we agreed on a code phrase that she'd text to the Jameson Carter number. Then I'd miraculously walk in for a meeting.

Olivia was nowhere near ready for this.

I sent her in anyway.

Because I had to. Because better people needed me to.

# 14

---

Olivia McEvoy returned to Sunshine Sports Collective just before three. She parked her rather inconspicuous—for Miami—purple Porsche 718 in the garage across the street and crossed Grand Avenue with purpose. I watched her from a bench in the plaza across from the office.

She was inside for a little over an hour, and when she emerged, I could tell from across the street that she was rattled. Olivia didn't come right to me—instead, she entered a shop and pretended to browse for a few seconds before leaving out a side exit. I hoped her anxious demeanor didn't cue an overzealous security guard that she was a potential shoplifter.

We met in the plaza, where I could still keep an eye on the parking garage in case Ruiz left. "How'd it go?"

"If my breath smells like mouthwash, it's because I just threw up."

"Let's debrief. It's important we do this right away, while the information is fresh. It'll give you something else to focus on."

"Right. Okay."

"Try not to look over your shoulder so much," I said. "I've got an eye on the door. Ruiz can't see us from here."

"He's not the one I'm worried about. Farrier is being weird."

"Let's focus on Ray."

"I told him I was preparing for this year's tax filing, and I'm concerned about the anonymous donations."

I had my laptop out and transcribed as she relayed the conversation.

Ruiz: "They're not anonymous. That's just something we tell prospects. They're through holding companies."

Olivia: "Right, offshore ones, with bullshit names. I need to know who is behind them."

Ruiz: "Where the hell is this coming from?"

Olivia: "*Grand Cayman Venture Industries* doesn't even make sense, and *Sand Diver* is a fish. Which I had to look up. We don't necessarily have to disclose their identities to the IRS, but we need a good answer if they ask. You ducked it last year. You brought me in here to, and I'm quoting you, 'get the house in order.'"

Ruiz: "I told you GCV is a group of Miami alums who wanted to donate to the collective and keep their names out of it."

Olivia: "Great. Just tell me who they are so I know."

Ruiz: "Maybe we need to revisit what confidentiality means."

Olivia: "Do you have NDAs on file that I don't know about? And at any rate, the IRS doesn't care what it means. Now, I need to know because I need to have an answer ready if they ask where the money came from."

Ruiz: "They won't."

Olivia: "You don't know that, and that's not good enough for me."

Ruiz: "Where the hell is this coming from? You never gave a shit about all this."

Olivia: "I did, but I didn't feel comfortable bringing it up with you because I thought you'd react just like you are right now. And like I told you, I'm asking these questions because I just started working on the tax filings. Which I'm delayed on. I suggested we bring in an outside group, and you freaked. So, I'm handling it, but if I'm going to do that, I need to know everything. Or I can quit, and you can sort it out on your own."

Ruiz: "Let's not get hasty, Liv. Look, GCV is an old friend of mine. He's going to court with his business partners. I don't know who is at fault—everyone is kind of suing everyone else. He wanted a safe place to park some money until the legal stuff sorts itself out. I told him I'd help him out. I don't want to disclose his name until his situation gets resolved. If it works out, he'll start getting his money back once we have enough in the coffers from other investors that we don't need it."

Olivia: "So, what about Sand Diver?"

Ruiz: "That's Alves Pacheco."

Olivia: "And who is that?"

Ruiz: "A guy with money."

---

Ray screeched out of the parking garage in his Aston Martin, and if it wasn't for heavy traffic, he'd be a spec on the horizon by the time I got in gear. It was hilarious to watch him blast out and then haul off on the brakes. I could see the impotent gesticulations of rage from where I sat on the street. It was the only entertainment I'd get that day.

"I have to go," I said, snapping up my laptop. "You did great. I need to see where he's going." I dashed for my truck.

The benefit to following someone driving a $200,000 SUV was that it was pretty easy to pick them up.

A fact worth remembering.

I merged with the oozing traffic and followed Ray north.

Turned out, we weren't going far. It still took forty-five minutes to get there, because...Miami.

He was headed to Little Havana.

Little Havana in general and Calle Ocho in particular, though it could feel a little fabricated and touristy, was deeply important to the city's Cuban population. For many, it represented a deep connection to the Motherland and pre-Castro Cuba. Little Havana was vibrant color splashed on low, cinderblock buildings with the smell of strong coffee and cigars permeating the air. I followed Ruiz into his slow neighborhood orbit as he looked for a parking spot.

Me driving a $200,000 SUV following a guy in a different $200,000 SUV, both looking for street parking.

The patron saint of private detectives must be laughing their ass off right now.

Since the car I was in wasn't exactly inconspicuous, I grabbed the first nominally legal spot I could find. There was a low-slung condo building a block off 1st Street, and I blasted down a side street to snag the spot as soon as I saw it. Ruiz made two trips around the block we'd been on, and he didn't give any indication that he was trying to shake a tail, so I reasoned his destination was on this stretch. I keep a variety of items in my truck to break up my silhouette or create an improvised disguise. I grabbed a navy ball cap and a pair of aviator eyeglasses like Redford wore in *Three Days of the Condor*. Yeah, I know it's a little on the nose, but I'm a sucker for nostalgia. Plus, the lenses are treated with a material that obfuscates my eyes on video surveillance.

Out on the street, I picked up Ruiz, who'd finally found a space of his own.

He ducked into a restaurant in the middle of the street called El Havana. The front windows had been retracted, opening the small, crowded dining room to the sidewalk, where they had a handful of tables. I pushed my way into the happy-hour-packed room and weaved through the crowd, Cuban music blasting loudly overhead. I caught a flash of Ruiz as he disappeared into the back.

I was quickly approaching an officially bad idea. From where I was, I couldn't see what was in the back room. I didn't know if it was another dining room, a hallway, or what. I could quickly find myself in a bottleneck with Ruiz looking right at me.

No other way to see who he was running to, though.

A passthrough and a thin wall separated the restaurant's back room from the front. There was a small alcove with a server's station tucked away, which had the machine they used to enter orders and process checks. I pulled the bill of my ball cap lower and got my phone out, tabbing the camera. The back room wasn't as full as the front. There was a semicircle of tables occupied mostly by old locals. What struck me though was how the tables were arranged. It looked like a hemisphere around one table in the back with a pair of silver-haired Cuban men. Ruiz stood with his back to me, addressing one of the men at that farthest table. The bluster and impatience with which he'd driven here had been let out. His body language wasn't exactly hat-in-hand, though it also wasn't alpha dog.

I filmed the interaction, pretending to tap things on my phone screen.

Someone took notice, because a presence filled the picture after a few seconds.

"This is a private area," he said. I looked up. He was older muscle, probably forty, but experienced. Loose, white button-down over gray chinos. I could make out the muffled shape of a pistol grip under the shirt on the right side.

"I'm just the Door Dash guy," I said, not looking up, still pretending to interact with some app. Though I made sure to hide the screen from the heavy's view.

"Don't care. You need to get out."

"Only here for a couple of sandwiches."

"My man, I don't think you're hearing me."

Oh, rest assured I was. He took a step forward.

"You work here?" I asked.

"No."

"Cool. Then I don't care."

I took a step back just as he was about to get physical. Last thing I needed was to cause a ruckus and draw Ruiz's attention. The phone went back into my pocket with about ten seconds of unobstructed footage and another thirty with that asshole flexing on me.

If you want to make espionage a lifestyle, one of the most important skills to develop is a well-honed sense of when you're about to be in deep shit.

Making my way out of the restaurant, I got my phone back out and turned the camera on selfie mode. Now able to see behind me, I noticed the heavy was following me out to the street. And he had a friend.

I hit the sidewalk and pushed into the street. Traffic wasn't moving, and I could weave through the crawling cars easily enough. I texted Flash the video while I walked. Once I was on the other side of the street, I chanced a look behind me, as though I were trying to find my way. The pair of trouble brothers were weaving through the traffic.

Cars seemed afraid to run them over, which was not a good sign.

I quickened my pace and looked for a place to duck into. My car was on the other side of the street—maybe crossing had been a tactical error.

Coffee shop ahead, and I ducked in, thinking it'd be fairly busy and I'd have some safety in the crowd.

It wasn't.

Shit.

I beelined to the counter. "Can I get a tall coffee?" Then, "Y'all got a bathroom?"

The kid behind the counter distractedly motioned to the back of the store—I probably hadn't needed the ruse of a purchase. And he wasn't going to be much use as a witness either, as he never looked up from his phone. Like most places of this type, the restrooms were along a hallway that stretched to the back door, which I shoved open. My nose was assaulted with the sickly-sweet reek of garbage. I was in a narrow alley between the buildings on either side.

I realized my error too late. I should've gone farther down the street before cutting through. In my haste to shake them, I didn't recognize there was a parking lot one space down from the coffee shop. A mistake punctuated by, "Hey, motherfucker, I want to talk to you."

I didn't bother with the coffee shop's back door—it'd be locked on this side.

Instead, I rabbited.

There was a vine-covered, wrought-iron fence separating the properties. I could probably scale it, though not before the thug caught up to me.

Last time, I'd taken out two of these guys at once. Of course, I'd had a gun, and that evened the odds.

I chanced a look back, just to see what I was up against. The heavy came at me like a swarm of pissed off hornets. He ran like an old-school linebacker, all shoulders and lumbering strides. He seemed to take up the entire alley.

There wasn't a great exit. The heavy came at me from the left like an escaped bear. That iron fence was straight ahead, and to the right, the alley continued. However, I had to clear the building to my right, which pushed deeper into the alley than the one I'd just come out of. To get clear, I'd have to cut across the onrushing heavy's path. Given his velocity, I wouldn't make it before he got to me.

Better to stand my ground.

And like I said, I'd taken two of these low-rent clowns out at once. I'm sure I could do the same *mano y mano*.

Landing a hit with the momentum of a run behind it was not easy to do. Unless the person throwing it had practice, and this one did.

To put a new twist on an old saying, sometimes you take the punch.

Sometimes, the punch takes you.

# 15

My head spun around so hard I wondered if he'd disconnected it from my neck. Then I went stargazing.

I stumbled, looking everywhere for my footing and finding it nowhere. Somehow, this guy had managed to tilt the whole street. Great, I was fighting Cuban Paul Bunyan.

I'd just about gotten my feet under me when he drilled my midsection with an uppercut that nearly lifted me out of my shoes. This would be the ideal moment to reach for a gun and impress him with some witty banter. If I'd remembered to pack either one.

Which I did not.

I got my arms up and assumed a defensive stance.

The third punch I actually blocked. He was a street fighter with some jail-yard boxing, not a trained combatant. A dangerous opponent, nonetheless. And he had about thirty pounds of muscle on me. The next punch got around my guard. It landed on the side of my head and knocked me back several steps. He followed that up with a lunging uppercut with his right. I stepped into that, grabbed the wrist with my left hand, and used the momentum to overextend his arm. Then I chopped with my left hand, hitting his Adam's apple. He coughed, struggling to breathe. Better, I controlled his right arm. I stepped back and drove my left leg into his knee. It was like kicking a bowling ball.

He thrust back hard with his right elbow, breaking my grip and connecting with the outside of my midsection. It was a glancing blow, but I still gave up half the air in my lungs and nearly my lunch. Standing behind him now, I punched his kidneys as hard and as fast as I could, before jumping backward several feet, just to put some space between us. The guy was undaunted. He spun on his back leg and lunged, grabbing for me. I blocked his hand with my left and landed a knuckle punch to the temple.

Then my head snapped back. He'd thrown a cross-body punch over his other arm, and I'd missed it entirely.

Something didn't look right.

Then I realized I was on the ground.

Being kicked in the ribs.

"Gimme your fucking phone!" He repeated this suggestion a few times in between kicks, and it didn't wind him much.

Must be a soccer player too.

Thrusting my legs out, I wrapped them around his in a scissor-like move and torqued my body over, throwing all my weight with it. He pitched forward and fell, bringing his hands up at the last minute to prevent his face from bouncing off the pavement. Unfortunately, our legs were intertwined, so I couldn't stand, though I had leverage. It took a few drowning-swimmer kicks to untangle our legs. I got my feet under me, stood, with my legs still loosely entwined with his, and dropped my knees into the small of his back. All the air went out of his lungs with a fierce rush. I drove one of my knees into his kidney for a little extra relish and stood.

I heard the squeal of an old door opening, though I managed to get one good kick into the side of his meat-slab chest before I heard an awkward, "Uh, did you still want that coffee?"

"Guess it's UberEats from now on," I grumbled to myself.

I followed the kid into the shop and closed the door solidly.

The kid told me he heard the commotion and thought someone got jumped. I took the coffee and a bag of ice, for which I tipped him fifty bucks, and staggered to my car. Thankfully, the Defender was exactly where I'd left it—and unscathed.

I had a text from Flash, and he said we needed to talk right away. I told him where I was, and he told me to meet him at Regatta Park, which was just a few blocks south of Little Havana in Coral Gables and steps from Sunshine Sports Collective's office.

I headed south to meet Flash.

Regatta Park was a wide stretch of tree-lined green along Biscayne Bay with a large public dock and yacht club. I parked, grabbed my laptop bag, and went to where Flash said to meet, which turned out to be a berth alongside a quay. "Hop in," he said from the cockpit.

I stepped off the concrete and onto the diving platform of Madigan's boat, *The Green Flash*. No sooner than I was climbing the steps, he was throttling us into the bay.

Flash navigated through the barrier islands and passed the rows of boats at anchor. He cut the engine and dropped anchor. We had an amazing view of Miami's electric skyline. I was seated at the table in the aft deck, just behind the cockpit cabin. Flash stepped out, took one look at me, and walked back inside. He returned a moment later with a bottle tucked under his right arm, two tumblers pinched between his fingers, and an ice pack.

I gratefully accepted the pack and applied it to my face while Flash uncorked the bottle and poured.

He slid one across the table. It was good scotch and eased the edge, just a little.

I gave Flash the context as to how I got the video and how I'd flushed Ruiz out of the pocket.

"The man in the video you sent me is Cesar Marrero," Flash said and picked up his own tumbler.

"Who's that?"

"Marrero represents the remnants of *La Corporación*, which was one of the city's largest organized crime outfits going back to the aftermath of Bay of Pigs, basically."

That felt like a missing puzzle piece.

"If Ruiz rushes to meet him right after his funding stream gets threatened, it's a good bet that's his money," I said.

"That's a reasonable guess," Flash agreed.

"Does the name Alves Pacheco mean anything to you?"

Flash shook his head. "Can't say that it does."

I got my laptop out of my bag and fired up EchoTrace. I entered the name and "Sand Diver," which returned a PO Box in North Miami, registered to Alves Pacheco. That sent me to a different address, which turned out to be an assisted living facility. Correlating some other public records, I learned Mr. Pacheco was eighty-three and suffered from dementia. I then used the link analysis function to connect the name with any known criminal associates. EchoTrace was hooked into law enforcement databases and could make connections between the search subject and any known associates. A link tree appeared onscreen with Pacheco in the center and connected to family members, business associates, and, if applicable, anyone with a criminal history. I turned the screen to show Flash.

"Now, that name," he pointed, "I do know. Jorge Acuna, Pacheco's nephew, it looks like. Acuna runs one of the Cuban gangs here. I don't know him personally, but I know his reputation. He's supposed to be a total psycho."

"What do you want to bet that young Jorge here used his uncle's name to open up some holding companies for *La Corporación*?"

"Not a chance," Flash said immediately. "So, last time we talked, I gave you a crash course in Miami's organized crime scene, right?" He took a sip of his whiskey and looked toward the horizon. "Today, it's pretty balkanized. The Russian mob has a large presence here, as does the Mexican Gulf Cartel. Back in the day, Miami was what the mafia called an 'open city,' meaning no one family controlled it. They all had interests here, and there was a sort of truce. After Bay of Pigs, you had a bunch of pissed-off, disaffected people—with guerrilla training and a healthy dislike of government—settling here. More than a couple of them turned to crime. One of those outfits, which came to be known as *La Corporación,* started here, moved up to Jersey, and came back in the '80s. The Mariel Boatlift brought a ton of refugees and a lot of criminals, because Castro opened the prisons up and sent them here. These guys form smaller gangs, which come to be called *marielitos*. The *marielitos* were heavy into the cocaine trade and would regularly shoot it out with the Columbians, with each other, whomever."

"Scarface," I said.

"Exactly. So, by the '80s, the Corporation is also into cocaine trafficking. The Columbians are supplying everyone but also have their own distribution here. There's fighting between all these factions. Miami turns into Thunderdome. Anyway, so by the time the '90s hit and a lot of these people are dead or in jail, it more or less distills down to the Corporation and all of these *marielitos*. The Corporation gets dismantled around 2000, and the bosses all go down."

"But not Marrero?"

"Nope. They'd always kept his name clear so assets could be transferred to him in the event other people got busted. The Corporation's leaders at the time didn't expect they'd all get life sentences, or near enough. Before then, they'd all gotten a bunch of short stints and usually got out of them. At this time, the Russians move into Miami in a big way."

That much I did know.

"Once they'd broken up the Corporation, the FBI only really cared about the Russian mobsters. So, you've got dozens of these *marielito* gangs that have been operating under the radar for forty-plus years that no one is paying attention to. I don't know very much about Cesar Marrero other than the word is he was the number two behind a guy named Enrique Aragon. Aragon starts rebuilding the Corporation around 2010. Again, the FBI isn't paying attention to them either, because...Russians. Fast forward nine years or so. Enrique Aragon goes down," Flash said in about as loaded a way as he possibly could without overtly admitting he had something to do with it.

He took a big gulp of his drink and continued. "Marrero is basically clean, and he takes over. He sees himself as the inheritor of the Jose Miguel Battle, a.k.a. *El Padrino*, empire and, thus, is the godfather of Miami. The *marielitos* don't see it that way. They've been fighting for years. What this looks like to me is your buddy Ray Ruiz is double dipping. He's got something with Cesar Marrero and also with Acuna's gang."

"I take it those two bosses wouldn't be happy if they found that out?"

"Acuna was part of the Corporation back in the day. Aragon didn't trust Acuna but wasn't strong enough to eliminate him. Once Aragon got sent up, Acuna tried to take over. Marrero blocked it and kicked him out. Acuna didn't have the muscle to mount a full coup, so he took the ones loyal to him and left. Since then, he's consolidated his power by absorbing some other gangs. Those two outfits *hate* each other. I don't know what in the hell Ruiz is doing working with both of them, but it's like playing with matches at a gas station. If either one found out, it'd be all out war. Though, between us, I'd be more worried about Acuna."

Several datapoints coalesced in a single, terrible picture.

A theory formed.

Ruiz needs, maybe even just wants, more money so he convinces Jorge Acuna to funnel money through SSC. Somehow, Acuna gets to Cody Portman. Possibly even though Ruiz. Acuna tells Portman to throw the game or else. Portman does his part, except the team plays a lot better than expected and keeps it close. Portman throws what he expects to be a near miss, only he sinks it instead. Acuna torches his parents' house for the trouble. He doesn't go after the kid, because now there is a bigger game with bigger stakes. I bet Ruiz didn't know anything about this beforehand, except now he realizes who he's in bed with. He can't go to Marrero for help. Marrero would probably kill him to keep this quiet. So, when I had Olivia go in and start asking questions about where the money was coming from, that inadvertently kicked over a hornet's nest.

She might be in danger, and I needed to warn her.

This was all hypothetical, though it was the most complete theory I'd come up with so far.

I asked Flash to take me back to the dock.

"One question," I said as he'd taken up position at the helm. I assumed that's what one called it. I didn't have a lot of experience with yachts.

"Shoot," Flash said.

"You told me before that you thought someone was watching you, and we had that whole dance with the phones. Then, tonight, you pick me up in —" I waved my arms "—all this."

Flash laughed to himself for a bit. "Yeah. I'm not on great terms with *La Corporación*. The reason Marrero is in charge and not Aragon is that I may or may not have set Aragon up for a certain Miami-Dade lieutenant to take down. They don't *know* for certain, but I'm pretty sure they suspect, and I think they've had a guy on me for a while. And the FBI—not Danzig—is looking into the whereabouts of a misplaced fortune belonging to a certain deceased Castroite hit man." Flash shrugged.

"And yet you stay right where you are?"

"I like the irony of living on a boat and not going anywhere."

I laughed a lot harder at that than I probably should've.

Flash dropped me at the quay.

"Hey—I owe you one, and I mean it," I said. "If I can help you at all, just ask. Without your help, I wouldn't have gotten this last piece."

Flash descended from the cockpit to see me off. He extended a hand, and we rapped knuckles. "You got it, brother. I'll take you up on that favor once this is all said and done. Though if you can bring down Marrero and break up whatever's left of the Corporation, that solves a lot of my problems."

I nodded and stepped off the boat, telling him I'd keep him posted.

My video of Ruiz meeting with Marrero was the key. That let Flash connect the dots in a meaningful way, to show who could be involved and how this would work. My research provided the part on Acuna, and that painted the picture of how volatile a situation we were actually in.

It was late, and there was a lot to do.

First, I made sure no one—like Farrier—was following me as I walked across Regatta Park to the Defender. I made a quick sweep with my hands in the usual places to check that nothing had been tampered with or added to it. Then I drove back to my hotel, keeping my head down because I looked like I just got my ass kicked.

Because this was the way the day seemed to be rolling, there was a conference at the hotel, and I shared an elevator with two businesswomen riding open-bar buzzes. They couldn't help but stare at the condition of my face and clothes. Finally, I turned to look at one of them and met her open-mouth gape. I said, "Mosh pit. You're never too old to rock." I held up the heavy-metal horns as the door opened to their floor.

Once in my room, I started making phone calls.

My first went to Silvestri. Straight to voicemail, and I told her I had information that I needed to share.

I honestly wasn't sure what to do about Olivia.

Ruiz could easily conclude that her asking uncomfortable questions about where the money was coming from wasn't coincidental. I didn't know why Marrero's people got so aggressive with me, other than my ruse about being a delivery driver wasn't terribly convincing. All that suggested Marrero might want to close ranks.

As I sat there, contemplating my next moves, I shockingly found myself wanting to be wrong about Ray. I wanted to give him this information and see him with the same shocked expression that had spray-painted Olivia's face when I'd told her. Maybe he didn't know. Or maybe he'd taken the money because he had to and was looking for a way out.

That either explained the murder and the attempt or it was me selecting the facts that bolstered the conclusion I'd already made.

I needed to warn Olivia either way.

My read on Olivia McEvoy was that she'd take every opportunity she could get, even the ones that cat-scratched against the illegal. She probably thought Ruiz had found a loophole to exploit, and while it might become illegal in time, it wasn't *now*, so fire away.

There was no way she could turn a blind eye to what was going on at that place. The notion of the lifetime contracts alone was shady as hell.

That didn't mean she deserved to have her life in danger.

I called her.

She took it better than I expected.

"Matt, can you come over? I don't want to be alone."

Well, at least I knew it'd be a short trip.

# 16

"Olivia, I think the thing you want to do is pack your bags and take an impromptu vacation."

"If I do that, Ray is going to know I talked to you. Especially after the fuss I made about tax prep."

She wasn't wrong.

"I can't promise that I can protect you," I said. "I think your best bet is to leave until the police are ready to talk to you. You can also quit. Tell him his answer wasn't satisfactory and that you want out."

I'd recruited her because I thought I could use her to get information on who Ray's investors were. In a way, we'd done just that. If it weren't for Olivia asking questions, Ray wouldn't feel the need to talk to one of those investors, who I got on camera and used my connection to confirm was a mob boss.

She'd done what I'd asked her to do. It just happened a hell of a lot faster than I'd expected. Now that I knew organized crime was involved, and that they'd shown no reluctance to use murder as a problem-solving tool, getting Olivia out of here seemed like a good idea.

Olivia said, "Maybe we could discuss this in person?"

Most of the time, terrible decisions don't give you advance warning. This one popped smoke and practically called in its coordinates.

"I understand you're scared, and you have every right to be. I want to be there for you, though I think my time is best spent working on the case. Thanks for your bravery today. I have what I need to involve my friends in the police department. Can I take a rain check?"

"Of course," she said, words behind a cold front.

"Olivia, I do think it would be best if you could find a way to get out of town for a little bit. Maybe go stay with your parents. If nothing else, it gives you some deniability for what happens next."

"What happens next?"

"I'm going to cause some problems for some dangerous people. They tend to react poorly to that."

---

I'd avoided a career-limiting move with a beautiful woman. Maybe I *was* learning something.

Or I just didn't trust her and was unsure that the story I got from her was exactly what had happened earlier with her boss. No way to know, other than Ray's reaction.

That had ended up with me getting an ass-kicking.

After I got off the phone with Olivia, I exported the link analysis from EchoTrace to a mind-mapping app, which allowed me to create a visual representation of Ruiz's illicit financial network. I showed the money coming in from the two shell corporations, whom they were registered to, or in the case of Marrero, whom I believed they were registered to. Outflows from SSC showed the transactions in the gig economy site as well as the "encouraged donations" for their athletes, which SSC made on their behalf with the money supposed to be paid to their clients.

By midnight, I had a comprehensive chart.

The next morning I was at it early. I woke myself up with a fast swim in the pool and a faster breakfast. I hadn't heard back from Lieutenant Silvestri yet and was kind of stuck regarding next moves. There wasn't much more I could do unofficially. I tried her again midmorning and, again, went straight to voicemail.

I didn't think another stakeout of Ray Ruiz's office was going to net me much. I'd already followed him to a meet with a mob boss and got it on video.

So much of this job was leading horses to water.

A call from Cyrus Brown saved me from pacing around my room.

"Good morning, Cyrus. What can I do for you?"

"We need to talk."

Twenty minutes later, I was burning time and gas in downtown Coral Gables looking for parking near the place Cyrus wanted to meet.

The morning was warm and overcast. I wore a loose-fitting Tommy Bahama aloha shirt that covered my holstered Glock well enough that I decided this was going to become my permanent look. I ordered a coffee and found a table in the front of the shop. Cyrus walked in a few minutes after I did, nodding once he caught sight of me.

He said, "Mind if we take a walk?"

This was shaping up to be good news.

"What's going on, Cyrus?"

When he didn't answer me immediately, I knew it wasn't going to be good. I could see his jaw working when I looked over at him.

"Matt, there isn't an easy way to say this. You're fired. I don't want you anywhere near my son or my family, ever again."

"This is quite a shock. Where is this coming from?"

"You aren't the man I thought you were. Jimmy trusted you, and maybe he was wrong in that. Or maybe he just has a different standard than we do."

"What the hell are you talking about, Cyrus?"

Cyrus fished his phone out of his pocket and opened it, searched for something with a few angry swipes of that giant finger. He held the phone out to me with so much force I thought he was going to break my nose with it.

The image on the phone occupied the entire screen.

It was a photo of me and Olivia that night I went to her townhouse. The photo was her moving in to embrace me, only in this version she wasn't wearing any clothes.

She sure as hell had been when she tried to hug me.

Farrier.

He'd followed us to her place, must have had a drone with a camera on it. That was the only way he'd have gotten this shot.

"This is a fake," I said.

"Don't look fake to me," Cyrus said. Of course it wouldn't. "Only thing fake around here is you. You take our money and say you're only going to work for us. Then you take a contract with some friend of Jimmy's to do the same damn thing. *Then* you go and sleep with Ray's partner. What *got-damn* side are you even *on*?"

"Did a man named Felix Farrier send this to you?"

"Not saying where I got it."

"Fine. Don't answer. I know who took the photo. In case you don't know, Farrier is a private security operative who works for Ray Ruiz. He's an ex-spook, like me. The kind of person who knows how to doctor a photo."

"You really expect me to believe that?"

"I did go to Olivia McEvoy's townhouse, and she did try to sleep with me. I wanted to get information from her."

"That what you call it?"

"For Christ's sake, Cyrus. Farrier must have had a camera on a drone outside her window."

"What were you doing at her place to begin with?"

"Interviewing her," I said flatly, checking my anger. "She's the best person to tell me what Ruiz is up to. I met her at a bar. She said she'd let me look at her corporate files, but that they were on her computer, which was in her condo. Farrier must have followed us back to her place. You can only get a shot like that with dedicated surveillance. Notice he didn't send you any pictures of me looking at her laptop. Yes, she did hug me like that. Farrier must have doctored the photo and replaced it with this one. Computers can do that."

How Farrier knew I'd agreed to work with Elena Mendoza, I had no idea, unless he or Ray had connections in her agency. I supposed that wasn't hard to believe.

"I don't know about any of that. All I do know is you aren't the person we thought you were."

"So, it doesn't matter to you that this image is faked?"

"See, that requires me to take you at your word. 'Fraid I can't do that. Even if that's faked, you were still there."

"How in the hell do you expect me to learn anything if I don't ask any questions? She wanted to show me the financials, which we couldn't do in a bar. Farrier must have been watching us." It didn't matter what I said. Farrier had fabricated a story, and there was no talking Cyrus out of believing it. For someone who didn't understand what computers were capable of, it would be a steep climb to explain what Farrier had done. Especially since Cyrus wasn't receptive to it.

"Cyrus, someone had Jimmy Lawson—your *son's agent*—murdered. Someone tried to kill me. I have Ruiz connected to two different organized crime figures. I saw him meeting with one last night. Now, Ruiz's security guy gives you this picture and tells you I slept with Ray's partner, so you'll do exactly what you're doing right now. You're being manipulated."

"Only into trusting you."

"I don't think the money Ray is paying your son is clean, and I don't think most of SSC's money comes from donors. If Ruiz gets busted, the government could take it all back anyway."

"He said you'd say something like that."

"Who said that—Ray?"

"Yeah, right after he paid us the rest of the money he owed on the contract."

"Wait, Ray just paid you—" I did the math "—what? $400,000?"

"That's right. So you can see, we won't need you around anymore."

"These are some dangerous people. I have reason to believe they threatened another athlete." When I could see Cyrus wasn't swayed, I added, "That's on top of getting your son's agent killed."

"I don't know about all that. What I do know is I don't want anything to do with you ever again. Stay away from my son, stay away from me. You got me?"

"Good luck, Cyrus," I said.

If you'd have asked me to put money on whether this conversation was being watched, I'd have taken that bet and doubled down.

I called Elena.

"The Browns just fired me," I said.

"What?"

I explained about the photo and how it must've been taken. "Ray Ruiz paid the Browns the remainder of the money on the contract. They just got a $400,000 check. That isn't all of it, I guess the rest of it is coming. That's going to let the Browns keep their house, among other things. Probably more money than they've seen in all their working years."

"Which Ruiz damned well knows," she said.

"Which Ruiz damned well knows," I echoed. "Silence, bought and paid for."

"What are you going to do now?"

"You've still engaged me to find out who murdered your colleague," I said, pausing to give her a chance to jump in and fire me too. "It's all related, Elena. And now I have conclusive evidence that Ruiz is connected to the mob. I've got it on video."

"You need to take that to the police," she said.

"Believe me, I'm trying." Short of emailing it to one of those "crimestoppers" shows, I wasn't sure what else I could do if Silvestri wouldn't return my call. There was nothing more cosmically frustrating than being "right" and having to convince people in authority to do literally anything about it. I understood bureaucracies well and knew they were lumbering giants slow to act. People were overworked, cops especially in this environment. Budgets shrank and departments were understaffed. There wasn't money for the kind of overtime some investigations require. Bad things slipped through the cracks when there weren't enough watchers on the wall.

"What are you going to do now?" Elena asked.

"Make the police pay attention. Failing that, I don't know."

"How are you holding up? I mean, someone tried to kill you. That's not normal."

"More than once," I said.

"What?"

"Not today. I'm not so much of a problem that someone is going to try to murder me before lunch. I tailed Ruiz last night and followed him to a restaurant where I caught him meeting with a local mob boss. One of his heavies didn't buy my story that I was a delivery driver. We tussled."

"Oh Christ, Matt." I started to say something else, when she interrupted. "If the Browns fired you, does that mean you're giving up on Jimmy's case?"

"Not a chance," I said. "I was already stupefyingly stubborn. Now I'm also pissed."

She sighed into the phone, the kind of sigh she wanted me to hear. "Well, how about I make dinner, and you can bring me up to speed on your investigation?"

"Can I at least bring wine?"

She said I could.

I had to admit this was an incredibly stressful and emotionally taxing case. A night off the wall would probably do me some good. We set a time, and Elena gave me her address.

I drove back to the hotel. Still nothing from Silvestri.

I'd still contact Special Agent Danzig as well. While this wasn't within her jurisdiction, the FBI had a substantial presence in Miami. If Silvestri wasn't going to act, maybe the Feds would. Problem was, with the Bureau starting from zero, assuming I could get them in gear, it could be a year or more before we'd see arrests.

Losing the Browns as clients hurt. Especially since it was based on a lie.

And I hate getting outmaneuvered.

Felix Farrier and I had a reckoning coming.

By the time I got back to Brickell, I called Danzig.

Danzig didn't pick up right away, so I left a voicemail outlining what I had and that I wanted to talk to her about it. The financial crimes task force was run out of a division of the state AG's office. I put a call in to them as well.

I needed something to do while I was waiting for the alphabet soup of law enforcement activities to return my calls.

I decided to pay a visit to Cody Portman's family.

What's the worst that could happen?

Well, given that Cody's Sweet Sixteen game was in two days, maybe I didn't want to answer that question.

# 17

Adding to the list of things in this case that didn't make a lot of sense was the house I found Cody Portman's family in.

It was a normal middle-class home on a curved residential street in Pembroke Pines, about thirty-five miles north of Miami. The thing that shook me was that so soon after the fire, the insurance company got them into a rental property. I'd have assumed they'd spend a few weeks in a hotel first. It was a little shady how I'd figured out the address, though we were pretty much past that concern by now. One of the fun things you can do with EchoTrace was to use it for "internal security audits." Since SSC was such a small operation, they didn't have any central IT, which meant they didn't have anyone managing their systems for them. Once I'd created a tunnel back into Olivia's machine, I set up an admin account, and this allowed me to deploy EchoTrace's monitoring software. Once that was in place, I could read emails and view any websites they visited, among other things. So, I could see the flowers and food delivery they sent to the Portman's rental house and, therefore, the address.

I'd been referring to the fire at the family home as Cody's "parents' house," though I couldn't find anything about his father, and the kid had seemed to skirt around any mention of a father in our short conversation. I had Mrs. Portman's phone number from the records I'd borrowed from

SSC. I called a few times, left messages, and by midafternoon, none of them were returned.

I parked the Defender a few doors down from the Portman's house and waited.

Say this for smartphones, they sure make stakeouts easier to manage.

Back in the day, you'd have to stare surreptitiously over a magazine or a newspaper at your surveillance target. Now you just pop some headphones in and listen to something while staring off into space. That faded you into the background faster than a periodical.

Since idling a Land Rover for two hours would have a measurable impact on the environment, I killed the engine, rolled the windows down, and listened to some music. At this point in the case, I didn't need any additional research on NIL, particularly since I'd puzzled out Ruiz's scheme. So, I put the Winery Dogs on low and bobbed my head absently to the tunes.

I was looking forward to seeing Elena that night. She was intelligent and witty and knockdown gorgeous. I'd need to play it easy, given she was technically my client now, and I'd made that mistake once before. Still, nothing against just seeing where something might go. It would be a welcome diversion from a maddening few days.

Donna Portman arrived home at five-twenty with her sixteen-year-old youngest son, book bag slung over his shoulder and the teenager's perpetual slouch. Cody's younger brother looked like he was well on his way to joining his brother. They moved like people who'd been sentenced, a slow trudge to the inevitable.

I watched the lights activate in the home, charting their movement through the house. I'd give them a little while to get settled before approaching. It's not like I was the cops and trying to catch Donna Portman while she was completely off guard. I didn't want to get them in the middle of dinner or while she was cooking, because that was an easy out for her not to talk to me. Without knowing the pair's evening routine, I just had to guess.

Speaking of the cops, it was at that moment Lieutenant Silvestri opted to return my call.

This was not great timing as I had a narrow window to speak with Mrs.

Portman. I also didn't know how long it would be until I could get Silvestri on the phone again.

"Lieutenant, how are you?" I said.

"Hey, Matt. Sorry it's taken me so long to get back to you. I'll let you pick your overworked cliché of choice—I'm too tired to come up with one. I got your voicemail...and one from Flash. What's up?"

"You remember me telling you about Sunshine Sports Collective?"

"The NIL thing, right?" She did sound tired, and I knew she was calling me entirely out of courtesy. I maybe had two minutes to land this.

"Right. It's run by this guy named Ray Ruiz. Well, I think I can connect Ruiz with two organized crime figures, and I believe I have a convincing case that Ruiz is using SSC to launder money for those mobsters."

"Who do you think he's connected to? And how do you know?"

"Cesar Marrero and Jorge Acuna. For the latter, I used some software I've got to trace SSC's financials back to a shell corporation chartered in the Caymans. It's registered to an Alves Pacheco, who, it turns out is an eighty-year-old man with dementia in a Miramar nursing home. Probably not running a company. His maternal nephew is Jorge Acuna, and Flash gave me some history on him. Flash also identified Cesar Marrero for me. I'd snapped a photo of Ruiz talking to him."

"Shit," she said. "How'd you get the financials?"

"I've recruited someone on the inside to help. She let me take a peek."

Silvestri let a long, throaty sigh escape her lips, and I didn't know if that was for my benefit or for hers. Then she said, "Okay," like it was three words.

"Is there a problem?"

"No," she said, weary.

"Michelle, listen, I know that you don't know me from Adam and just took my call as a favor to someone who is, at best, a frenemy." She snorted at that. "I think I'm onto something here. If this isn't in your jurisdiction, do you think you could introduce me to someone that I could talk to?"

"Well, if this is legitimately connected to organized crime, then it would fall in my division. The department also has a criminal conspiracy unit—it could fall to them. I suppose it depends on who's driving the train, you know? Sorry, I'm not trying to blow you off, but we already have a full docket, and I don't have any officers to spare. If we were going to take this on, it might be a while before I can assign anyone. Still," Silvestri's voice trailed off, overcome by whatever conversation she was having with herself.

"I think they killed my client. They also tried to get me. And all I've done is ask some questions."

"What?"

"My client was a local sports agent, representing one of the people SSC has on contract. He was gunned down two days ago. They called it a drug deal gone south."

"This is James Lawson?"

"That's right. I've spoken with people who know him well, and they think that's bullshit. The same night, one of SSC's...I don't know what you call them, sponsors? He called me and said he wanted to meet. I'd spoken with him before and told him I was looking into the collective. I showed up at his warehouse. He wasn't there, but there were a couple of heavies in his place. Followed me, rear-ended me, and tried to make it look like an attempted carjacking." I paused to give her a second to process. "I talked to the MPD officer investigating it. He wasn't much interested with what I had to say."

"Typical."

"I'm convinced they tried to take me and Jimmy out in the same night, both incidents looking like something else. I have money coming from shell corporations connected to organized crime figures moving into SSC and moving out as payments to athletes, which is above board, and to investment schemes and high-paying gig economy jobs, which probably aren't."

"How'd you put all that together?"

*Because I'm good at this shit.*

"I've got some software that helped me make the financial connections. Though this is also the kind of operation that unless someone can view it in total, it would be hard to put together. If I hadn't convinced Ruiz's number two to share SSC's financials with me, I'd just be trying to piece together some bad luck."

"What was the name of the guy who set you up?"

"Charlie Garcia. He runs Miami Fitness Source."

"The gym-gear chain?"

"Yeah," I said.

"I know it. His commercials are terrible. All right, this is what we'll do. I need the name of that MPD officer you spoke with. I'll speak with our criminal conspiracy squad, see what their load is. My group is kind of tapped out, though this is something I might be able to use as justification to get my people off sweeps and back into cases. One thing I can tell you for sure, no one is looking at Cesar Marrero, not since we put Enrique Aragon in prison. He was always clean by design. His name hasn't been associated with anything more than a dice game in thirty years. I can talk with the Bureau, too. See if they've got any interest. If there's a money-laundering scheme involving offshore, they might want a piece of it. That'll help. Where are you right now?"

"I'm up in Pembroke, about to interview someone."

Based on the immediacy of her next words, I wasn't sure Silvestri had even heard my response. "I'll need a couple days to put something together. In the meantime, try not to do anything stupid or illegal."

She hung up before I got to promise her that I wouldn't. That meant I could treat it as a suggestion.

So, I got out of my Land Rover and prepared to interrogate a single mother about how someone had burned down her home because her son didn't throw a college basketball game.

In my defense, Silvestri had not specifically defined "stupid" or "illegal."

I walked across the street to the Portman's rental. It was a single-story, peach-colored home in an L-shape with a screened-in front door and a token palm in the corner where the house meets the garage. I stepped through the screen door and hit the doorbell. Through the door, I could hear Mrs. Portman directing her son to answer it, and given the delay between the bell and the opening, she must have given up and done it herself.

Donna Portman was in her early fifties, white, and ground down by life and circumstance. She was raising two behemoth sons on her own, and I couldn't imagine what her grocery bills had been when both of them were under her roof. She carried twenty extra pounds and looked like sleep was not a thing she got much of. You had to work at being pale in Florida.

"Mrs. Portman," I said calmly. "My name is Matt Gage, and I am a private investigator. I was wondering if I could have a few minutes of your time."

Paranoid and enemy security service officers had given me less scrutiny than Donna Portman did in that moment.

"I'm afraid this isn't a very good time. I'm sorry."

"Mrs. Portman, I was hoping to speak with you about what happened to your home."

"I don't have anything to say," she said, and I could sense tension, anxiety, and possibly fear.

"I don't believe it was a gas leak, or if it was, it had some help. I think you believe that too. Did someone threaten you?" Portman didn't respond. "Did someone threaten your son? Did they ask him to throw that game?"

"I think you need to leave," she said, her tone final. Her eyes flicked to the street behind me, and I understood.

I pulled my card wallet out and, using my body to block the view, extended it in front of me. In low tones, I said, "Please take my card. If you decide you want to talk, call me any time day or night. I will answer. I'm just trying to make sure what happened to you doesn't happen to anyone else."

The door was closed and locked before I'd made the step to the screen door.

I always kept my phone on silent when I was interviewing people, and I found I had a missed call. A cold shock ran through me when I read the voicemail transcript.

The call was from Dalton Bream.

The message was short and entirely business, just a request to return the call and said in a tone that made it seem less of a request.

"Mr. Gage," he said when he picked up. "Thank you for returning my call."

"Mr. Bream," I said tentatively. "What can I do for you?"

"That, my friend, is an excellent question. Are you free now? I'd like to see you."

"I'm not really free now."

"How about we meet at my office downtown? Say, thirty minutes?"

Either he hadn't heard me or wasn't used to being told things he didn't want to hear.

"Appreciate the offer, Mr. Bream, but I don't have the time tonight. Happy to schedule you in tomorrow. Or we could just talk about it now."

"I prefer not to discuss sensitive matters over the phone."

*I'll bet you don't.*

Had to admit, I was intrigued now.

"All right, Bream. I'll hear you out. Can't say I can make it in thirty minutes, though."

"I'll be here, Mr. Gage."

Bream gave me the name of the building, which, consequently, was the same as the address: 830 Brickell. I plugged it into the GPS, grateful to discover it was near my hotel. I settled in for the long drive back.

An hour later, I was pulling up to blue glass monolith that reflected a blazing orange sun going down. I parked, eventually found the lobby and took an elevator to the fifty-third floor. The elevator, whose acceleration could easily be mistaken for a Saturn V, dropped me in a warm-wood and gray-metal hallway. There was a smoked glass door with the words *Donaldson/Bream Development Group*. I'd learned from researching him that the "Donaldson" part was his maternal grandfather, who'd started the business. Bream kept the man's name on the letterhead to honor him. I entered. A young woman sat behind a large, curved desk. She stood as I stepped through the doors.

"Good evening. Mr. Gage?"

"That's right."

"This way, please."

The girl led me through the open-air office space. I spotted a few people still at their desks working, throwing furtive glances toward the boss's suite as if waiting for their cue to leave. The receptionist showed me into his office. "Mr. Gage is here to see you," she said.

Dalton Bream rose from his desk, plastered smile on his broad face. Bream was a large man, six-two and a frame to match. Impeccably tailored suit, though at his height, I supposed it had to be. Bream had reddish-brown hair shot with gray at the temples, a manicured beard, and a watch that could've paid my college tuition. His dark eyes gave little away. They reminded me of a shark's, utterly black and utterly soulless.

His office was amazing. I could see my hotel from it. The outer wall was floor-to-ceiling glass showing a blazing skyline at sunset. It followed the wood-and-steel motif from the lobby.

Bream greeted me with an overhand, power-move handshake and pumped it once to let me know he still had a grip. "Thank you for coming on short notice. Can I offer you a drink?"

I'd have turned him down, but I imagined he was profoundly stocked, and it had been a long drive.

"If you're having one, I'll join you," I said.

"Good man." Bream sauntered over to a wet bar, pulled a scotch from the shelf with a label I couldn't recognize, and poured a healthy amount into a pair of oversized Baccarat tumblers. He handed me one and sniffed his. "Bottled the year I graduated," he said.

I took a sip. Cream soda with a honey floater, oak and pepper, peaty smokiness. It was amazing. Probably the best I'd ever tasted. For a bottle of this, I'd agree to whatever he called me up here for. I suspected that was the point.

"I was sorry to hear about Mr. Lawson," he said. "Your employer, yes?"

"That's right," I said. I was surprised Bream knew about the lives of lesser mortals.

"If you don't mind my asking, what are you doing now that you have no client?"

"Why would I mind your asking?"

"Just being polite, Mr. Gage."

"As it turns out, a few people weren't happy with his early exit. Wanted to see something done about it."

"Seems like that would be the police's job, no?" Bream said, and he took a long, languid sip.

"You'd think so." I took another sip myself. I found myself enjoying it less and less, now that it felt like it had a cost. "What'd you want to talk to me about, Mr. Bream?"

"Ray Ruiz," he said. He walked over to a pair of dark brown Manhattan chairs on the far side of the office. It took us some time to get there. He motioned for me to sit. "Ray is trying something new, and I commend him for it. He's found a novel approach to monetizing sports and is probably years ahead of the game. Unfortunately, I think Ray has gotten over his skis a bit."

"That's one way to put it. What's your interest in it?"

"Ray and I go back a long way. I'm invested in his venture now, both materially and personally. I've been mentoring him."

"Dalton, the most charitable explanation is that Ray is taking advantage of kids." Life flashed into those shark eyes, a starburst of anger. It faded just as fast. Still, I could tell he only liked being called "Dalton" by the people he deemed were his peers. "The worst is that he's *intentionally* preying on them."

"I'll acknowledge that he's made significant missteps. I think his heart is in the right place."

Not a strong argument for positioning, if you ask me.

"I'm not sure taking mob money counts as a 'misstep.'"

"Gage, I'd like Ray to have a chance to correct his mistakes. I want him to turn his business around and do it the right way. He can't do that if he's constantly dodging you."

"So, what...you're asking me to go away as a favor to you? The scotch is good, but it's not *that* good."

"You misunderstand me. I'm not trying to scare you away. On the contrary, I'd like to offer you a job. You're tenacious and resourceful. I could use someone like you. More to the point, so could Ray."

"Isn't that what he's got Felix Farrier for?"

Bream shrugged and looked out the window. "Farrier is a bad influence on him. Come work for me. I can handle Farrier. *Matt,* I can certainly pay you more than your going rate. I also think you'd tell me what I *need* to hear, rather than what you think I *want* to hear. Which is more than I can say for most of the people who work for me."

"How much are we talking?"

"As the head of security for Donaldson/Bream? That's $300,000 a year, plus incentives."

"That's quite a lot of money," I said.

"Imagine how quickly you could resolve Mr. Lawson's murder if you didn't have to worry about hamstringing Ray Ruiz."

I finished my scotch in one go and set the glass down, then stood.

"You've certainly given me a lot to think about, Dalton. Thanks for the drink." I shook his offered hand at the risk of him thinking it was a deal. I made sure I didn't burn one neuron on that offer as long as I could still see the view from his office. Three hundred thousand a year. For the near term, it was to keep Ray out of trouble long enough that he could fix his problems. Maybe I could even influence him to do what Jimmy had wanted—modify the endorsement deals so they terminated when the athletes turned pro. Jimmy would call that a win.

I'd get Felix Farrier out of town on a rail.

I'd have long-term employment.

And I would have the time to dedicate to finding Jimmy's killer.

Those all stacked up pretty high on one side of the scale.

On the other was the knowledge that no one ever paid you to do the right thing.

## 18

I drove back to the hotel.

During the ride, I put everything Dalton Bream just offered me out of my mind so I could recenter on the case. All I could think about was Flash warning me that Ruiz was probably running funds for two different gangsters, who had grudges going back twenty years. If they found out Ruiz was doing it, the best outcome was a bunch of murders.

Once I was back at the hotel, I cleaned up and changed. Then I found a liquor store nearby where I could pick up a bottle of wine. All that done, I walked to Elena's condo. It was about a half mile from my hotel, and after so much time in the car, I needed to stretch my legs.

I knocked on Elena's door and was greeted by a very large man that was not her.

"You must be Matt," he said with a big grin, putting his hand out between us. He was six-foot-three and corded muscle coiled underneath a deep tan. He had sun-bleached, sandy-blond hair that went to his shoulders and a precise amount of stubble. He wore a light blue short-sleeve shirt, and I could practically hear the sleeves crying for mercy when the right biceps extended to take my hand.

It took me a second to recognize him.

Gavin Monroe was the LA Dodgers' third baseman and led the National

League in runs batted in last year. Looking at those arms, I could see why. Some sportswriter had nicknamed him "the Gavel" as a notionally clever play on his name.

I'd tried to make good on my adopted home and, as something to do, started following almost all of LA's sports. I wasn't the biggest baseball fan, though I do really like seeing it live at a ballpark and would admit to skipping out to Dodger Stadium on slow workdays. It was hard not to be just a little awestruck in his presence. And believe me, that guy had one. He'd be standing next to Joe Buck, calling the World Series, once he was done playing.

Maybe he was Elena's client? Or maybe he had some connection to Jimmy? That might make more sense since Jimmy started his career in LA. I found myself desperately hoping it was one of those two things.

Elena's call from deeper in the condo answered that question. "Is that Matt, baby?"

Oh, of course it's her boyfriend. That's exactly how this day would go.

"Sure is," he said over his shoulder, smiling. Gavin turned back to me. "Come on in, man. It's great to meet you."

Elena appeared, wringing her hands in a kitchen towel. "Matt, this is Gavin."

"Oh, I know," I said and hoped I didn't sound stupid.

"My God, what happened to your face?" Elena asked when she got close enough to see the condition Marrero's thug had left me in.

"Occupational hazard," I said dismissively.

Elena mouthed, *What happened?*

I replied, "Later," soto voce.

"Gavin, this is Matt. He's the private detective I told you about."

"It's really nice to meet you, Gavin," I said. "I don't normally look like a tackling dummy."

I did quick calendar math, and my brow furrowed.

"Wait, the Dodgers don't have spring training here. It's in Phoenix, right?"

"Glendale, but yeah. It's not public yet, but I was just traded to the Marlins. I just got here today. I think I've only got another four years left, and I wanted to be out here with Elena."

"I was *not* moving to LA," Elena cut in. "No offense, Matt."

"None taken. I can barely stand it myself."

"That sounds like a conversation we'll need this for," Gavin said, taking the bottle of wine from my hand.

Well, *that* was a situation I didn't read correctly.

In her defense, I'd have picked the Gavel too.

"Gav, will you see what Matt wants to drink?"

They had a bottle of wine open already, so I opted for that. Gavin and I made small talk while Elena finished the meal. Whatever it was, it smelled amazing.

Gavin and I stood on her balcony, which offered a stunning view of Biscayne Bay and the triangular-shaped Claughton Island. The sky had long since turned to violet, and the sunlight was replaced by the electric night of Miami's nocturnal skyline.

"Elena said you were a spy."

"She did? How'd she know?"

"I guess Jimmy told her. Thing about agents, man, they can't keep secrets for shit."

"I was a spook," I said.

"That's badass."

"There were parts of it that were exciting, absolutely. It's also a lot of waiting around for something to happen and praying a bunch of something else doesn't happen. People outside think it's the coolest job in the world. Parts of it were; other parts were mind numbingly boring. You can probably relate more than most."

Gavin laughed and said, "Yeah."

"Every guy in the world would trade places with you at gametime, but they probably don't appreciate the training, the conditioning, and all the other scrutiny that goes along with it."

"Yeah, the games make it worthwhile. I can leave a lot of the rest of it."

"Got a World Series ring out of it," I said.

Gavin laughed. "That's one of the parts I'll take. You miss it?"

I considered the glass in my hand. "Some of it. Our stations are all at embassies, right? So, to maintain cover—because most countries are spying on us too—you typically have a day job for the State Department. You do that for eight hours and then go spy at night. It's not always like that. At the larger embassies, like Vienna or Berlin, our stations are fairly big. The smaller ones are where you're pulling double duty like that. I don't miss pretending to be a full-time, half-assed diplomat on top of being a spook."

Elena called us in, and we sat. Gavin poured the wine. Elena passed dishes around the table, spiced pork over red beans and rice with plantains on the side. Everything was delicious. She said the recipe—and how to cook it *just so*—had come from her grandmother.

"Gavin, do you mind if I ask you some questions? You have an insider's perspective that I'm not likely to get anywhere else."

"Of course."

"Can you tell me a little about your impression of NIL?"

"This is going to come across as bitter or petty, and it's not meant to be, but I don't really care about it. It wouldn't have made a difference for me."

"Really?"

"For the most part, the only ones making real money are the football and basketball players at big schools. You need to have a large donor base and, usually, some big movers. Of course, you've got individuals with big social media followings, and they might be making real money. Hell, if you're not a baseball fan, you'd never have heard my name until I signed in the majors. Honestly, I don't like the idea of college players making money at all. At some point, it's supposed to be about the sport. Maybe there's a problem to solve in how much schools make off these revenue-generating sports, but I don't know that the answer is paying players. I'd rather they changed the rules, or policy, or whatever, so the money gets reinvested in facilities or maybe some of it goes to a general scholarship fund."

Elena said, "Between undergrad and law school, I had over a hundred thousand in debt. That's what landed me a job at a sports management firm, so I can afford to pay that debt off, but those first couple years when I was working my way up was lean. Meanwhile, the players I represented—" Elena threw some playful side-eye at her boyfriend "—they all just coasted through."

"Exactly," Gavin said. "Most kids don't have the opportunity or the ability to play a college-level sport and get the scholarship money that comes along with it. A lot of people are resentful over how much resources schools put to athletics. They feel left out, while they or their families are paying tens of thousands to go there. I don't blame them. This thing is not the answer. And there's no accountability."

That I could believe.

I said, "So, part of my investigation might be branching into illegal gambling. Do you know anything about point shaving or game fixing? I imagine that sort of thing is hard to pull off now, right?"

"It is. Also, games are heavily scrutinized these days. Every single play is analyzed to death. Still, sports betting has blown up now that its legal to do online. There are so many bizarre side bets, or parlays, or whatever they're called. You can literally bet on anything. We have people from the front office come in and give us scared-straight talks before every training camp."

"What do you mean?"

"It's like this. You could place a bet on the odds that I'll throw a no-hitter or have a shut-out inning. If you wanted, you could bet on my percentages against specific batters."

"What do they cover in these scared-straight talks?"

Gavin chuckled. "Every club will have a compliance team, and I imagine it's the same for other sports. Because the betting is so complex now, the casinos have these handicappers—they're like spotters. Their whole job is to watch for patterns that don't make sense, ones that might be influencing the outcome of a game."

"Like throwing one?"

"Exactly. The betting industry analyzes every sport, team, and player they take action on. They have spotters watching the games for outliers. If someone falls outside the performance norm, they get alerted and take a closer look. Everything is recorded, and you've usually got multiple angles on key plays. People still try, but they don't get away with it for long."

"Would it make sense for an underdog to lose intentionally?"

"I really want to play the dumb-jock card here," he said and flashed a charming smile. I got why the cameras loved him. "You'd want to talk with an oddsmaker, but I don't *think* so. I guess, maybe, to see who might be willing to take a dive? That would have to be a pretty sophisticated operation. I mean, like the stuff the mafia used to do in the NFL in the '70s. However, if you're talking about an activity that's spread around, I'm talking a couple of teams, it might be possible to manipulate the results. There was a ref who'd tried that a few years ago, I think."

There was more to this thread I wanted to pull on, but I was mindful that I was a guest here, and that wasn't why Elena had invited me over. Nor was that her case. Still, I wondered if what Acuna was doing was testing out the system, seeing what tripped the regulators. Knowing what they were watching for was the first step to knowing what they weren't. Gavin's point about multiple teams was sound, though with any operation...there always had to be a first one.

That's basically what Ruiz had done with his collective.

Elena picked up on my change in mood and steered the conversation into more benign territory, and I was grateful for it.

After dinner, Gavin offered to do the dishes, which gave Elena and me a moment to talk business. We walked out to the balcony, and she asked for the story of what happened to my face. I told her.

"I can definitively connect Ray Ruiz and the collective to two different gangsters," I said.

"Have you told the police?"

"I have, and I think they're finally paying attention. There's a jurisdictional question. They murdered Jimmy in Miami PD territory. My connection is with Miami-Dade's organized crime squad. She's going to try to connect the dot there."

"You don't sound convinced," Elena said.

"I'm not trying to sound cynical. I just got a really dismissive vibe from that Miami detective. Some of those dudes don't like private eyes, even though a good number of them end up doing it when they leave the force. Others just don't like anyone asking questions about their work, offering suggestions, whatever. I saw that time to time in the Agency. You're an expert, so you don't think anyone else is capable of a good idea—that kind of thing." I drained what was left of my wine. "Things are starting to pick up speed quickly. I am fairly confident that between the police and now maybe the Feds, they'll unravel SSC's mob connections. That's the good part."

"What's the bad part?"

"Parts," I corrected. "The first one is that one of these gangs is dangerous. Like, dangerous for mobsters. They're trying to edge in on the other group's gambling monopoly and are doing it by forcing SSC players to throw games. Right now, we've got a warning arson. Something tells me it doesn't stop there. Then there's what happens when these two rival gangs find out Ray Ruiz is dealing with both of them. My other contact here says that could touch off a gang war."

"Oh my God," Elena said.

"Yeah. The worst part is, while I think they roll up Ruiz and SSC and maybe even one or both gangs, I'm really worried Jimmy's murder will fall through the cracks."

"Why would you say that?"

"They set it up well, and it's easily explained as a drug killing. An overworked police department can write that one off and focus scarce resources on something else." It pained me to tell her that, but she deserved the truth. "I'm going to do everything in my power to make sure that Jimmy sees justice, I just want you to be prepared for, well, something else."

"I understand. Thank you."

"My contact with Miami-Dade is going to get back to me in a few days."

"What are you doing until then?"

"She was very clear that I was not to do anything stupid."

"Why do I get the feeling you're not going to take that advice?"

"I think the police and I grade on different scales."

I declined her offer of an after-dinner drink and thanked them both for a nice evening. I told them it was a much-appreciated distraction from what I'd been slogging through recently. Elena admonished me to be careful, and I said something to the effect of "careful people don't get answers." She gave me a hug at the door and squeezed my arm as I left. It felt like electricity.

I left her to her adonis professional baseball player, who was also a good-dude boyfriend.

Back at the hotel, I contemplated a drink when the phone rang.

Turned out, I was hearing from Lieutenant Silvestri sooner than I'd expected.

"Charlie Garcia is dead."

---

Their best guess, it happened like this.

Garcia got into his Audi Q8 and left his North Miami store at approximately six thirty that evening. He stopped at a gas station two miles from his home, according to a credit card transaction that his wife verified and was confirmed on camera. Also on camera was a black Cadillac Escalade, though it didn't get close enough for the gas station's video surveillance to catch the license plate. Garcia turned off Biscayne Boulevard into his neighborhood and made his first left. There, he was rear ended by the Escalade. It happened in a residential street and was over in less than a minute.

Garcia got out of the Audi and went to inspect the damage.

Unclear whether he suspected anything. I'd told him how they tried to get me in a similar trap, and I have to believe that by the time he saw who hit him, he knew what was going on.

The Escalade's driver put two bullets in Garcia's chest, got into his Audi, and drove off. Someone in the Escalade moved into the driver's seat and sped away. The police only know this because an eye wit went to their window after the gunshot and saw both vehicles disappearing with Garcia bleeding out in the street.

Garcia never regained consciousness and died in the ambulance on the way to the hospital.

Given the altercation I'd had with him, and the very understandable reason for disliking Mr. Garcia, Silvestri wanted to know exactly where I'd been.

At six thirty, I was driving back from Pembroke Pines, which could be verified by the GPS on my phone, and I agreed to send that to her. I gave her Elena's phone number to verify that I'd been there for dinner.

"Are you arresting Ruiz?"

"With what? We have absolutely nothing connecting him to this."

"And it goes right through the cracks," I said. "Just like Jimmy Lawson."

"I don't need this from you, Gage. We're doing our best."

*And you wouldn't know any of this if it wasn't for me*, I wanted to say, and it took every ounce of self-control to bite back the words. I gave it a long string of seconds before I spoke again.

"It's obvious they're closing ranks," I said. "Jimmy, the attempt on me, and now Garcia. Anyone connected to that is either dead or in the crosshairs."

"You may have a point. Who else knows?"

"Olivia McEvoy. She's Ruiz's number two at the collective."

"Does he know she knows?"

"No idea. I asked her to keep it quiet."

"Well, why the fuck did you tell her in the first place?" Silvestri thundered.

"I had to convince her to work with me. She wasn't responding, so I had to convince her that her boss was a threat. That worked." Now, I had to come clean about how I'd gotten her to push Ruiz into getting scared enough that he'd driven straight to see Marrero.

It's hard to read a cop over the phone unless they're swearing at you.

Luckily for me, Silvestri removed the ambiguity.

"Goddamnit, Gage. You are a fucking piece of work." It wasn't clear if that was directed *at* me or if she was just stating it for the record.

"Hey!" I shouted into the phone, breaking off her rant about the mathematical inverse correlation between my abilities as a private detective and my ability to cause problems. Lieutenant Michelle Silvestri was dangerously silent on the other end. "I have been trying to get yours and MPD's attention since this thing started. Both of you gave me some flavor of the same excuse—that no one cared college kids were getting ripped off. Like they deserved what they had coming because they get paid to play sports. When my client was killed, I offered everything I had to Parr at MPD, and he couldn't be bothered. You, at least, returned my calls. But you cannot tell me I didn't warn you that something was happening. Now I've connected Ruiz with some mobsters, and there's a good bet one of them burned down Cody Portman's house."

"What did you say?"

"Cody Portman is a basketball player who has an endorsement contract through Sunshine Sports. His team is playing in the NCAA tournament. Couple of nights ago, he made a last-second shot to upset a heavily favored team. The look on that kid's face was sheer terror. Like, 'My God, what'd I just do?' You can YouTube it. Two days after that game, his mother's house burned to the ground in a 'gas leak.'" Talking on the phone undermines the sardonic effectiveness of air quotes, though I was sure she could hear it in my voice. "That wasn't an accident—it was a message. I spoke with Portman. He wouldn't say anything because...message received, right? His mother wouldn't say anything either, and she kept checking the street the whole time I was talking to her. I know what it looks like when someone thinks they're being watched."

"That is wet-napkin thin," Silvestri said.

"Given my experience with cops in this town, I didn't bother contacting the arson investigator. Bet it'd be an interesting conversation. I also bet that, right now, they're leaning toward arson, and they're going to blame the family for setting the fire as an insurance scam."

"You have a vivid imagination."

"No, I have long experience watching people get screwed. And that's exactly what Cody Portman said the cops were doing. Are you going to do anything about this or not?"

"Gage, I am willing to admit you captured Ray Ruiz on camera talking with an organized-crime figure. I have agreed to review what you've collected regarding alleged money laundering, and if I determine there's probable cause, I will begin an investigation. You're—"

"They wanted Portman to throw the game because there was a betting scheme attached to it. When he didn't do what they wanted, they torched his house. Flash told me Jorge Acuna's group was moving into gambling, and they're probably looking to make a big splash saying they got March Madness wired."

"I never should've introduced the two of you. I knew that was a mistake."

"Are you kidding me? That's where the pieces came from."

"Matt, I'm only telling you this once. You're done here. Pack up and go home. You've done enough. Thank you for the lead. The real cops will take it from here."

"Real cops? You wouldn't—"

"Your client is dead. Whether it was part of this thing or he was in the wrong place at the wrong time, he's gone. And so, there's no reason for you to be here."

"Other than not wanting to see an innocent kid get hurt."

"That's *my* job."

There was a lot more I wanted to say to that, and none of it would've helped, so I opted for silence. Turns out Silvestri beat me to the punch, because all I heard was dial tone.

---

I'd made an overly passionate plea for something I desperately believed in, and it got me alienated from the one person who could help.

Weird.

Apparently, I loved reruns.

I'd said enough dumb things to women before to know that calling Silvestri back right away would only make things worse. I'd try her again in the morning. As much as I wanted to wait a few days for her to cool off, I didn't think we had that kind of time.

I texted Kristin Danzig and asked if she had time to speak, that I wanted to get advice on my case and see if I had something to refer up to the Bureau.

Then I texted Elena and asked if she was still awake. It was only nine-thirty, and I didn't want to interrupt her night. She said she and Gavin were just having an after-dinner drink and asked what was up. I called her.

"Charlie Garcia is dead. He's the SSC donor who'd set me up. I think these guys are cleaning up their mess. No one knows you've hired me, except my police contact. I felt like you needed to know, though."

"Thank you," she said, and I could hear the worry seeping into her words.

My next call went to Olivia. She didn't pick up.

The night passed slowly, and at some point, I fell asleep. I had a couple of things that kept swirling around in my mind. The first was I didn't know who'd killed Jimmy and Garcia. Ruiz was in bed with two different mobs, and it could've been either one of them. Then again, the two murders could be unrelated. Based on what Flash told me, my money was on Acuna's group for Cody Portman. That seemed like the logical play for them. However, if I went after them for everything, and I was wrong, I would burn what little time I had chasing the wrong shadow.

At some point in the night, I walked over to the minibar and poured a bottle of whiskey in the dark, desperately hoping it wasn't Dewars. Turning on a light would have solved that problem, but it seemed to do so would only bring more questions somehow. I sat in the room's one plush chair, because drinking in bed is an indicator of deeper problems, and I tried to process my thoughts on Charlie Garcia.

He'd tried to have me killed.

Well, nothing about his character suggested it'd been his idea. He'd also have no reason to. However, he let someone push him into it when warning me or going to the police were perfectly good options. Which suggested he was far more afraid of them than he was trusting of either me or the cops.

He was, presumably, a decent husband and father, who loved his family. He probably used that love to justify taking mob money to keep his business open. I couldn't know that was true. He might've been just another asshole looking for a shortcut and hadn't taken into account the consequences of that action.

Ultimately, he'd set me up to get shot in the street, and I found it hard to squeeze sympathy out of that particular stone.

Eventually, I drained the tumbler, set it aside, and crawled into bed.

Morning brought no better answers.

Nor did it bring me any returned calls.

The phone rang at 9 a.m., and the discordant tone took a second to register, because it wasn't my usual ringtone. It was the app Mickey had given me to backstop the Jameson Carter legend.

That meant it could only be Ray Ruiz.

I watched the phone ring, feeling somehow like I'd just been caught doing something I shouldn't.

I debated letting it go to voicemail. There was no good reason to speak with Ray Ruiz.

Maybe it was genuine curiosity, maybe I was desperate for clues or just wanted to land this plane before it crashed. I answered it.

"This is Jameson," I said.

"Jameson, hi, it's Ray Ruiz." The usual bravado was gone, replaced by a wary hesitation.

"Ray, good morning. What can I do for you?" I tapped the speaker function and started moving around the room, picking things up and making it sound like I was in the middle of something.

"I was hoping you were still in town. Do you have some time to meet?"

"Unfortunately, I don't have any white space on my calendar today and am heading back to Dallas soon. Maybe I can have my assistant find some time next week. Does that work for you?"

"Jameson," he spoke the name as though he were unloading something heavy. "Are you really Matt Gage, the private detective?"

# 19

The cardinal rule for not getting burned in the field was stick to your cover, no matter what.

Admittedly, once I'd involved Olivia McEvoy, it was fair to assume the clock was ticking on the Jameson Carter legend.

I had less time to consider my options than I did to describe them. I'd been in this situation before, realizing I was compromised and having to convince someone I was who I'd pretended to be.

Admitting what Ruiz suspected had dangerous consequences for me and, possibly, Olivia McEvoy.

"No, Ray, and I don't know what you're talking about. I already told you I retain an investigative service for due diligence. I also told you that work was completed."

*Run this down. How could Ray know it was me?*

Farrier starts surveillance on Jameson Carter, follows me to my meeting with Olivia and then back to her place.

Farrier takes the photo, alters one version, which he shows to Cyrus Brown. Cyrus confirms it's me in the photo and that I'm the PI they hired. Farrier shows him the doctored photo and tells him I'm sleeping with Olivia McEvoy.

Farrier then shows the original version to Ray and said, "I think this is the detective snooping around. Cyrus Brown just confirmed it."

I got outplayed by a third-tier collector. It's a good thing the Agency wanted nothing to do with me, because I'd never hear the end of this.

"I know who you are, Gage," he repeated. "I want to talk to you."

Ruiz suspected my real identity, but he didn't *know*. I'd been in this position before and knew how to recover from it. Still, I had a choice to make. I'd pretty much gotten what I could out of the Jameson Carter legend. However, if I broke cover now, I risked alienating Ray entirely and shutting him down.

I decided to admit he'd guessed correctly. Ray believing he had the upper hand had its own value, and I didn't think there was anything else to be gained with Jameson Carter.

"There is no Jameson Carter, Ray. My name is Matt Gage, and I am a private investigator. Jimmy Lawson hired me to look into your business."

"That right? Well, he was full of shit."

"He asked questions, and it got him killed. Playing tough isn't what you want to do right now, Ray. You're swimming in deep shit, and you don't have a snorkel."

Since I woke up on that side of the bed, I seriously considered hanging up then and just leaving Ray with that imagery.

"I want to talk to you," he said again. "In person."

"Why?" I asked honestly.

"I...need your help."

"No, you need a lawyer, possibly a priest, and you need to talk to the police. I can facilitate one of those things."

"Mr. Gage, I'm desperate."

"That's what you've got Farrier for." I barked out a harsh laugh.

"What's so funny?"

"You and Farrier, you've both got alliterative names."

"I don't see why that's funny," he said.

"Never mind. Let me see if I've got this right. You knowingly make deals with mobsters who murder my client and try to kill me to cover it up."

"I had nothing to do with that," Ray protested.

"Of course you didn't. Then one of your investors gets killed. You're done, Ray. There's nothing I can do to help you. More to the point, there's nothing I'm *willing* to do to help you. After all, this is what you pay Farrier for."

What this was actually about was whether I could flip him and deliver him to Silvestri. Ruiz was the linchpin. I just didn't want him to know that. If he was going to play, he needed to know that I was his last, best hope to stay out of the grave. If I was going to do that, I had to isolate him.

"Please. I need help."

"No argument there," I said. I let Ruiz twist for a few seconds. "I'll agree to meet you, Ruiz. Here's the deal. I'll tell you when and where. It's going to involve you driving around a little bit, to make sure I know you aren't followed, or that you don't have any of your friends waiting. Understand? If I catch a whiff of mobster, or Farrier, I'm gone. You get me? Also, you should know I'm working with the police and the Feds. If I disappear, they'll know, and they'll have a good idea why. Are we clear?"

"Yes."

"Good. Where are you right now?"

"My office."

"Wait for my call."

Time for Mr. Ruiz to chase some wild geese in his zero-miles-per-gallon Aston Martin.

---

I waited two minutes and texted him, instructing him to go to Claughton Island. Claughton was a small, triangular-shaped manmade island connected to the Brickell neighborhood by a curved bridge traversing Biscayne Bay. It was mostly high-rise condos bunched around sporadic green space. I posted in a parking lot on the corner of Brickell Key Drive just in time to catch Ruiz racing over the bridge to meet me. I gave him a few minutes to hit the island's traffic circle, then I called with his next destination, the parking lot across from Miami's Freedom Tower.

Ruiz turned north on Brickell Avenue to take the bridge into downtown, and I pulled into traffic behind him. At a red light, I texted Ruiz an address in South Miami, basically the opposite direction along Brickell Avenue. I could practically hear him swearing as he pulled into the stadium's vacant parking lot to turn around. Ruiz threw me a curve that I hadn't expected—he'd headed north to pick up I-95 south instead of city streets. The address I'd given him was just one block up from the interstate's off-ramp at the Rickenbacker Causeway. I wasn't worried about him picking up the tail at this point, so I followed him to the on-ramp and through the grinding end of morning rush hour.

I called and gave him the exit just in time to make it.

"Stay on the line," I said. "Just don't talk."

"I don't—"

"I don't want you calling your friends."

No way to prevent him from texting—this was the next best thing.

We exited the interstate and crossed under it, heading back toward the water. "Stay on the causeway," I said. Rickenbacker Causeway connected the mainland with Virginia Key, one of the string of channel islands in Biscayne Bay. We drove over the bridge onto the causeway proper, with a long band of yellow-sand beach on our right, before hitting a second bridge.

By now, it'd be obvious to him where we'd be going, so I had to make the meeting quick. I assumed Farrier was typically just five minutes away from his boss.

"Pull into the stadium," I said, giving him just enough time to make the turn. "Park in the front."

We turned left into the nearly empty parking lot, and I followed Ruiz's Aston Martin across the pavement to stop in front of the derelict stadium.

The Miami Marine Stadium was built in the 1960s as an outdoor venue for watching water sports, boat races, and concerts. Hurricane Andrew had leveled it, and it'd been more or less condemned since. Various groups tried to resurrect the stadium, even getting it listed on the national historic registry, but the bond initiatives to repair it always seemed to fail. The strip of land that held the stadium had a marina and boat launch on the northern side and a marine science academy to the south. We parked facing the water.

Before hanging up the call and getting out, I said, "Lower all the windows in your car."

He did.

I stepped out of the Defender, tapping the door panel where I kept the Glock. Shielded by the car door, I clipped the holster to my belt and draped my shirt back over it.

"Open your back door and the hatch," I said. He did, and I gave it a quick once-over to make sure we were alone.

There was only one way into the parking lot unless it was by boat, so I'd see if he tried to call in backup. Not that I planned to be there long enough for anyone else to roll in.

Ray wore an off-white linen suit and a lime-green shirt opened two buttons too low, his hair slicked against his skull. He had on a pair of designer sunglasses and a giant watch. All in, he was probably wearing close to $10k. He looked like *Miami Vice* central casting, just forty years too late.

He stood there beneath that monolith of granite and graffiti, waiting for me to speak, to move.

"Why am I here, Ray?"

"What the fuck was all that driving around about? Why'd you have to waste my time like that?"

"I explained that already. Take your sunglasses off," I said.

"Why? What business—"

"Ray, I'm going to ask each question exactly one time."

He removed his glasses, showing me wide and bloodshot eyes. My guess was a few rails of coke to bolster his nerves.

"You don't want to play the tough guy here. Mostly because you can't back it up. I'm also not afraid of your mob buddies. I've seen way worse."

"Okay, hardcore."

"Ray, I used to know this officer in the Egyptian security service. He had a rather brutal way of getting at the facts. He was trying to root out members of the terrorist group, Egyptian Islamic Jihad, and that was about the only thing we had in common. I watched him line possible collaborators up against a wall, then he asked a question. When no one answered, he shot one of them in the head. Everyone else started tripping over their tongues to tell him whatever he wanted to hear. He looks to me and says, 'You see, my friend, we are only ever one bullet away from the truth.' Now, that's not the lesson I took away from that. See, if someone is scared for their life, they'll tell you whatever they think will save their ass. It's the basic reason why torture doesn't work in interrogation. My big concern, here, is that I cannot trust you, because you're scared shitless and looking for whatever scrap of floating debris you can cling to in this shipwreck of a life you have. If I'm going to help you, you need to convince me you're worthy of it."

My little soliloquy served two ends. First, to let Ray know I was at least as dangerous as the other parties in this equation. Second, to set the tone of our relationship from here out.

Ray's bravado went to the back burner, though it didn't fully cool. He started to speak, and I held up a hand. "It's not your turn to talk, pal. We have to set the table before breaking bread. Jimmy Lawson hired me because he believed you were running a Ponzi scheme, collecting money from donors, and pretending to pay athletes. I started asking questions and, in all honesty, some pretty softball ones. Jimmy is dead. That same night, someone took a swing at me, so please don't give me that bullshit about Jimmy having a drug problem. Since then, I've connected you, financially, with Cesar Marrero and Jorge Acuna. As I understand it, these guys hate each other's guts. As soon as they find out you're taking money from both, they're going to come after you and then probably each other. From what I hear, it'll be a kind of land grab. So, you're not wrong in asking for help. Your problem is, unless you've got something tangible to trade, no one is going to help you."

"I can give you Acuna," he said, too quickly.

"How?"

"I can set him up for you, and then your police contacts can arrest him."

"You don't *know* I have police contact. I just told you that. What were you hoping to get out of this? Why did you call me?"

"I don't know, Gage," he said, his voice taking on a plaintive character. "I wanted to see if you were really Jameson Carter or the private detective."

"Why?"

"Because I needed that money! When you said you and your partner would invest in my firm, I thought it was a way to buy out Acuna and Marrero. I never wanted to take their money. Was forced into it."

"By whom?"

Ray shook his head. "No way. We're not there yet. I turn on anyone, and it gets me killed."

Now that was something.

"All right, we'll table that one for now. But if I agree to help you, you will need to come clean about that point. You're afraid of getting killed? Only the police can help you. You want that, you have to turn on everyone. Understand?"

"I do."

"Fine." There were questions I needed answers to. I knew that in getting them, I might jeopardize the evidentiary value of anything that might be used in a legal action. If this got to trial, a good lawyer could argue that I'd coerced Ray into admitting something he didn't do. Whether Ray had done it or not. However, considering my status with Silvestri was up in the air, I couldn't count on the Miami-Dade Police Department. And no one anywhere seemed to be interested in solving Jimmy's murder.

"Ray, who killed my client?"

"I don't know. Honest."

"Did you know it was going to happen?"

"No. Swear to God." he said, emphatic, though that could also have been the coke.

"Do you know who tried to kill me? Who ordered it?"

"No."

"You're not giving me a lot to go on," I said.

"They don't tell me anything, Matt. I swear to you, I didn't know."

"Did Farrier kill Jimmy?"

There was a very long pause, and then Ray finally said, "No."

My instinct was that Ray knew more than he was letting on. It was clear to me there was more going on behind the scenes than I knew about. This was far more complex than I'd first appreciated. It seemed likely Ray knew about the hits, but not that he'd ordered them. Ray was not a shot-caller.

I decided not to press him on this. The case had just taken an abrupt and sharp turn, one I hadn't anticipated.

On the surface, it looked like Ray was trying to find a way out. It also looked like Ray was trying to play pieces on both sides of the board, and until I knew for sure, I wasn't going to trust him. Nor would I try to push him too far.

I said, "We're going to have to come back to Jimmy's murder before this goes much further." Ray let the fear speak for him, and he nodded his understanding. "What now, Ray? What do you want out of this?"

"I already told you. Acuna is dangerous. I can set him up for you."

"Did you know about Cody Portman?"

"What are you talking about?"

My fingers wrapped into a fist, and I'd started cocking my arm back to throw a punch before I'd even realized it. I caught myself before it was too late, but that was as lucky as Ray was going to get today. "You got to play dumb on Jimmy Lawson, but you don't get to do that with Cody Portman. He's one of yours. His house burned to the ground. His mom and little brother lost everything. The police think it's arson, which it clearly is. It's just that their leading theory is Cody's mom set the fire so she could use the insurance money to push herself into middle class. So, no, Ray, you do not get to play dumb here. You knew. And if you didn't, you're probably too dumb to save, in which case I'm doing humanity a favor letting Acuna remove you from circulation."

He opened his mouth to speak, and I saw the words forming...

I waved a dismissive hand. "Spare me. I got it. You didn't know. Good luck," I said then turned to leave.

"Matt, wait."

I turned back to look at Ray, mindful now of the time we'd spent here. If he'd told Farrier or Acuna or anyone else that we were meeting, this was probably long enough for them to find us.

"If I tell you, I give up the only thing I have to trade,"

"It doesn't work that way. You need to bring solid evidence to the police, or they won't deal," I said. "Right now, I'm not convinced you even know what's going on. I've seen it a hundred times before. You put your head in the sand and pretend you don't know about the horrible things happening around you. Then when—"

"Acuna made me give him the names of all the athletes we had on our roster," Ray said. "But he kept me out of his deals. So, I really don't know for certain that he did it. That's why I'm offering to set him up for you. Goddamnit, cut me some slack, I'm making this up as I go."

That makes two of us.

Ray was panicking. He'd played too many sides of the board and gotten caught. Now that he fully understood those consequences would get him killed, he was looking for a way out in a hallway of rapidly closing doors. Because I'm paying for past sins, Ray Ruiz landed on me.

This is good, because I was starting to think this case was too straight-forward.

"You're moving money for Acuna and Marrero. Why?"

He flashed a withering look, like I'd asked a stupidly obvious question. When I didn't say anything, Ruiz snapped, "For all the reasons a couple of mobsters would want to hide money."

"Is that why you created SSC?"

"Uh-uh. I'm not saying anything else until we have a deal."

"If I agree to take out Acuna, what are you planning to do about Marrero? You know that you don't get to go back to business as usual, right?"

"I need a little time to figure that out. Marrero isn't going down. He's clean. His name isn't on anything. He's never been arrested. And he's connected." Meaning, he probably had his own cops. Or worse.

"How are you proposing to set up Acuna?"

"He's pissed that it takes so long to clean the money he gives me."

I didn't let on that I knew how that part of the scheme worked, because I was afraid he'd figure out how I knew. Instead, I just nodded.

"So, I was thinking I'd introduce him to, you know, Jameson Carter. He'll offer to invest a bunch of money in your business, and you spring it."

"Meaning I should have this arranged with the police in advance? Wear a wire, something like that?"

"Yeah."

"And you know when this is all over, you *will* have to testify?"

"I do," he said.

"I'll talk with my contacts and see if this works. Remember my contingency plan. That never goes away. If anything happens to me, I light this whole goddamn thing up. Are we clear?"

"I understand."

I doubted very much that he did.

"You have until the end of the day," I said and walked to my Defender.

Ray was taking a hell of a risk. Even if we succeeded—meaning I not only convinced Silvestri to go along with this thing, but we pulled it off—that still left Marrero, and it would be obvious Ray was working with the police.

The chance that Ray was a double agent didn't escape me. Perhaps Marrero already knew Ray was playing both sides of the street and had offered him a way out by running his money. A stretch, though not impossible.

I improvised a surveillance detection route on the way out. Once I'd done a few circles through South Miami neighborhoods, I called Silvestri.

To my great surprise, she answered.

"I'm sorry for what I said last night. I was out of line," I blurted out before she got to tell me why she'd answered.

"I appreciate that. Look, I'm sorry, too, for blowing up at you the other night. There was some stuff going on in the background, and I let it get the better of me. Apparently, Ray Ruiz has some well-connected friends, and they made some calls to the mayor and others."

"Let me guess. One of them is State Senator Frank Rizzo."

"Yep."

"And the other is a Palm Beach real estate titan named Dalton Bream, who probably kicks a lot of money to all of the reelection funds for the mayor and city council?"

"Congratulations. You get the prize. The mayor's office sent word down through the department and started yelling before we even got this off the ground. The only reason I can figure out how the brass got to me so quickly is that I'd called that MPD homicide cop, Duane Parr. He's a piece of work, by the way."

"Ruiz has a private security consultant working for him named Felix Farrier. He's an ex-spook like me, Army, and a short stint with the DEA. He's dialed in with local police, and I know he spoke with Parr."

"That must be it. So, everything had just come down on me when we spoke the other day. We got ordered to back off Mr. Ruiz. So, what's up?"

"You're going to love this. I just met with Ray Ruiz. He wants to play ball."

"He wants to do what?"

"Jorge Acuna scared him enough that he's willing to cooperate." I relayed everything Ray had said about Acuna not being happy with how fast or how much clean money he was getting."

"He admitted to laundering?"

"Yep."

"And he'll testify?"

"He said he would."

"And you're willing to wire up? Go undercover for us?"

"Michelle, I've got more undercover time than any five people in your department combined." I said it like it was a fact, because it was. "That's not what I'm worried about. I want to make sure you guys are there if it goes south. Better that I'm the lead, but you guys maybe have someone in there with me, act like a business associate or something."

"Let me talk with my captain. No promises, given the shit sandwich we just ate, but I'll see. Dangling Acuna might just do it."

My phone chimed with an incoming call. I looked down at the screen. It was a number I didn't recognize.

"Michelle, can I call you back?"

"I've got enough to run with here. Hit me if you hear back from Ruiz."

"Will do. And thanks." I flipped the call over. "This is Matt."

"Mr. Gage, this is Donna Portman. We spoke yesterday. You gave me your card."

# 20

"Mrs. Portman, what can I do for you?"

"Mr. Gage, can you really help me?" This was a woman who carried some serious weight on her shoulders. That much was obvious in the few words she'd spoken.

"I don't know yet," I told her honestly. "I don't have half the facts I need to make that call. All I can promise you is I'll do everything in my power to. Are you safe right now?" The image of her looking beyond me to the street was burned into my memory. That was a visceral kind of fear.

"I-I don't know," she said.

"Can you tell me what happened? I was right, wasn't I? The fire at your house was no accident."

She broke down into tears. "They wanted Cody to lose that game. They told him he had to."

"Who told him?"

"Some men. They said it was part of the deal. Those were the words they used."

"Part of what deal? His contract with Sunshine Sports Collective?"

"I wasn't there, Mr. Gage. This is just what my son tells me."

"I understand." I assumed they'd be smarter than to tell him outright that throwing a game was in his contract, but you never can tell.

"They told him bad things would happen if he didn't. Then someone came to see me. He...he showed up outside my work. He told me to make sure Cody understood 'the terms.' That's exactly what he said. I threatened to go to the police. He told me if I did, Cody's playing days would be over. They'd hurt him, and he implied he'd hurt my younger son too. Words to the effect of "we didn't know what else to do" came out, but they were so muddled by her sobs I could only guess if that was what she had said.

"Take your time."

Eventually, the tide of fear, sadness, guilt, and self-recrimination ebbed enough, and Donna Portman could speak again. I couldn't even comprehend what this woman was carrying.

"Cody tried to, you know, do what they told him. But the team played their best game of the season. And at the end, they put it in his hands because he was the best three-point shooter, and he was open. He didn't think it was going to go in. He thought if he could make it close, it'd be good enough. Those men, they didn't care. As soon as it ended, I got a call on my cell phone. They said they had been clear, and now there will be consequences."

There was a longshot chance the police could trace the call from the cell phone records, though I doubted Acuna or whoever had used a permanent phone.

"The fire happened the next day while I was at work. The police think I did it for the insurance money." Her voice broke up again.

"Donna, I'm working with Miami-Dade to investigate Sunshine Sports Collective and potential ties to organized crime. I think I know who did this to your home—at least, who gave the order. Would you be willing to speak with the police?"

"They told me if I spoke to the police, they would know. I think they're watching the house now. That's why I couldn't talk to you when you were at the door."

I doubted a local gang had the knowledge or the resources to run dedicated, round-the-clock surveillance. It was possible they had a hidden camera somewhere, though I doubted it. Still, I wasn't going to minimize Donna Portman's fears. Those were real. Knowing whether she'd talk to the cops was probably an empty threat, but *she* didn't think it was, and I would act accordingly.

Because there were terrible consequences if I was wrong, and they wouldn't be for me.

"Donna, I worked for the CIA for almost twenty years before I was a private detective. If there's one thing I know how to do, it's to get a brave person from one place to another without the bad guys knowing it. If I can guarantee your safety, will you meet with my police contact?"

She took a long time to answer.

"They said they'd know. What if they're watching me?"

"I'm trained in this—they are not. I've gone up against the Russians and the Chinese, the Venezuelans, and most of the secret police in the Middle East. I can outsmart some local thugs. Will you trust me?"

"What do I need to do?"

As I was speeding to the parking garage at Fort Lauderdale International Airport, I called Silvestri. I knew this was backward. I also didn't want to put Donna Portman through a bunch of bureaucratic shuffling back and forth. She had actionable intelligence, and we needed to act on it.

She exhaled. "What's going on? Ruiz isn't backing down is he?"

I could tell she was in the middle of something.

"I just talked to Cody Portman's mother. Her son was the one I told you about, who Acuna tried to, uh, convince to throw the basketball game."

"Their house burned down, right?"

"That's right. I went to see her the other day, and she was scared shitless. Still is, but she's willing to talk. Can we meet you somewhere?"

"You flipped two people in a day. That's got to be some kind of record." It was impossible not to notice the sardonic tone in her voice. "When and where?"

"Two hours. I'm going to get her now. She's convinced that Acuna's people are watching her. They told her they'd know if she talked to the police."

Silvestri considered this. "I doubt they have someone in the department on their payroll, but let's not take a chance. I'll get us an interview room at the Intracoastal District station in Aventura. That'll be well outside Acuna's turf."

---

I met Donna Portman on the third level of the short-term parking garage. She got into the Defender, and we headed south. I explained what a surveillance detection route was, how we would drive in circles, occasionally looping back to see if we were followed. How we'd take a circuitous route to our destination that was designed to shake any tails we may have had. I told her about how sometimes in the Agency, you might spend five, six hours or more on an SDR using a combination of cars, trains, buses, and walking to make sure you weren't followed, just to have a five-minute meeting.

I told her I'd never been caught.

And that was mostly true.

It seemed to put her a little more at ease.

We arrived at the Miami-Dade Intracoastal District station where Silvestri met us just inside. She wore a black suit and blue blouse. Her hands were at her hips, pushing the sides of her jacket out like wings and displaying the badge clipped to her belt. There was a younger officer, maybe mid-thirties, in a gray suit.

"Mrs. Portman, my name is Lieutenant Michelle Silvestri. I want to thank you for coming in to speak with us today. I want you to understand how much we appreciate your bravery. This is Detective Sergeant Beecher."

"Hello," Portman said.

"Can I get you a cup of coffee before we get started? It's not very good, but it's coffee," Silvestri said with a thin smile.

"No, I'm fine, thank you."

Silvestri turned to me. "Thank you for making this happen, Matt. If you'll both follow me, please." She led us into an unused conference room. "Ed and I are not based out of this station. I understand from Matt that you've got some concerns about whether the people who threatened your family might be watching you."

Ray had told me Acuna had cops on his payroll and said something about the jails. Since those were administered by Miami-Dade, we had to be cautious wherever we met. That said, Jorge Acuna was not John Gotti. He might have a few policemen in his pocket, but the odds that he had eyes and ears in every substation in Dadeland were so low they didn't bear calculation.

"Yes. Mr. Gage took some pretty elaborate steps to make sure we weren't followed here."

Silvestri regarded me for a moment with an appraising look.

"I can speak with the police department in Pembroke Pines about having them include your home in their patrol."

Portman nodded.

Silvestri set her phone on the table and started the recording function.

She began the questioning by asking our consent to be recorded and then stated the names of everyone present for the record. Guided by Silvestri's questions, Portman relayed the story she'd told me earlier over the phone. This time, she amplified it with details about the physical description of the men who'd threatened her son and who'd confronted her. She agreed to meet with a sketch artist as soon as it could be arranged.

Silvestri asked, "Mrs. Portman, I understand your son's next game is tomorrow. Is that correct?"

Donna nodded heavily. "And has anyone contacted you or your son with a threat about the outcome?"

Donna nodded again and said, "yes."

That was news.

"What happened?" Silvestri asked.

"Someone was waiting for him outside his dorm when they returned from Charlotte. He just walked up and said, 'Don't do that shit again.'"

I noted they didn't actually threaten him in an obvious way. Nor did they instruct the kid on how much he should throw the game by. That was the big hang up with my points-fixing theory.

"Where is your son right now?"

"He's in Dallas with the team." Silvestri shot me a look that I couldn't read, which I took to be a placeholder for some future conversation that I wouldn't like.

After about an hour, Silvestri asked me if I'd join her outside while Detective Beecher asked some follow-up questions. We went to the break room, and Silvestri poured us each a cup of coffee. It was as bad as she'd said it would be.

"Well, I'm certainly convinced someone threatened her. I need to talk to the arson investigator at Pembroke, but I don't think that woman set her house on fire." Silvestri looked at the cup in her hand and the acrid, luke-warm contents it held. "It's clear to me the threat was *implied*. They were careful about it being a direct *quid pro quo*."

"You mean because a scary-looking dude said, 'Don't do that shit again'?"

"Right," Silvestri agreed. "We get exposed to numbers games and rackets a lot on the OC detail, especially now that we've got a casino here in town. They've got people who look for patterns, like if there are parlay bets for a particular player to score, stuff like that. Which is to say that if this is a sophisticated operation, they wouldn't run their betting enterprise on just this kid's performance. This feels more like these guys are testing the waters for something bigger. The other part that bothers me, Matt—and I kind of knew this going in—is that there's no tangible link to SSC or Ray Ruiz. If I can find the people who torched her house, we can certainly make them swing for arson." Silvestri shook her head. "Ruiz's lawyers are going to argue he had nothing to do with it."

"Not even if we show the court that Ruiz is laundering the money for those same gangsters that are pumping into his business?"

"It could be a completely separate thing. In all likelihood, it is. I'd be willing to bet Ruiz didn't know anything about trying to fix the game in advance."

"What if they forced Ray to give up the names of his athletes, so they could see who might be vulnerable?"

"Maybe," Silvestri said.

"You're not letting Ruiz off the hook, are you?"

"God no. I just want you to appreciate how complicated this is. The arson happened outside of my jurisdiction. I have to give what we've got to the Pembroke PD detective and convince him to run with it, make sure he knows that poor woman isn't trying to run an insurance scam. We focus on connecting Ruiz with the gangs. This, though…there's only so much I can do."

"I understand jurisdictions, Michelle. I just don't know that *she* does. When you explain it to her, please make sure she knows this isn't going to fall in between the cracks. Or that something will get missed in the hand-off, then the bad guys get tipped and the Portmans get hurt. Whether it's justified or not, or rational or not, that woman is scared for her life and for her family. We cannot let her leave here thinking she was wrong in coming forward."

Silvestri's eyes flared, and I knew I'd pushed it too far. I could practically hear her asking who I meant by "we." She clearly didn't like the implication that I had some kind of official position here.

"I will take care of it," she said. "We probably don't need the cloak-and-dagger routine to get her home."

"I can do it. Her car is at short-term parking in Fort Lauderdale. That's a little bit outside your route."

"We can handle it. I'll let her know when she's done with my guys. You need to focus on getting Ruiz on board and ready."

I nodded and walked out of the police station.

I got in my car and called Special Agent Danzig. This time, I got her.

I summarized the case to date, adding, "There are two parts of this that I don't think fit with the local cops. The first is this point-fixing thing. If we've truly got an organized crime group trying to fix the basketball tournament, that's got to be federal, right? The first game was in Charlotte, and the next one is in Dallas."

"That's where it gets complicated," Danzig said. "Yes, if this kid goes through with it and tanks it on purpose, a crime is committed in that location. But we also have to consider where the threat was made. So, two or three states at least. Yeah. Now, I've got to caution you, Matt. This stuff takes time to get rolling. If I can get a deposition from you, summarizing everything you've found, I can probably get it in the hands of one of our mob squads."

"Kristin, this kid doesn't have that kind of time! He's playing *tomorrow*."

She sighed into the phone, probably for effect. "Matt, you know the power of bureaucratic inertia better than anyone."

I was thinking, *Yeah, an organization at rest tends to stay at rest*, but I didn't say a word.

"I promise you I will do what I can," she said.

"Thank you. Now, the other part of this that doesn't fit with the locals is the financial side. I know there's a state-level financial crimes task force down here but—"

"But you don't trust them," Danzig finished for me.

I ignored that statement, though it was basically true. "From what I've told you, what's your read?"

"I can't fault your conclusions. Of course, I haven't seen any evidence, but from the way you describe it, it certainly sounds like a money-laundering pattern. I can connect you with my old squad. Fair warning, it'll take them some time to get spun up on this, and I'm not sure what the current case load is. I also...well, that job was a penalty-box assignment for me, and I treated it that way."

"So you're saying you burned some bridges on the way out?"

She laughed. "And on the way in and some of the parts in between. We left on good terms, though everyone agreed I was better on the street, with a squad catching bad guys and not in an office running spreadsheets. I've still got some friends there, so let me make some calls."

"Thanks, Kristin. I owe you."

"Be careful, I'm the type who collects," she said, and I knew her well enough to know she meant it. "I'll get back to you. Keep me posted on the kid."

Danzig disconnected, and I headed south to Miami.

---

It was late afternoon by the time I got back to the hotel and Ruiz's call.

"We need to talk," he said. I could hear the alcohol in his words.

"Where are you?"

"I'm at home. I'm pretty sure you can figure out where that is, Detective."

His words were bitter and dark.

*I'm sure this will turn out fine.*

## 21

Miami Beach had manmade fingers of land clawing out into the water so they could stack more thirty-million-dollar homes on land not made to support it. Ray's was midway down one such finger. I'd been here previously, trying to stake him out, though I'd found that a little problematic and gave up quickly. Stillwater was a single street with houses on either side and no gap in between. There was a cursory turnaround at the end of the street for those unwashed masses who got to the end and realized they didn't belong. Ray's house was on the northern end of Miami Beach and, with traffic, a good forty minutes from the hotel.

It was a single-story, midcentury home, probably first sold for five grand in the 1950s and had appreciated on a level commensurate with diamonds or lithium. I pulled into the carport behind his Aston and walked to the front door. Giant palms shielded the carport from the sun. I hit the doorbell. Ruiz told me through the box next to it that he had unlocked the door and was out back. I entered and made a fast line for the back, eager to get this over. He'd decorated the place in a modernist aesthetic, somewhat matching the exterior—white, gray, and colored glass. A sliding back door opened to a pool deck and, beyond that, a wooden dock and a boat. That's where I found Ray.

He sat in the fading afternoon light, a tumbler of something brown in his hand. The boat looked to be about thirty feet long, black with red accent lines and teak trim. It wasn't large enough for a full cabin belowdecks, though there was a pass-through to seating at the bow. That's where I found him.

Ray reclined in one of the seats, facing south, the sky's light burning away.

I didn't see Farrier anywhere.

"What's up, Ray?" I asked as I rested one arm against the windshield glass.

"Have a seat," he said. I found a spot next to him. "Drink?"

"No thanks. What am I doing here?"

"Acuna's people agreed to the meet. They're interested to hear how 'Jameson Carter' and Apogee can clean their money faster than I can." He said it with a flourish of simmering anger.

"This is your best way out, Ray," I said, hoping that'd bring the temperature down a little.

"My way out was supposed to be the money from Apogee."

"Ray, that was never real."

"Yeah, I get that now. That's what I was going to use to pay off Acuna and cut ties. Now that it's all bullshit, I got no choice but to take whatever you serve up, huh? I guess that's how it works with you people."

"If Marrero finds out you're double dealing, he's going to kill you. Working with the police, you've at least got a chance to get out of this with your life intact."

His lips curled in spite, and he barked out a laugh. "A chance. Fuck your chance. You don't know shit about what's happening here. I help you and Acuna finds out—and he will, because he's all over the cops—they're going to kill me. You're probably going to tell me that if I cooperate..." I could smell the rum coming off him now. "If I cooperate, they'll give me a lighter sentence, right? You don't think he's got people in the jails here? How the hell you think he's never served time? Huh? How come not, asshole? You got all the answers—how come he's never served jail? Because he's bought 'em the fuck off is why. And you want me to go walking right in there with a snitch jacket?"

"Ray, I'm not going to bleed out sympathy for you. You're laundering money for two criminal gangs. That's bad enough, but you're exploiting kids to do it. Whatever happens, this is your own doing."

"Whatever you think, Gage, I didn't set out to do that. I wanted to create a collective. You know what the dirtiest secret in college sports is? They all goddamn do it. Every school has a bag man. Usually it's a booster, or maybe someone connected to one. He pays the big names under the table, gets them to come or keeps them from leaving. All I wanted to do with SSC was use it to bring recruiting out into the open. The government seems to agree with me, by the way. There's two cases," Ruiz held up a pair of fingers, and I was impressed by how straight the lines were. Ray didn't continue and must have assumed whatever he already said stood on its own merits.

But after a couple of beats of silence, he did continue. "I didn't know about Marrero, at first. I know how to make deals. I don't have a lot of experience in fundraising, and I needed the seed money to get it started. I had a few classmates who did pretty well for themselves, and they helped, but we just needed a lot more. If you don't have a ton of bank to start with, it's kind of a catch-22. The big boosters don't want to kick in because they want to see you've got connections with the kinds of endorsements that are going to get kids excited—Nike and Gatorade, whatever. And without a big donor pipeline needed to get top-tier talent, none of my contacts with big-name sponsors would do anything but say they'd wait and see. So, I talked to Frank Rizzo."

"We've met," I said in a sandpaper tone. Ray seemed to be in a state of mind where some details were going to slip through the cracks.

"Right. Well, Frank said he had some connections that would help out, local businesses that would want to, you know, advertise. He said that would give me the cash I'd need to attract bigger players on both sides. It sounded good, so I did it. I didn't know *who* was behind it until much later. Once they were kicking money in, someone came to see me. He said they wanted to know how to get their money back out. I said, 'You don't. It's an endorsement. You get paid back from new business coming in because of that endorsement.' That ended up being not the right thing to say."

Ruiz drained his tumbler and refilled it. "Once you approached me about contributing, I thought maybe I could make you an investor in the firm. I'd use that money to pay back Marrero and Acuna and get clear of them."

I doubted the mobsters would've seen it that way.

"How'd Acuna factor into this?" I asked. "Way I hear it, those guys hate each other. Why take on that risk?"

"They sure do. I don't have all the details—" Ruiz looked over at me "—and I don't want 'em. What I *do* know is Acuna used to run a crew in the Corporation. He was sort of a rival of Marrero's, resented the fact that Marrero's name wasn't on anything, and resented the fact that he didn't take any risk. Acuna broke off to start his own thing and went after some of Marrero's interests to spite him."

Seemed like Ruiz knew an awful lot about that backstory for not wanting any details.

"Is that how you got involved with Acuna?"

Ruiz shrugged his shoulders. It was a sad, resigned gesture. "Not exactly. He'd heard that I had a way to clean money and wanted in. He didn't know I was working with Marrero. I almost told him. Maybe I should've. Acuna doesn't negotiate with people—he just tells you the outcome he wants. Once I got in with him, he then tells me he wants to see who I'm working with, the players. You know, to know whether the operation was legit." Ruiz stopped to give a chuckle at his half-drunk attempt at irony. "I told him some of the names I had. Was scared not to. I didn't know he was gonna... do what he did."

I suspected there was some solid truth in Ruiz's story. No one wants to be the villain in theirs, and I bet he'd painted over several key details in the telling. Not that it mattered much at this point.

"Is Cody safe?"

"I don't know anything about it. I told you." Ruiz corked his face to look over at me. "I want immunity, Gage. Or I don't do shit."

"I'm not the district attorney, Ray. I can't promise that."

"Make it happen, or I vanish."

"Where are you going to go?"

He gave me a sour look and gestured at his boat. I just closed my eyes.

"This isn't a yacht. You've got nowhere to sleep, and anyway...if you run, the first call is going to the Coast Guard."

"Ha! If they could catch boats, Miami wouldn't have a coke problem."

There was some logic to that, and I conceded him the point.

"I spoke with my police contacts," I said, "and they are willing to move on Acuna if you can set it up. I don't know how long it takes to put immunity together or what those rules are. We need to be clear on this. I cannot make any promises on that score."

"There's no deal without it."

"You want to think on that, Ray. Because they've got you on money laundering. There is a reasonable case for accessory to murder. Cody Portman is a whole different set of bad. Probably, Jorge Acuna doesn't have hit men in the kinds of jails they send money launderers to. Still, you want to consider the time you'll do in city lockup, waiting for trial, and the possibility of either of these two gang bosses deciding they don't want to risk your squawking."

Ruiz threw his hands up and realized a little too late that one of those hands held a tumbler full of rum. Luckily for me, the booze mostly landed on the seats in front of him. "All right, all right," he said. Ray considered his empty glass dejectedly and set it aside.

"He's got a place in Little Havana, the Son Cubano," Ray said. "He wanted to do the meeting at my office, but that's obviously out of the question."

"Is it, though?"

"I can't have gangsters at my place of business."

"You let Frank Rizzo in," I said.

"No."

I much preferred this meeting take place at SSC's offices. As would the police.

"For a whole host of reasons, not least of which are my personal safety, you need to reconsider that," I said. "If Acuna is looking for an air of legitimacy, he's better served if this meeting happens at the logical place—at SSC. What'd you tell him about Carter?"

"Just that you were a businessman. I implied you could invest his money in something lucrative and then give him a good, clean return."

"That was the phrasing you used," I said.

"Jesus Christ, Gage! You think I said, "Park your money at the illegal laundromat"? Are you an idiot? This was a bad idea. You're going to get me killed."

"The only thing that's going to get you killed, Ray, is not listening to people who know more about this shit than you do."

Ray looked out over the water. "I'll talk to him," he said.

"How does Olivia McEvoy factor into all this? Does she know what's going on?"

Ray shook his head emphatically. "No. She's got no idea."

"Never asked questions about where the money came from?"

"She had no reason to."

"If we do this meeting at your place, is she going to be a problem?" I still had no idea where she was, and she hadn't returned any of my calls. I'd gone from being ghosted to seriously concerned about her safety.

"She won't be a problem," Ray said in a tone I didn't like.

"Given some of your pals, I don't like the way that sounds, Ray."

"I haven't talked to her in a couple of days, though I haven't been in the office. I'll call her."

"Best not to say anything. Don't draw any attention. Also, keep Farrier out of this."

A long, sullen moment passed before Ruiz finally said, "Okay."

I got up to leave. "I'm going to speak with the police right now. Be ready to meet with them tomorrow." I decided to keep the specific law enforcement agency out of it until I felt Ray could be trusted. Given that Silvestri had already taken some heat from the brass over this, I didn't want Ray leaking any of it to his pals. If he pulled out, got scared, or whatever, I wanted to maintain an organizational element of surprise.

"Immunity, Gage," Ruiz said. He must have been a practiced drunk, because his words were now sharp and clear.

Something about his repetition of "immunity" hit me exactly the wrong way. It smacked of the foreknowledge of terrible things. I snapped. I lunged for him, and in Ruiz's half-drunk state, he couldn't even get a hand up in time. I grabbed him by the collar and yanked him to his feet. Somewhere on his outfit, fabric ripped. I jerked him once, threatening to send him over the side.

"Listen to me, you miserable fuck. The only reason you're walking is because you've got something to offer that might save some lives. I swear to you, if anything happens to Cody Portman or his family..." I yanked Ruiz closer, to within inches of my face, dousing my nostrils in the rum stink of his breath. "If *anything* happens to him, they will *never* find your body. Are we clear?"

The size of Ray's pupils told me he got the message.

## 22

A long and agonizing night followed.

I regretted losing my cool with Ray. Pressure builds and it's got to go somewhere, still I've never lost my composure like that on the job before. It saps objectivity in dangerous ways and leads you down dark roads better left alone. Granted, Ruiz wasn't in his right mind, but the way he played with immunity as though he were entitled to it...

The other thing that continued to haunt me into the low hours of the morning was the comment Ray had made about counting on the money from Apogee Partners. In both our conversations, he carried on as though that money had been a real thing that he'd somehow lost.

A precious few conclusions came to me in the night. The one that sang out, though, was that Acuna's point fixing had to be a target of opportunity, a spark of dark inspiration that made him wonder if he could pull it off. This was not a systematic, long con, like its predecessors. The simple explanation was that Acuna realized what he had, and once Cody's team made its improbable way into the tournament, he'd created a fairly unsophisticated betting scheme. First, Gulf Coast was a huge underdog in each of their games, so betting against them would yield considerably less return than if they pulled the upset. Which they did in the Tennessee game. Of course, with Acuna running his own numbers racket, he could set whatever odds he wanted. Still, this didn't reek of savviness.

The other thought that kept circling was Acuna had a different play here and was using Portman to see what he could get away with. The first step to beating any security system is to test its weaknesses.

Both theories meant Acuna was more likely to toss his used-up resource aside when he was done with it. They wouldn't let the kid go with the knowledge they'd forced him to throw a game and punished him when he didn't. The blowback would go to Ruiz and Sunshine Sports Collective.

So, what I was looking at was the very real possibility that, if I couldn't bring this case in, I might save Cody from a short-term danger only to set him up for a longer one that would haunt him the rest of his life. These things always got out, and he'd be ruined. A prosecutor would just as likely paint him as a willing partner as a victim, especially if it got headlines.

Gray light came into the room through the crack in the curtains, and I realized I must have fallen asleep. I pulled the curtain back, revealing an overcast morning. They were high clouds that held no rain.

The Gulf Coast game was later today, six in the evening. I checked my phone, and there were no messages from Donna Portman. She said she'd notify me if anyone from Acuna's gang approached her.

I hated to admit it, but in that moment, I found myself thinking about Dalton Bream's offer. Take the money, focus on finding Jimmy's killer. Ray is a dirt bag, and he took mob money, and maybe I should just leave him to the consequences. Of course, I couldn't get rid of the suspicion that's exactly why Bream had offered me a job. I was a problem for Ray. Bream could afford to throw money at me and make that go away. Maybe use that as leverage to force Ray to rethink his business model. Still, I couldn't escape the "why." Bream wouldn't be invested in Ray's success for altruism, so why did he care?

My initial instinct was probably correct. No one offers you a ton of money to do the right thing. There's no easy way out here. Silvestri needed Ray Ruiz to get me in front of Acuna so the police could nail him.

Silvestri called and said we'd meet with Ray at the department's Doral headquarters. I got into my Defender and made the crawling trek through Miami's miasmic traffic up to Doral. It was a concrete monolith lording over an expanse of St. Augustine grass, resembling a fortress. After signing in, a uniformed sergeant escorted me to a conference room where we waited for Ruiz to show.

Chewing the clock with me were Silvestri and the five other members of her squad, whom she introduced to me. Also present was an assistant district attorney named Anthony La Barca. He was average height and fit enough for golf, with a tan suggesting he played a lot of it. La Barca wore a beige, tropical-weight suit, white shirt, and dark blue tie, clearly pushing the boundaries of conservative dress for a civil servant. La Barca spent a lot of time checking his watch, as though the expression on his face wasn't enough to tell us he had somewhere he'd rather be. By thirty minutes in and no sign of Ruiz, he'd taken to explaining to Silvestri that "this thing was so hastily cobbled together the duct tape wouldn't even stick."

Silvestri shot me a questioning look, and all I could do was lift my shoulders in response. I didn't have any more answers than they did.

The conference room was on the third floor and had a pair of windows propped open. There were three rows of tables that each held six chairs, with a lectern and a wall of whiteboards at the front. One of Silvestri's team had rolled in another whiteboard, on which they'd drawn a pyramid diagram with pictures indicating Acuna's organization and what they suspected each member was responsible for. Silvestri had confirmed for me something Flash told me early on, which was there were dozens, maybe even hundreds of these *marielito* gangs operating in South Florida, with most of them so far under the law enforcement radar they didn't even blip.

"How much longer are we going to drag this out, Michelle?" La Barca wanted to know. Forty-five minutes had now passed.

Silvestri looked at me.

"Ruiz told me he'd be here," I said.

"Well, I don't like being jerked around," La Barca said.

"Calm down, guy," I said, and Silvestri's hand immediately went to shield her face. "In about four hours, Gulf Coast is going to tip off their game in the Sweet Sixteen. After the last one, their star player's house got torched. You want to know why? Because Jorge Acuna told him to throw the game or else. Acuna—" I pointed at the whiteboard "—is trying to fix the tournament to support his burgeoning numbers racket. Now, there is no set of circumstances that has us nailing Acuna and any of his goons in the next four hours. Which means that kid and his poor mother, and to a lesser extent me, are riding on pins because we know what these assholes are capable of. I'm sorry if you don't make your tee time, Counselor, but try to muster a little empathy for some people who are really goddamn scared this afternoon."

I watched a carnival of emotions march across La Barca's face until he finally settled on concession.

"Right. I just wanted to get this moving is all."

I'd pretty much killed the vibe in the room, and no one said much after that. Eventually, Silvestri's squad started muted conversations, passing time the way operators the world over do—small talk and bullshit.

Ten minutes later, La Barca's phone rang.

He looked at it, grimaced, and then answered.

There was a short conversation, a shorter argument, and the proffering of threats. Once I heard the phrase "twenty-four counts of fraud, conspiracy and racketeering," roll off La Barca's lips, I knew who he was talking to. Sunshine Sports Collective had twenty-four signed athletes, and the State of Florida would be charging Ruiz with one count of everything for each one. Amazingly, the word "arson" didn't seem to turn the tide of the conversation. La Barca ended the call, and his phone just hung limp in his hand.

"Ruiz isn't coming."

"What?" Silvestri and I said at the same time, though I may have added "the" and something else after.

"That was the eminent attorney, C. Edward Cathcart." La Barca pinched his eyes shut and rubbed his temples. "It appears Mr. Ruiz has elected to retain counsel."

The waves of expletives from the assembled cops was tsunami level.

Silvestri looked over at me, knowing I was a step behind. "Cathcart is probably the most successful criminal defense attorney in South Florida. He made a name for himself in the '90s defending some high-profile drug dealers. Actually won a few of those cases too."

"So, he's dirty?" I offered.

"No," La Barca said with resignation. "Just the opposite. I know him personally. Interned at his firm. He is a constitutional absolutist. What I mean is he genuinely believes in the presumption of innocence and holds the government accountable for doing its job. If you were wrongfully accused of something, he is 100 percent the lawyer you'd want in your corner."

"How can Ruiz afford him? Isn't his money tainted? That's against the law, right? You can't pay for attorneys with stolen money?"

"That's true, but that only applies to the money the government has already seized or has otherwise proven to be illegally acquired. Which..." La Barca spread his hands to show they contained nothing.

"So, where does that leave us?" I asked.

"Down shit's creek and swimming," one of Silvestri's squad said.

"It's 'up shit's creek,'" another one said.

He looked over at her and said, "You don't think downstream is worse?" His squad mate nodded, conceding the point.

"Question remains," Silvestri said.

"Folks, there's nothing I can do about Ruiz. If you have enough to charge him, bring it to me, and we can go see the judge. Is it possible to go after this Acuna without Ruiz?"

It was a subtle thing, but La Barca adding "this" before the name told me he didn't know who the guy was. That's not a knock—Miami has a lot of gangs. I'd imagine keeping track of it all must look like LAX's air traffic control radar at Christmas.

"Ruiz was our way in. We don't have much without him," Silvestri said.

"The point to Ruiz helping us was so he didn't get charged with all that other stuff. When does that get triggered? If he's not going to help, aren't we going to nail him to a wall?"

"With what?" La Barca said.

"Money laundering, fraud, racketeering," I said.

"How do you prove it?"

"I've got all of his financial records," I said.

"And you're not a cop. I'm not taking that to a judge. We need someone who can testify to that."

"Didn't you have someone on the inside?" Silvestri asked me.

"Yes. I didn't steal those files. Ruiz's number two gave them to me. She thought something was off and shared. I analyzed them and concluded there was."

"And you're qualified to do that?" La Barca asked.

"Yes," I said flatly.

No one spoke until Silvestri said, "Mr. Gage was in the CIA and used to run down terrorists and stuff, people who did this sort of thing. I trust him. He was recommended to me by a Bureau contact."

"Okay, well, if you can find this number two—"

"Olivia McEvoy," I said.

"Right. Produce her, get a deposition, and I'll see what I can do. Oh, and Mr. Gage, don't threaten witnesses. I don't want to hear that kind of shit again."

Silvestri leveled a narrowed-eyed gaze at me. "Matt?"

Ruiz must have complained to his eminent lawyer. "I didn't threaten him," I said. I mean, I *did*, but that was probably mostly hyperbole. "Ruiz called me last night to talk about today. He was a few drinks past being a reliable narrator by the time I saw him. I wouldn't put much stock in his recollection of the evening."

"In any event..." With that, La Barca left.

"Well," Silvestri said, watching the door closing behind him. "That happened. Guys, give us a minute. I'll meet you back in the squad room."

Her team shuffled out, and Silvestri slid a leg onto one of the tables to half sit.

"Were you able to get a hold of someone at Pembroke PD?" I asked.

She nodded. "I explained what was happening, and they're going to have a cruiser at the front of the house for the next couple of days."

It wasn't great but, under the circumstances, was probably the best I was going to get.

"What are you going to do now, Matt?"

"Find Ray and ask him a few questions," I replied.

"You should not do that. I don't want you going anywhere near Ray."

"Fine. Wish I could understand what was going through his head. Yesterday, he's desperate for help." That was for Silvestri's benefit. I think I knew the answer to that question already. Ray believed he had a have-cake-and-eat-it way out of this when he thought that I was a rich whale with money to burn. When that fizzled, Ray went to his Plan B, which was lawyering up.

With Dalton Bream's lawyer.

That explained why we hadn't heard from the guy until now. It wasn't until Ray realized there was no possible way he was getting out of this on his own that he went to his benefactor for help.

"Oh, none of this is too surprising," she said. "It's a little curious that he'd agreed to do this before he retained counsel. Though, if he was as drunk as you say, probably had something to do with it."

"I don't think Ray and Cathcart were acquainted before. I'll bet that came from his pal Dalton Bream, or maybe Senator Frank Rizzo."

"Possibly," Silvestri allowed. "You still didn't answer my question. What are you going to do?"

Maybe Ray was a red herring...and maybe that was the point. He was the convenient scapegoat for his shadier partners. I'd kept after Ruiz because that was what Jimmy hired me to do—well, more specifically, investigate the SSC—and I'd hoped that by exposing Ruiz, the truth about Jimmy's murder would flush out with it. I believed this was all connected and that if I'd solved one mystery, the dominoes would fall.

It's just that you can't tangentially avenge someone. It's an all-or-nothing proposition.

What I had now was the responsibility to find Jimmy's killer. Everything else was in the police's hands. Or it wasn't. Either way, Ruiz had stopped being my concern, it seemed. But that wasn't true—not by a long shot.

"Ray told me he didn't know who killed Lawson, or who'd ordered it done. Not sure I believe him, but here we are. I have to find that out."

"Don't quit on Ruiz just yet," she said. "Cathcart is trying to show his client isn't afraid of the charges. La Barca is going to hit them back with everything we've got. You showed that he's tied to an offshore account that we can connect to a known OC figure." Silvestri shrugged.

"OC?" I said, thinking this was something I should know.

"Organized Crime," she said. "That's not nothing. He also lied about who those accounts belong to when McEvoy had asked him about it, so we need to get her deposed. Heads-up play to figure out Acuna used his elderly uncle's name to open the account."

"Thanks," I said.

The way I'd figured out Acuna was involved was by following the paper trail of SSC's donors. One of those corporate donations was from a shell company allegedly owned by a man named Alves Pacheco. Mr. Pacheco was an eighty-something living in an assisted living facility in Pembroke Pines, and his maternal nephew was one Jorge Acuna. "We need McEvoy. Otherwise, the defense will claim you stole the files in question, and it'll be your word against theirs. That doesn't mean it's over, and La Barca knows that. I've worked with him before. He's a good guy, just a little high strung. He's also going through a nasty divorce right now, and his wife is an attorney. They each know each other's tricks and, between the two of them, have almost all the lawyers in the county as connections. It's like two scorpions in a jar."

"One question," I said, because this had been gnawing at me for days. "Detective Parr, he's the MPD guy with Jimmy's ticket. I called him to say I had information, told him who I was, and when we met, he took my picture. Said it was for the field interview card, some new policy. You ever heard of that?"

"I have not. Was the attempt on your life before or after that?"

"It was before."

"What was his first name again?"

"Duane."

"I'll see what I can find out. In the meantime, if you're going to stick around, I'd focus on trying to find Olivia McEvoy. That'd be a huge help to me, because it means I don't have to do it. Stay away from Ruiz. I mean it. No calls, no drop-ins. He calls you, don't pick up the phone. La Barca trusts this Cathcart, but I don't."

I promised to ignore Ruiz, and we agreed to check in with each other tomorrow. She also admonished me to not interfere with the official investigation into Jimmy's murder. She couldn't stop me from looking into it on my own, particularly since I had a contract, but suggested I give Duane Parr a wide berth. And not do anything to get myself killed.

I left the headquarters building and got in my car for the slog back to downtown. I had a long string of minutes to contemplate my next move.

Searching for Olivia was, fundamentally, the same problem as trying to figure out who Jimmy's killer was. I had nowhere to start. I couldn't access her home for clues nor could I get her phone records. I doubted there would be anything in the office, though looking there would just tip Ruiz anyway.

And there was the little problem that I'd actually *told* her to disappear for a few days for her own safety. I'd just thought she would respond to my numerous texts and calls.

I got back to the hotel by three thirty and pulled up EchoTrace on my laptop to run some link analyses on Olivia. The app would, in addition to other things, mine her social media profiles for any recent posts. I assumed she was smarter than that, but it was still worth checking. With EchoTrace working in the background, I went down to the pool for a quick swim. I showered and changed in the spa locker room and then went to the bar for a quick bite.

Portman's game would start in about an hour, and I couldn't bring myself to watch it.

Returning to my room, I found that EchoTrace had a report for me. Olivia hadn't posted anything since she'd vanished and generally wasn't active on social media anyway. Her parents lived in Naples, and now I had a phone number for them.

They still had a landline.

"Hello," a man said.

"Mr. McEvoy?"

"Yes. Who is this?"

"Sir, my name is Matthew Gage. I am a private investigator working with your daughter, Olivia. I am trying to reach her and haven't been able to connect with her for a few days. I was hoping maybe you've heard from her."

"Is this some kind of a scam?"

"No, sir. As I said, I'm working with Olivia on an investigation. I'm happy to provide my investigator's license as a reference. She's been assisting me with information. I haven't spoken with her in a few days, and she hasn't returned my calls. I was hoping maybe you could pass on a message."

"If she wants to talk to you, she will."

He hung up.

Can't say that I blamed him. Some anonymous man wanting information on his daughter? I could understand why he'd think it was a scam. The call might still prompt him to contact Olivia to report the conversation, and she'd confirm I was who I said I was and call back.

Assuming she was in a position to call back.

Needing some air and wanting to be away from a television so I didn't have to fight the compulsion to turn the game on, I left the hotel for a walk. It was two blocks up from the water, so I headed down there and strolled along the sidewalk facing Biscayne Bay, watching the fading sunlight. At some point, I stopped and sat, feet over the edge of the walk and resting on the rocks below, water lazily lapping the piled stones. The air felt like a warm bathrobe.

I hadn't realized how much I'd missed this.

My father ran a fishing-charter business in Sarasota, and most of my formative years were spent on small boats, cruising the Gulf. I loved the water. When I wasn't out with my old man, if I had free time, I was usually at one of the city's waterfront parks, reading or just daydreaming. I loved to watch the thunderstorms roll in off the water in the summer.

It was the first time since leaving that I'd seriously considered coming back to stay. California wasn't for me. Square pegs, round holes. And the Pacific was too damned cold. What the hell's the point of living near the water if you needed a wetsuit to enjoy it?

Eventually, I resumed the walk, my path taking me north along the water with some slight deviations where the walkway ended. I kept moving until Cody's game was over and curiosity got the better of me. I checked my phone. As much as she wanted to be there for her son, Donna Portman hadn't traveled to Dallas to watch Cody play because she was afraid of losing what little she had left. Goddamn those people for doing this to her.

Gulf Coast won close in another upset. They were moving on to the Elite Eight, the "Cinderella" narratives already blossoming across the internet.

Funnily enough, I didn't know if that outcome was good or bad.

I'd done what I could for the Portmans. It wasn't enough, but I'd at least convinced some sympathetic cops to get others to take notice that yes, that fire was probably arson, just not caused by the Portmans. People were looking out for them now. I'd have to hope that was enough.

Now to unravel the two mysteries at hand. One—who killed my client? Two—where was Olivia McEvoy?

Little and less to go on. The call that got Jimmy into that seedy neighborhood would've come from a burner, so no point tracing that. However, he'd said it was a prospective client. That might mean he'd logged the call with an assistant or put it in a tracking system. Also, if the firm issued his phone, their IT people might be able to trace records. I assumed the call had come from a burner, but I really didn't know for sure and had to run that down. I would check in with Elena and see what internal support she could provide.

My phone rang.

I didn't even look at the number, my head was elsewhere, and I just answered it.

It was Ray Ruiz.

My promise to Lieutenant Silvestri to totally ignore him lasted about four hours. Maybe I was getting better at this.

## 23

Most of the things I wanted to say to Ruiz were violent, and I reminded myself this conversation could well be recorded. If his lawyer wanted to undermine the state's case against his client, getting something sketchy on the phone would be a good way to do it.

With that in mind, I said, "Before we begin, I need to tell you that I do not consent to this conversation being recorded." Again, I'm not as conversant in Florida's privacy laws. In California, that would stop him cold. Just in case he hadn't taken my advice, I said, "Ray, you agreed to join me at the Miami-Dade Police Headquarters today. Remember how we were going to talk about an undercover operation, which you agreed to support, in exchange for the consideration of immunity to a litany of crimes they want to prosecute you for?"

The scene of that recording being played in a courtroom brought a smile to my face.

"I couldn't go there today," he said.

"Why?"

"Because they can't protect me. My lawyer said as much."

"So, he knows you're working with Acuna and Marrero?" I said, you know, for the record.

"Cathcart knows about Acuna and how I didn't know who he was, or what he wanted, until it was too late."

Convinced Ray wasn't mugging for any potential courtroom playback, I decided to drop the act. He'd never admit to any of that if he thought this might come back on him.

So, Ray's attorney knew about one gangster and not the other? Was Ray keeping that one hidden? More to the point, why does he think he can keep it that way? He knew I knew about Marrero. Which meant he had to know the police were aware of it too.

The obvious answer was that he was protecting that relationship with Marrero, because he expects to come out of this with Acuna in jail and himself absolved of any wrongdoing.

But that felt too easy.

And, if someone was trying to throw me off the tail of Jimmy's killer, what better shiny object to chase in its place than this.

"Why am I talking to you, Ray?"

"I can still help you out. I'm just not taking that deal. The cops are going to go back on it, put me in lockup to scare me. As soon as they do, Acuna's people get me. Forget that. I'll help you take him out, but I'm not officially involved."

"When did Acuna contact you?"

"Today. He wanted to know when he was meeting with my guy, Jameson."

"And you didn't tell him anything about the police?"

"No."

Listening for stress indicators over the phone was possible but rarely conclusive. Most of the unconscious indicators of deception are physical rather than verbal. Without being able to see him, I'd have to take him at his word.

"He wants to talk to you tomorrow night at his club."

"No, we do this at your place. You need to have skin in the game."

"Out of the question. Cathcart says that'll be like admitting guilt."

"Guilt," I said glacially slow. "But you actually *did* do this shit." Before he could protest, I said, "What does your attorney think about you setting up a mobster like this?"

"Don't be an asshole, Gage."

"Ray, if you took any more sides, you'd be a fucking octagon."

"Cathcart keeps me out of jail, which is best for my near-term survival. Taking Acuna out is best for my long-term survival, so I'm willing to work with you and the cops to do that. Are you going to be there or not?"

"I'll let you know," I said. "I need to clear this with the police and make sure they're still willing to work with you. And why am I the go-between? Shouldn't this offer to help be coming from your lawyer?"

"I don't trust the police."

"Ray, not showing up today was stupid. You and Cathcart could've rolled in and made any deal you wanted. You kept going on and on about immunity, and you might have pissed that away by standing them up. I can't broker you a deal. I'm not an officer of the court. Cathcart has to work that out with La Barca. The best I can do is tell Silvestri you're willing to cooperate in nailing Acuna. But, Ray, and I'm serious here, they are going to need you to give up some names. You hinted before that someone forced you into this, that they pushed you into the arrangement with Acuna and Marrero. Was that Rizzo? Was it Bream? Was it someone else?"

"I told you I'm not saying a word about that until I have a signed immunity deal. You people want me to risk my life, and then you're just going to throw it away."

This was one of the few times in my life when I was generally confounded by someone.

"What happened to you?" I said.

"I don't understand."

"The first time I met you, I figured you were someone who, maybe, was going to be caught speeding. I'm having a hard time reconciling the stat-quoting sports junkie with a mob money launderer."

"I keep telling you, Gage. It wasn't me."

He hung up.

I didn't feel like talking to anyone right then. I'd let Silvestri know Ray called, because she told me to stay away from him and I didn't want it getting back to her that Ray and I had spoken. Though unless Cathcart and La Barca could find some kind of arrangement, it didn't much matter.

As I found my way back to the hotel, I realized I might have a way to track Olivia, or at least her laptop. I had the computer's IP address, which would show me the device's last known location. I just prayed the thing wasn't in a landfill somewhere. Once I was in my room, I fired up a trace program and found her device easily enough. The lat/long return showed the last time the device accessed a network was at her condo. It wasn't currently connected. Probably something I should've tried earlier.

What I needed was access to her phone. I knew she used a MacBook, so if the laptop was on, I could also use that to find her phone.

It was questionable, but I was also running out of options.

There were other ways to get that information, and none of them were legal.

Unfortunately, the laptop wasn't on, so all I had was its last known location.

Trying to put those thoughts out of my head, I called Silvestri and filled her in.

"This case reverses one more time, I'm going to file a worker's comp claim for whiplash," she said.

"What do you think? Is it worth pursuing? Do you trust him?"

"Immunity is probably off the table now, and La Barca won't go for it anyway without Ruiz convincing us he knows something earth-shatteringly good. Right now, he's got nothing to bargain with but Acuna."

"That's what I told him," I said.

"I have a vested interest in taking Jorge Acuna off the streets. What's your stake in this?"

"I'm sure either Acuna or Marrero ordered Lawson killed. More pressing is the situation with Cody Portman. Irrespective of Jimmy, we know Acuna did that."

"Allegedly. But I get you. Your logic isn't wrong. Though I don't see what Acuna gets by killing Lawson."

"Other than ending the investigation into his money-laundering operation. I don't think Ruiz could pull a trigger."

"You've got a soft spot for this guy," she said.

"No, I know the type, and he's not it."

"Desperate people do stupid and dangerous things. The way you've described Ruiz to me, he's terrified and using drugs and alcohol. These are not the foundations of sound decision making. Push him far enough, and he snaps."

"I mean, you're not *wrong*. I don't know. I just don't see it."

"Forest from the trees, Gage." Neither of us spoke for a while. "Look, if you're willing to go undercover for me, I'm grateful for the assist. I'll call La Barca and try to talk him off the ledge. Don't—"

"Do anything stupid, I know."

"One more thing. I have enough that I can go to a magistrate and get a wiretap authorization for Ruiz's phone. And now for this club in Little Havana where Acuna allegedly has his headquarters. That was information we didn't have an hour ago." Silvestri paused, and I couldn't exactly hear the gears grinding, though it seemed an awful lot like they were. "I will call La Barca and get his thoughts. Fair warning, immunity will be a tough sell. If Ray doesn't go for this, we'll need to walk away, and I don't want you going rogue on me."

"Michelle, there isn't a lot of time on this."

"It's my next call, Matt. But don't push it. You're lucky I'm willing to even entertain this. I'll be in touch."

She called me back within the hour to say La Barca had signed off on me meeting with Acuna and Ruiz

I called Ruiz, letting him know I'd be there and that Jameson Carter would have his assistant with him. I could front, but Silvestri had to have one of her cops present to make the bust.

"Are you out of your damn mind? You want to get us all killed? You go, and you go alone. That's the deal, man."

"No, Ray. There's no flex on this. We're willing to bend on not doing this in your office, but you have to convince them to let me bring someone with. It'll go better for you, if you do."

"What do you mean?"

"You need to show the police you're willing to work with them."

"Acuna will immediately think something is up. No way. It has to be just you and me or there's no deal."

"If there's no deal, Ray, you get arrested."

"Do you want this guy or not?"

We could circle the drain on this point for hours, and I knew we wouldn't make any more headway. It wasn't my fight. Deciding to leave this one for the DA, I asked, "What time?"

Ray said, "Nine."

---

I was at the Doral HQ early the next morning. The desk sergeant paged someone from Silvestri's squad, and the female detective I'd seen the last time I was here met me at the front. Ava Baptiste was her name. She led me back to their squad area and offered me a fresh cup of coffee, which I graciously accepted.

"You sure you're up for this?" she asked as we walked.

I'd told Silvestri that I had more time undercover than any five cops in this department combined, and I believed that stat was accurate. It didn't change the fact that I was going into a dangerous situation with my violent death as a likely outcome. I was doing this for the Portmans, and I was doing this to get answers about Jimmy. So, I spared Detective Baptiste the bravado and just said, "Yeah. I'm ready."

Silvestri pulled me aside before the briefing started.

"No dice on getting an additional person. La Barca spoke with Ruiz's lawyer and said it's not possible. Ruiz said they are only willing to meet with him and you."

"Okay," I said. "So where does that leave us?"

"We can still do this, but you'll have to wear a wire. We've got some decent toys, probably not as good as what you're used to. We're just a humble, small-town police department." She gave me a wry smile.

"Where did they land on immunity?"

Silvestri shook her head. "La Barca said it's not inked yet. Ruiz has to deliver Marrero *and* Acuna. La Barca gave Ruiz's attorney a conditional approval, though it hinges on what happens tonight."

We assembled in the squad room, and Silvestri briefed the team, bringing them current on the information I'd given her the night before.

"Team, this is fast, even for us. We would not normally do it this way, but the DA's office and I both agree it's likely our best bet to connect the Acuna *marielito* with Ray Ruiz and his operation. Mr. Gage, posing as a businessman, will enter the Son Cubana with Ruiz at nine p.m. The intent is to offer Acuna an option to expand the money-laundering operation. Ruiz will facilitate that. Mr. Gage will describe the ways in which he'll be able to reallocate and distribute Acuna's money. We move in once we have confirmation that Acuna has accepted the terms. Once we've got him and his people in custody, we're going to hit them with the four other murders we suspect them of."

Silvestri had explained to me earlier that Acuna's group was implicated in several homicides. They just lacked sufficient proof for a charge. Once they had Acuna and his key people in custody for racketeering, they hoped to start flipping the underlings to rat out the boss.

Silvestri finished with, "Okay, let's review assignments. Ava?"

Baptiste, the cop who signed me in, was about five-three with a brown complexion. "I checked the club out last night after the LT told me it was on." She went over to the whiteboard and drew a diagram, showing the bar, the stage, and the back office where she assumed the meeting would be. Baptiste also marked where the "bouncers" were positioned, which she assumed were Acuna heavies. "I could've rolled the lot of 'em up for guns, I can tell you that. They keep the music loud, and its typical Latin, lots of drums and horns. A mic wouldn't pick up shit on the dance floor. I did step into the ladies' room and make a quick voice recording on my phone."

"That's not fair. Every time I make a recording in the ladies' room, I get written up," a brick shithouse detective named O'Connor said.

Baptiste flipped him off and smirked.

"How'd the recording turn out?" Silvestri asked.

Baptiste shrugged. "Lots of background noise. I could hear myself okay, but the distance test wasn't great. It was a small space, just one toilet. So I set my phone on the sink and moved about five feet away. You can make out my voice. Is that going to be good enough for a courtroom? Who knows?"

"Mostly, I'm worried about our being able to pick up Matt's duress call. I get what you're saying, though. I think our mic is a little better than the phone," Silvestri said.

"I'm still not comfortable sending an informant in like this," a detective named Tran said.

"I'm not an informant," I said.

"Maybe we shouldn't go in on something so half-assed, then," Tran said.

"You got a better idea?" I asked.

"Yeah, we stuff this shit and go back to our regular caseload. This wasn't even on our radar a week ago. Sorry some kid's house burned down, but maybe he shouldn't have taken mob money."

"Not sure if they teach fraud at the police academy here, but typically the marks don't know the money is tainted," I said.

"That's enough," Silvestri barked. "Tran, knock it off. This case is good enough for the DA, so it ought to be good enough for you. I expect best effort out of everyone. If you can't do that, I'll find someone who can. Matt, you're a civilian now. And there's a direct relationship between the thickness of the ice you're standing on and how heavy your steps should be."

I nodded once and said nothing else. I hoped Tran wouldn't be backing me up.

Baptiste wrapped up her briefing on Acuna's club. She'd found an office on the second floor, accessed by a stairway at the back. She'd made it most of the way up the stairs, claiming she was looking for a bathroom, before someone caught her and steered her back down.

Silvestri showed me the mic we'd be using. It was built into the outer shell of a ruggedized smartwatch, which she explained would provide omnidirectional pickup. Under normal conditions, it could reliably record conversation ten feet away. It was better tech than I'd guess a police department would have, though she explained it was left over from their multi-year operation with the FBI.

We rehearsed the meet several times, with Tran playing Acuna's part. I assumed Silvestri did that on purpose since he was already hostile and didn't want to be here.

Silvestri looked at me. "Let's review the radio signals. We'll be listening for it, but just in case it's not clear from the conversation, once Acuna agrees to the terms, you say, 'It's a deal.' We should be there within sixty seconds. 'Thunder' is the extraction code. That means you're in imminent danger, and we'll come running, regardless of whether you got evidence or not."

"Got it," I said."

"This is important. You need to get Acuna to say exactly what he wants and, if possible, how much he's willing to pay."

"Understood. Where will you be?"

"We'll have an undercover unit in the alley behind, and two on the street out front. O'Connell and Baptiste will be in the bar with concealed earpieces. If you make the call, we're there in less than a minute."

A lot can happen in a minute when guns are drawn. I also knew that was a pretty good response time.

We broke in the early afternoon to get ready.

Before I left, Silvestri said, "I shouldn't need to remind you of the rules, but it's you, so I will. You're a civilian. You cannot have a weapon on you. They'll frisk you anyway. Don't do it."

"I understand."

Silvestri told me, again, that I didn't have to go through with this.

I told her, again, that I would.

## 24

I wore a dark camp shirt, tan pants, and white canvas sneakers. A suit would look too much like I was trying to hide a mic, so I opted for the outfit that would take that question off the table. Our showtime was 6:00 p.m. I paid a visit to Ray at his office to make sure he was going to be there tonight.

No word from Olivia. She hadn't checked in at work, and the security guard at her building had no record of her either. Silvestri was coordinating with MPD for a wellness check. My needle moved from "generally concerned" to "seriously worried" about her well-being.

Six o'clock.

Silvestri ran a tight briefing. Everyone confirmed where they'd be, by when, what their jobs were, and what they'd do if one of the danger codes came over the net. This was a good operation, for as hastily as it'd come together.

And it was so full of holes it wouldn't even float in a bathtub.

I left at eight to get ready, running a full SDR just to make myself feel better.

At eight thirty, Ray picked me up at a park in Brickell in his Aston Martin SUV.

"Where's your boy?" I asked.

"Who?"

"Farrier," I said. "Assumed he'd be here."

"Not a lot of good he's doing me right now," Ray said in a way that wasn't convincing.

We drove in silence after that. He parked two blocks away from Acuna's club, and we walked through the nighttime streets of Little Havana. It was a warm night, and the sounds of music from half a dozen venues poured out into the street, mixing with the smells of tobacco and Caribbean food. Like most neighborhoods that centered around an expat ethnicity, nighttime belonged to the locals.

Ruiz stayed quiet. I didn't try to make small talk, though I did try to hit him with some softball questions just to make sure his head was still in the game. As it was, I thought he'd vibrate out of his skin. Couldn't say I blamed him. Ruiz had played a dangerous game—and one that was wholly out of his league. This was a desperation play, a crooked Hail Mary. I couldn't say that, in the moment, Ray fully grasped the stakes or what was about to happen.

Son Cubana was in the center of the block and painted bright orange with an equally loud yellow awning. A stubby line extended from the front door like a fat caterpillar, undulating slightly to the loud echoes of music from inside. There was a tobacco shop on one side and a bodega on the other. Word was Acuna owned the tobacconist, and the bodega paid protection through the nose, even though it would be suicidal to hit a place next door to Acuna's headquarters.

We stopped at the bouncer, a big dude with a napping squirrel for a mustache. Ruiz leaned in and told him "Mr. Reyes" was expecting us. They didn't use Acuna's name in public, I noted. Good tradecraft. The bouncer nodded and waved at the door. We stepped inside and plowed into a wall of music. The place was packed, and while I could make out the bar along the far wall, I couldn't see O'Connell and Baptiste. I also didn't see how they were going to hear a radio call unless it was delivered by field artillery.

Ruiz pushed his way through the throng to the back of the room. It was a big club with a live band tonight. They played on a stage set along the back wall, and judging by where the stairs were, the stage was right beneath the office. So, perfect for recording a conversation with a clandestine microphone. Right.

We found another bouncer at the back stairs. Looked like he came from the same factory as the guy out front. It was too loud to exchange words, so he just jerked his chin up a few degrees when he recognized Ruiz. The heavy pointed at me and jerked his thumb at the stairs. I was two steps up when I turned to see that Ruiz wasn't following. The bouncer was blocking the door.

I gave both a questioning look and then pointed at Ray.

The bouncer said, "Jus' you," loud enough for me to hear.

I took a step down, closing the gap. "He's supposed to be there. He set this whole goddamn thing up," I shouted.

An index finger that might've belonged to Zeus throttled me in the chest. "Jus'. You."

The words of an old teacher and mentor flashed into my mind.

Jackie Kerr was a legend in the Clandestine Service. His covert operations career, which spanned nearly thirty years, constituted a black epic that would astound people if they knew even half of what he'd accomplished on behalf of this country. He'd retired from active service by the time I met him, but the Agency brought him back as a contractor. When I'd been attached to a black ops unit, Jackie trained us in his dark arts. Among the many nuggets of wisdom he dropped on us, there was a particular favorite about walking into known dangerous situations. Jackie would tell you, "There are three rules for walking into a trap. Number One: you know it's a trap, stupid—don't do it. Two: failing Number One, have a Quick Response Force on immediate standby to bail your ass out. Three: see Rule Number One."

Jackie would kick my ass if he saw me walking up those stairs. Because I knew better, and he'd trained me to know better.

I went anyway, because I'm either cosmically rooted to uncovering the truth or pathologically stupid.

Or both.

Probably both.

There was another goon at the top, and the door was on the left. He pressed his bulk into the corner somehow so I could pass by without touching him. The guy pushed in right behind me and knocked twice on the smoked-glass office door. It opened, and he shoved me inside. There were four men in the room. One next to the door to my immediate left, two on a couch who were now standing, and a fourth lounging against a desk. They all looked to be between twenty and forty, except the guy leaning against the desk, in white pants and a blue and white guayabera. I recognized him immediately—Jorge Acuna. He was about fifty, squat, powerfully built but also a little pudgy. At the same time, naked aggression practically oozed out of his pores. He was the living embodiment of a chip on a shoulder. I also recognized one of the others from the photos in Silvestri's squad room. The space was stuffy and poorly lit with a tired yellow light. It smelled like old cigars. There was a glass tumbler with the ghost of a drink on the desk.

The door closed behind me, with the goon stepping back outside. Most certainly to continue his guard on the other side. That ruled out me making a break for it.

There was no question of what this was.

The guy to my left gave me a pat down and then had me lift my shirt to show I wasn't wearing a wire. Which is what happened when you learned about this stuff from watching television.

"Good evening...Mr. Carter, was it?" Acuna said.

Fast recon of the room.

The one who had patted me down was young and of average build. I could see the imprint of a pistol grip tucked into his waistband beneath his shirt. The two guys on the couch were a little bigger—they'd be the muscle. I couldn't immediately place the weapons on them, but I would assume they were armed anyway.

Acuna smiled, and it was an ugly thing. I could see in his eyes he was no stranger to violence. The desk he leaned on was nothing special, just black metal and hard corners. There were three windows behind it, with shades drawn. I knew from their position in the building they overlooked the alley behind the club. Silvestri should be parked maybe a hundred feet from where I stood.

I said, "So, what is this exactly? Ruiz said Mr. Acuna was looking to invest some money. Is that you? I assume so, since you're doing the talking."

"Ruiz talks too much," Acuna said, and I had to strain to hear him over the noise from the band beneath us.

I continued the charade, saying, "I'm told this was Acuna's idea." I looked down at my watch, hoping Silvestri was picking this up in the van. "This also isn't the only meeting I've got tonight. Are we talking business or what?" I splayed my arms and looked around.

"Busy man," Acuna said to the others and chuckled.

"What's your name, chief? Are you Acuna, or not?"

If he thought he was being recorded, I could see him not admitting to it.

Again, that forced chortle. "Sure."

"Great. So, Mr. Acuna, do you handle the business or is that going to be someone else?"

"Listen, Mr. Carter, there isn't going to be any business."

"Then what the hell am I doing here?" I said with just enough force.

"We wanted to talk to you about your association with Mr. Ruiz. You seem to be asking a lot of questions. Like, cop-type questions. You a cop, Mr. Carter?"

"I'm not a cop. What I am is getting pissed off for having my time wasted."

"Ohhh," he said and punctuated it with a dirty, manufactured laugh. "We don't want that."

"Ruiz said you wanted to do business. He said you have money to invest in one of my businesses in exchange for a very favorable rate of return. And a...call it a service fee. So, what the hell is this? I came here in good faith."

"Oh, I doubt that very much."

"Then what am I doing here?" Shaking my head, I turned to leave. The guy to my left put an arm up across the door. I turned back around.

"That's a good question, Mr. ...Carter." Acuna looked to the other men in the room, unspoken signals exchanged. "See, what we want to know is—"

"Yeah, I'm not interested in what you want to know," I said. "I'm not here to answer your questions, pal, unless that question is where do you send the check? If you're not going to do it, I'll thank you for wasting my goddamn time and call it a night. That good enough for you?"

"Playing the tough guy...well, that's not what you want to do here."

"Oh, and what do I want to do?"

"You want to tell us who hired you to spy on us. See, we don't think you're here to 'do business.' We know someone hired a private detective to stick their nose where it don't belong. You know what they say on that kids' show—one of these things don't look like the other one. I look around for the thing that's out of place, and that looks like you."

*Stick to your cover.*

"I don't know where you're getting your information from," I said, playing on the chance that they weren't sure about Jameson Carter's bona fides and this was a pressure test. If they were serious about laundering money, they'd want to make sure it wasn't a trap.

"Like I said, Ruiz talks too much," Acuna said with a dismissive shrug.

"What about Senator Rizzo? He talk too much, too?" I asked with a slight smile. "Or just enough?" Acuna didn't respond immediately, and I could see the math happening behind his eyes. He wasn't used to being outmaneuvered *and* wasn't used to having to think on his feet. This was a guy who made statements and, I suspected, didn't spend a lot of time listening to the responses. He'd get wrecked on a witness stand. "I understand a few things from Frank and a few other things from Ray. Rizzo connected the two of you, and business was probably fine for a time, though it wasn't going as fast as you'd hoped. Ray also wants out of the game, so he offered to connect you to a bigger fish—which would be me—in the hopes that I could move your money at a higher volume. How am I doing so far?"

Acuna stayed quiet. Just glared at me through narrow slits.

"You didn't know Ray wanted out, did you? I can see by the look on your face that's news."

"I don't know no Frank Rizzo. I don't vote," Acuna said, and his lackeys chuckled because they were expected to. "But if I did, he'd probably say you were a nuisance."

So, Acuna *did* know the senator. That was useful. I really hoped Silvestri was getting all this.

"Tell me, Jorge, you following the basketball tournament at all?"

"Ray really does run that fuckin' mouth of his, doesn't he? Might have to do something about that too. I've heard enough outta you. Carlos, show Mr. ....Carter out. Wait, was it Carter, you said your name was or—" Acuna looked down at a piece of paper on his desk "—Matt Gage?"

The thug on my left reached out and dropped his meat paw of a hand on my right shoulder.

I'll give Ray this, he was a cunning little bastard. He wouldn't have told Acuna that I was working with the cops, because that'd get Ray killed just as surely as it would me. Instead, he'd have Acuna take me out, and the police would just follow the breadcrumbs, hook Acuna for my murder, and now Ray was clear of all his problems.

"Tell me, how do you hear yourself think with that band? Sounds like thunder."

Acuna shook his head slowly. "Now, Carlos."

Assuming they heard me on the radio, allegedly I had sixty seconds before this place was surrounded by cops.

I prayed it would be fast enough. Acuna was raw malevolence. He was a true psychopath. Other lives didn't register on any meaningful scale. They were simply things that existed and could just as simply cease to exist if it suited him.

"What's your game here, Acuna?"

"Game?"

"Why bring me up here?"

"That would seem...obvious, no?"

"Explain it to me," I said. "You owe me that much."

"I don't owe you shit."

"What are you doing with Cody Portman?"

"I think you're asking a lot of questions you got no business asking," he said.

"You're not going to let me out of here anyway, so why not just answer me? I care what happens to the kid and his family."

Acuna shrugged. "Okay, tough guy. Kid's got nothing to worry about as long as he does what he's told."

"Where is Olivia McEvoy?"

"Who?" Acuna asked, and his face looked like I'd just asked him to explain string theory. He genuinely had no idea what I was talking about.

I did my part and chewed up clock. Still, there were no cops to be seen. Even if they'd heard me, the two at the bar had to charge through a crowded dance floor, past a pro wrestler at the bottom of the stairs and another at the top. That would take a minute. I needed more time.

I saw motion out of the corner of my eye.

Okay, here we go.

The smoked-glass door was at my back.

You know what electricians tend to put right next to doors? Light switches.

Carlos was to my immediate left. I pivoted on my left foot and used the momentum to drive the heel of my right hand into his jaw. His head snapped back and bounced off the wall. With my left hand, I grabbed the pistol beneath his shirt.

I don't have a lot of sympathy for people stupid enough to stick their guns in the front of their pants.

Because accidents happen.

Or someone with a higher degree of hand-to-hand combat training and faster reflexes grabs the weapon first and pulls the trigger.

Ruiz was right about one thing. I *am* an asshole.

The gun's report was second only to the man's screaming. I didn't know if it was pain, terror, or both. I ripped the gun free—he wasn't fighting at this point—and saw a smoking hole in his pants. I didn't see any blood, so maybe I'd missed the goods.

While the other three were fumbling for their weapons, I hit the light switch with my elbow. The room plunged into darkness, save the dim glow of the streetlight. Coming through the shaded windows, the outside light gave a mottled, dark silhouette to the men in front of me.

I fired twice at the floor, close to where I'd seen the others standing. I didn't want to hit them necessarily, just back them off. I also wouldn't lose any sleep if one of them lost a toe. Then I put four rounds into the farthest right window in a tight clockwork pattern.

Confused shouting and hasty instructions to kill me ensued.

Carlos was still screaming next to me.

Two ways out of this room, and neither option was particularly good. There was a guarded door behind me, and by the feel of it, that guard was trying to come through. My weight against the door held him back for now. Even if I did manage to get past him, the stairs were next. And that meant I'd have to shoot my way out. It also meant I'd be running down a dark stairwell, relying on an amped-up cop to make the right split-second decision that I wasn't a bad guy. The other option was the window, which I'd hopefully just made easier to get out of.

Window it would be.

The three in front of me couldn't see me as well in the dark, whereas I had the contrast of their shapes against the windows. Three fast steps had me across the room. Acuna's gun came up. I blocked it with my left hand, knocking it away just before a round escaped the chamber. Twisting my hand to wrap my left arm around his, I pivoted and used all my weight to swing him around me.

And into the window.

Acuna staggered backward, reaction-firing twice, both shots missing. He crashed into the window I'd shot out, and I surged forward, hitting him hard in the chest with both hands, one of which still held a pistol. Acuna fell through the broken glass and crashed onto the roof. He'd cleared most of the obstruction for me, so all I had to do was step through it. Shards still clinging to the frame scratched me as I passed.

The other two thugs would have clued in by now and were probably running toward the window. Figure the one on the other of the door was with them.

I was on a thin strip of rooftop before it dropped off to the alley. The buildings on either side were single story with a short, jumpable gap between them. Acuna writhed at my feet. Probably had a lot of cuts on his back.

Maybe there's a morality tale for not murdering strangers.

What I did *not* see were police cars charging in with lights and sirens.

Criminal organizations have a lot in common with terror cells. The bosses make all the decisions and delegate action to the grunts, who are typically below average intelligence. These aren't people used to thinking on their feet or making decisions, because questioning the boss will usually get you killed. So, it didn't surprise me that the three still inside burned a precious few seconds figuring out what to do next. They probably knew they needed to catch and kill me, the *how* was evading them. No doubt, Acuna had given strict instructions not to draw attention to the club, so they were debating whether to shoot or chase. Those precious few seconds had allowed my escape.

Acuna was moving now. I could hear him behind me. Too bad, he had just enough awareness to not roll over and, subsequently, off the roof.

Navigating the roof as quickly as I could, I made my way over to a wider section so I could pick up speed.

Shouts behind me. I didn't need to turn and look.

The club's second floor included just Acuna's office, so the roof was mostly level with the two buildings on either side. I jumped the short gap between the club and the tobacco shop and aimed for the alley, where Silvestri was supposed to be.

Adrenaline has a way of overestimating human performance.

Running at a full clip, I put one hand down on the edge of the roof and sailed into the air.

The fall took long enough for the "oh shit" to register in my brain.

The hard shock of striking asphalt informed me I'd hit the ground. Some back corner of my mind remembered to roll with the impact, though there wasn't a lot about jumping off a building that one could practice. The pistol clattered somewhere in the darkness.

Pain followed as soon as the body realized what I'd just done.

Everything hurt, and I'd landed hard on my right leg. It didn't feel broken

All I wanted to do was lie there and bleed. Voices on the roof shook me out of it. I rolled over onto my stomach and pushed myself up to all fours, then stood, staggering backward into the yellow-orange lamplight behind the tobacco shop. I pushed myself against the wall at the edge of the light where I knew it would be the darkest.

Acuna's goons were directly overhead. My Spanish was good enough that I could make out they had no idea where I was—also that they thought I was nuts. They weren't jumping off that roof. They were, however, coming after me. Give it two minutes, tops, for them to make it back inside, down the stairs, and out the back door. Assuming they didn't run into O'Connell and Baptiste inside.

Speaking of...

I looked down the alley in both directions.

Silvestri was supposed to be in the command-post van monitoring traffic in the alley.

There wasn't a van to be seen.

That's...not good.

## 25

There would be time to sort out what in the actual holy hell happened to my law enforcement backup...assuming I survived the next three minutes.

The thugs were still on the roof, planning their move.

I could hear Acuna barking orders out the shattered window and a hell of a lot of commotion.

Unfortunately, these guys were slightly smarter than I'd first given them credit for, because they'd decided to leave one of them behind on the roof as a lookout.

This wasn't an alley so much as it was a box canyon made of cinderblocks and chain-link.

To the left, there was a building extending all the way through the alley, effectively cutting it off. In front of me, there were a line of tall, leafy trees that gave a little barrier between the businesses and what looked like residential property. I could now make out a wooden fence, about seven feet tall, just behind the trees. I wasn't scaling that without help. The only way to go was to the right.

Just to be sure, I tested the tobacco shop's back door. It was locked.

I didn't know where the gun had landed and couldn't see it in what little light there was. Looking for it was going to get me shot. Instead, I broke into a dead run.

My right leg didn't like that idea.

Pain shot up from my foot—I must have twisted or sprained something. Still, my foot held the weight, so I'd sort out whatever problem that was later. Running as fast as I could manage, which was a limping gait, I heard a curse from the roof and then three rounds splitting the air.

Stupid.

You could maybe hide the sound of gunfire in a building with overly loud, thumping music. Outside, one shot might sound like a car backfiring. Three shots would only sound like gunfire.

By the time I'd cleared the adjacent building, the door was open and there were shouts in the alley, plus commands from the roof. It didn't take long to figure out why Silvestri wasn't where she'd planned to be. Someone had parked a delivery truck across the alley, sealing it off. There was enough of a gap between the bumper's rusty edge and the building next to it, and I squeezed through. Bullets dinged off the rusted metal.

There was a stubby parking lot on the far side of the dumpster. I hit that and accelerated. The obstruction slowed my pursuers enough that I could put some distance between us. Running, I shouted into the watch, "Thunder! Thunder! Fucking thunder! Where the hell are you people?"

I cleared the parking lot before the first pursuer made it through the thin gap, and I was over the chain-link fence on the far side.

I hit the ground and rolled, pushed myself off the ground, and took off.

The night cracked with two more shots.

More shouting behind me.

I made the far side of the lot, vaulted that fence, the tops of the chain link digging painfully into my palms.

Streetlights and asphalt. I'd made a cross street.

Was I safe, though?

Chancing a glance back the way I'd come, I could see forms in the darkness running, seemingly in all directions. At least two were scaling the first of the two fences I'd just topped.

Calle Ocho was right in front of me. Nine thirty on a weeknight, and the street was still busy and bright with both pedestrian and vehicle traffic. I started off, and my leg told me in no uncertain terms that it'd run as much as it planned to. I waited for a car to pass and crossed the street, now about half a block away from Acuna's club.

I heard a shout from behind me and turned. Couldn't make out what was said.

One of Acuna's hoods stood on the corner beneath a streetlight, pistol raised. The wall behind him was plastered with faded and torn handbills, and the street was bleached gray from constant sun exposure. The still-shot image of a man aiming a gun at me frozen in my mind.

I froze, couldn't move if I'd wanted to.

Then Detective Tran crashed into the guy with a flying, open-field tackle and put the guy's face into the street.

Since I could hear it from this far away, I had to assume it hurt.

The night exploded into lights and sirens as police cars swarmed the street.

---

Because this was their jurisdiction, Miami PD handled crowd control and blocked off the street with half a dozen squad cars. By now, the crowd from Acuna's club had been ushered out to the pavement, and cops were taking statements. I also saw officers weaving through the crowds with printed pictures, presumably of Acuna and his enforcers.

After first talking with Miami Police's on-scene commander for a good while, Silvestri sent word through one of her officers that we were going to meet up at the van.

"All right, let's first start with what we know," Silvestri said. She was joined by a thick-set cop, balding with a mustache, whom I hadn't met yet. "This is Detective Morales from Miami PD's organized crime unit." He nodded. Silvestri continued. "Matt, I'm sorry, we couldn't hear you over the radio. We didn't get the duress call until you were already outside. We did hear the bullets and responded then. Again, I'm sorry. I appreciate you taking a risk for us. We have three people in custody. The one Detective Tran tackled, one of the men inside, and another with, ah, some curious powder burns and a leg wound." A pause for the laugh track. "We've also got all of the staff rounded up, though I'm not expecting much."

"Acuna?" I asked. Something in the air told me I already had that answer.

Silvestri shook her head.

"We don't have him. He could've gone out through the window and over to an adjacent building, out the kitchen, or just waited on the dance floor with everyone else."

"Acuna dove out the window. There's no way he went back in and hid on the dance floor," I said.

"At any rate, Detective Morales's people are out knocking on doors and working informants, but frankly, the odds of us finding Jorge Acuna in Little Havana are laughably bad."

So, what she was really saying was the mobster psychopath was in the wind and they had no leads.

"The three we do have...those will be gun charges, though I'm not sure that's enough to flip them."

"The guy with the shot to the leg? Acuna ordered him to kill me."

"Did he use those specific words?"

"No, but it was pretty obvious from context."

"Walk us through it, please."

I described everything from the point where Ruiz and I walked into the club to when Detective Tran faceplanted Acuna's heavy into the pavement. "So, you didn't get any audio at all?" I asked.

"No."

"Then you didn't hear Acuna acknowledge knowing Senator Frank Rizzo or that Cody Portman was safe as long as he did what he was told?"

Silvestri shook a negative, and I didn't rub it in.

They couldn't hear me, but they did hear the gunshots in the office and that had gotten them moving. The reason the *marielitos* were able to make it outside was because it was too loud inside the club for O'Connell and Baptiste to hear the initial radio call. It wasn't until they didn't roger the first one that Silvestri screamed onto the net, and they finally heard it.

Ruiz was also in the wind. Silvestri had posted someone on the street to watch the door, but Ray never came back out, so he must've gone to the back. They made a tactical error in not having someone at the back of the building, instead staying at the end of the alley. I can only assume Silvestri believed they'd be covered by having a van in the adjacent parking lot. I also had a sneaking suspicion Acuna had that truck parked there on purpose.

They hadn't had the exits covered, and that was on them.

Silvestri put her hands on her hips. "We can't prove it was a setup. Ruiz will claim he had no idea because the bouncer wouldn't let him up the stairs. I think we can get the bouncer to flip, though, especially once we start talking 'accessory to attempted murder' charges. Same goes for the heavies. I'll talk it over with La Barca, make sure he's on board. If any of these idiots have priors, we can play that too. We'll shut the club down for a good while. I'll have my people going over it. We'll get to look at their books. My guess is the club will come out clean. I'm going to ask the county health inspector to make problems for the place, and we can get them shut down for a while. It'll at least take away some of his money-laundering vectors."

Seemed like Silvestri was trying to make a good showing in front of the MPD cop. Unless those hoods were already on their second strikes, getting them to flip their boss over gun possession charges would be a tough sell. Maybe they could bump two of the charges up to Assault with a Deadly Weapon—that would help. Still.

Acuna getting away was an embarrassment.

"Matt, why don't you go back to your hotel and get some sleep? We'll need to do a formal deposition with La Barca tomorrow."

"Okay," I said. "Thanks for being there."

She nodded.

"Make sure you see O'Connell on the way out. He needs to print you."

"What for?"

"We need to clear you on that gun. Also, for what it's worth, I think it's highly unlikely Acuna does anything with this Portman kid. We just raided his headquarters. He's going to turtle up for a while."

I wished I had her confidence. I did not.

By the time I'd finished with statements and fingerprints and driven back to the hotel, it was about twelve thirty. I showered and availed myself of the minibar's regenerating whiskey supply.

I found sleep eventually.

The worst parts of a terrible thing have a way of only coming to light after daybreak. Night confuses things, hides them, rounds the sharp edges. Daylight hides nothing. When I woke, I knew how bad it was. Silvestri and her team took a long shot at a violent criminal and came up short. Acuna knew they were onto him and could now go to ground, hide his moves.

Though I'd confirmed Acuna was behind the points-fixing scheme, it was for my ears only. The goons Silvestri arrested last night might know something about it, though chances were they didn't.

On a positive note, Acuna didn't know anything about Olivia McEvoy—his reaction to my question as to her whereabouts had been genuine enough. That told me Marrero had her, if anyone did. The twisted, mobster logic was clear to me now. If Marrero had Olivia, she couldn't go to the cops, and Marrero could use her as leverage over Ray. The other darker possibility was that Marrero knew Ray had taken money from both him and Acuna. I could see Marrero using her as a bargaining chip to have Ray transfer all Acuna's money into Marrero's control.

Well, that's a great way to kick off a gang war.

I chose to believe Olivia was still alive. Certainly, Marrero might kill her to keep her quiet, but I chose to believe otherwise. And I had a good idea, too, on where I should start looking.

But there was something I needed to do first.

I messaged Brashard.

I suspected he was already in classes for the day and wouldn't pick up. He and his family needed to know about Ruiz. Somehow, I had to convince them to go to the police. It seemed like the only way to keep this thing alive. Even more than that, I needed to warn them. Ruiz had set me up to get killed last night. When Garcia had done it with that bogus meeting, I could *maybe* give Ruiz a pass that he didn't know. He'd have told his mob sponsors someone was kicking around, and they'd said they would handle it. If he did know, perhaps Ruiz convinced himself they were just going to scare me off. When it became clear that wasn't the case, he'd come forward out of some semblance of guilt, trying to make right. Maybe.

Last night, though, there's no way around what had happened and no possible explanation other than he was complicit in Acuna trying to bury me in a swamp.

I won't pretend to understand why Ruiz had made that decision in the end, other than Silvestri's justification that desperate people did dangerous, stupid things.

The message app showed the rolling ellipses of an inbound text. It stopped, picked up again, and stopped. Brashard was thinking about what to say, or if he should. Finally, the reply was, *They said I can't talk to you anymore.*

I would have asked who, but I already knew the answer, and it didn't matter.

Instead, I called Cyrus, and it went straight to voicemail.

"Cyrus, I need you to call me back. It's important. I have reason to believe Brashard might be in danger. Please call as soon as you get this."

To my great surprise, he did.

"What's this about, Matt?"

"Ray Ruiz tried to kill me last night."

"This shit again? Everybody ain't trying to kill you, man."

"Well, Miami-Dade police have a different interpretation, Cyrus. I told you before I had evidence that Ruiz was in bed with some mobsters. Well, last night he set me up to meet with one of them. I agreed to work under-cover for the police." I realized how confusing this must sound to him. Cyrus didn't know that Ruiz, up until a few days ago, had thought I was Jameson Carter, a Dallas businessman. "All the times I interacted with Ruiz, I was using a cover identity. He didn't know I was a private detective."

"Then how—"

"I will explain everything in detail, later. It's not important. What is important is that he had me go to a meet and then disappeared. When I showed up there were about four armed men, and they tried taking me out. I was working with the police, wearing a wire. I escaped, but so did Ruiz. Now we don't know where he is."

"Sounds like something for the police to sort out."

"Do you know where he is? Has he tried to contact you?"

"Why the hell would he do that?"

"Because he's now wanted for attempted murder, Cyrus. He's looking for alibis. He's looking for protection."

"Okay, so what makes you think he'd talk to me?"

"Because you have a vested interest in his survival."

The words were out before I could fully think through the implication of them.

"What's that supposed to mean?"

"It means that after I started looking around, all of a sudden Ray decided to move the money from your contract out of his bullshit investment and pay you cash. And then told you not to talk to me if you wanted to keep it."

"You saying he bought me off?"

"Goddamn it, Cyrus! They murdered your son's agent."

"He got shot buying drugs," he said with a thunderous intonation.

"No, Cyrus, he didn't, and I think you know it. Wake up, man. I understand you're protecting your family. I know the money Ruiz paid you is more than you've seen in your whole life."

"That's money my boy *earned*."

"That doesn't change anything."

"The hell it doesn't."

"Cyrus, I've said it before, and I'll keep repeating it until it sinks in. Ruiz is mixed up with dangerous people. They killed Jimmy Lawson. They threatened one of his colleagues to scare her off. They've tried to kill me, twice now. And they are trying to fix the basketball tournament. Jesus Christ, Cyrus, what more do you need to *see*?"

"You really think Ray killed Jimmy?"

"I don't think Ray did it himself, no. I think one of his mobster connections did it to throw us off the trail. It's all going to come out, eventually."

"Why are you telling me this?"

"First, because I'm worried about your son. The people Ruiz is in bed with...they burned a kid's house down because he didn't tank a game like they'd asked him to. What happens if they try to do that to you when Brashard's season starts? Second, Ruiz is going down. It's just a matter of time. When he does, all that money goes away. If you come forward now, tell the police what you know, maybe you can cut a deal and keep what he paid you."

"It's our goddamn money," Cyrus said, seething. "You talking about cutting *deals* like we had something to do with this bullshit."

"That's mob money, Cyrus. The government is going to seize it."

"I think you'll forgive me if I don't feel comfortable going to the police."

I was losing the already tenuous grasp I'd had on this relationship. There was so much more at play here than I could truly hope to understand. He didn't see, or chose not to, that Ruiz paying his son with dirty money would result in government seizure when this was all over. There was even a chance the Feds might consider the Browns complicit in the scheme because they'd been warned it was illegal and kept it up. A prosecutor could allege they were just another avenue to clean Acuna's cash. It wasn't true, but it would play with a jury. Especially one comprised of people scraping by.

"And here's one more thing. Jimmy only wanted to hire you because my son's contract with Sunshine Sports meant less money was gonna go to him. Yeah, we signed a bad deal. Didn't know no better. But the money was good, and what we have is because of Ray Ruiz. These rules change so fast we don't even know he's gonna be in business in five years, ten years, whatever. I don't think for a minute this lifetime contract is going to be around half that long. And once Brashard goes in the first round, we can hire a decent attorney and get out of it. I already got two different lawyers telling me the contract won't stand up. So, yeah, lemme tell you about your pal, Jimmy Lawson. He just wanted to dip his hand in the till like they all do."

No one, in any of this, had asked Brashard what *he* wanted.

I had no doubt Cyrus Brown believed he was acting in his son's best interests. But did Brashard?

Now that Jimmy was gone, there was no one truly objective about the kid's career. No one whispering in Brashard's ear with the good advice he needed to be considering right now.

No one telling him that his father might just be driving him off a cliff.

"You don't want to talk to the police, Cyrus. I appreciate your reasons. Maybe consider this. When this story gets out, and it will and soon, what is Brashard's university going to think? Mob money, murder, points shaving...."

They're going to wonder whether Jorge Acuna had his hooks into your son. Or maybe they'll just want to distance themselves from anything and anyone connected to Sunshine Sports Collective. They can find another starting quarterback. Can your quarterback find another school?"

"You stay away from my boy," Cyrus Brown growled, real menace in his words.

This would only end badly for most of the people involved.

# 26

Lieutenant Silvestri hadn't specifically told me *not* to look for Ray.

By now, Acuna would've told him that I survived.

Which meant Acuna's people could also be looking for Ray.

What I could do with him if I found him, though, was up for some debate. I couldn't take him into custody because I wasn't an agent of the court.

Well, focus on finding him first and *then* worry about getting him into custody.

There were a few things working in my favor here. First, as a criminal, he wasn't that bright. This was his first toe-dip into the underworld, and he was rapidly running out of options. Ray was making this up as he went. He'd hide somewhere he felt safe.

Best guess, Ray was holed up at one of Dalton Bream's properties or a hotel.

The smartest thing he could do right now was to take his boat down to one of the Keys and hide out for a few days. But then what? He'd have to return at some point.

I decided to check off the obvious places.

First, I called SSC using another app Mickey designed that would ghost my phone number from caller ID.

When the receptionist answered, I said, "Good morning, my name is Barry Golden. I spoke with Ray a couple weeks ago, and we agreed to meet up in the future. I represent an athletic beverage company called Dash. I don't suppose Ray has any time on his schedule today?"

"I'm sorry, Mr. Ruiz hasn't been in yet today," she said. A different answer than "he doesn't have time."

"Are you expecting him?"

"I am. I thought he'd be in by now," she said.

I thanked her for her time. I hadn't thought he would go to the office, but it needed to be crossed off.

One try to flush him out. I dialed Ray's phone from my cell rather than the app. Maybe he'd respond to a lifeline. I had to count on this being played back in court, so I kept the accusations to a minimum.

"It's Matt, pick up. Acuna tried to kill me last night, though I suspect you knew that. He also knows I'm working with the police, which is going to have him wondering if *you* are too. The cops have about six of his people. One of them will flip. There's a straight line back to you now. Your best chance is to come in. Acuna is out looking for you. Do yourself a favor, Ray, and come in. I can help you."

I hung up.

Then I called Flash.

"Matt, hi," he said.

Tension and frustration expelled from my mouth in a harsh bark of a laugh.

"That good, huh?"

"It's not the easiest thing I've ever done, that's for sure," I said.

"So, what's up?"

"I was wondering if you could help me out. Should be about half an hour of your time."

"Probably. What do you need."

"A ride."

Flash picked me up in his boat along Miami's Riverwalk. He pulled up, put some buoys alongside the boat so he didn't damage the hull, and I hopped aboard. Once I was on, I pushed us off, pulled the buoys back in, and met him in the cockpit.

"Where we heading?"

I gave him Ray's address on Biscayne Point in North Beach. Traveling by boat was a hell of a lot faster than driving. On the way over, I chatted about the Ruiz and gang situation. He reminded me that we'd covered some of it already. Honestly, it'd been such an off-the-rails mine-cart ride since I'd spoken to him last, I forgot what Flash already knew.

"Man, Ruiz is playing with fire here," he said. "Once Marrero finds out that idiot is mixing his funds with Acuna's, all hell is going to break loose."

"Why is that such a big deal?"

"Part of it is just this stupid machismo thing that Cuban gangsters have. But those two also *hate* each other. I think I gave you some of the details already. Acuna wanted to strike out on his own, and Marrero wouldn't let him, said he hadn't paid his dues. With the Corporation's original leadership all in jail and many of their original businesses rolled up, Marrero was worried the organization wouldn't survive if they split like that. Acuna told him to go to hell. Marrero thinks Acuna is a reckless hothead, which he is, and that any scam of his is doomed to fail because he's going to take it too far, too fast."

"Not an injudicious assessment from what I've seen," I said.

"Right? So, the big reason Marrero won't want his shit mixed up with Acuna's is because he knows Acuna's reckless as hell and he'll eventually get found out."

"What do you think the reaction would be?"

"Not good. Once he finds out, Marrero will move quickly. He's quiet and deliberative for a Cuban. He'll murder Acuna and his men in their sleep, take their money. Now Marrero has something over Ruiz for the rest of his days. He'll keep this thing going as long as is practical, maybe years. Eventually, he's going to pull his money and kill Ruiz for the trouble. Of course, if there's a bunch of heat on this, and it sounds like there is, all that moves faster."

"And if Acuna finds out?"

Flash just shook his head. "Then he burns anything Marrero touches right to the ground."

"There is a very good chance that is already underway."

Flash pulled back on the throttle and angled the boat to the right as we approached Biscayne Point. Golden morning sun pressed down, scattering diamonds across the green surface of the bay. It was pleasant now, in the upper seventies, but the day would be hot. Biscayne Point consisted of two manmade peninsulas, the southern of the two large enough to support two residential streets. Ruiz lived on the northern smaller one. Each home had a dock, and most of them had boats attached. Flash's fit right in. He motored us toward Miami Beach and then pulled a U-turn, slowing to an idle, and brought me up next to Ruiz's dock.

The plan was I would get off here, and Flash would float nearby, picking me up when I signaled.

I stepped off *The Green Flash* and onto Ruiz's dock. His boat was in the water, but tied up, so Ruiz hadn't made good on his threat for a water escape. Large palms and shrubs hid the house's front from the road, but the back was largely exposed to take advantage of the stunning southern view. I walked up the dock and to the patio, the pool filter burbled softly. All else was quiet. The blinds were all closed.

Ruiz had a Ring camera on his front door, though that was the extent of his home security.

You'd think someone with as much cause to fear for his life would have a decent alarm.

I was trying very hard to hold to my promise to not break the law. However, personal change takes time, and the statistics of recidivism from cold-turkey quitting aren't great. I'd brought my lock picks and a pair of disposable gloves with me, just in case, and was through the patio door in about fifteen seconds. I slid it open a crack, listened, and then stepped in.

The house was cool, musty, and dark.

First, I checked for signs of recent occupation.

The sink and faucet were both dry. The coffee pot had a cup or so left in it, and the brew was long cold. A half-full cup in the sink had a film over the top. I walked over to the front window and peered through the blinds. No vehicle in the driveway. Creeping down the hallway, I checked Ruiz's bedroom. It was empty and showed the general dishevelment of a man who lived alone. I was convinced the place was empty, but just to be thorough, I did a quick search of his room—nightstand drawers, dresser, that sort of thing. People tended to hide their best secrets in the spaces where they felt the safest, and for most, that's their bedroom. I didn't find anything of use, other than a half-empty vial of what I assumed was cocaine. That'd certainly track with the behavior I'd seen the other night.

Finished in the bedroom, I made a quick check of the other rooms, finding nothing.

Ruiz did have an office, and in that office was a laptop.

More to the point, it was a MacBook. Which meant it was likely connected to his phone.

Most people didn't lock their computers at home. Why would they? The odds of an ex-spy breaking into your home to search it for clues were laughably minute. Even if you had it coming and should know better, like Ray.

I opened the screen and woke it up. A quick scan showed 547 unanswered emails, not surprising for a CEO neglecting his business. The eighteen unanswered texts drew my attention. I tapped iMessage and scanned them, acknowledging I was in dangerous territory, legally. Again. Nothing I uncovered here would be admissible as evidence, and if I were ever deposed on the subject, it could jeopardize the entire case. Certainly, my credibility as a witness, which was what most of the legal strategy hinged on right now. I decided not to look at the texts or any of the messages. Doing so would show them as "read," which would tip Ray off that someone was spying on him. Instead, I opened up the Find My app and quickly scanned his devices.

Ray had his phone off, which explained the unanswered messages. Smart. He probably watched enough TV to know the police could, with a warrant, track your phone by triangulating its position relative to cell towers on the carrier's network. His AirPods, however, were last reported in Little Havana. I had a guess where that would be, so I opened Maps, because that would show his vehicle's last known location. Sure enough, that matched the AirPods. I wondered if he was trying to square things with Marrero before they got cosmically out of control.

Figuring I'd found what I needed—and all I was likely to find anyway—

I closed up and left, locking the sliding door behind me. A minute later, I was on Flash's boat heading back out into the bay.

"Where to now, chief?"

Now, I was off to find Ray Ruiz and/or Olivia McEvoy with the one person I believed could answer to their whereabouts.

Cesar Marrero.

## 27

I drove to Little Havana. My first stop was at Ruiz's Aston.

He'd parked it on a residential street a block and a half off Calle Ocho. It was just after eleven now, and the side streets were relatively clear. Ruiz's SUV was right where the app said it would be. We had some rain early this morning, and there were still beads of water on the Aston's paint. That meant it'd at least been here since then.

Maybe he'd been summoned to a damage-control session with his "investors."

That would make some sense.

There was another possibility, which was that Ruiz had sought Marrero's help in shedding his Acuna problem. It would take a subtler hand than I gave Ruiz credit for—particularly if he was strung out and paranoid from doing lines all night. That didn't mean it was beyond the pale. Ruiz had known Acuna was dangerous all along, though it seemed he'd miscalculated just how much.

The game-fixing scheme jeopardized everything Ruiz was trying to do. I could see him going to Marrero with a story that Acuna was trying to push his way into the money-laundering operation. It would be just a few degrees off the truth, as the best lies are. Ruiz would be betting the speed of

Marrero's assault on his rival outpaced his learning Ruiz took Acuna's money.

Ray was taking a heavy risk, and it could easily backfire on him. Though, from his view, what other option did he have?

Beyond going to the police and doing the right thing, that is.

The next round of the basketball tournament was in two days.

I still did not share Silvestri's optimism that Acuna would just roll over and hide because we'd raided his club. Based on what I knew about him, this would only make Acuna swing harder. It was so much worse than Silvestri thought.

Gulf Coast was a Cinderella sliding into the Elite Eight. There would be a lot of gambling action, most of it betting that Gulf Coast would lose in a close game. That was something Acuna could influence—a close game. A handicapper might have a hard time proving outside influence.

As much as I wanted to believe this was someone else's problem to solve, I couldn't just walk away from that kid and his family. Especially without hearing someone in authority saying, "We've got this."

Acuna needed something to focus on that wasn't Cody Portman. Even after last night, I wasn't a big enough pain in his ass to divert his attention away from his dealings with Cody. I was henchman fodder to him.

The owner of El Havana wasn't.

Well, to be fair, I didn't know if he actually owned the place. Probably, it was more of a fiefdom.

Whatever.

Common with many of the restaurants in this neighborhood, El Havana served food by day and transformed into a live-music bar at night. Which was a good way to move illicit cash.

Like the day I'd followed Ray here, El Havana had its windows retracted so that the front dining room and bar opened to the street. Afro-Cuban jazz pumped onto the sidewalk, and an early lunch crowd was already flowing in.

Avoiding eye contact with the hostess, I weaved my way through to the back room where I'd first seen Marrero. This time, the door was closed. I opened that and walked through.

What's that line?— "Here comes the new boss, same as the old boss." As

Flash had explained, the Corporation was on its third iteration of leadership. Not bad as far as crime syndicates were concerned. And Marrero had the distinction of never having been arrested or associated with any illegal activity. This was a man who'd go to some lengths to keep it that way.

I could use that.

It could also get me killed more quickly.

Marrero sat at the same table in the back, chomping on a cigar and reading the paper. An empty coffee cup sat in front of him. A lieutenant hovered nearby.

A bodyguard clocked me as soon as I entered the room and stepped up to challenge me—one of the assholes who'd jumped me the first time, when I'd followed Ruiz in. While he was still getting to his feet, I folded my fingers back to the knuckle, forming a fat blade and punched him in the throat. It wasn't enough to crush the larynx permanently, but breathing would take all his concentration for a while. While he was gasping for air, I kicked him in the chest, knocking him onto his back and then dropped to a knee on top of his chest. I found his pistol and liberated him from the liability of an unlicensed firearm. Just to make sure no one got dumb ideas, I field-stripped the gun and dumped the pieces on the floor.

I stood and walked over to Marrero.

"Seniõr Marrero, do you remember me?"

He looked up from his paper, uninterested, and went back to it.

"No," he said.

Marrero was tall with an average build, a little paunch visible through the shirt. He was deeply tanned and mostly bald with some wispy holdouts on top of his head. Dark eyes over darker bags gave the impression he was looking at you from a swamp.

"You tried to have me killed, twice," I said.

I'd figured out that Marrero had been behind the first attempt—when his two heavies rear-ended my Defender. Then there were the trouble boys who followed me out of this place after they caught me snooping on Ray and Marrero. The initial clue was that Ruiz had come here first, and the other was that I could make some loose connections between Marrero and Charlie Garcia. Garcia told me once he'd needed money to keep his business open. That was the kind of thing the Corporation was good for. Acuna would've given him a twenty-five percent vig and blown his business up when he missed the payment.

"That so," he said, not looking up. "You, coming in here like this, disrespecting me.... You're gonna wish I hadn't missed the first time."

"Hire better muscle. You want to know why I'm here, or you just going to make idle threats and pretend to read that paper?"

Marrero exhaled and set the paper down slowly. The cigar shifted slightly in his mouth. He inhaled, the cherry brightened, and then pushed out a cloud of smoke.

"What do you want? You want a truce? I'm not gonna do that because I don't even know who you are."

"I'm a private investigator. Your friend Ray Ruiz isn't very discreet and doesn't cover his tracks half as good as he should for the kind of operation he runs."

"That so."

"I saw his car. It's kind of hard to miss. He here?"

Marrero made a show of looking around the room and then back at me, like I'd asked him an idiotic question.

"So, you're not going to tell me where he is?"

"You got some cojones, Mr. Private Detective, I'll give you that. To come in here, hurt one of my men..."

Marrero looked at the guy I'd taken down. There was an ever-so-slight head shake, which I took to mean "not yet."

I looked over at the muscle. He was on his feet now, fists balled and vibrating with restrained rage.

"I wouldn't," was all I said in warning. Turning back to Marrero, I said, "That? I think we can call it evening a score. The last time he came at me, it was three to one."

Marrero shrugged, as if accepting my logic. "So, you want to know where Mr. Ruiz is, and I tell you I don't know. It's as simple as that."

"Is it? What about Olivia McEvoy?"

"I don't know that name."

"She's Ruiz's number two at SSC. Someone who wanted to find out what's going on at Ruiz's organization, someone with questions about what he's doing with his money and where it comes from...well, that person might want to talk to her."

Marrero's eyes narrowed. "What do you mean?"

"I mean exactly what I said. Let's say an interested party—an *investor*, we'll call them—had concerns about how Sunshine Sports Collective was using his money. Let's say that investor had reason not to trust Ray Ruiz, like he felt he wasn't getting straight answers. Said investor would, logically, want to speak with Ray's partner, no?"

Marrero pushed back his chair and stood. He scissored his cigar with the fingers on his left hand, inhaled once more, and blew the smoke out before removing it. For the first time since I'd walked in here, I felt like he was actually looking *at* me.

"I don't know where the woman is. And I'm not hiding Ray. You, though, have some things to answer for."

"That may be, but not to you. You won't care, but the people Ray is taking advantage of, the innocent people who are going to lose everything because of him, hired me to get them out of it. I mean to do it. You can stand in my way and get swept up with all the rest, or we can make a deal."

Marrero laughed at that...and hard.

"You talk a big game, Mr. Private Detective, for someone who doesn't have good odds leaving here on his own."

"My odds are better than you think," I said.

"Okay, tough guy. Well, I don't have the information you want. You've got nothing that *I* want, so all we have is you wasting my time."

"The other reason an investor might want to ask questions is because they know—or maybe they don't—that Ruiz is not careful enough about whose money he takes."

"You don't think my money is good enough for him? That it?"

"Oh, I'm sure it's dirty enough for his little laundromat. That's not what I'm talking about. I mean your old pal, Jorge Acuna. Ruiz is double dipping. I've seen his books. I know the account you use. I also know the shell corporation Acuna uses that's in his uncle's name. You'd be amazed at what we private detectives can do. Oh, the other thing is that my friends in the FBI, Metro-Dade, and some news outlets all know what I'm doing, and if I don't show back up later, they'll know why. Just in case your boy back there gets any dumb ideas."

"You told the Feds you were coming here? That wasn't smart, my friend."

"I didn't tell them anything, yet. I have emails triggered to go out from a virtual server that you'll never find. If I don't turn it off within the hour, messages go out to the people I mentioned along with a clone of my iPhone that shows its last reported location on the network. Trust me, if you know how—and I do—you can track those things even if they're off." I gave him a knowing smile. "Ruiz is also moving Acuna's money. Jorge, as you may be aware, is making some very loud moves right now. He's using Ruiz's business to try and fix the college basketball tournament. You know what kind of attention that's going to bring? The FBI, for starters. Every national news organization. If I could backtrack your accounts in a few hours with a computer, what do you think *they* can do? More to the point, what's going to happen to you when they roll Acuna up? Do you really think the attorney general, or a jury, will differentiate between your gang and his? I'm willing to bet you had nothing to do with his scam, but they won't care. You will get rolled into that and you, all of you—" I waved a hand to encompass everyone in the room "—will die in prison. And the jury won't be here in Miami, where you might find people sympathetic to fellow Cubans or people you can intimidate or buy off. No, they'll hold this in Texas, where the tournament is, because the government could make the case that's where the crime is committed."

It's fun watching people argue with themselves in their heads, debating their odds for survival.

He didn't respond, and I hadn't expected him to.

"Well, it's been fun getting to know you, Mr. Marrero," I said. I took a few steps backwards. Then I drew my pistol and leveled it on the guard next to the door. "Hey, Ace, why don't you take about ten steps that way?" I motioned with the barrel. He did, without looking at his boss for confirmation.

Before I left the room, I turned for one last comment. "Cesar, your people tried to kill me. I recommend you don't try that again. If something happens to me, ever—because of you or Acuna, it doesn't matter—a thousand angry badges come swarming into this place like a biblical plague."

That was a damned good line. I was going to have to remember that.

It'd be better if it was even remotely true.

"Mr. Gage," Cesar said in a way that iced my blood. It was the first time he'd said my name. Now, I was certain he was the one who'd sent his goons to take me out after Charlie Garcia sent me on a bum steer. Acuna hadn't known who I was until later. Cesar Marrero and I locked eyes. "You came in here, and you threatened me, disrespected me. When this is over, Mr. Gage, we will have words."

I doubted very much that words were what he wanted to trade.

In return, I gave Marrero a nonchalant shrug and said, "When this is over."

I left El Havana without making it look like I was running for my life. Hard to do at a walking pace. Marrero was the type who moved—and fast —when he smelled blood in the water.

I was not followed.

However, I drove out of there like I was.

Once I was certain I was clear, I called Donna Portman as I drove.

"Mrs. Portman, I wanted to check in on you. Do you still have your police protection out front?"

"Hi, Matthew. Yes. They're still there."

"Has anyone made any new threats against your son?" It just occurred to me that we'd never contacted the police in Ft. Myers, or Cody's campus, to keep watch.

Donna Portman was quiet long enough that she didn't need to answer my question.

I said, "They told him if he spoke to the police, they'd know. Didn't they?"

She just broke down into tears.

The racking sobs subsided long enough for her to say, "I haven't been to work in five days. I don't have very much vacation time. At first, my boss said they were sympathetic of my...they called it 'my situation.' It feels like it's a problem for them."

"Donna, I've told you this before, but I really need this to sink in. Jorge

Acuna cannot monitor your phone. His gang will not know if you contacted the police. Ever."

"They told Cody they would know."

It's amazing to me how so many people don't have a basic understanding of how their devices work. I was so frustrated I wanted to scream into mine. Of course, that would help no one, least of all the panicking single mother on the other end who I desperately wanted to help. Are there organized crime outfits that specialize in hacking? Absolutely. I've taken a few of them down. Most of those guys were also trained by the GRU, Russia's military intelligence department. I didn't believe for a second that a spinoff *marielito* gang could hack into an email account, let alone conduct sophisticated digital surveillance.

"Donna, I'll say this again, and I really need you to believe me. They cannot monitor your cell phone. They are trying to scare you into doing what they want. Frankly, it would be hard even for the police to monitor your phone. I also don't think these guys are a big enough organization that they've got someone watching Cody twenty-four hours a day." I paused and gave her a moment to process. There was no value in a deeper technical explanation. I just had to trust this was enough.

"I don't know about all that," she said.

"Donna, you're right to be scared. These are dangerous people. What you *do* about that is what matters. They want to harm your son. They probably will if you don't do something about it. I'm not a cop, so there is only so far I can take this. I need you to call Lieutenant Silvestri and get her in touch with Cody immediately. Can you please do that for me?"

"You're sure there's no way they will know?"

"I will gladly explain how it's impossible, but I think you'd find it pretty boring. I'll just say that it takes a level of sophistication with computers that these people do not have. They're a street gang, not the Cuban intelligence service."

"Okay, Matthew. I'll call her. Right now." She paused. "Can you protect my boy?"

"I'll do everything in my power."

"That's not a yes."

The best thing would be for Cody not to play. Explain the situation to the coach and sit out, say he's injured. Neutralize Acuna's threat entirely. Though trying to convince a kid with a once-in-a-lifetime chance that he should sit the game out would be about as easy as convincing Acuna to reform himself for the greater good.

"I am not ever going to lie to you, and I'm not going to promise you something I can't for certain deliver. However, I aim to make a big enough problem for Jorge Acuna that there's no way he can harm your son in the next three days. Just distract him long enough until the police get their shit together." Maybe I shouldn't have said that last part—or maybe I just thought Donna Portman deserved a little honesty.

I hung up and made for Coral Gables. Brashard was probably finished with classes and would be at lunch before afternoon practice.

It was a little after twelve thirty by the time I made it to campus. I found a metered spot on a side street and made long strides to the athletic complex. I called Brashard on the way. Straight to voicemail. Hoping he was scanning calls, I left a message. "I need to talk to you right away. It's vitally important you call me back. I'm on campus now. I only need a minute." Then I followed that up with a text saying essentially the same thing.

While I waited for Brashard to call me back, I scanned the area for anyone who looked like they didn't belong here. While Acuna's goons might blend into greater Miami, they would stick out on a college campus.

Brashard called me fifteen minutes later.

"Matt, I'm not supposed to talk to you. You gotta stop this shit."

"Where are you? I need to talk to you right now."

"I can't do that. My dad..."

"Your dad is making a mistake. Now where are you?"

"Walking to the practice facility."

"Meet me at the bridge."

"I can't, man."

"Damn it, Brashard. We're running out of options, not to mention time to put them into play. Your agent was murdered. The same people tried to do me, twice. Ray's business partner is now missing. We have a chance to get the people who did this before they hurt anyone else. I need your help to do it."

"I have to be in pads in five minutes."

"I only need two."

Because I wasn't cleared for any of the athletic facilities, I had to run the long way around to the footbridge that spanned a green waterway alongside the practice field. I turned north when I came to the green-painted metal fence and followed that to the footbridge beneath leafy trees and what looked like cypress trees. I found Brashard standing in the center of the bridge, like he didn't want to come all the way across. He wore a black Miami football practice shirt and white practice shorts that hung below the knee, his hands hooked around his backpack straps.

As soon as I stepped onto the bridge, Brashard looked over his shoulder, as if checking behind him. For what?

I didn't waste words thanking him for showing up. By now, it was his goddamn duty.

"Ray Ruiz is taking money from two different gangsters and laundering it so the authorities can't trace it. That's how he got his business started, because he couldn't find enough legitimate investors. He paid you with illegal money."

"So? What do I care? My money now."

"No, Brashard, it's not. What happens with these kinds of cases is that the government seizes all of it as evidence. This could break badly for you. If you don't come forward now, the government can say you were part of the scheme."

"What does that even mean?" His tone went aggressive quickly, and I could hear his father in it.

"It means the government can take it back."

"They gotta talk to the bank for that shit. My dad paid the mortgage with it. That money gone."

I knew Brashard was a smart kid. The staggering amount of information a college quarterback had to process in the span of a few seconds made the difference between a completed pass and eating turf, which is what made this conversation so damned frustrating.

"Just because you spent it doesn't mean it's 'gone.' That actually makes it worse for you. If the government thinks you spent money you knew was illegally acquired, they'll say you were part of this."

"Man, that's bullshit. We have a contract. If Ray's doing illegal shit, it ain't on me. I didn't do anything wrong."

"No one said this was fair, kid. You got taken up in a scam. Ruiz promised to make you rich, and you signed with him. If you want out, if you want to make sure your name isn't tainted by this, you need to contact the police with what you know."

"Matt, I don't know shit. I'm just playing ball!"

"Did Ray Ruiz give you $400,000 in exchange for firing me?"

"It wasn't like that."

"Okay, what was it like?"

Brashard looked away. "Fine, it was *mostly* like that. But there were pictures of you and that woman."

"Those were faked, with a computer. I explained that to your dad, and he elected not to believe me. That woman, by the way, is now missing." I let that sink in for a second. "Last night, Ruiz arranged a meeting for me to meet with one of his gangster backers. It was supposed to be an undercover sting where the police moved in and arrested everyone. Instead, it was a setup. Ray disappeared, and those guys tried to kill me. The police need to talk to Ray so he can flip on this gangster before he hurts anyone else. If you want any hope of keeping that money you earned, you need to tell the police what happened."

"How come I ain't heard from the police?"

"I thought you were more likely to listen to me than some cop you didn't know."

Brashard pushed most of the air out of his lungs, loudly for my benefit, and pressed his eyelids together while he thought it through. This was the critical moment in a recruitment, and I elected to stay silent. Anything else I said now would just push him away.

"What do you need me to do?"

"First, call this number. This is Lieutenant Michelle Silvestri. She runs the organized crime squad for Miami-Dade. Tell her we spoke and then tell her everything about your relationship with Ruiz. I mean *everything*. Most importantly, you need to tell her about the payment." I texted Silvestri's information to him. "Then I need you to call Ray."

"Why I wanna do that if he's as bad as you say? I don't want anything to do with him."

"He's hiding, Brashard. He knows he's in deep shit, and he's just trying to ride this out somewhere. Now, he's desperately trying to hold on to whatever he can. So, you call him and tell him you're signing with someone else. Tell him you talked to a lawyer, and they can get you out of the contract. That should flip him out pretty good. He'll come running to convince you not to, or say you can't. Either way, he'll want to talk to you. Set up a meeting place somewhere here on campus. Tonight, or tomorrow at the latest." I didn't like the idea of using the kid as bait, but we were rapidly running out of options. I was afraid if Ruiz didn't see Brashard when he showed for the meeting, he'd think something was up and slip out.

"What if he won't?"

"I'm counting on the idea that you're too big for him to let go of. He wants to save his business and assumes his criminal pals will take me out. I'm worried if we don't bring him in, one of these mobsters will kill Ray to keep him quiet. I don't want that to happen. For one thing, it means we can't hold him accountable for what he did. For another, it makes it harder to get your money."

"Yeah. I get you," he said and then gave a short, brittle laugh. "You're crazy, you know that, right?"

"Probably a little. You're a good kid, Brashard. I don't want to see you lose your shot."

He looked away—I assumed because there was something in his eyes he didn't want me to see.

"What is it?" I asked.

A shrug. "Nothing."

"You're saying 'nothing' when you clearly mean 'something.'"

Everything about his demeanor had changed when I'd said I didn't want him to lose his shot.

"I got a gun," he said.

"You did *what?*" He still wouldn't look me in the eyes. "Brashard, give it to me right now."

Finally, his gaze met mine. "I don't have it with me," he said, like I was stupid for asking. "It's in my room."

"What in the actual hell are you doing with a gun?"

"It was what you said about Cody Portman, that basketball player. Figure if one of these assholes tried to get me to throw a game or whatever, we'd have a whole different conversation if I was strapped."

"Brashard, listen to me and listen good. If you get caught with an illegal firearm, you will face some life-altering consequences. Do you know what happens if you threaten someone with a gun? Your playing days are done."

"Just standing my ground, man. And the piece isn't illegal. It's my dad's."

"What is your dad doing with a gun?"

"You live in the places we used to live, you'd have one too."

"What do you think the chances are of a black kid with a gun getting off scot-free in court? Don't be stupid."

Shame, embarrassment, and more than a little righteous anger washed across his face, and this time, he didn't look away. He was daring me to stare him down.

So I did.

He blinked first.

"Look, I know you didn't ask for my help, Brashard," I said. "Jimmy did. So, I understand why you think I'm just some random guy barking at you. Just think on this one thing. I'm now the only person here who isn't financially invested in your success. And I'm telling you to sneak that thing back into your parents' house and don't think about it ever again."

I'd be painting myself a hypocrite if I told him to trust the system. God knows I didn't. Sometimes the logic of the moment was enough.

"You'll call Silvestri?" I said.

"Doing it right now," he said and turned, walking back to the practice facility.

I watched Brashard go then headed back to the Defender.

I needed to stay moving.

---

I burned several hours and more gas driving unnecessarily elaborate SDRs across the Dadeland area. Deciding I needed a break and some food, I found a dirt road beneath some trees on a thumb of land sticking out into

Silver Blue Lake in Miami Shores, halfway between Miami International and the ocean. I seriously had no idea what to do next, other than finish the Cuban sandwich I'd bought at a food truck.

By now, I had to assume Olivia was dead.

Several calls a day went unanswered, from the police and from me. I'd tried her parents again, this time saying I was afraid for her safety. Her father hung up on me. I don't know which one of us he didn't want to hear from again, maybe both. Silvestri hadn't had any luck with him either.

Olivia's disappearance left a blacker pit in me than I cared to admit. I got her involved, got her asking questions. Probably, Marrero had her silenced, which meant Ray's chances weren't looking good either.

Or, for that matter, mine.

For now, I'd stay on the move.

There were two gangs scouring the area looking for me. Just needed to stay mobile until the police moved on one of them.

My phone rang as I was looking for a trash can.

It was Dalton Bream, and because I'm a glutton for punishment, I answered.

Bream spoke before I even acknowledged the call. "This can all go away, Gage."

"You'd need a lot of clout to make a promise like that, what with all the cops involved now"

Without missing a beat, Dalton Bream said, "And you're wise to remember that. You didn't accept my offer. That displeases me."

"Sorry to disappoint," I said.

"I won't waste your time—or more importantly, mine—on idle threats. Help me get Ray back under control, calm the waters, and I can quiet certain elements. You don't want to work for me, that's fine. I can still make it worth your while."

"That sounds a lot like you're trying to buy me off."

Bream sighed hard into the phone. "You really insist on doing things the hard way, don't you? I would have thought solving your client's murder would be a more important outcome for you."

"You're telling me you don't know anything about it? For someone who just tried to pay me to, what was your phrase, 'quiet the waters,' sure seems like the opening move would be to silence the guy who put all this in motion."

"You can have my word that I knew nothing about Mr. Lawson's death. It's entirely why I made you the offer that I did."

Telling him what I thought of his "word" would just be wasted air, so I spared it.

"This is my final offer, Mr. Gage."

"Dalton, I'm going to tell you something I suspect you've never heard before."

"Oh, and what's that?"

"Fuck off."

I hung up and thought hard about tossing the phone in the water just to make sure he couldn't call back.

---

This was the second time Bream had tried to use the prospect of solving Jimmy's death as a carrot for me. The only explanation was that my instinct about Bream proved correct. He was trying to buy me off to protect Ray. Or, rather, to protect his involvement in Ray's business. Bream didn't care about Ray the man. He cared about the flashing red light of criminal liability Ray represented.

I might not have gotten there if Bream hadn't used finding Jimmy's killer as the lever. That's when I knew Ray hadn't been involved in Jimmy's death. Bream wouldn't give me license to find Jimmy's killer if he knew that would ultimately connect back to him somehow.

Ray wouldn't have killed Jimmy. Perhaps I could now envision a world where he would pull a trigger, but only when he was backed so far into a corner that he needed to shoot his way out.

Felix Farrier was still the obvious choice. Ex-Army, spook, ex-cop, someone who knew the law well enough to break it and get away with it. I mean, his job was to make problems go away. The reason it didn't fit was that it was *too* obvious. While Farrier absolutely had the skills to murder someone and make it look like anything else, it was a huge risk for Ray to take on. If that backfires, Ray loses everything and goes to jail forever. If

Jimmy hadn't been murdered, the only risk Ray takes on is the chance that I prove SSC is breaking the law.

Could Farrier have acted without orders? Taken his mandate to protect Ray to a lethal extreme? Maybe, but why? It's not like he's got some unimpeachable loyalty for Ruiz. They didn't come up the hard way together. And Ray sure isn't paying him "disappear bodies" kind of money.

Bream could, but he wasn't.

My mind started doing a kind of free association with random facts. Images, fragments of conversation started coalescing. It was the thing I'd just heard that tipped the first domino for me. Bream offering to buy me off so I could solve Jimmy's murder. If Bream had been shepherding Ray Ruiz, SSC had nothing to do with it. Ray was connected to mobsters, and I can't imagine Dalton Bream didn't know about it. Neither Acuna nor Marrero would know or care about Jimmy Lawson. Any legal threat to Ruiz's business would be his problem.

If I eliminated Ray Ruiz, Dalton Bream, Felix Farrier...who remained?

Oh God, no.

Brashard: *The gun was my dad's. You live in the places we used to live, you'd have one too.* Liberty City, one of Miami's most dangerous neighborhoods. And the place where Jimmy Lawson was shot.

The phone was ringing. I don't know how long, just that it was going a bit before the sound registered. I was entirely focused on the implications of the connection I'd just made.

I just stared at the thing for a while until some distant part of my brain recognized I needed to answer it. Probably because I knew "answering" would quickly turn into "answering for."

Turned out I was right.

"What in the actual holy hell did you do?"

# 28

"I'm going to need some context," I said.

"You must not have been watching the news last night, Gage, because half of Miami was lighting itself on fire," Silvestri said.

"The hell are you talking about?"

"Charlie Garcia's warehouse went up in flames."

"Garcia is dead."

"Yeah, and you know who owned a third of his business?"

"Cesar Marrero," I said. "Why would Marrero torch it? Would he really extort the widow to get his money back?" Actually, that seemed like something he would do.

"No, we think Acuna's people did it."

Oh.

"Four liquor stores got firebombed last night too."

"Let me guess, all of them belonging to the Corporation," I said.

"That's right," she said. "About twenty years of bad blood between Marrero and Acuna just blew up in our faces. We're looking at the kind of gang war Miami hasn't seen since the early 90s."

Holy shit. And I'd walked right into Marrero's headquarters and acted like I was a cop with backup.

There are a few times in life you realize, only after the fact, that you'd gotten away with your life when you probably shouldn't have. A sickening, stomach churning sensation.

"What's happening in Little Havana?" No way in hell I was telling her I'd just come from Marrero's.

"Word is Little Havana is off limits," Silvestri said. "Both gangs have their headquarters there, legitimate businesses and safe houses. Plus, there are too many ties to count. Cubans generally won't narc out their own, unless it's for good cause. Any beef Marrero and Acuna have with each other is going to be carried out everywhere else."

That explained why Marrero didn't have a ton of soldiers hanging out. Marrero had no reason to be afraid there.

"Has Marrero retaliated yet?" I asked.

"You know how Acuna is trying to build his own numbers game?"

"Yeah," I said, not really wanting to know the rest.

"Someone firebombed a counting house, with people placing bets inside. The message was pretty clear. Not even civilians doing business with Acuna are safe. And it's only going to get worse. Not to mix too many metaphors, Gage, but have you ever seen what happens when you try to put a grease fire out with water? That's what we expect it to look like tonight."

"Really?" That sounded dubious to me. "Acuna has, what, a squad? His gang can't be more than ten, fifteen people."

"We don't know how big his organization is. They've mostly stayed under the radar, and if I'm being honest, no one was paying attention to them. There are so many of these *marielito* gangs, and their membership is so fluid, it's hard for us to keep an accurate count. We think Acuna has been attracting other smaller gangs. And to be fair, most of our resources—and the Feds—are aimed at the Russians and Mexican cartels. The *marielitos* are like the cancer you didn't know you had because you were so busy treating something else. The Corporation isn't anywhere near what they were in the '90s, but I bet they could still put fifty soldiers on the streets if they had to. Where are you right now?"

"Gathering no moss," I said.

"Right. Where is that, specifically?"

"I'm at Silver Blue Lake, near the airport."

"Don't go anywhere. I'm on my way," she said and hung up. I got out of the Defender to stretch my legs and think about what I was going to say when Silvestri arrived. Maybe I was being pessimistic, but if she knew that I'd basically goaded these guys into going to war, she would either arrest me for obstruction of justice or threaten to and then escort me to the county line.

Could I blame her?

---

Silvestri arrived half an hour later in her undercover ride. It was about three now, and the full bore of tropical sun laid down on top of us like a dying elephant. My weather app told me it was eighty-two, but it felt closer to a hundred.

Silvestri pulled up on the grass next to me and got out of the car. She was decked out in a Miami-Dade polo, chinos, and aviator shades.

"Not the best place to hide out, Gage," she said, looking around. "Water on three sides. You're boxed in."

"Figured I'd shoot my way out," I said.

She smiled dryly. "I talked with Donna Portman this morning. We conferenced in her son. He told me everything that had happened. It's a credible threat," she said with the finality of a judge leveling a sentence. As if anticipating my next question, Silvestri said, "I've contacted campus security and the athletic department at his school. I've also spoken with Fort Myers PD. Protecting him during their game is going to be a little more problematic, though we don't think Acuna would send someone to Boston, where the next game is. I called Boston PD anyway, and they'll have their organized crime unit at the stadium. Pembroke is going to put an additional detail on Portman's home. With the threat against Portman and the arson on the family home, we've got enough to arrest Acuna. I've got two detectives running the warrant to a magistrate right now. We couple that with the firebombing last night, we've got Acuna on a host of RICO and conspiracy charges. I'm in contact with the Feds, too, for this tournament thing. It's going to take some time to get them rolling, though. This is a little convoluted because the extortion happened outside Miami-Dade's jurisdiction. I spoke with the arson investigator in Pembroke Pines, gave him what I had and he agreed to drop their suspicion charges on Mrs. Portman."

"That's great news," I said. I pushed a great mass of air of out my lungs. The Portmans were going to be okay, it seemed. One of my biggest fears in all of this was that they were going to fall through the cracks in the half a dozen jurisdictions this case seemed to span. Every agency would think it was someone else's problem to solve.

I didn't know if my telling Marrero about Ruiz also working with Acuna was what set this off or if it had been a long time coming.

In another context, Silvestri had described Marrero and Acuna fighting each other as "scorpions in a jar." I wished that was the extent of the damage this could do.

It wasn't.

It wasn't over. The wave hadn't crested yet.

They also didn't have Acuna in custody. There was a lot of damage that maniac could cause between "now" and "then."

Pray he goes out like Tony Montana and only shoots up his own house.

"Did Brashard Brown get ahold of you?" I asked.

"No, why. Was he supposed to?"

"Yeah," I said in a voice that was at once tired and annoyed. "Brashard is our best chance to find Ruiz. I think Ray believes he can still save his business. Don't ask me why—it's just a hunch. If Brashard tells him that he wants to talk, he'll show up."

"Why won't Ruiz think it's a trap?"

"Because he gave the Browns $400,000 to fire me. He'll assume that took." Especially if he was getting a report on my last conversation with Cyrus. Fresh questions bubbled to the surface about whether Ray knew Farrier had faked those pictures of me and Olivia. I said, "Ray salted the earth pretty good with me and the Brown family. He won't see this coming."

"Will the kid do it?"

"I'm not sure."

"You're putting him at risk," she said.

"Ray won't hurt him."

"Matt, Ray is on the run, and it wouldn't surprise me if one or both gangs want to take him out. You've also described him as being desperate and using narcotics. We shouldn't assume he's stable." She wasn't wrong. I couldn't believe Ray would hurt Brashard, though. "And the family...you're sure they didn't know anything about Ruiz's money-laundering operation?"

"Not until I told them. Why?"

"We had a case a few years ago. Wasn't my squad—I just knew about it. It was a real estate developer that was trying to park money in a bunch of places to hide where it was coming from. He'd find families that would be willing to help him do it. Now, this wasn't laundering. This was tax evasion. Doesn't matter how the scheme worked, just that there were some people who were complicit because they'd known and didn't say anything. The smartest thing for the Browns to do right now is to come forward and offer testimony, get it on the record that they didn't know."

Pretty sure I now knew why they hadn't volunteered anything to the police. All this time, I thought it was the easily explainable reason of "he's a black man who doesn't trust the cops."

"Believe me, I've been trying. They've conjured this kind of willful ignorance. The father thinks because they didn't know, the government will just let them keep it."

Silvestri laughed, though not in the fun way.

I continued. "They didn't have much to start with. Brashard's NIL contract got them the first house they'd ever owned. They can't return the money because they spent it on the mortgage. " I shrugged.

After Silvestri had her share of silence, she asked, "So, you don't know where Ruiz is now, and you're hoping the kid can draw him out. That it?"

"Yes. He vanished after setting me up at Acuna's club. I haven't heard from him since."

"I'm ready to arrest him for attempted murder. Acuna's bouncer said during questioning that Ray knew he wasn't going upstairs that night."

"Up until he disappeared at the meeting, I was 60/40 Ray was going to cooperate. He didn't really appreciate what he was getting into, or he overestimated his ability to get himself out. Ray thinks he's this master dealer. I hope its dawning on him, that he understands how much trouble he's in, and maybe that gets him to flip on our mobster friends."

"You're going to some serious lengths to protect this guy, Gage, and I'm not sure he's worthy of it."

"Let's be clear, I'm not protecting Ray. I just think he's the one person who can flip on everyone. He's the link between Marrero and Acuna, and he's connected with Senator Frank Rizzo and Dalton Bream."

"Who?"

"Bream is a land developer. He's a silent partner in Ray's business, and I think his interest is in using SSC to launder money. He's tried to buy me off, twice, by the way. If we get Ray, we get the whole damned thing. And some of these people might get the money that's promised them."

"Matt, that money is going to get seized by the Feds."

"They're victims of fraud, I'm assuming there's some recompense here." Made me sick to my stomach, but that also wasn't my problem to solve.

"In any event," Silvestri said, "La Barca told Ruiz's attorney, in no uncertain terms, we will arrest the shit out of his client and deny him bail. He's denied knowing where Ruiz is, of course. Though he's probably talking to the son of a bitch right now. Oh, and I've got the marine unit and the Coast Guard alerted to Ruiz being a flight risk. There's a marine unit boat orbiting in the bay near his house."

"How can I help?" I asked. The waves seemed to have calmed, and I could tell she was as eager to move past it as I was.

"That's what I wanted to talk to you about. The one thing we've got working for us is that everyone involved in this thing wants you dead."

My eyebrow lifted a touch. "Remind me how that helps?"

"Because you're the only one who has all the pieces. Whoever is left in this thing already knows they can't buy you off."

"They might if they knew what my rent payment is."

The look Silvestri flashed me suggested now wasn't the best time for my unique brand of insight. She took a mental lap before speaking again. "Knowing they can't buy you off leaves just one option. Someone is going to contact you...and soon. Whoever that is, that's the person Marrero has a hold of. It'll be a set up."

"How do you know?"

"Because this is a big city. Marrero doesn't have the resources for a manhunt."

"No, I mean, how do you know it's Marrero?"

"Because we raided a bunch of Acuna's businesses and his home about an hour ago. Word is all over Little Havana by now. Acuna is running, he's not worried about hitting you, much as he'd like to."

"Why are you convinced that Marrero is going to do it?"

"Because he already wants your head. And he's got a bunch of money wrapped up in this thing."

"Marrero doesn't—"

"Matt, his bartender is an informant of mine. Try to remember, for a moment, that I run an organized crime unit. I know all about that stupid shit you did this morning. However, that might be the thing that lets us round these assholes up for good. You pissed Marrero off something good, insulted his honor, yada yada. Acuna is running out of places to hide. We'll have him soon, and we put the word out that it's because of his association with SSC. Marrero knows he's got one chance to silence this thing, and that's to take you out."

"Well, you know I like to be helpful," I said. "So...what, I just sit around and wait for someone to call?"

"Basically, yes. Then I want you to call me. They'll be asking for a meet, which will likely be an ambush. I expect Marrero will have hitters there. We just need to grab them before they get you. Then we've got him."

"Oh. Is that all?"

"Matt, we think Marrero will be closing ranks...and quickly. That means we expect he's going to take out Ray tonight. Maybe Brashard and his family."

"Why on earth would Marrero go after them?"

"If they took money from Ruiz that they knew was tainted, Marrero won't know if they knew how far back the money trail went. He'd rather take them out than risk it. Innocent people are nothing to a guy like him. If you want to help them, you need to get them to come forward and help me."

So, there's that.

---

I didn't tell her about my suspicions regarding the Browns and Jimmy's death. Not yet. I needed to be sure.

And there was something else.

Jimmy hired me to protect Brashard, to make sure he had a chance. When you stripped away all the money and the endorsements, the possibly fraudulent royalty contract, what this was about—for Jimmy—was shielding Brashard from everyone who was trying to get a piece of him before he really had anything to give.

If I came forward with this, if I was right, Brashard was done. Even if he had nothing to do with it, no school would touch him. Not with clear links between him, a mob-run money-laundering and point-fixing scheme, and the murder of his agent. Good luck finding representation after that, kid.

Kind of hard to ask my client which end he wanted me to serve now.

I needed time. Time I didn't have.

At least I didn't need to run anymore.

Silvestri had convinced me that I'd be just as safe at my hotel as I would be driving around and wasting gas. I drove back to the hotel. I was not followed. I hit the pool for a few laps, needing to work out some nervous energy. There were no calls while I was in the pool. After I toweled off, I went down to the hotel bar for a burger and a beer, only marginally interested in either. Confronting Marrero earlier had been a stupid, risky move, and I should know better. The knowledge that Silvestri had an informant in his organization, or at least close by, made me wonder what else she knew and hadn't let on.

So, Cesar Marrero was the one we needed to worry about. I'd made the unforgivable mistake of focusing on the obvious psychopath at the expense of the subtle one.

I could only hope it wasn't too late.

Thin hope was what I had left.

The guy behind the counter at the hotel bar was new. After he handed me my beer, I asked him, "Are you a CI?"

He didn't have a response.

I nursed my beer because this would be the only one. Silvestri seemed sure I'd get a call today, and I had to be sharp when it came.

A little after five, it did.

I just wasn't ready for the caller.

Olivia McEvoy.

## 29

I signaled for the check.

"Olivia," I said, sliding off my barstool and heading for the stairs. I didn't want to lose connection in the elevator. "Are you okay," I asked while walking.

"I'm fine. I suppose."

"Where have you been?"

"Hiding. Where in the hell do you think I've been?"

"Hey, I'm on your side here. I've just been worried about you. You disappeared, and I thought something happened to you. I called your parents, and they didn't know. Or wouldn't say. I called you several times a day, and the police checked your townhouse. What was I supposed to think?"

"I asked my parents not to say anything," she said.

I reached the hotel's patio bar and moved as far away from others as I could. "Why did you ghost me?"

"I didn't know if I could trust you, Matt."

"That's insane. Of course you could."

"Ray told me you were working for Acuna."

"What? That's insane."

"I know. I know. It sounds crazy. I didn't know what to believe. Ray has this way of getting in your head."

That, I could believe.

She continued. "Ray told me Acuna hired you to figure out if there were any holes. He said you used to be a spy or something, and that's how you'd know if I was talking."

"Did you tell him you shared information with me?"

"Christ, no! He'd have had me killed. That's why I went into hiding... and why I didn't return any of your calls."

"What convinced you I was on the up-and-up?"

"Had a lot of time to think. It just didn't seem to fit. You wouldn't have cared as much about Brashard Brown's dead agent if that was just a ruse."

"Where are you now?"

"My cousin owns a marine repair business. He's been letting me stay on one of the boats."

"Why didn't you just go to a hotel and ask them not to confirm you were staying there? That's what every celebrity in the world does."

"I don't know this world, Matt! Jesus Christ, you act like people just know this shit."

Her end went quiet, and for a moment, I thought I'd lost the call.

Finally, she said, "Can you come and get me?"

"I can come get you, but you need to speak to the police."

"I don't trust the police."

"Oh, for the love of—"

"What? I'm supposed to sit around in some station somewhere for a few hours until someone gets around to taking a statement? For all the good that'll do. Then what? They send me home, by myself. Ray has completely lost his mind. And those people you told me he was in bed with—those gangsters—their names are all over the news, like there's some kind of mob war in the city. I don't feel safe."

I could acknowledge her fear, even if I didn't think it was justified. She'd just been thrown into a terrifying and dangerous world. I also had to acknowledge Ray's rapid descent into oblivion. He'd really believed he could talk "Jameson Carter" and Apogee Partners into giving him a desperately needed lifeline. Once he'd learned none of that was true—that Jameson, the company and the money were all fabrications designed to get to him—he must have had some kind of breakdown.

The coke didn't help.

"You're right, and I'm sorry. I completely appreciate why you're scared. I'll get you some place safe, and we'll stay there until the police arrive. Does that work for you? Or I can drive you to your parents, and you can speak with my police contact over the phone until things cool down here."

"No...no let's just get this over with."

"Okay. Where are you?"

"Poseidon Marine Services. It's on 12th Street, on the Miami River. It's like a service station for boats. I'll text you the address."

"Hold on," I said as I looked up the address. We were getting close to evening rush, and traffic was already starting to bulge. "I'll be there in a few," I said and hung up.

I might've encouraged her to stay in hiding, but not in a marina of all places. Silvestri was right. Miami was a big and dangerous city. We needed Olivia to testify, and we needed her to unravel SSC's finances. Better that we get her into protective custody now.

And not hiding on a boat that wasn't in the water.

I headed out to the garage and into the afternoon crush.

I called Silvestri from the road.

"I got the call," I said. "At least, I got *a* call. Olivia McEvoy has come out of hiding. Said the reason she went underground was because Ruiz convinced her I was working for Acuna."

"We need to get her into protective custody right away," Silvestri said. "Will she testify?"

"I think with some convincing. She's pretty concerned for her safety."

"Are you going to meet her now?"

"Yeah. She said her cousin owns a marine service business. She's been hiding out on one of the boats there. Seemed weirdly paranoid to me, but... whatever. I'm going to pick her up now."

"That's a strange place to hide out."

"This woman was scared. She's the one who showed me the books in the first place. She wouldn't do that if she'd been involved in it." She'd also tried to seduce me, but that was either a function of my dashing good looks and rakish wit, or covering the bases—so to speak—to make sure I was on her side. Or she was scared and vulnerable and just needed someone.

Olivia put herself at risk by sharing the collective's financial data with me. Without that, I'd never have made those essential connections between SSC and the offshores or with the real estate investments or that political action committee. Looking at this situation from her eyes, I could see how she'd be terrified and want to go into hiding.

When Silvestri didn't say anything else, I said, "Unless you're telling me not to get her."

"Against my better judgment, I am not. You are already way more involved in this thing than I'm comfortable with. I'm hugely concerned about what happens if this ever gets to court. All that aside, I don't have a unit to spare right now."

"What's going on?"

"Cop stuff. Jesus Christ, Gage, you don't get to know everything that happens on this side of the fence. When I have information that's relevant to you, I'll share it."

"Ease off. Sorry."

"Just get her to the headquarters building in Doral. Wait for me. Don't do anything else."

"What about when Brashard calls about Ruiz?"

"Why would he call you?"

If he's anything like his father, it's because he doesn't trust cops. "Let's just say he does. He knows me—he doesn't know you."

"Forward it to me, and I'll handle it."

"You don't think I should be there?"

"I absolutely do not."

I told her I'd call her as soon as we were at headquarters.

Poseidon Marine was wedged into the north side of a stubby cul-de-sac in the shadow of an elevated section of I-395 and the Miami River's South Fork. A bridge over that narrow channel formed the border on the left side. There appeared to be another larger marine service business on the right with a fence and thick trees between the lots. On the other side of 12th Street was the back side of a shopping center that ran the length of the block. Twelfth ended in a turnaround halfway into the block and was every bit the bottleneck.

When I approached, I decided to avoid 12th. Instead, I turned onto 11th, which didn't directly connect with it and looked for a spot to park. That's when I found something interesting.

It was about six now, and the marine business had wrapped up for the day. The sky above was already turning to glowing pastels and the place on 11th that shared a wall with Poseidon, M & L Marine, had their lot lights on already. This looked like a high-end place, by contrast. They had a ten-foot wall of stucco concrete surrounding their large compound, and over it, I could see some legitimate yachts on trailers or support structures.

Once I got close enough to see Poseidon Marine Services, I understood why their neighbors put in the visual barrier of trees. Where M & L Marine were luxury watercraft and floating condos, the lot at Poseidon looked like a tornado singled it out with prejudice.

M & L Marine occupied a lot of real estate. The lot went all the way from 11th Street back to the river, and both the shopping center and Poseidon shared a fence line with it. I found a narrow alley between M&L and the strip mall, a mostly overgrown finger of broken asphalt that led to the 12th Street turnaround. I moved quickly down the alley. There were three dumpsters pushed along the fence, so it wouldn't have been possible to get my Defender down it. Good thing I'd parked where I had.

Poseidon Marine had an eight-foot chain-link fence with a green vinyl security barrier on it, which was ripped in several places. Poseidon was more a nautical graveyard. The place was a maze of boats, racks, and low buildings. I'd have no sight lines on the ground and could get boxed in easily. The vehicular gates were all closed, but I spotted an entry in the fence on the compound's far right side.

I walked up to the gate and tried it. It was unlocked.

I slid through the opening and onto the compound. I walked across the lot, staying close to the far-right side and the edge of the security lighting fending off the growing dark. There were two boats in front of me on trailers, and I squeezed through those, moving toward the river. Olivia told me she was in one of the boats moored on the dock.

There was no activity in the yard, and no sign of anyone. I spotted a panel van and a pickup near the office, which was dark, save for the exterior security lights.

Sometimes when walking through a place, you get the sense that you shouldn't be there. This was one of those times.

First, this was a business day, and there wasn't anyone here. True, I hadn't checked if they were closed today for some reason, but all the other businesses were wrapping up for the day.

Poseidon Marine had a dock that ran the uneven length of the water-front. There was a boat moored right in front of me and several more—perhaps seven—moored along the docks. Some were parallel to the dock, others perpendicular, following the contour of the shore. Closer to the office and the covered storage, there were docks extending into the brackish and murky water with small- and medium-sized power boats tethered. On the far side of the channel, there were houses, and most had a boat tied up to a dock.

"That's far enough, Gage."

I knew that voice, and it wasn't Olivia's.

Felix Farrier stepped out of the shadows, and he had a gun.

# 30

---

There are some things you realize you should've seen coming.

I missed this one by a mile.

Farrier wasn't dressed for murder, though, admittedly, I didn't know him that well. He wore a brown linen suit and a cream-colored collarless shirt, probably silk, and those sneakers that people think are okay to wear with suits now.

I did not move.

Well, my mouth did, because…it's me.

"Olivia?"

Farrier shook his head. "She's not coming."

"I didn't suspect her of making a play. Should've once she told me that *farkakte* story about sleeping on a boat."

"I told her that was stupid," he said.

"What—"

"No," Farrier said heavily. "Left hand behind your head. Right hand, lift the gun out of your holster with two fingers and drop it on the ground. I see you so much as twitch, I'm putting you in the dirt."

Farrier was an operator. If he were going to kill me, he'd have done it without identifying himself. The fact that I was still alive meant they needed me for something.

"Ruiz fire you, or did you switch sides on your own?" I asked as I put my left hand behind my head.

"You don't know what the hell you're talking about," he said.

That's stalling.

I said, "I figured you weren't in the picture when Ray summoned me to his house the other night."

"The gun, Gage. Now."

"I'm reaching beneath my shirt now, as you asked. And I am removing the pistol. I have to grip it to remove it from the holster."

"Turn around."

I did and released the gun from the holster with the typical push-lift motion. Once free, I used the first two fingers as instructed to lift the gun out. I extended that arm out to my side.

"Toss it," he said.

I flipped my wrist, and the gun went flying. I brought my right hand up to meet the left.

"Don't shoot me. I'm turning around." I pivoted back around, and he didn't kill me for it. "My read on you," I said, "when I didn't see you at Ray's, was that you'd bend rules, but you wouldn't break them. That tells me Ray knew our conversation would be about his mob buddies and didn't want you hearing about it. Or you already did know, and that was the end of it. How close am I?"

"Not far," Farrier said.

And then I understood, at least this part of it.

"So, Olivia was never hiding out on a boat in here. That was all bullshit."

"Safety Harbor Spa," Farrier said with a short laugh. It was a famous resort on the north end of Tampa Bay. Much more her speed than living on a moored boat for a couple of days.

"Let me see if I've got this right. Olivia wants Ray out of the picture because she plans to take over the collective. Once she heard that Ray fired you—"

"I quit."

"Fine, you quit. Once you quit Ray, Olivia hired you to, what? Make sure

I didn't interfere? If you were going to kill me, you'd have done it. What's the deal here?"

"Just keep you busy until Olivia explains things to Ray. After that, you're free to go."

"Are you fucking kidding me?"

Farrier actually had the audacity to look confused.

"All this," I waved my hands, which I realized in retrospect was stupid because he had a gun on me and told me not to move. "All this was to stall me long enough for Olivia to talk to Ray?"

"Some things really are as simple as they appear, Gage."

"There's a couple things you ought to know, Felix."

"Oh yeah, what's that?"

"The police know I'm here, and if I don't check in with Olivia McEvoy in tow, they're coming for you."

"Bullshit," he said, stretching the word like it was rubber.

"Fine. You're welcome to call Lieutenant Michelle Silvestri with the Organized Crime Division and confirm it. Or not. I don't care." It was a good bluff, and one he couldn't call in the moment. I didn't need him to believe me necessarily. I just wanted to introduce enough doubt that he would second-guess pulling the trigger. "This thing doesn't end without you talking to the cops, one way or the other. Silvestri is leading the investigation into SSC and the people Ray is moving money for. Silvestri knows who you are and what your background is. There are a lot of loose ends in this case that can conveniently get tied up by attaching them to your name." Time to test a theory. "Thing is, Detective Duane Parr with Miami Homicide, whom I believe you are acquainted with, is convinced Jimmy Lawson's murder was a drug thing. Lieutenant Silvestri is *not* convinced. In fact, seeing you here holding me hostage—which is a felony, by the way—is going to lead her to wonder what other problems you made go away for Ray. Problems like Jimmy Lawson. You see, we can link the attempted hit on me to Cesar Marrero. The one on Jimmy, though, was a pro job. And I'll tell you, Felix, from what I've seen of your resume, you're the only one here with those skills."

"That wasn't me, and I am *not* taking the fall for it." What I'd expected was an urgent plea. An emphatic denial. What I got was a calm and measured response, like someone reading the answers out of a teacher's edition. "You're pretty good, Gage. I'll give you that, smarter than I took you for, given how you crashed into this case at the start. Once you got going, though, you're weren't half bad. But you don't have all the answers yet."

"And you do?"

Farrier only nodded.

"I really hope you're planning on sharing some of that with me, because the way this looks to the cops is that Ray hired you to make problems disappear, and the biggest problem he had was Jimmy Lawson hiring me. You're former Army intelligence with some law enforcement training. You could easily set up a murder."

"It wasn't me," Farrier said with some force.

"Let me break this down for you. Ray pays you to make problems go away. You've already taken photos of a woman and used CGI to make her naked, so it looked like she was seducing me. And you have a background that's almost as redacted as mine. You know what the public thinks about people like us." I allowed him to marinate in the imagery for a second but not enough time to respond. When his mouth opened, I said, "Despite your extracurricular hobbies with photography and computers, Felix, I think you've got a moral compass. Of a sort. To borrow from Sam Spade, you want your reputation to be a little sketchy because it brings in high-profile work and the expectation that you get results. In reality, that's a fiction you let persist, and you're not dark enough that you're ethically compromised. It's just that Ray Ruiz called your bluff. The police are going to think you killed Jimmy. You're perfect for it, and I already outlined the reasons why. If I'm right about you, then convince me you didn't do it."

"Pretty speech, Gage. Like I said, you're missing some key pieces, and you've got nothing left to trade. You said you've got cops waiting to pounce. If you did, they'd be here by now. It's just that you're not one of 'em, and I don't need an interpreter. I don't need you to prove I didn't kill Lawson— that'll all come out in the wash. I just need to keep you here long enough to let my client do her thing. Then you're free to go."

"You sent your client into a trap," I said. "There's one last little nugget that you and Olivia don't have. Cesar Marrero is making the problems go away. He's got people like you. They're just faster, more efficient, and they don't worry about staining the furniture. The cops have a citywide dragnet for Marrero and his gang, so it's a race to see who catches whom first. Olivia and Ray don't know any of this. Marrero's people are out looking for them both. And they know where to look because Ray is so desperate to save his ass, he's probably told them where he is because it's a chance to wipe out everyone else who can talk to the cops There's only so many places he can hide. Now, we can sit here and argue with each other, or we can go help some people. Which is it going to be?"

Now we'd know how good of a spook Farrier really was. Could he tell I was bluffing? If he could, I was certainly leaving here with more bullets in me than I'd intended.

No words left either of our mouths.

We heard evening traffic on the bridge, boats in the channel, industrial equipment next door. Car horns, distant and faded conversations in English and Spanish. Too far away to make out the words, just that they were happening.

Farrier lowered his pistol and holstered it.

I dropped my hands and tried to get some circulation back into them.

I'd lied about my intuition on Farrier. I thought he was a dirt ball who would do anything to keep his client out of the spotlight. We had people like him in our industry, especially in LA and Washington. They either did dirty things to keep their clients out of trouble, or dirty things to dig up the horrible facts about their client's enemies. The one common denominator was filth.

Felix Farrier was no different.

I wondered what Olivia McEvoy had used to buy him off?

But he appeared not to want to shoot me at the moment, so here's to being a born-again good guy.

"Who killed Jimmy Lawson?"

"I don't know," he said.

"I'm sure that'll play well in court."

"It's the truth. Believe it or don't, " Farrier said and waited for me to pick up the thread. When I didn't, he added, "Ray found out from the news, same as everyone else."

"So, who did it? Marrero?"

"Not exactly. Ray had a lot less contact with Marrero than you think. It was mostly just money. Ray went to Dalton and told him someone was snooping around and that Lawson had hired him. Dalton told him he'd take care of it. The guy looks at me like, 'This is your job,' or some shit. I might bend some rules for a client, but I'm not killing anyone to protect a secret. Dalton was pissed that Ray let him get exposed. That's when I started following you. Ray wanted to clean his mess up so he didn't get too sideways with Dalton. We didn't find out about Lawson until it was on the news, swear to God. And only after that did we learn they'd also tried to kill you."

"What else am I missing?"

"You were right that Ray hired me to keep him out of trouble, but you were wrong about why. He knew Marrero and Acuna were bad news. I was supposed to shield him from that, run interference with them, and make sure nothing happened to him. Swear to God, I didn't know about Cody Portman beforehand either. I tried to get Ray to go to the police." Felix shook his head slowly. He looked like a Doberman scanning a yard.

"When did you walk away?"

"Little bit ago. When Ray first learned that Lawson hired you, we thought this was just the Browns trying to dig up dirt to get the kid out of his contract. I thought you were some gutter dweller. I checked into you, and your reputation with the Agency ain't great, you know? Once you kept it up after Lawson died, I asked myself why. Look, I knew about the money stuff. Ray made a stupid mistake, and I was trying to keep him out of trouble until he could correct it. When you stayed in the picture, it kind of woke me up to the fact that this whole thing was just dirty. Olivia offered me a way out. Everyone else goes down, she takes over and rights the ship. The point to hiding out was so she could distance herself from whatever the hell has been going on these last couple of days."

"You said Olivia went to confront Ray. Where is that happening?"

"She said Ray was meeting up at Frank Rizzo's place, and that's where she's going."

"Oh Christ," I said, already moving to pick up my gun from the ground.

"What?"

I grabbed the gun, holstered it and turned to face Farrier before taking off. "Rizzo is the one who connected Ray with Marrero in the first place."

Again, Farrier shook a negative.

I knew Farrier was drawing this out to give Olivia time to confront Ray, but he was filling in valuable gaps for me, and I wasn't going to pass this up.

"Not quite. He did, but only because Dalton Bream told him to. Bream always works through intermediaries."

I made to leave.

"I'll go with you," Farrier said.

"Felix, I think it's better that you're nowhere near this."

"I want to see it through. I want to protect Ray."

I couldn't see why, but maybe they'd been friends.

"I think Ray might be beyond saving at this point. I'm calling this in right now, and hopefully, the police will get to Rizzo's house before I do. You probably don't want to be anywhere near there when they arrive. You probably also want to get an attorney."

Farrier sized me up, then nodded and said, "Thanks. I wasn't expecting that."

They usually don't.

Back in the Defender, I checked my phone. I needed to call this in to Silvestri so she could roll units to Rizzo's place.

"Matt, what happened with McEvoy?"

"She was a no-show."

"That's not great," Silvestri said.

"Why do you say that?"

"We just got a tip from my CI in Marrero's organization. They found where Acuna is hiding, and Marrero's sending hitters to take him out. Word is he's going to be there to finish the job."

"Where is this?"

"Acuna's got a safe house in Hollywood."

An hour outside her jurisdiction in the wrong direction.

"Michelle, it's a setup."

"What are you talking about?"

"The information is bogus. You're being fed."

"What? Why?"

"Because I just learned that McEvoy is going to confront Ruiz. They're meeting at Frank Rizzo's home in Coconut Grove. I bet Marrero knows you have an informant, and he's feeding the guy some bullshit to get you on the other side of town." I'd looked up Rizzo's home and office locations when I'd first learned his name. "Marrero and Rizzo are connected. That's who connected Ray with Marrero in the first place. Where are you now?"

"I-95." Even if they turned around right now and did some *Moses at the Red Sea* kind of driving, they were still an hour out. Which was way out.

I was just north of Little Havana, and it could be thirty minutes this time of day, since I was taking residential streets.

"You've got to turn around. It's going down tonight, just not where you think."

"I'd never make it in time. I also can't go back on an informant's intel because you have a hunch. Coconut Grove is MPD's turf. I can make a call, but...Gage, you have to be certain. We cannot go raiding a state senator's home on just your word."

How do I say the information came from someone who was just like me? A master manipulator who would know exactly how to set me up for a career-ending disgrace. That whole scene at the marina could've been a setup to force exactly this. Get us to react, raid Rizzo's house, and—surprise —the senator is entertaining the mayor.

If I'm right: I get there, hopefully in time, and stop Marrero from killing everyone.

If I'm wrong: I ruin Silvestri's career and the case, and my reputation takes an acid bath. And then Marrero kills Olivia and Ray anyway.

"I'm *mostly* sure."

"You need to do goddamn better than that," Silvestri said.

"I'll go scope it out. If it is what I think it is, you have people on standby and roll in. If it isn't, the only thing out is me."

"I don't have anyone on standby, I've told you this. I'd need to call Miami PD and have them send a patrol car out. My team is tied up. What are you going to do, Matt?"

"We are several minutes past the 'I have a plan' stage."

"That's not good enough for me. Not now."

"All I'm going to do is make sure Ruiz, McEvoy, and Rizzo are all there. If they are, I'll call you, and you can send a squad car over. However you need to do it. MPD can hold them until you get there."

"Next time, lead with that, not the 'I don't have a plan' shit."

I disconnected the call and plugged Rizzo's address into my phone's GPS while I weaved through traffic. *I'm a professional, kids—don't try this at home.*

Silvestri didn't call me back, so I took that to mean she'd either accepted my plan or written me off entirely. I had even money either could be true.

---

In addition to being a state senator, Frank Rizzo was a noted attorney with a highly successful practice and lived in an affluent neighborhood on the water. Maybe that went without saying here.

The home was a two-story, L-shaped structure that looked like an abstract art sculpture of a Polynesian hut. You could barely make out the house from the street because of the jungle-aesthetic landscaping. The home was sandwiched between a pair of McMansions. They all backed into a channel that spilled into Biscayne Bay and faced east, giving them a nearly unobstructed view of a Caribbean sunrise.

A concrete wall wrapped around the property with thick foliage behind it. The only entry points appeared to be a closed metal gate or through the ten-foot wooden gate across the driveway. No way to tell if Rizzo was home and I didn't see Ray or Olivia's cars on the street.

I got out of the Defender, holstering my Glock.

Interestingly, the neighboring three-story house did not have a wall around it. I crept through the neighbor's yard, careful to avoid windows. The owners were home, though all seemed to be indoors, so I moved quickly along the wall and past their patio. There was no cover. If anyone walked outside or looked down from one of the floors above, they'd see me. The wall terminated at the water's edge. This would be fun.

Grabbing onto one side of the wall, I leaned over to look around to the other side. There were some metal bars I could hold onto. Unfortunately, this exposed me to the back side of the house across the channel that was maybe fifty feet away. The waterway was about as wide as a residential street. That house, naturally, had a back wall that was entirely glass and had a great view of Rizzo's backyard. The curtains were all pulled back, and there were lights on in every room. People were moving about, looked like they were getting ready for dinner.

I crouched next to the wall. I chanced a look behind me and saw that the bottom-floor curtains were open too.

A man appeared in the window across the channel, holding a tumbler of something and staring into space. He didn't have direct line of sight on me, probably couldn't see me because of the wall. However, if I climbed around to Rizzo's place, he would. Worst case, he called the police, and I'd bet in this neighborhood, they had a pretty fast response time. It just wouldn't be the "right" police. If Miami PD rolled in and not on Silvestri's top, I'd just be an armed trespasser at a politician's house. By the time Silvestri and her crew showed up, whatever advantage we might have had would be burned.

The guy in the window raised the tumbler and took a drink. He had a western-facing window. Body language suggested he was watching the sunset.

Christ, he could be standing there for twenty minutes.

He turned his head to one side, said something to a person behind him, and went back to the sunset.

*Go help set the table, you asshole.*

Rizzo's house had jungle-like clusters of palms and other plants, erupting in green geysers from the ground. Great cover, if I could get to it.

A sliding glass door opened on the house behind me. Someone was coming out to the patio. With no other options, I would have to chance being seen. I reached up and around, grabbed one of the metal rails on the other side of the wall, and swung myself around. Keeping low, I dashed for the shadows beneath one of the palm clusters. I looked back across the channel.

The scotchy sunset gazer saw *something*, but the look on his face said he didn't know exactly what. He craned his neck forward, and I could see the squint from here. One more call over the shoulder, and he looked back in my direction. I picked up some conversation from the patio I'd just evacuated. Sounded like a post-dinner drink on the water.

I also picked up the beginnings of a conversation on Rizzo's patio, on the other side of this wall of foliage.

"Well, Raymond, it seems I've got *another* uninvited guest tonight," a voice said in a high-strung tone. I recognized it from my meeting at SSC. That would be Frank Rizzo.

Worth noting that my cover was good, but it wasn't total. I could see through the fronds, and presumably, they could see me too. The landscaping consisted of clusters of coconut palms that rose up above the home's second floor, with saw palmetto and bottle palm at the base to give more cover at ground level. The palm wall, for lack of a better term, extended some distance into the patio. Olivia stood facing two men, whose backs were to me, about thirty feet away. I could make out some of what they were saying, though it wasn't clear. She looked aggressive and agitated.

The house's long side terminated a few feet from me. Olivia and Rizzo stood on the far side of a circular pool, beneath an overhang from the second floor.

Ray paced back and forth like a caged animal that knows the bars aren't as strong as advertised. He was nervous energy and aggression—with a cocaine chaser.

"Neither of you should be here," Rizzo said.

"Dalton won't return my phone calls, so I'm talking to you," Ray said, a little too loudly. His words were mushy, like he was speaking through a sponge.

"This is not the place," Rizzo said.

"I already know, Frank," Olivia interjected.

"Jesus Christ, Ray. How fucking stupid *are* you?"

"Don't call me stupid," Ray countered in some dangerously loaded tones.

The air had a static charge that I could feel from here.

I got my phone out and texted Silvestri that I'd been right, and they needed to roll, right now. Then, I made sure the phone was on silent in case she tried to call.

"Well, you brought her into this, what am I supposed to think?"

"He didn't 'bring me in,' Frank. I figured it out for myself."

"You had help," Ray spat. "Who told you? Was it Gage or that lying snake Felix? Or maybe you just fucked 'em both."

Oliva took two long strides, extended an arm, and slapped the spit out of Ray's mouth. Ray cocked both arms back and shoved her with all the force he could muster. Olivia fell backward onto the deck. Rizzo looked down at her, but he didn't move to help her up. The son of a bitch didn't even set down his drink.

"Ray, you need to leave. Immediately. And when I tell Dalton about this, Cesar Marrero is going to be the least of your problems. I told him you couldn't handle it."

"Shut. Up," Ray said and punctuated that by pulling a gun.

Weapons in the hands of untrained civilians rarely, if ever, defused a situation.

And that was if they were calm. And not coked up.

Ray said, "I told Dalton I could fix this. And I will. Turns out, I don't need any of you. While you assholes have been running around, playing with your mobster pals, what have I done? Nothing. I just built a goddamn business. I'm the proverbial tortoise, and I will outrace you all."

I think Ray was off base far enough to be out of the stadium, though I could see the fuzzy logic through his eyes. Stacked up against the people around him, what he'd done was some low-level, white-collar stuff. It wasn't murder, and God only knows what in the hell Acuna's and Marrero's gangs were doing to each other right now. Ray figured he could wait all of them out, let the dust settle, and when it was all over, probably make a reasonably convincing argument that he was an unwitting victim in all this. And Shakespeare couldn't have written a more effective double-cross than Olivia McEvoy.

"Hey, guys, hope I'm not interrupting anything," I said, moving out from the wall of greenery.

Rizzo almost dropped his drink when he saw me, though he recovered quickly enough to dryly utter, "Thank God, the asshole cavalry is here."

Rizzo stood closest to me, with Ruiz to his right. There was a small, circular pool between us and Olivia, who stood closest to the house. And she'd since picked herself up off the ground.

"Don't let me interrupt you, Frank," I said. "You were saying something about Mr. Bream?"

There was just one piece of this I didn't have, which was the connection between Bream and Rizzo and how that factored into Marrero. There was a rough map sketched out in my head, and I was hoping Rizzo would fill in the gaps to save his skin.

"You're trespassing, Mr. Gage," Rizzo said and lifted the drink to his lips. That was an expensive crystal tumbler he had there. "Whatever you have to add to the conversation, you can save it for the police."

"Oh, I'll be speaking with them shortly. Just not the ones you've got a hook into."

Rizzo's eyes widened just a touch; otherwise, he hid it well.

"No one is calling any police," Ray said. His face was flushed, and he was sweating, breathing heavily. The guy looked like he was one hot minute away from a stroke.

"Put the goddamn gun down, Ray," Rizzo said.

"Or what?"

"You want all this out in the open? Fine. Let's have it your way, Raymond. I warned you not to come here. You showed up anyway. You're assuming because you have a gun that Dalton will take your call? You're dead to him, Ray. It's over. You couldn't handle it, and now you're done. You are going to go to jail, and it will be your word against ours. Oh, and you can assume that Mr. Cathcart will not be representing you in this matter, as he's a close friend of Dalton's."

A low growl formed deep in Ray's throat.

"And you," Rizzo turned his megawatt stare on Olivia. "Your plan was, what? Tell us you'd figured out the scheme? Nice work, Nancy Drew. It's going to get you precisely shit. Between the pictures of you and Gage and the simple fact that as SSC's chief operating officer, you couldn't hope to convince a jury of your ignorance."

This guy was saying all my lines, and it was kind of pissing me off.

"I'm going inside now to call the police. Anyone left here when they arrive can explain it to them, or you can do us all a favor and get the fuck off my property. You sicken me, Ray. You were only ever just a tool to us, especially to Dalton."

Ray's growl escaped his mouth in a full-throated roar with some expletives buried in it.

And he fired.

# 31

When I think of them now, these are single images frozen in time. Even when I play it back, it only looks like an old movie of stitched-together stills.

Frank Rizzo fell backward into the pool.

The crystal tumbler hit the patio and exploded into a billion shimmering pieces.

Olivia screamed because she'd never seen anyone shot before.

Ray's expression didn't change, even as the recognition of what he'd done punched through the chemical shield around his brain. Maybe he was too far gone, or maybe he just didn't care.

Ray turned to look at me, though he didn't see me. His eyes weren't just muddled from coke and booze, I think he was...unmoored.

He turned his gun on me and fired. The shot was wide by a mile—I was pretty sure—but I dove anyway and landed unceremoniously in a cluster of bushes. I heard the scraping of footsteps on pavement running away.

Damn it.

By the time I pulled myself out of the landscaping, Ray was gone.

Since I didn't see his car on the street, I guessed he'd parked in the carport. That gate would take time to open. There was still time to catch him. But then what? A shoot-out?

I decided to let Ray go. Mostly because I had a good idea where he was heading, and that would give me time to get Silvestri involved.

Hoping I'd made the right decision, I ran over to the pool and pulled the bleeding Frank Rizzo out. He was still alive, so I dropped him on the deck.

"I need a doctor, damn it," he said, spitting blood.

"You sure do," I said. "I think Marrero has hitters on the way here now."

"Why do you think that?" he said, grunting through the pain.

"Because he basically told me he did. Did Dalton set you up, or is Marrero just pissed at everyone? Your answer matters. I'm working with Miami-Dade, so I can help you if you help us. If not, you can take your chances. I doubt you're connected enough for this."

"Dalton," he said with some effort. "It was Dalton. Marrero is just a tool. The son of a bitch."

"I'm going to get you to the hospital."

"Olivia, grab some towels from the kitchen," I said and went back to triaging the senator. Ray had hit him in the chest, but it was on the right side. Rizzo probably had a punctured lung. Olivia reappeared with the items, and I made a makeshift bandage, then helped him to his feet. He sucked air in through his teeth. I turned to Olivia. "I need you to drive him to the hospital."

"Mercy," Rizzo grunted. "About two miles that way." He motioned to the north.

"Can you take him there?"

"I can," she said. "Won't the police..."

"I'll make sure the first people you talk to are the ones I'm working with."

"Okay," she said, adding, "Ray is gone." At least he hadn't tried to kill her on his way.

I helped Rizzo outside to the carport. He had a Tesla Model X and a Corvette, both back-in parked so they faced the gate. Olivia's Porsche was off to the side in the wide turnaround.

"Your keys in the car?" I asked.

"No way," Rizzo said, voice hoarse.

"Your blood, your car."

"Tesla," he croaked.

There were sirens in the distance, but not close enough to know if they were coming our way. Had to believe first responders would be here soon enough. I wanted to control the situation and make sure the ones who got the first crack at Rizzo and Olivia were Silvestri's people. I doubted Rizzo had Coconut Grove or MPD cops on the take—the city just wasn't wired that way anymore. That didn't mean Rizzo wouldn't have political connections he could use. The mayor and chief of police would both be on speed dial. And I couldn't stay with him to stall any authorities who might arrive.

I helped get Rizzo into the Tesla.

Rizzo, impatient, hit the button for the carport gate.

Olivia got behind the wheel.

The gate was halfway open.

Two soft snaps cracked the silence, and two holes appeared on the windshield. Spiderweb cracks burst out like silent lighting, and Frank Rizzo's chest exploded. A suppressed pistol sounded like a light crack on the wind.

Olivia screamed, and a third round went through her side, she bounced in the seat then slumped forward.

The carport gate finished its slow crawl to the left, revealing Felix Farrier in a shooting-range stance with his suppressed pistol.

He couldn't see me because I was standing next to the car on the driver's side.

I sighted him and fired.

Farrier never saw it coming. My aim wasn't great, though, and I hit him in the upper chest. Farrier whipped around like I'd spun him, but he didn't go down.

The gate started its return trip, so I ran to Rizzo's Corvette for cover. I reached in and hit the button to open the gate again. The massive door jerked once and reversed course. When it opened, the plan was for Farrier to think I was hiding next to the Tesla. I was already running for the door set into the wall to catch Farrier from behind. Pulling the door open, I popped out, pistol first and using the wall for cover.

Farrier was watching the gate, and I had the drop.

I took off at a dead run, accelerating as fast as my legs would push me, and leaped off the ground in my best impression of a flying tackle.

We locked eyes just before I hit him. I registered genuine shock in his.

I wasn't giving this son-of-a-bitch an easy out. We landed on the pavement, and Farrier's head bounced off the street. I cocked my left arm back and gave him a left hook to the side of the face. Farrier recovered fast. He hammered my midsection with knuckle punches and then went for my gun.

I kneed him in the crotch to get some breathing room.

And because he deserved it.

Farrier brought his legs in impossibly fast and kicked me in the stomach, driving me off with serious force. I flew a couple inches and landed hard. The gun slid out of my reach. Farrier jumped to his feet. I charged before he had a chance to get planted. He had a kick in the air by the time I closed the distance. His shin hit my ribcage, then he grabbed my shoulders for leverage and brought his knee into the same spot.

Farrier thrust a second time with his knee, and I let him do it.

Since he was grabbing my shoulders, he couldn't block. I shot a palm strike up to his chin, snapping Farrier's head back, followed by a flat-knuckle strike to the trachea. He staggered back as he fought for his breath.

Two steps back and he was ready to go.

I'd give him this, the guy recovered fast.

A red stain blossomed out on the left side of Farrier's shirt from where I'd shot him, though it must have been a graze. Clearly, he was still mobile and throwing punches.

I lunged forward. Farrier anticipated my right-hand jab, blocking it. He tried to mask the tight-lipped wince of pain as he brought his left arm down. I punched with my left, and he down-blocked it. I countered with an open-hand strike aimed right at his wound. I connected with the knuckle of my thumb and drove the point into the wound. I could almost see the shockwaves of pain radiate out from that spot. Maybe I'd done better than just clip him.

Farrier countered with a feint, which I fell for, and then landed a punch to the side of my head. My point of view changed immediately, and now I was looking ninety degrees in the wrong direction and had just taken up astronomy. Farrier followed that up with a kick, landing it in my midsection.

That hit to my head had scrambled my circuits, and I wouldn't be on my feet any longer if I took another. That kick had robbed me of the wind in my lungs.

He fought pretty well for a man with a leaking bullet hole.

But I'd discovered something too.

After my strike, Farrier wasn't using his left arm.

His right arm lanced out in an attack that might as well have been telegraphed in advance. I grabbed the wrist with my left hand, driving it down, and sent a flurry of rapid strikes to the side of his neck and face with my right. I pulled Farrier in closer, causing him to lose balance, then I stepped into the gap and jammed my right elbow into his throat. He fell over my right thigh and crashed to the street.

I took a couple steps back to get space to catch my breath.

Farrier rolled with the impact and was on his feet faster than I would have thought possible.

And now he had a knife in his hand.

It was a small tactical blade favored by special operators and many of the Agency's paramilitary officers.

Farrier closed the distance between us, fast. The knife blade shot out like a snake.

My left wrist shot up, smashing him below the hand, and sending the blade off its mark. A hot lance of pain on my forearm told me *not by enough*.

Farrier's left hand hung not-quite limply at his side.

I lunged for his left hand with my right, grabbing the thumb and cranking it as hard as I could. Farrier yelped in shock and pain as I corkscrewed his arm around. A second later, I had his left arm pinned behind his back. He flipped the knife in his hands so he could make a downward slash at me, which I anticipated and stepped to the side to dodge. He kept at it, now panic stabbing.

I went as far to his left as I could without losing my grip on his arm and brought my right foot down on the side of his kneecap. Farrier couldn't even scream. His mouth and eyes went wide, and he dropped the knife. I adjusted my grip, releasing his arm so I could get him in a choke hold.

I squeezed until I felt his body go limp and then held for a bit longer to make sure he wasn't faking it. His body collapsed, and I let him go. Farrier sank to the street, out cold. I kicked the knife away. The smart thing to do was field-strip the gun or throw it over a wall, just in case he woke up. Both of those things would leave my prints on it, and that would only complicate things. I kicked the gun away too.

The national average response time to an active shooter call is fifteen minutes. This is from the time someone hears shots fired and calls 911. Most of the rounds fired in this thing were from Farrier, and he'd used a suppressed pistol. If someone was inside with the windows closed, they wouldn't hear a thing. But the first shot fired had been from Ray. I assumed I had less than five minutes before the first cops were on scene.

I ran back to the carport.

Frank Rizzo was dead, no question. I heard soft wheezing coming from Olivia. A quick search of the Tesla revealed a roadside assistance kit with a small first aid box. I tore that open, found the bandages and did my best improvised field dressing. I spoke to Olivia in as soothing a voice as I could while I worked, asking if she could hear me, telling her to hold on, reassuring her that help was on the way. I had to be out of here before the police arrived or all of this was for nothing. Ray would find Brashard, and after what I'd seen tonight, I honestly didn't know what he would do. So why was I burning precious minutes on Olivia?

Because even though she'd made mistakes, she didn't deserve to die because of them.

If I was lucky, I now had two minutes until police arrived.

There was nothing about this case that suggested I had any luck left.

## 32

Rizzo's neighborhood was an L shape with water on three sides.

I fought the urge to *bat out of hell* it out of there. The only hope I had was the police blasting by me to respond. I turned right onto Fair Isle Avenue, the main artery connecting the neighborhoods on this small peninsula with the mainland, and saw three Miami Police Department squad cars scream around the corner from Bayshore onto Fair Isle. I pulled over to let them by.

Driving a restomod early '90s Land Rover that looked like a rich guy's toy probably made the difference between them blitzing past me and an uncomfortable conversation at the wrong end of a service pistol.

Wasting no time, I throttled down the street and made a left before more cops arrived.

The realization of things I'd set in motion hit me like a slap in the face. After Ray turned up missing, I'd told Brashard to call him, believing the kid was the only one who could get Ruiz out of hiding. Things went vertical after I'd met Farrier at the boatyard, and there hadn't been time to tell Brashard to call it off.

My first call went to Silvestri.

"Gage, what the hell is going on? Radio is blowing up with shots-fired calls in Coconut Grove. Please tell me you're not involved."

"I don't have a lot of time to explain."

"Goddamn it, Gage!"

"Listen to me," I shouted, cutting her off. "Felix Farrier, Ruiz's private security guy, just shot Frank Rizzo and Olivia McEvoy. Rizzo is dead, I've got a dressing on Olivia, and she might make it if she gets medical attention immediately. Ruiz got away."

"Wait, I thought you said Farrier was working with McEvoy. Like, the two of them were switching sides or something."

"Yeah, well, I didn't exactly have a lot of time to ask him what he was thinking."

"Where are you *right now*?" Her tone suggested she didn't entirely believe me.

"Driving to Coral Gables."

"Listen to me loud and clear, Gage. Stop the car. Get out and wait until I get there."

"I'm not doing that." Silvestri started shouting at me again, and I cut her off. "Hey, Ruiz lost it, okay? He snapped. He got away in the gunfight and is going to confront Brashard Brown."

"Why would he do that?"

"I told you, he's lost it. I've seen him, Michelle. Ray doesn't know what reality is right now."

"Is that your clinical diagnosis?"

I see now how constant sarcasm can be perceived as being unhelpful.

"I suspect I have some similar training as you to spot someone in crisis," I said and left it at that. "Ray thinks he can survive by outlasting the bad people around him in this race to the bottom he's kicked off. He's going to meet Brashard, who set this thing up. Which we asked him to do, remember, because we thought that was the best way to get Ray into the open. We are not letting this kid twist in the wind now. I'm going to stop Ray from harming Brashard—and stop Brashard from doing something life-alteringly stupid to defend himself. If you'd like to take it up with me in person —and I really hope you do—I'll text you my location as soon as I have it." I hung up.

Silvestri called back, and I didn't answer.

I dialed Brashard and prayed I wasn't too late. Ray had at least five minutes on me. Brashard didn't pick up, which for a nineteen-year-old almost certainly meant either ghosting or incapacitation. As I was setting my phone back down to concentrate on aggressive driving, I saw that I had voicemails. Ignoring the ones from Lieutenant Silvestri, I saw Brashard had called while things were going down at Rizzo's.

Brashard: "Hey, Matt. Uh, haven't heard from you, but I...ah, did what you asked. Called Ray. Didn't seem like we should do this on campus, so I told him to meet me downtown Coral Gables. Seemed like he wouldn't do stupid shit if there were a lot of people around. I told him Alhambra Plaza. There's a fountain there, Columbus something."

I told Siri where to go, and the GPS updated. Fifteen minutes. I voice-texted the location to Silvestri and turned my attention to the road.

I turned right on 22nd and floored it north.

Had to hand it to Brashard, this was a heads-up play. Good move getting this off campus and putting Ray in a situation where there were people around. Might just get Ray to think twice about violent options. Streetlights and taillights streaked by me in their respective blurs. The phone said fifteen minutes. I did it in eight.

Turned out this place had a lot of fountains, and the one Brashard referred to was the Galiano-Alhambra Gazebo Fountain at Columbus Center. I had to park about a block away. My hand hesitated on the holster as I got out of the Defender. Ray was armed, unstable, and had already shot one person tonight. If I brought a gun, the likelihood of this ending badly increased immeasurably. If I didn't, though, I was relying on my ability to talk him down or stall him until the police arrived.

Against my better judgment, I took the gun.

The Galiano Fountain was a long, rectangular pool flanked by palm trees. There was a salmon-colored restaurant and brewery next door, and the looming Alhambra Tower was to the left. Behind the fountain looked like either a condo building or an upscale hotel.

I crossed two lanes of slow-moving traffic and saw Brashard immediately. He stood on the tiled plaza, the pool behind him a soft backlight of glowing blue-green. He was dressed in team workout gear. I climbed the two steps to stand next to him.

"Thank Christ you're all right," I said. "Where's Ray?"

"Man, you gotta explain what the hell is going on here."

"I will. The short version is that Ray is in bed with some mobsters—I've already told you that part. Everything just came to a head. Some people were killed. Originally, this was about you getting Ray to a place so the police could arrest him."

"Lemme guess, that ain't the plan now?"

"Yeah, we're kind of at the winging-it stage."

"You look like you got your ass kicked."

"That's about right. Ray had a security guy working for him, and the guy dragged my face across the street a bit. Where is Ray?"

"I don't know, man. Called him, like you said."

"You should go. Ray is in a bad place right now, and he's dangerous. You did your part."

I got my phone out to call Silvestri. She had to be, what, an hour away when I'd first called her? Even if she had believed me when I told her the tip she'd been chasing was a red herring, I figured it was twenty minutes for me to get from the boatyard to Rizzo's. That whole shitshow was another fifteen, between my sneaking around and the fight with Farrier. Another ten to get here?

No way to know.

"What are you doing here?" If there was any more poison in his words, it'd need a warning label. Brashard and I both turned to the sound of Ray's unmistakably slurred voice as he came up from the cross street to the fountain's other entrance. From our vantage point, it looked like he was rising up out of the water. He stepped up onto the side of the pool, where it was slick with backsplash from the smaller fountains that arced water into the pool at evenly spaced intervals.

I couldn't see the gun.

"It's over, Ray," I said as he approached. I kept my hands wide and to the sides to show I wasn't armed. Ruiz turned his head at the sound of my voice. He was still flushed, and there was a wild look in his eyes. I faced his left side, and he stood at an angle. I still couldn't see the gun. "Frank Rizzo confessed to everything. He said Dalton Bream set you up. We can all go home now." I decided not to hit him with the knowledge that Rizzo was dead.

"What are you doing here, Gage? This is a private meeting," Ray said. "Brashard wanted to talk. This doesn't include you."

"I'm here to help you, Ray."

"When have you ever helped *anything*? Everything you do is lies. You lied about who you are. You lied about the money, about helping me. Then you fucked my partner, turned her against me."

"That was not me. I didn't touch her. Felix doctored those pictures with a computer."

Ray laughed, the way you think villains do in a comic book. It was loud, maniacal, and off balance. "Right."

"Farrier was working for Dalton Bream, Ray."

"No, he wasn't. He worked for me until I fffffired him." Ray walked closer to us, staying on the fountain's marble outer edge. He passed behind a palm tree and then put one foot up on the raised planter. He was, maybe, ten feet from us now and a foot above our level. "You shouldn't believe anything he says, Brashard," Ray said with some effort.

"Maybe you ought to come down from there, Ray," Brashard said. "Let's talk this out."

"What is there to talk out? You called me here to...what? Fire me? We have a *contract*. Contracts are binding. They're binding." He repeated that a few times.

"Look, man, I think it's best if we all just chill. Why don't we have a seat right here?" Brashard pointed at a spot near us.

"We can talk. Gage has to go."

"I don't feel comfortable with that," Brashard said.

"Why is everyone betraying me?" Ray shouted, and now he had everyone's attention. He lifted his shirt and pulled the pistol out of his waistband.

The pitched whine of a siren broke in the distance, and it was quickly joined by more to form a chorus.

Someone must've seen the gun because there was a scream and a person shouting, "He's got a gun!"

Thanks for the hot tip.

"Ray, please put the gun away. The police are coming. If they see that, there's no way out. We can fix this. Rizzo confessed to Dalton setting you up, to his connection with Cesar Marrero."

*Of course, your attack dog shot him in his driveway thirty minutes ago, so he's not sharing any of that with anyone...*

Adding that didn't seem helpful.

"Rizzo...he's such a snake," Ray said, and the words clawed at his throat, sounding half like a plaintive wail and half like a growl. "He's the one the police have to talk to."

"I agree," I said. "Now please put the gun down, and we'll talk to the police together."

Ray's head cocked to the side, and for a second, I thought he'd heard something that maybe I hadn't. Then he shook it, as if answering his own question.

"Your dad...he negotiated your deal with me. Negotiated. Ha! He didn't even *read* it. I jus' told him how much the money was, and he said you'd sign it. He didn't care."

"Leave my dad outta this, man," Brashard said, and there was an edge in his voice I didn't like.

"Did he even give you any of it?"

"Gents," I said slowly, though I didn't know that either of them heard me. Took a step forward to get between them and then thought better of it. "Let's all take a step back."

"You're just a predator, Ray!" Brashard blurted out. "A goddamn leach. You wouldn't have shit if it wasn't for me and people like me."

"You ungrateful shit. I made you rich. You're a millionaire 'fore you're even twenty years old." Ray's slur was getting worse. He had almost an extra syllable at the end of every word now.

"Yeah, and you get a cut the rest of my life."

"That's the goddamn deal!" Ray shouted. We had a crowd now, though they were a distant ring. "Read the fine print. Not my fault. Terms and conditions. Isss not my fault."

Police sirens getting closer.

I didn't dare look away to see if I could spot the cop cars.

"Nobody wanted to sign you, Brash...Brashard. You were jus' some kid. You think you're Ken Dorsey or somethin'? You don't have a *name*. *I* made you what you are. People know you cuz of *me*. Stupid little shit."

"You threatened my family," Brashard said.

"I didn't threaten nobody. Jus' told that two-faced sack-of-shit father of yours that...terms and conditions."

"You told him you could have me cut and have to pay back the money to you."

"Terms and conditions," Ray repeated. I knew he was gone.

Brashard's hand went to the hem of his shirt.

Oh shit.

Ray raised the gun.

I drew my Glock and fired twice.

Ray managed a shot before I hit him.

Brashard was on the ground.

Ray's head snapped back, and he fell backward into the pool, landing with a wet crash.

I just stood there, numbly holding my pistol, wisps of smoke trailing off the barrel like ghosts. The pool wasn't deep enough for Ray to be fully submerged, but the water around him was already turning a cloudy red. No question he was dead.

I turn to check on Brashard. He was lying on his back and frantically patting himself, like he was trying to squash a loose ember. "Are you hit?"

"I don't know. I...don't think so."

There was a gouge in the tile next to him, where it looked like Ray's bullet had hit, missing the kid by inches. With Brashard safe, I shot a quick glance at Ray. Still dead.

"He all right?" Brashard asked.

I shook my head. "What in the hell were you doing?" I said.

"What are you talking about?"

"You were going to lift your shirt to show Ray your gun."

"I don't have a gun. I left it in my room. I was going to get my phone to play the message Ray left my dad."

"Ray thought you were going for a gun. That's why he shot at you," I said.

I holstered my pistol and sat on the lip of the pool as the sound of sirens reached ear-splitting levels. Lights, like red and blue phantoms, painted the building across the street, and then the plaza was flooded with law enforcement vehicles. Police stormed out of them.

All the police.

—————

Silvestri arrived with one of her detectives, Baptiste, a while after the first wave of police. I didn't know exactly how long because I was face down on the pavement and couldn't look at my watch. Eventually, they let me up, and I sat on the lip of the fountain hearing nothing but the gurgle and rush of the water. I was not even dimly aware of what was happening around me.

I'd already played the scene back a hundred times in my head.

Yes, Brashard would've been killed if I hadn't taken the shot. Without question.

That wouldn't make any of this easier to accept.

It must have taken Silvestri a few tries to get my attention. I heard her speaking my name and, at some point, she'd started snapping her fingers. The words just didn't register in my brain as something I needed to acknowledge. Maybe there was another "Matt Gage" here, and Silvestri was talking to him.

Eventually, I looked up and saw her, hands on her hips. The lieutenant had a tactical vest over a department polo and chinos. The black ball cap dropped shadows on her face that made the lines of her scowl drop almost to the street.

"What the actual absolute fuck, Matt?"

I stood.

I looked Michelle Silvestri dead in the eyes, and I said, "I just shot a man that I shouldn't have had to."

She was a detective and could figure out the implication of my words on her own.

—————

Thirty people saw it go down.

They saw Ray waving a gun and shouting. They saw him shoot, and they saw me shoot him to protect Brashard Brown.

The accounts weren't unanimous, because eyewitness accounts never are, but there was enough for a quorum that the Coral Gables homicide detective responsible for the scene decided it wasn't murder. We spent several hours making statements to the Coral Gables PD and then to Miami-Dade in the scope of the broader investigation. They separated Brashard and me. I'd done what I could for him, and he was now on his own.

A Miami Police Department patrol sergeant arrived at some point to speak to Silvestri.

That would be about what happened at Frank Rizzo's.

The part of my brain that was rarely helpful wondered if I would get a prize for involving three different jurisdictions in one night.

Hat trick.

It was long after dark by the time someone handed me a bottle of water and Silvestri asked me if I wanted something to eat. I did not.

"We need to go to Rizzo's house and talk with MPD," she said, joining me on the marble.

"Did Olivia make it?"

"She's at Mercy Hospital in critical condition. Someone did a pretty good field dressing, which likely saved her life." Silvestri paused and considered her next words. "Why didn't you wait with her?"

"If I had, Ray would have shot Brashard."

"You don't know that," she said, the way cops do.

"Wait until the toxicology tests and tell me if you still think that," I said, not taking my gaze from the street below. "And I was making sure Brashard didn't do anything stupid."

"Like what?"

"Like shoot first. He'd told me earlier that he had a gun, for protection. He didn't bring it, but I didn't know that until after everything went down."

The cop in her wanted to tell me that I'd fled a crime scene; the human in her stayed her tongue.

Silvestri got up and walked over to the Coral Gables homicide cop and had a couple of words, then she handed him a card, and I saw a head nod. She jerked her chin at me, indicating it was time to go.

As we were walking to her car, I saw Cyrus Brown in the crowd. There was only blame in his eyes.

We drove in silence, other than Silvestri admitting, "You were right about Hollywood being a ruse."

We arrived at Rizzo's home, and it was an unsurprising shitshow. Miami PD kept the media trucks out of the cul-de-sac, though it took a lot of honking, light flashing, and siren squawks to get us through them and the police cordon. We parked, and she told me not to move until she said otherwise.

There was a gaggle of uniformed brass with a lieutenant I took to be the on-scene commander and some plainclothes detectives. Silvestri walked up to that group, and I could tell even from here the conversation was... animated. After a good fifteen minutes, one of her guys, Detective Tran, sauntered up to the car. "They're ready for you, Gage," he said.

The detective escorted me over to the group, and Silvestri broke off to intercept us.

"You don't want any part of that," she said.

"Did they arrest Farrier?"

"He's in custody. Nothing more until you talk. Tell me everything. Leave nothing out. No bullshit, Matt."

I started with the boatyard meeting with Farrier and how he convinced me that he was working with Olivia, how he basically convinced me to come here. She interjected only to ask small clarifying questions. When I got to the Rizzo shoot-out portion of the day, she said, "Walk me through it. Let's go."

I led her through the carport. Rizzo's Tesla was still there, with forensics techs buzzing around it. I walked Silvestri through the sequence of events. The three-way argument, Ray pulling a gun and shooting Rizzo. We walked back to the carport, and I described what happened with Farrier. How I had to fight him even after I'd shot him once.

"Ray had fled by this point. Rizzo was shot and needed medical attention. Instead of chasing after Ray, I decided to stay and offer aid to Rizzo. I wanted him alive to testify. I asked Olivia to drive him to the hospital."

"Why not just call 911?"

"I knew Rizzo was dirty. He claimed to have police connections." Silvestri nodded and didn't probe further. I continued. "We opened the gate from afar, and Farrier was there waiting. I could see him, but he couldn't see me. He shot Rizzo first, then Olivia. I took my shot, hit him in the side. I left through the gate, and he was right there. We fought. I was able to maneuver him into a headlock and render him unconscious. I calculated the MPD would be here within minutes. I saw that Olivia was still alive and used the first aid kit to do what I could for her."

"Back up a second. Earlier, you go to this boatyard because that's where McEvoy says to meet you," she said.

"Right."

"Only she's not there. It's Farrier. He convinces you to come here?"

"Yes. He admitted he and Olivia were working together. Farrier told me he'd quit working for Ray. Olivia figured Ray would get arrested and she could take over SSC. Probably rename and relaunch, and in a year, no one even remembers Ray Ruiz. She'd seemed genuinely horrified when I told her about Cody Portman."

"Then why did Farrier shoot her?"

"Your guess is as good as mine," I said.

"After all this goes down," she said in a way that seemed to neither acknowledge nor discount what I'd just told her, "Miami PD responded to the shots-fired call, and they found Felix Farrier with a suppressed pistol and a combat knife. He seemed pretty out of it to them. If you're trying to convince officers responding to a multiple homicide that you're just wrong place, wrong time...that's not the look to go for. Thankfully, Farrier did not try to shoot his way out. I think if they'd only responded with one car, Farrier would have. He's not saying anything. MPD has him in an interview room right now, waiting on his attorney."

"Cathcart?"

"Don't know," she said. "I can all but guarantee you that Farrier will say you shot those people, because you fled. That's also not a good look. Now, matching the bullets to the gun they found will undermine that argument, but what do you want to bet the gun can't be traced back to him? It comes down to prints and any powder residue on his skin. And your testimony against his."

She didn't have to tell me any of that.

I'd have to get a lawyer, for certain, and would likely face some consequences for leaving the scene. I'd done the right thing, whatever those consequences might be.

"I know why you did it," she said. "I think I know you well enough to understand your rationale. None of that will matter to the MPD people we need to speak with now. You need to be clear on that."

"Do you think I was right?"

"I think *you* think you were right."

I appreciated Silvestri prepping me for the conversation with the Miami homicide detectives. I didn't ask what the latest on Marrero or Acuna was. Honestly, I didn't care anymore.

I'd been forced to shoot a man tonight, and it was the inaction of others that had put me there.

When she felt I was ready, Silvestri introduced me to the pair of murder cops handling the investigation. Thankfully, neither of them was Duane Parr. We did a field interview, and they informed me we'd be going to the station for a more in-depth conversation. One of them tried the typical interrogation judo, trying to get me to trap myself with my words. If I'd have seen that play any further out, we could've had air traffic control at Miami International guide it in.

It took a long time to sort out, but the net result was that I wasn't arrested.

Between Silvestri explaining I'd gone undercover for her and Brashard saying I'd risked my life saving his, it convinced the Miami cops that things had played out the way I'd described them. I had a credible self-defense argument. And I'd applied lifesaving aid to a victim. The only thing I did that they could really hammer me on was leaving the scene.

But I still had to go to the station for a formal interview, and they wouldn't let me push it until the morning.

Since my Defender was still over at the *other* crime scene, Silvestri offered to give me a ride. I paused before I got in the car. She looked over at me.

Jimmy hired me, ultimately, to protect Brashard from the people around him. To give the kid a chance. That got Jimmy killed, just not for the reasons I'd thought. Or by whom.

Elena hired me to find out who'd killed Jimmy.

The choice I had to make was which end did I serve, because I couldn't do both.

"Something on your mind?"

"If you search Brashard Brown's dorm room, you're going to find the pistol that I told you about. It's his father's. Even money on whether it's registered or not. If you analyze that gun, I'll bet it matches up with the one that killed Jimmy Lawson. When Brashard told me it belonged to his father, that he kept it for protection from when they lived in Liberty City, I put two and two together. Brashard had taken it after I told him about Acuna's people threatening Cody Portman."

"You're saying Brown's father killed Lawson?"

"Cyrus never wanted Brashard to sign with Jimmy in the first place. Ray convinced him it was just splitting the pot. When I first met Cyrus, I thought he'd turned the corner and realized Ray was ripping them off. Apparently, Ray convinced Cyrus they were going to lose everything because of Jimmy and me. I think Cyrus called Jimmy to confront him, got him to Liberty City, a place he knew well. His turf, you know? I don't think it was premeditated. I think he just wanted to scare Jimmy into giving up on representing Brashard. It just didn't go the way he planned. This whole time, I'd thought it was Marrero, because it happened so quickly after I'd spoken with Charlie Garcia. Again, I didn't put it all together until Brashard told me where he got the gun."

Silvestri stared at me over the top of the car.

She reached into the car, grabbed the radio, and called it in.

Whatever happened next to Brashard was out of my hands. I'd protected him as long and as best as I could. Wherever he was, I hoped Jimmy understood my decision. I could have covered this up. With Ray dead, Sunshine Sports Collective would disintegrate...and their contracts along with them. Brashard would be clear, but so would his father. And I could not let him walk for Jimmy's murder.

# 33

We have happy endings in fairy tales because the real world so rarely has them.

I spent the better part of a week in interviews with the Miami-Dade, Miami, and Coral Gables police departments, working through the events that led up to that horrific night. After the first session, I knew they weren't charging me with anything serious. Miami PD would eventually hit me with some misdemeanors. That was the most they could get.

The nights were the worst. When I did sleep, all I could see was Ray Ruiz bringing up a gun to shoot Brashard.

Ray's soul, if he'd had one, was a black pit of nothing. He was rotten all the way through. But what he deserved was to sit in a courtroom and answer for everything he did.

Instead, I had to live with the fact that I'd been forced to shoot him.

This would haunt me for a long time.

Everyone involved in this had believed Sunshine Sports Collective would be a hundred-million-dollar operation within five years. It wasn't hard to imagine why. College sports was big business in Florida, with three of the nation's most successful and storied university athletics programs. National championships in major sports, pipelines to all the professional leagues,

Olympians.... Certainly, as the transfer rules eased, the smaller programs were increasingly more like feeders or a minor league system for the Power Five schools. There was so much money flying around, and SSC, by not being tied to any single institution, was positioned to capitalize on all of it.

I turned over the financial analysis I'd done through EchoTrace. This would eventually go to a state financial crimes task force for them to fully unwind. That would take some months because of the number of shell corporations and offshore accounting. However, in time, the task force would be able to connect enough dots to Dalton Bream that they could impanel a grand jury.

The police had a hell of a time piecing it all together, and I didn't envy them the task. I also didn't feel an ounce of sympathy for them. Maybe if they would have collectively got their asses in gear sooner, we could've prevented some of this, *any* of this.

When the debriefings were done, Silvestri told me she'd coordinated with the other departments and confirmed I was free to return to Los Angeles. She met me as I was checking out of my hotel, and we had a last conversation on Miami's Riverwalk.

"McEvoy survived her surgery and has been recovering in the ICU. We got to question her finally. Once we could play her and Farrier off each other, it cleared up a lot. You were right that she thought she had a chance to take over SSC. She assumed Ray was going down and tried to distance herself from it. The plan was basically to continue what Ruiz was doing all along. She thought she could use you to get Ruiz out of the picture. When that didn't work, she talked Farrier into it."

"Then why'd he shoot her?"

Silvestri laughed. "After you turned Dalton Bream down, he bought off Farrier. That thing at the boatyard, the showdown at Rizzo's...that was all to clean up the mess. Farrier's idea. He suggested that if they made it one giant clusterfuck, we'd be unlikely to sort it out. Interestingly, he thought you were in the car, not Rizzo. Everyone flipped on Bream. They're scrambling to cut deals with the prosecutors because they know how good Bream's legal team will be."

"What a shitshow."

"Yeah. Thanks for that," she said dryly. I didn't know if it was a joke or a rebuke.

"I didn't get a chance to thank Flash for his help. If you see him, buy him a beer for me, will you?" When this started, Flash was worried that either the Feds or the mob was still surveilling him on account of old remembered sins. Safe to say he was clear of the latter now. I think that made us even.

"Sure. Though I suspect you'll be back here before too long, if you want to tell him yourself. You'll be testifying as a material witness in about eighty trials." Her mouth twisted into a kind of frown. "We arrested Marrero yesterday. He was hiding out in someone's closet. Got most of the organization too. I didn't want to tell you this the night everything went down at Rizzo's because you were already rattled enough, but Marrero figured out where you were staying and had some people waiting there. You were right that he was cleaning up, just wrong about the location."

Jesus.

"One question," I said.

"Go for it."

"Why did you help me? You told me that your squad was reallocated to other work, and your detectives sure groused about the additional workload. You also told me no one was going to care about Sunshine Sports Collective ripping college kids off. Why'd you do it?"

"Look, Gage, you might be a pain in the ass...and for the record, you are. You were also doing the right thing. Every now and again, we need to be reminded of what that is. We've been after Cesar Marrero for twenty years. This was the best chance we'd ever had at nailing him." Another wry smile broke across her lips. "And Danzig said she owed you one. Said she'd owe *me* one if I listened to you and took you seriously. You should not repeat that, by the way."

"I won't," I said.

"Good luck, Matt," Silvestri said.

I checked out of my hotel. The bill was stratospheric.

Jimmy had paid the tab up until he was killed. I was on the hook for the rest.

Elena Mendoza and I met for coffee my last morning in town. Her boyfriend, unfortunately, couldn't join us because he was at the season opener. I, again, lamented that she'd found someone who'd won the genetic lottery, was worth about a hundred fifty million...and was a genuinely nice dude. Son of a bitch also ran a charity.

Elena was someone I could've fallen hard for, had seemingly a million other things worked out in my favor.

"So, Cyrus Brown killed Jimmy," she said, gazing long into her cappuccino. I'd reported everything I learned to her. There hadn't been a signed contract between Jimmy and Brashard, just a handshake. "I still can't believe it," she said.

Silvestri's detectives found the pistol in Brashard's room and turned it over to Miami Homicide. Their forensics team connected it to the bullets found at Jimmy's murder scene. They arrested Cyrus Brown for second-degree murder. He was in custody now, awaiting a hearing.

It was a tragedy all around.

Elena asked for an itemized list of expenses. I'd done what I said I would.

We sipped our coffee in silence for a time. We were seated outside and had a view of the Miami River from the Brickell side. Skyscrapers hid the sun.

"What's next for you?" she asked.

"I'm heading back to Los Angeles. Today," I said, adding with a forced smile, "I'll be back, though. To testify. A lot."

"Thank you for holding course for Jimmy. It means a lot to us. Everyone loved him."

We finished our coffee, and I told her I needed to be moving along. We stood and embraced. Elena gave me a soft smile that was slightly sad.

Closure is rarely happy, and never comforting. It just is.

"Jimmy and I dated for a long time," she said. "And we were pretty serious."

Now that part about hiring me made sense. I remembered something he said at dinner one night, about having found someone out here and caring a lot about her.

"Eventually, it ran its course, but I'll always care about him. Thank you."

Elena squeezed my shoulders, and I watched her leave.

I'd wanted to see Brashard before I left, but he made it clear he wanted nothing to do with me ever again. He couldn't appreciate the choices I'd had to make, could only see it through the lens of the consequences for him and his family.

I got back into the Defender and settled in for several days in a straight line.

---

A week later found me floating off the Santa Monica beach in my kayak. I found some much needed calm in the gently rolling waves.

Everyone involved had assumed that Bream would have a top-tier defense—and he did—so they all scrambled to cut deals and sell him out to the prosecutors. Well, everyone except Jorge Acuna.

The police tried grabbing him the day after the shoot-out at Rizzo's. He did not go quietly.

Blaze of ignominy.

Cesar Marrero was the easiest deal to make.

Turned out that Mr. Bream had interests with *La Corporacion* that went back to the early'90s. He used them for "resolving" labor disputes and undermining his competition with convenient accidents. The respective trials between him and Cesar Marrero would be some hilarious finger-pointing.

Bream introduced Ruiz to Marrero as a potential "investor" to his burgeoning business. This came from Marrero—Bream wasn't talking. The prosecutor's working hypothesis was that Bream wanted to see if this would be a viable money-laundering scheme and was testing it out with the mob first. That helped convince Marrero to talk.

Because Ray and Acuna were both dead, they couldn't get ground truth on how that connection truly happened. No one left alive knew—or they just wouldn't say. I heard some speculation that Ray thought he could play Acuna and Marrero off each other. That didn't seem right to me. I felt certain it was more like he got in over his head and still believed he could buy his way out with the money he thought was coming from my fabricated private equity firm. When he realized that was all fake, he snapped.

Acuna's attempts at point fixing were a test run to understand the system and see what he could get away with. He'd figured there was a lot of money to be made on these side bets and wanted to see how much he could make if he controlled a player. He planned to have a stable of players in multiple sports that he could put action on. The intent in the tournament wasn't for FGCU to lose, necessarily—it was on the action that the team would score less than 80 points. It was one of the most diabolical things I'd ever heard of in my life. The world was better off without him in it, and if that made me ignoble for saying it, so be it.

The situation with Olivia and Farrier was a little harder to unpack. We wouldn't get the full details until the trial.

My meeting with Farrier at the boatyard had been staged, as I thought. A master manipulator who was truly skilled at his craft, Farrier gave me a mixture of truth laced with lies so I would go to Rizzo's place. The intent was to get me, Rizzo, and Ray all in the same place. When I went there, I'd assumed Olivia was trying to negotiate an out for Ray. Farrier, now working for Bream, had manipulated her into thinking she could talk Ray into quitting. Farrier gave me enough of a head start that I'd get there first, and so he wouldn't have to worry about me spotting him tailing me there.

The story Farrier told at his deposition was that Bream offered him five million to eliminate Rizzo, Ruiz, Olivia, and me. Farrier said he was going to disappear and live out the rest of his life in Panama or Costa Rica under an assumed name. However, in his trial, under cross-examination, it would come out that *he'd* pitched Bream on the plan to resolve all of Dalton's problems and staging the Rizzo scene to look like one giant murder/suicide with Ray as the easy perpetrator. Farrier pled guilty to murder to avoid the death penalty, but after prosecution unearthed this reversal, the judge hit him with life without parole.

As the head of an organized crime outfit, Marrero would get multiple life sentences for ordering the firebombing of Acuna's gambling parlor.

Olivia was charged with several counts of criminal conspiracy and money laundering. The prosecution argued that she knew Ray was breaking the law and didn't come forward, even after I'd identified myself as a private investigator working with law enforcement. If she had, she'd have been spared. As it played out, the state argued that her giving me the financial records was her first step toward framing Ruiz. But I thought her desire to take over SSC and make it right had come from a good place. At least, I hoped so. Of course, she'd gone about it in a spectacularly horrible way. So, there's that. I wanted to believe that she was a good person who'd lost her way. If for no other reason than someone in this twisted saga had to be redeemable. Maybe I could ask her one day.

I'd have to wait five years for that.

The one person that the legendary defense attorney, C. Edward Cathcart, did represent was Cyrus Brown. It went down, more or less, like I'd suspected. Cyrus confronted Jimmy over hiring me, saying that he was jeopardizing the whole thing, that Ruiz was going to drop Brashard if he didn't fire me. It got heated. Cathcart painted a convincing picture at trial that Jimmy was the aggressor. I didn't believe it for a second, but the jury did. And it's not like Jimmy was there to defend himself. Cyrus's behavior after the shooting could best be explained by, first, not knowing what to do and then wanting to put as much distance between him and me and the investigation as he could. The prosecution would try to paint a picture that he and Ray were somehow colluding. That blew up in their faces spectacularly. Cathcart got Cyrus knocked down to manslaughter, called it a crime of passion. The judge gave him seven years, and he'd serve three of that at a minimum-security prison.

It didn't feel like justice to me.

In keeping with my promise, I gave Mike Pusatera, the journalist I'd spoken to at the start of the case, everything I had uncovered. We spent hours on the phone together as I recounted the twisted events that led up to Ray's death and the unravelling of Sunshine Sports Collective. Mike wrote a series of scathing stories that served as a hard indictment of the effects of money in college sports, the complete lack of accountability by the governing bodies. How things like this would only continue. Mike also covered the trials as part of his series, and we saw each other frequently during my trips back to Florida. News outlets across the country picked his story up and ran it. He got a lot of great exposure. There would be a book... because there was always a book.

The one thing I'd gotten really wrong was that I figured the Hurricanes would quietly part ways with Brashard to distance themselves from the scandal surrounding him. Instead, the team, the school, and the community rallied around the kid. As the story of Ray Ruiz and Sunshine Sports Collective's predations grew, and the public learned the full measure of the mob's involvement, it was clear Brashard Brown, Cody Portman, and all the rest were victims. Even after the news broke that Brashard's father shot and killed his son's agent, the team stuck by Brashard.

I took a small measure of solace in that.

Ray Ruiz's death would haunt me for a long time. It was so unnecessary. A life should never be taken so easily, and his death marked the easiest way out for him. A complete dodge of accountability for what he'd done. Worse than that, it was a burden I'd forced myself to carry for the rest of my days.

Maybe I'd feel better if the man I'd killed was worth the bullet.

Lightning Strikes Twice
Book 3 in The Gage Files

**What is more dangerous than the truth? Matt Gage is about to find out.**

When investigative reporter Jennie Burkhardt uncovers a link between
Russia and the mysterious "Havana Syndrome" attacks, she enlists former
CIA operative-turned private eye Matt Gage to verify the source—a Russian
defector with ties to a shadowy military intelligence unit. But as Gage
plunges headlong into the investigation, he realizes the opposition is far
more organized—and closer to home—than he expected.

Gage's case pulls him into an international hunt, making him the target of
powerful adversaries determined to bury the secret. And as the investigation continues, he realizes they'll stop at nothing to bury him, too.

With powerful forces closing in, Gage faces a harrowing choice: reveal the
truth, risking worldwide chaos, or become complicit in hiding a dark
conspiracy, betraying his values and humanity.

Get your copy today at
severnriverbooks.com

# AUTHOR'S NOTE

Money in college sports is not new. Certainly, one of the primary goals of the Name, Image, and Likeness (NIL) initiative is to bring much-needed transparency. Before NIL, many programs would use influential boosters to act as deniable intermediaries to incentivize athletes to play for a school. If they got caught, it was usually the player who took the fall. One of the most notable examples of this were boosters offering money to the family of University of Southern California quarterback Reggie Bush, which cost him his Heisman Trophy (until its 2024 reinstatement). Texas A&M quarterback and Heisman winner Johnny Manziel has talked openly about schools having a "bagman," someone who would deliver payments to a player's family, allowing the school to maintain the semblance of deniability. While not exactly the same as "pay-to-play", in the 80s and 90s, Luther Campbell of 2 Live Crew, allegedly paid Miami Hurricanes players bounties for hits on rival teams.

College athletics are incredibly high-stakes endeavors for universities and athletes alike. And with high stakes comes big money. For a major Division 1A school, the proceeds from their football program may fund the rest of their sports. It is also a significant factor in recruiting, even for regular students. For student athletes, an athletic scholarship could mean the difference between an affordable education or tens of thousands in debt (or no education at all). Athletes argue that their schools make money by virtue of their participation in sports, from selling jerseys with their names on them or having video games with their likenesses. This is a gross oversimplification, but I hope it at least illustrates the complexity. The National Collegiate Athletic Association (NCAA) attempted to solve this problem with the NIL rules, which allow players to be financially compensated by a third party, called a "collective," which is funded by private citizens and not officially connected to the university. However, it's also fair to say that in implementing such a massive change to collegiate athletics, the NCAA has not put up sufficient guardrails to manage the process. With that as a backdrop, I thought it was a compelling and timely subject for a crime novel. It has all the elements of a spectacular criminal story, with the additional layer of the personal risk and cost for the athletes involved.

The main risk in tackling this subject is how quickly it's evolving. Even as I was writing it, there was a class-action suit decided in favor of athletes seeking compensation that is sure to have seismic implications for college sports. There was also a second lawsuit that appeared to change the rules on whether NIL collectives could be used to recruit players (the original policy stated they could not).

The other risk is that it's a highly charged topic, and nearly everyone who follows college sports has a strong opinion on it. I have always believed that one of the most important things fiction can do is to challenge our ways of thinking. In this, I have tried to present the majority of viewpoints on the topic of money in sports and collegiate athlete compensation. I have kept my own opinions on the subject out of the narrative, and I don't advocate for any one position. My job is to tell a hopefully interesting, compelling, and exciting story. I'll leave it to you, the reader, to decide what's right. Whether you agree with the idea of athletes being compensated or not (and there are valid perspectives on both sides), I hope that after reading this book, you have a sense of the scope of the problem and a sense for why it matters.

The one aspect of this dynamic where I will interject my personal feelings is that I worry that, with NIL, we are ending the era of amateurism in sports. This may be a nostalgic take, but I think there's value in playing sports for the sport itself. For the spirit of competition, for being on a team, for fitness, for fun, or to be able to pay for an education. That's an important tradition, and one where the United States is unique in the world. I hope we don't lose it.

# ACKNOWLEDGMENTS

This book is dedicated to some of my oldest friends, classmates from high school through college, and with whom I have now talked, debated, argued, laughed, cheered, and extolled endlessly about college sports for some thirty years and counting. I am lucky and grateful to call you friends. For Samantha, Mike, and Joe, I love you all and wouldn't have traded it for anything. Go Gators! Especially Joe.

I would also like to extend my heartfelt gratitude to my publisher, Severn River, for giving me the opportunity to bring the Gage Files to life. I've had this character in my head for twenty years and am so grateful to finally tell these stories. Thank you, Andrew and Cate. And also for assembling a crack editing team, who understood exactly what I was going for and worked tirelessly to help me realize that vision. For Randall and Janet, thank you.

# ABOUT THE AUTHOR

Dale M. Nelson grew up outside of Tampa, Florida. He graduated from the University of Florida's College of Journalism and Communications and went on to serve as an officer in the United States Air Force. Following his military service, Dale worked in the defense, technology and telecommunications sectors before starting his writing career. He currently lives in Washington D.C. with his wife and daughters.

Sign up for Dale M. Nelson's reader list at
severnriverbooks.com

Printed in the United States
by Baker & Taylor Publisher Services